Lavanyadevi

Kusum Khemani (b. 1944), well-known writer, critic, translator and social activist, has a large and eclectic body of work to her credit. She is best known for her fiction, especially her four novels *Lavanyadevi* (2013), *Jadiabai* (2016), *Gatha Rambhateri* (2018), and *Lalbatti ki Amritkanyayein* (2019). Her short-story collections include *Sach Kehti Kahaniyan* (2012), and *Anugoonj Zindagi Ki* (2015). Her non-fiction includes a biography *Ek Shakhs Kahani Sa* (2009), *Hindi Natak ke Paanch Dashak* (2011), and *Kahaniyan Sunati Yatrayein* (2013). She has also translated works of Bangla fiction into Hindi, including Shankar's *Jan Aranya* (1975), Ashapurna Devi's *Chashma Paltey Jaye* (2016), and short stories of Jyotirmoyee Devi (2007). Her stories and articles have been published in dailies and literary journals like *Dharmayug*, *Dinman*, *Kadambini*, *Desh*, and *Hans*. She has also been working with diverse social causes and institutions for decades. Her last novel *Lalbatti ki Amritkanyayein* was born out of her experiences of working with sex-workers in Sonagachhi, Kolkata. President of the Bharatiya Bhasha Parishad, and editor of its journal *Vagarth*, she is currently overseeing the publication of the Parishad's ten-volume *Hindi Sahitya Gyankosh*.

Banibrata Mahanta is Professor of English at Banaras Hindu University, Varanasi. His recent works include *English Studies in India: Contemporary and Evolving Paradigms* (2019) co-edited with Rajesh Babu Sharma; and the forthcoming *Evolving Perspectives in English Studies: Views from the Northeast and Beyond* and *Narrative Universes of Disability: Global Perspectives*. His research interests include Indian writing in English, Indian nationalist thought, contemporary literary theory, disability studies and rights in India, and translation. He translates from Bangla, Hindi and Urdu into English. His translation of Kusum Khemani's *Lavanyadevi* won the PEN/Heim Translation Fund Grant (PEN America) for 2021.

Amritjit Singh is Langston Hughes Professor Emeritus of English, Ohio University. His recent works include the co-edited volumes *Feminism and Diaspora: Critical Perspectives on Chitra Banerjee Divakaruni* (2022), *Revisiting India's Partition: New Essays on Memory, Culture, and Politics* (2016), and *Interviews with Edward W. Said* (2004). He has also translated the poems of Gurcharan Rampuri. His research interests include African American Studies, postcolonial fiction, South Asian literatures, and migration studies. He is currently working on a documentary history of South Asians in North America.

Praise for *Lavanyadevi*

"...a fascinating tapestry of a complex intergenerational narrative that unravels the richness of cultural diversity intertwined with linguistic plurality....[and] includes a gender perspective alongside the dichotomies of personal/impersonal, material/spiritual...A very readable and relevant story homing well in its English avatar!"

—SUKRITA PAUL KUMAR

"...an entire history of migration, settlement and social life...of the Marwari diaspora in Kolkata...particularly significant for it is also [told] by and through a woman's life...it nuances the predicament of a merchant community in a shape-shifting colonial and postcolonial India...to provide [a] detailed and granular picture....an important text for both historians of India...as for scholars of literary fiction. Banibrata Mahanta's translation is sensitive to the imprint history leaves on words....a startlingly multilingual translation...also a useful illustration for translation scholars...."

—RITA KOTHARI

"...a truly complex work...steeped in the language of Indian traditions... saints, gods and sacred texts. In [keeping]...both the tonality of folktales as well as the cadence of Indian languages, this translation [is]... almost like a collection of Buddhist Jataka tales...that one can dip into repeatedly to find a different facet of an ostensibly simple story."

—OMAIR AHMAD

"Banibrata Mahanta deserves our gratitude and adulation for his excellent translation of...an intricate narrative written in Hindi by a Rajasthani writer settled in West Bengal, whose polyglot fluidity...the tone and texture of the narrative, its atmosphere, the range of experience and the suspense that pervades it are all very ably captured...A real contribution to the grand repository of Indian language literature in English."

—K. SATCHIDANANDAN

Lavanyadevi

KUSUM KHEMANI

Translated from the original Hindi by

BANIBRATA MAHANTA

With a Foreword by

AMRITJIT SINGH

Orient BlackSwan

LAVANYADEVI

ORIENT BLACKSWAN PRIVATE LIMITED

Registered Office
3-6-752 Himayatnagar, Hyderabad 500 029, Telangana, India
e-mail: centraloffice@orientblackswan.com

Other Offices
Bengaluru, Chennai, Guwahati, Hyderabad, Kolkata,
Mumbai, New Delhi, Noida, Patna

Originally published in Hindi as *Lavanyadevi* (New Delhi: Rajkamal, 2013)

First published by Orient Blackswan Private Limited 2024

ISBN 978-93-5442-857-9

The artwork on the title page is a Lithograph by James Princep, 1832, titled *View of the Ganges from the Phatuk or Gate at the Top of Punchgunga Ghat* (Varanasi).

041369

Typeset in
Dante MT Std 11.5 / 13.7
by Le Studio Graphique, Gurgaon

Printed in India at
Avantika Printers Private Limited, New Delhi 110 020

Published by
Orient Blackswan Private Limited
3-6-752 Himayatnagar, Hyderabad 500 029, Telangana, India
e-mail: info@orientblackswan.com

Contents

Foreword by Amritjit Singh *vii*
Acknowledgements *xi*
Translator's Introduction *xv*
Lavanyadevi's Family & Friends *xxxi*

Lavanyadevi 1–235

Translator's Note 236
Glossary 243

Foreword

Among the many thought-provoking insights that Walter Benjamin offers in his well-known 1923 essay, 'The Task of the Translator,' the following appears quite relevant to Professor Banibrata Mahanta's work in this volume: "A real translation is transparent; it does not cover the original, does not black its light, but allows the pure language, as though reinforced by its own medium to shine upon the original all the more fully." Having read Kusum Khemani's novel *Lavanyadevi* in the original, and in Dr. Mahanta's translation, I can say with a degree of assurance that the multicultural competence of the author finds its match in the multilingual abilities of the translator. Banibrata's translation, finished over several years, does not cast a shadow over the original, instead it "shines upon the original all the more fully."

Banibrata has taken this challenging text up for translation and has produced an amicably just rendition. The translated text captures the various nuances of the linguistic and cultural diversity and the idiosyncratic style of the author that characterises the source text. This could only have been accomplished by someone who was fully aware of the fluidity in play here. Even for a reader whose mother tongue is Hindi and who turns to English only as a second or third language, I believe the translated text justifiably, and more significantly, recognises and communicates the philosophical depth of the Hindi text as well as the personal ideals proffered therein. In doing so, the translated text succinctly stands both as a work of translation and as an independent text in its own right. Hence, for me, *Lavanyadevi* in English goes beyond being either an *anuvad* or a *bhashantar*, to become a work of literature in its own right.

Lavanyadevi is an intriguing novel in its fascinating mixtures of tradition and modernity, idealism in action and reclusive spiritualism. It is also a politically incorrect work in fascinating ways: an exploration of the life and values of Bengali *bhadralok* in Hindi by a Marwari writer. The novel develops its themes primarily through its many women characters, including and especially the novel's eponymous protagonist. An exceptionally competent woman with unmatched qualities of heart and mind, Lavanyadevi is presented as an epitome of perfection, yet believable because she acts with the greater common good in mind, successfully transmitting that spirit to her grandchildren. Does the creation and glorification of such a 'superwoman' play into the hands of patriarchy? Is the idealisation of women's strength and the romanticisation of their selflessness a normalisation of patriarchal expectations? At the same time, are not the acts of conformity and defiance subtle indicators of empowerment, given that they are often based on choice not coercion? Are these not to be seen in the context of the larger trajectory of the novel—the quest for both individual and collective freedom that plays out through the character of the protagonist? Another notable aspect of the novel is how the bonds between women characters cut across class, region, religion, and on occasion national boundaries. These are some of the thought-provoking questions that the novel is likely to raise for its readers today.

I have been fortunate to experience Dr. Mahanta's sensitivity and sensibility since the summer of 2015, when we met first at the Indian Institute of Advanced Studies (IIAS) in Shimla. I was a Senior Visiting Fellow at IIAS from March to June, and Bani was one of the several college and university colleagues who were completing their multi-year residency funded by the University Grants Commission. There were plenty of opportunities for convivial conversations during the long days in and around the Library, even more so during our after-dinner walks.

Banibrata has kept in touch since 2015 and I have come to know him as a "radical centrist," as he sometimes describes himself. In a recent phone conversation, he quipped, "Being a radical centrist is not an oxymoron. You need to be an Indian today to figure out what it means to be one." Coincidentally, novelist Kusum Khemani's sensibilities appear to be in sync with Dr. Mahanta's challenging position in a world divided by unbending ideologies. Although the narrative in *Lavanyadevi* is shaped within the cultural framework of Hinduism, the idealism and 'purity' that the text advocates is not rigidly ritualistic and narrow. Instead, it is a broad and liberating humanistic sensibility that demands to be heard in early twenty-first century.

Mahanta has a natural flair for languages, and can read, write and speak Bangla, Hindi, and English. Comfortable in both Bhojpuri and Punjabi, Banibrata also has a smattering of both Urdu and Sanskrit. I know from our conversations how his interest in languages and literature was shaped early by his upbringing in the industrial township of HEC, Ranchi (where he was born) through extensive interaction with people from all over India. For me, Banibrata is an Indian citizen who demonstrates and connects actively with the communicability and intelligibility of the multiple layers that comprise and enrich India's cultural life. Despite visible setbacks, Nehru's conception of India as a palimpsest continues to lift itself into new formations with every generation.

I believe Banibrata is well qualified to undertake the task of the translations he has already done (such as Tagore's short story, 'Subha' or Syed Muhammad Ashraf's short story 'Ka'abey ka Hiran'), and now this translation of the Hindi novel *Lavanyadevi* (2013) by Kusum Khemani, a member of the Marwari community, long settled in West Bengal. Banibrata is also currently working on a collection of disability themed short stories in Bangla.

Translation can often be an act of transgression—an act of taking apart, dismantling the syntax and idiom of the original language and pulling it back together in received language.

While the product of translation may not be a transgression in every case, it almost always results in a literary work that signals new experiences and meanings all its own. The effect could vary widely—say, from the "murmurs" and "low sounds" in W. B. Yeats' 'The Lake Isle of Innisfree' and 'When You are Old' at one end to the "slow beast" and the "brute blood" in his 'The Second Coming' and 'Leda and the Swan' at the other. Mini Chandran (2016) has rightly argued that in the context of translations between *bhashas*, intracultural translation is often more fluent because of shared cultural matrices. Also, as I have argued elsewhere, because of the special position English has occupied in India since the 1830s, translations from Bangla, Hindi or Telugu into English too are quite distinctive and cannot be placed in the same category as, say, translations from Korean or Japanese into English (Singh 1982, 2019).

I expect this English translation of *Lavanyadevi* to find its way in the South Asian literary world, almost like Walt Whitman's child "who went forth every day, and who now goes and will always go forth every day, / And these become of him or her that peruses them now." I wish it well.

AMRITJIT SINGH
Langston Hughes Professor Emeritus of English,
Ohio University

References

Chandran, Mini. 2016. 'Into Bhasha and English: Comparative Study of Bhasha and English Translation in India'. *Comparative Literary Studies* 53 (2): 359–376.

Singh, Amritjit. 1982. 'Indian Literatures and Multilingualism'. *Indian Literature* 25 (1): 141–152.

———. 2019. 'Another Window on the World: English for Creative Expression in the Indian Context'. In *English Studies in India: Contemporary and Evolving Paradigms*, eds. Banibrata Mahanta and Rajesh Babu Sharma (Singapore: Springer).

Acknowledgements

It started with a phone call from Kolkata inquiring if I would be interested in translating *Lavanyadevi* into English. I was struck by the author's multilingual repertoire and her attempts to reconfigure the relation between tradition and modernity, between past and present. As I read on, I also attempted to visualise the protagonist—larger-than-life yet essentially human, empowered and empathetic, worldly yet detached from everything around her. When she met me in Varanasi a couple of months later, I realised that I needed to look no further than the author to visualise the protagonist. Intrigued by the challenges a multilingual text presented, I agreed to translate the novel. The author also agreed to my only condition: that I wanted to work at my own pace.

That was shortly after the novel was published in 2013. It has taken me a considerable amount of time since then to complete the translation. Work progressed sporadically, and it was only during the pandemic that I finally managed to complete the translation. Importantly though, I completed it the way I wanted to. There were numerous issues which often left me uncertain about the best way forward. I hope I have been able to resolve at least some of them satisfactorily and do justice to the work that inspired me to venture into translation. Although I have subsequently taken up and completed a few translation projects, *Lavanyadevi* remains special.

I am immensely grateful to Prof. Amritjit Singh, who has been a guiding light to me for some time now. As always, he has been generous with his observations and suggestions whenever I needed them. I am thankful to him for writing the foreword to this volume even as he contended with several health issues. I am also deeply indebted to Prof. Himadri Lahiri for always lending a patient ear and offering sane advice whenever I turned to him.

I have accumulated numerous debts in course of completing this translation. I must begin by putting on record my indebtedness to the students of the Indian Literature in Translation course, MA English (2019–2021), with whom I had several interesting discussions on translating this novel. I must also acknowledge the support I received from my former students, presently fellow academics: Atul Kumar Singh for the numerous debates and discussions that informed my approach to the task; Saumyadeep Bhattacharya for a few important observations on the initial draft; Sumitro Banerjee for the precision with which he helped me prepare the final manuscript; Anway Mukhopadhyay for the opportunity to talk about 'Translation as Experience', which helped me put my introduction together; Partha Sarathi Nandi and Saurav Kumar for putting up with numerous random requests for books and study material; and Amritendu Ghosal, for responding promptly to a last minute request. I am thankful to my colleague Umesh Kumar for his comments and suggestions, and my research scholar Aniket Ojha for his assistance during the final stages of my work. The help and support of my brother Bithin Mahanta has been a key factor in the completion of this project.

I am grateful to PEN America for supporting my project with a PEN/Heim Translation Grant, and to my anonymous reviewer at Orient BlackSwan, her/his commendation of my work and some valuable suggestions. And finally, a big, big thank you to my editor, Moyna Mazumdar, who believed in the project. It is primarily her expertise and support that has shaped the work into what it is. I am thankful to my publisher for bringing this translation to a wider readership.

This work is dedicated to 'my people'—my family. Your patience, support and love, present in the spaces between words and the pauses between sentences, are my lifeforce. They nourish every breath I take. I am happy that I am finally have the answer to a few questions that had, with passing time, metamorphosed from genuine concern to exasperation to a bit of a dinner-table joke: "*Hua? Kab tak hoga? Hobey toh*? Is it done? When will you complete it? Will you be able to complete it?" It wouldn't have been possible without you all.

June 2024 BANIBRATA MAHANTA
Varanasi

Translator's Introduction

Lavanyadevi (2013) is a novel by Kusum Khemani that chronicles five generations of a Bengali *zamindar* family as it transitions from colonial to contemporary times, with the eponymous protagonist as its principal focus. The author belongs to a community that was traditionally involved in trade and moneylending, migrated to Kolkata during the eighteenth and nineteenth centuries, and subsequently came to be known as Marwaris. The dynamics of construction of Marwari identity in the city, the evolution of its distinct character, and the very contours of the nomenclature 'Marwari' are a result of intricate processes of conflict, confrontation and conciliation that characterised the community's interactions with the new milieu and its inhabitants. These interactions between the migrants and the city unfolded against the backdrop of complex historical, political and cultural realities in the country and Bengal, particularly in Kolkata, of those times. The Marwaris' support of and participation in Hindi literary activities during the Indian freedom struggle played a crucial part in the formation of their identity. A Hindi novel about a Bengali family by a Marwari woman from Kolkata, *Lavanyadevi* is part of a significant outpouring of contemporary Hindi literature by Marwari women authors from the former colonial capital, made possible by these developments over the past three centuries—a phenomenon that merits thorough scholarly investigation.

To fully comprehend this phenomenon, it is essential to delve into the multiple meanings of the term 'Marwari'. Just who is a Marwari? How is a person identified as one? Variously interpreted in geographical, linguistic or cultural terms—as a word that suggests a connection with Marwar in Rajasthan, a people who speak a particular language, or those belonging to the desert—the relative homogeneity that these interpretations imply is, however, in sharp contrast to the startling diversity of the group it is used for (Timberg 2014: 4–5). "There was no pre-existing 'Marwari' community in western India before the migrations began. It is the fact of migration—and their diasporic location outside of Rajasthan—which makes the migrant Rajasthani business community into Marwaris" (Hardgrove 1999b: 732). Migration and the consequent geographical dispersal paved the way for the formation and public realisation of Marwari identity (Hardgrove 1999b: 726–727). The term Marwari was used by resident communities in Bengal for the migrant population from Rajasthan and neighbouring states, or traders from north India in general. It also included social and religious groups from and around the Marwar region in erstwhile Rajputana who migrated to eastern India, particularly Bengal, where they became prominent merchants and traders, those who joined these migrants to assist them and establish new firms, as well as other north Indian and Rajasthani traders who adopted Marwari identity due to the credibility attributed to Marwari businessmen in those times (Dugar 2021; Roy 2015). Ratan Shah points out that even among Marwaris themselves, there was a lack of consensus about the connotations of the term. It is in the new constitution of the All India Marwari Conference (published in 1958) that one finds for the first time a standard definition of the term, one that is accepted even today: "All people whose lifestyle, language, and culture are influenced by Rajasthan, Haryana, Malwa, and the surrounding regions, and who themselves or whose ancestors have settled in any part of the country or abroad, are Marwaris" (Shah 2011; my translation). The Marwaris are thus not a community; they are a group.

The evolution of Marwari identity has been shaped by the history of the subcontinent over the past 300 years. The expansion of the Mughal Empire in the seventeenth century, its gradual decline in the eighteenth century, the subsequent British colonisation, and a host of developments in India post-1947 are significant events that led to the formation of the Marwari trading community (Roy 2015; Timberg 1978: 18–23). Around the seventeenth century, Marwaris shared amicable relations with states in and around the region where they were settled. As Mughal power waned and the British consolidated their hold in India, Marwari traders, earlier concentrated in Rajasthan and northwest India, migrated to different parts of the country including Mumbai, Chennai and, of course, Kolkata—then the imperial power centre. Experiences of Marwari migration and settlement are, therefore, also varied across the country. The community established itself as a dominant presence in trade and commerce in colonial India, and continued to consolidate its position after 1947. Both pre- and post-Independence, these migration and settlement experiences, the increase in and diversification of entrepreneurial activities, and the community's well-thought out entry into business and politics enhanced their socialisation with other communities across the country, and the world, and shaped Marwari identity in important ways (Goswami 1989: 291–302; Roy 201).

This identity has been extensively documented. There is a rich corpus of literature on the Marwaris, focussed on their resilience and adaptability as merchants and traders, their entrepreneurial and organisational skills, and the success of Marwari business families. Many of these offer historical analyses of the community's growth and success (Birla 2009; Goswami 1985; Hardgrove 2004; Saha 2003; Taknet 1986; Timberg 1978), while some focus on particular business personages or business houses

(Kudaisya 2003; Kumar 2016; Piramal 1996; Timberg 2014). Some studies delve into economic dimensions in conjunction with community identity, engagement, and organisation (Babb 1999; Low 1991; Mukul 2015; Timberg 2014). Most available literature on the Marwaris documents their remarkable achievements and pre-eminence in industry and business, highlighting attributes like resilience, pragmatism, astuteness, thrift, and solidarity as key to their success, thus advancing an understanding of Marwaris as a predominantly mercantile community, and little else besides.

Representations of Marwaris by non-Marwaris underscore the complexity of their identity. Across India, particularly in Bengal, Marwaris have "suffered the stigmas and stereotypes of so many entrepreneurial minorities…due to their strong bonds, communal ties, and adherence to 'tradition'" (Parson 2012: 10). Their success in trade, commerce, moneylending and entrepreneurial endeavours, coupled with their closed and tightly-knit family life led to their being labelled materialistic, opportunistic, clannish and insular. Community stereotypes like the *kanjoos seth* (stingy businessman) and the *tangdil sahukar* (mean moneylender) became ubiquitous in Indian popular culture. Marwari women were largely seen as "heavily invested in the discourse of home, family, lineage, and domesticity": traditional, docile and homebound, their main duty was "to provide a stable household life for their husbands, sons, and brothers-in-law" (Hardgrove 1999b: 732).

The persistent focus on the Marwaris' economic success obscures other trajectories of their development. While Kolkata was undoubtedly an economic epicentre in their professional success story, and the city that forged the 'imagined-Marwari-community', it is also central to the shaping of modern-day Marwari identity beyond the dominant stereotypes. Marwaris' interactions with Kolkata and its inhabitants over generations have effected cultural, social and intellectual transactions, and advanced other dimensions of Marwari identity that challenge the narrow view of the community as merely a business-oriented, trading and entrepreneurial people.

The role of Kolkata in the shaping of contemporary Marwari identity is explored in a couple of recent studies (Mantri 2019; Parson 2012). Oftentimes disparagingly referred to in colloquial Bengali as *meros* and *khottas* and relegated to the domain of the Philistine, Marwaris are frequently represented in Bengali cultural imagination as shrewd and avaricious, or comical and uncultured, or both, with little interest in cultural and intellectual accomplishment (Chaudhuri 1990: 19; Saraogi 2023). The cultural and intellectual are claimed as domains of the Bengali *bhadralok* and the *buddhijibi* (Mantri 2019: 197). This distinction between the progressive, cerebral *bhadralok* and the regressive, inward-looking and tradition-bound Marwari is just one example of the consolidation of Bengali identity through contradistinction (Banerjee 2016: 644). The Marwaris' subsequent engagement with social, political and cultural issues can be understood as their response to and negotiation of these processes of community and identity formation. These and similar inter-community dynamics lead to the formation of hybrid identities.

A significant aspect of this hybrid identity is the Marwari adoption of the Hindi language. The rise of the Hindi movement and the incipient nationalist movement led Marwaris to adopt Hindi, marking a pivotal moment in the shaping of their social identity. Drawing on a detailed analysis of literary activity in Bengal in the nineteenth and twentieth centuries (Mishra 1983; Shambhunath and Dwivedi 1993; Sharma 1998), Rahul Bjørn Parson points to the existence of a 200-year-old tradition of Hindi in Kolkata that has not received as much attention as Bangla literary activity of this time. He goes on to note how the support of the Marwari business community in Kolkata was instrumental in giving rise to a "confident Hindi print community" which had "a major role in the promotion of Hindi as a national language" (Parson 2012: 1–10).

This warrants deeper investigation into the interrelations between Marwaris, Hindi literature and Kolkata. Marwaris made the switch from their own language to Hindi on account of several factors. The "supralocal character" of Hindi suited them as they spread out over the entire country. Hindi was also emerging as the language of the nationalist movement. Divided into orthodox and reformist factions, Marwari groups also patronised Hindi journals to publicise their respective points of view. Hindi thus became the medium for expressing social and cultural positions, including those on women's issues and nationalism. The Marwari readership of these journals was, in the process, drawn into these debates, and thus embarked on a course of modernisation and nationalisation. Over time, they started regarding Hindi as their own language (Parson 2012: 1–10). Their involvement in Hindi cultural and literary activities also contested the portrayal of Marwaris in Bengali popular culture as an uncultured community. However, this Hindi print community gradually went into decline after 1947.

From the 1990s onwards, there has been an efflorescence of Hindi literary writings by Marwari women writers from Kolkata. It is, in a way, a culmination of 300 years of Marwari migration to the city and 200 years of the Hindi print culture there. This surge of Hindi novels in the twentieth and twenty-first centuries by Marwari women in Kolkata such as Prabha Khaitan (1942–2008), Alka Saraogi (b. 1960), Madhu Kankaria (b. 1957), and later Kusum Khemani (b. 1944) and Renu Gourisaria (b. 1941) provide fascinating insights into the evolution of Marwaris, who were, until recently, viewed as an indistinguishable mass of tradition-bound people busy minting money while holding on to archaic values. Parson discusses how these novels by Khaitan, Saraogi and Kankaria, published in the last decade of the twentieth century (which is also the first decade of neoliberal reforms in India), diverge from mainstream majoritarian narratives of Kolkata's history and yet are distinctly urban and Kolkatan, thus laying claim to a share of the city's cultural space (Parson 2012: 7–9).

These literary works not only reflect the socio-economic realities and cultural shifts within the Marwari community but also delve into issues like gender, migration, and identity. They present a complex and nuanced portrayal of Marwari identity that combines history, memory and contemporary life. Through their narratives, these authors challenge the traditional roles ascribed to Marwari women, portraying them as active agents in the negotiation of their identities and social positions (Hardgrove 1999a). The exploration of domestic spaces, family dynamics, and tensions between tradition and modernity in these texts provides valuable insights into the lived experiences of Marwari women and their contributions to the cultural and intellectual life of Kolkata.

As a Kolkata-based Marwari woman writing in Hindi, Khemani is part of this group of writers engaged in exploring the migrant Marwari identity. However, what is noticeable in her work, especially in *Lavanyadevi*, where she focusses on the Bengali community, is her distinctively amalgamative approach. Instead of highlighting the schisms between Bengali and Marwari identity, her narrative emphasises a shared, plural culture and a composite, distinctively Indian women's ethos. This is seen "in the many friendships (mostly between women) in the novel that bridge disparate and contrasting worlds and worldviews (across communities, cultures and age-groups, if not always across class)—most notably, Marwari and Bengali. The camaraderie, laughter and common ground shared between the two, what they learn from each other, are vital, as are their differences. And, as revealed through these friendships, equally significant is the (firm, if gentle) debunking of the typically negative stereotyping and caricaturing of Marwaris by Bengalis, across representations, fictional, textual, and otherwise (including by sensitive auteurs like Ray)" (Mazumdar, email correspondence).

Reflecting on her life and the significance of her cultural environment, Khemani acknowledges the enormous influence that Bengal has had on her:

> Being born in the educated land of Bengal was significant for my consciousness. I developed not only a deep affinity for Bengali literature and culture, but also a profound interest in it. Love for classical music! Reverence for Shantiniketan as a pilgrimage! Discovering new dimensions of wanderlust! A cultured language! I will remain indebted to this land of Bengal for its refined culture and traditions. (Khemani 2023; my translation)

Bangla and Kolkata's Bengali culture became an inseparable part of her, as did the liberal ethos of the city. While her great-grandfather, grandfather, her mother and her spouse inspired and supported her commitment to social service, her dedication in pursuing an education and her appreciation of literature, the city also nurtured these values in her (Khemani 2023; Verma 2019: 60–66). Whether pursuing academic research as a married woman, appreciating classical music, embarking on a literary career rather late in life, or writing about spirituality, nationalism and women's issues, Khemani credits the soil of Bengal for cultivating in her a sensitivity to these pursuits (Khemani 2020). This deep connection with Bengal, familiarity with its culture and proficiency in Bangla effects a perfect synchronisation between the spirit of the author and the ethos of the text.

Lavanyadevi follows five generations of an aristocratic Bengali family of yesteryear as it transitions into modernity, from British occupation of India to the present. Diverse narrative strategies like flashbacks, diaries, letters and emails, history, memory, and the omniscient third-person narrator enrich its telling, lending it depth and range. The diary as metanarrative and the protagonist as reader/narrator are particularly effective, offering a telescopic perspective.

Lavanyadevi's rootedness and belief in the philosophical framework of Hinduism form the core of her being. They propel her to seek answers to questions of *satya* (truth) and *mukti* (liberation) that confront her in the latter half of her life, questions that transcend immediate, personal concerns to address larger, universal issues. These are not just philosophical questions about life, its meaning and purpose—they are questions that a whole system of values asks of itself. And the narrative does not foreclose its own interrogation. It is these questions and the quest for answers to them that the principal narrative and the various sub-narratives lead to. Lavanyadevi's transition from *grihastha* (householder) to *sanyasa* (renunciate) harkens back to the Hindu ideal of human life divided into four phases. However, contrary to the conception of life in isolation, Lavanyadevi, free of any kind of worldly considerations in this final phase of life, marshals material and human resources to create a strong network of *seva* (social service) across the country and even beyond its borders.

Lavanyadevi successfully transmits her values and ideals to her grandchildren, who carry her legacy forward. The strong bonds between Lavanyadevi and her grandchildren, who are referred to as Lavanya-*santaan* (Lavanya's children), demonstrate that moving forward does not necessitate a break from the past. These relationships reaffirm certain core values rooted in the cultural ideal of working for a greater common good. The benefit of this intergenerational dynamic is reciprocal—it leads to subtle reforms that fine-tune the attitudes of both Lavanyadevi and her "soul-children" (p. 234), unobtrusively ushering in change and creating space for diversity in relationships and ways of living. These changes are both individualistic and holistic, and cannot be analysed in terms of the regressive/progressive or traditional/modern binaries. It is this plurality, this in-betweenness that is eloquently captured in the novel and in these lines: "Bring more breadth and compassion into your vision, my child. Don't bring in rites and rituals, honour and tradition as impediments and make your life-path burdensome and inaccessible; use them as steps to take you forward" (pp. 81–82).

Lavanyadevi is foremost a novel about women. Khemani's vision of womanhood, in the words of the Kusumanjali Award (2016) citation, is "one that breaks age-old barriers and invents a future-oriented woman" who "lays the road for engendering life values for a new progress" (Srivastava and Bisht 2016). What ideals of womanhood, especially in the Indian context, does Khemani evoke in her novel? The women protagonists of Khemani's fictional world are exceptionally strong, self-possessed, clear-sighted, and graceful. But they are not just glorified as perfections: they dwell in the realm of the sublime. Their sublimity articulates an idealism that is larger than life even as the characters remain firmly grounded in reality. While some may find in such characterisation all the ingredients for how patriarchy constructs and validates women, that is not how Khemani sees it.

The polyphonic structure of the novel engages Lavanyadevi the granddaughter, the daughter, the wife, the mother and the grandmother in conversations with her preceding and her succeeding generations. These fine examples of intergenerational interaction (and in some instances, the lack of it) are occasions for the transference of codes of female conduct and are instrumental in validating both progressive and parochial elements of the past and present, offering alternative perspectives to both. This approach enriches feminist thought by addressing gendered and patriarchal practices from within the rubric of family and kinship, but without completely abandoning or adopting either tradition or modernity, thus blurring the distinction between them. The novel also raises thought-provoking questions about whether women's *seva* falls within the 'care' paradigm and whether renunciation allows them to transcend patriarchy, empowering them to engage with society and the world on their own terms. These layered questions enrich the narrative, adding nuance and depth to the exploration of womanhood and societal roles.

Lavanyadevi is also a deeply political novel and one which, apart from contesting colonialism and Western education and advocating indigenous, rural and ecologically sustainable approaches to life and living, emphatically distinguishes between Hinduism and its opportunistic political variant. While religion undergirds the philosophical and social discussions in the novel as well as the advocacy of sustaining livelihoods specific to geographical and socio-economic contexts, Khemani does not mince words when it comes to taking on cultural nationalist appropriations which interpret religion and its practices along narrow, parochial lines. It is also a forward looking novel as, in addition to chronicling change in women's lives across a century or more, it also brings in contestations of caste and sexuality. While not without inconsistencies, the novel's advocacy of humanitarian concerns above and beyond imposed and constructed borders—personal, familial, communal and national—makes it relevant across cultures and times.

What makes *Lavanyadevi* an extraordinary novel in Hindi is the language of its narrative, which is best described as *batras*—a joyful effusion of speech, the sheer delight of conversation—as Ekant Srivastava so aptly words it on the back cover of the Hindi original (Khemani 2013). However, given the implicitly essentialist ways in which classifications like 'Hindi writer' or 'Hindi novel' are generally deployed, these labels do not fully describe either the author or her work. Khemani's novel is a hybrid artefact, born out of multiple linguistic and cultural encounters. The presence of characters in the novel who speak in languages other than Hindi necessitates dialogues in Bangla, Marwari, Haryanvi or Punjabi. Khemani's own Hindi is distinctive—it does not adhere to a single grammar or lexicon. The fabric of her Hindi is interwoven with Bangla words and syntax, Haryanvi, Punjabi, and the occasional Marwari, embellished with Urdu and sprinkled with English. Proverbs from Hindi and its dialects, scriptural references in

Sanskrit and Pali are all part of its weave. Khemani's language is definitely not the purist's Hindi. Like Premchand, Krishna Sobti, Mahasweta Devi, Syed Mustafa Siraj, and so many others, it acknowledges the subcontinent's rich plurilingual realities and integrates sensibilities, both cognate and disparate, of multiple Indian languages.

Khemani's language is a perfect example of the "complex multilingual repertoires normal to those growing up in India" (Spolsky 2022: vii) characterised by naturally internalised linguistic and cultural transferences that are manifest in spontaneous linguistic alterations defined and classified as inter-sentential code switching, intra-sentential and intra-lexical code mixing (Crystal 2008, 83; Muysken 2000, 1–3), blending, phonological, syntactic and lexical borrowing (Hudson 1996: 53; Tay 1989: 408). The effortless fusion of languages, registers and subcultures in *Lavanyadevi* presupposes a certain familiarity with such repertoires on part of the reader, and functions at a degree of interculturality that takes negotiations between them as a given.

Translating such a narrative into global or even a pan-Indian English is always risky. While something is invariably lost in translation, the translator must guard against the co-optation of cultural nuance into the uniformity of a seductive cosmopolitan idiom, and strike the right balance between oversimplification and overexplanation. How Susie Tharu and K. Lalita approach the translator's task in their monumental two-volume *Women Writing in India* has been my touchstone: they "preferred translations that did not domesticate the work either into a pan-Indian or into a 'universalist' mode, but demanded of the reader too a translation of herself into another socio-historical ethics", taking pains "to preserve the regional grain of the work" (Tharu and Lalita 1993: xxii). In a world where we are increasingly confronted with expressions of difference, and often deeply divided by them, translation offers other ways of seeing and being that complement one's own, enabling and enhancing one's understanding of the world and locating oneself in it.

Spolsky underscores that "multilingual societies offer important lessons for humanity to discover harmony in diversity" (quoted in Sachdeva and Agnihotri 2022: xi). It is these considerations that made me resolve to retain some of the multilingual flavour of the original and thus to approach the intricate navigations between source language*s* and target language*s* in ways—outlined in my 'Translator's Note', and supplemented by a 'Glossary'—such that readers in India and elsewhere are able to savour just a tiny fraction of its many linguistic delights, in English. I believe there is much to be discovered and celebrated in the conversations between languages and sub/cultures in this novel. As Professor Amritjit Singh puts it in his 'Foreword', they warrant the two major meanings of translation in South Asia—*bhashantar*, altering the language, and *anuvad*, retelling the story—and much more besides.

References

Banerjee, Swapna. 2006. Review of *Community and Public Culture: The Marwaris in Calcutta, c. 1897-1997*, by Anne Hardgrove. *The Journal of Asian Studies* 65 (3): 643–645, August. https://www.jstor.org/stable/25076109 (accessed July 2024).

Babb, Lawrence A. 1999. 'Mirrored Warriors: On the Cultural Identity of Rajasthani Traders'. *International Journal of Hindu Studies* 3 (1): 1–25, April. https://doi.org/10.1007/s11407-999-0006-z (accessed July 2024).

Birla, Ritu. 2009. *Stages of Capital: Law, Culture, and Market Governance in Late Colonial India*. Duke.

Chaudhuri, Sukanta. 1990. *Calcutta: The Living City*. India: Oxford University Press.

Crystal, David. 2008. *A Dictionary of Linguistics and Phonetics*, 6th ed. Oxford: Blackwell.

Dugar, Prodip Kumar. 'Marwaris'. *Banglapedia* (Last modified 17 June 2021). https://en.banglapedia.org/index.php/Marwaris (accessed July 2024).

Goswami, Omkar. 1985. 'Then Came the Marwaris: Some Aspects of the Changes in the Pattern of Industrial Control in Eastern India'. *Indian Economic and Social History Review* 22 (3): 225–249. https://doi.org/10.1177/001946468502200302 (accessed July 2024).

———. 1989. '*Sahibs*, *Babus*, and *Banias*: Changes in Industrial Control in Eastern India, 1918–50'. *The Journal of Asian Studies* 48 (2): 289–309, May. http://www.jstor.org/stable/2057379 (accessed July 2024).

Hardgrove, Anne. 1999a. 'Hindi Literature as a Political Space: Marwari Women's Fiction in Calcutta'. *Economic and Political Weekly* 34 (14): 804–806. https://www.jstor.org/stable/4407816 (accessed July 2024).

———. 1999b. '*Sati* Worship and Marwari Public Identity in India'. *The Journal of Asian Studies* 58 (3): 723–752. https://doi.org/10.2307/2659117 (accessed July 2024).

———. 2004. *Community and Public Culture: The Marwaris in Kolkata c. 1897–1997*. New York: Columbia University Press.

Hudson, R. A. 1996. *Sociolinguistics*, 2nd ed. Cambridge: Cambridge University Press.

Khemani, Kusum. 2013. *Lavanyadevi*. New Delhi: Rajkamal.

———. 2020. 'Sakshatkar, Dr. Kusum Khemani'. Interview by Dr. Abhigyat. *Sahitya Samartha* 4 (13): 6–7, October–December.

———. 2023. 'Dr. Kusum Khemani: Atmakathhya'. In *Kusum Khemani: Ek Garimamay Vyaktitwa*, eds. Bimala Poddar, Rajshree Shukla, Shambhunath, and Sandip Awasthi (no pagination). Kolkata: Bharatiya Bhasha Parishad.

Kudaisya, Medha M. 2003. *The Life and Times of G. D. Birla*. New Delhi: Oxford University Press.

Kumar, Pavitra. 2016. *Bhujia Barons: The Untold Story of How Haldiram Built a 5000 Crore Empire*. India: Penguin Random House.

Low, D. A. 1991. 'The Forgotten Bania: Merchant Communities and the Indian National Congress'. In *The Indian National Congress: Centenary Hindsights*. Delhi: Oxford University Press.

Mantri, Swati. 2019. 'Marwaris of Kolkata: Community, Identity and City'. PhD diss., Department of Humanities and Social Sciences, IIT Delhi. https://shodhganga.inflibnet.ac.in/handle/10603/443462 (accessed July 2024).

Mishra, Krishṇabihari. 1983. *Hindi Sahitya: Bangiya Bhumika*. Kolkata: Maṇimaya.

Mukul, Akshaya. 2015. *Gita Press and the Making of Hindu India*. India: Harper Collins Publishers.

Muysken, Pieter. 2000. *Bilingual Speech: A Typology of Code-Mixing*. Cambridge, UK: Cambridge University Press.

Parson, Rahul Bjørn. 2012. 'The Bazaar and the Bari: Calcutta, Marwaris, and the World of Hindi Letters'. PhD diss., South and Southeast Asian Studies, University of California, Berkeley. https://escholarship.org/uc/item/7ng958qz (accessed July 2024).

Piramal, Gita. 1996. *Business Maharajas*. New Delhi: Penguin.

Roy, Tirthankar. 2015. 'Diaspora: Marwari'. In *Oxford Handbook Topics in History*. Online edition: Oxford Academic. https://doi.org/10.1093/oxfordhb/9780199935369.013.22 (accessed July 2024).

Sachdeva, Rajesh, and Rama Kant Agnihotri. 2022. 'A Word of Gratitude'. In *On Being and Becoming Multilingual: Some Narratives*, xi–xii. Hyderabad: Orient BlackSwan.

Saha, Narayan Chandra. 2003. *The Marwari Community in Eastern India*. New Delhi: Decent Books.

Saraogi, Alka. 2023. 'In Conversation with Alka Saraogi'. Interview by Owshnik Ghosh. *The Antonym*. https://www.theantonymmag.com/in-conversation-with-alka-saraogi-owshnik-ghosh/ (accessed July 2024).

Shah, Ratan. 2011. 'Marwari Samaj: Ek Tathyatmak Vivechan'. https://shahratan.blogspot.com/2011/03/blog-post.html (accessed July 2024).

Shambhunath, and R. N. Dwivedi, eds. 1993. *Hindi Navajagaraṇ: Bangiya Virasat*, 2 vols. Kolkata: Coal India Limited.

Sharma, Shyamsundar. 1998. *Hindi Prakashanan Ka Itihas: Bangiya Khanḍ*. Varanasi: Pracharak Granthavali Pariyojna.

Spolsky, Bernard. 2022. 'Foreword: A Note on Indian Scholarly Hyperglots'. In *On Being and Becoming Multilingual: Some Narratives*, eds. Rajesh Sachdeva and Rama Kant Agnihotri, vii–ix. Hyderabad: Orient BlackSwan.

Srivastava, Shivani, and Himanshi Bisht. 2016. 'Hindi Writers Kusum Khemani, Veerendra Kumar Awarded'. *The Pioneer*, 2 August 2016. https://www.dailypioneer.com/2016/india/hindi-writers-kusum-khemani-veerendra-kumar-awarded.html (accessed July 2024).

Taknet, D. K. 1986. *Industrial Entrepreneurship of Shekhavati Marwaris.* Jaipur: D K Taknet.

Tay, Mary W. J. 1989. 'Code Switching and Code Mixing as a Communicative Strategy in Multilingual Discourse'. *World Englishes* 8 (3): 407–417. https://doi.org/10.1111/j.1467-971x.1989.tb00678.x (accessed July 2024).

Tharu, Susie, and Lalita K., eds. 1993. 'Preface'. In *Women Writing in India*, Vols. 1–2: xvii–xxv. New Delhi: Oxford University Press.

Timberg, Thomas. 1978. *The Marwaris: From Traders to Industrialists*. New Delhi: Vikas Publishing House Ltd.

———. 2014. *The Marwaris: From Jagat Seth to the Birlas (Story of the Indian Business Series)*. New Delhi: Penguin.

Verma, Ravi. 2019. *Kusum Khemani ke Sahitya mein Samajik Sarokar.* Department of Hindi, Directorate of Distance Education, Kurukshetra University.

Lavanyadevi's Family & Friends

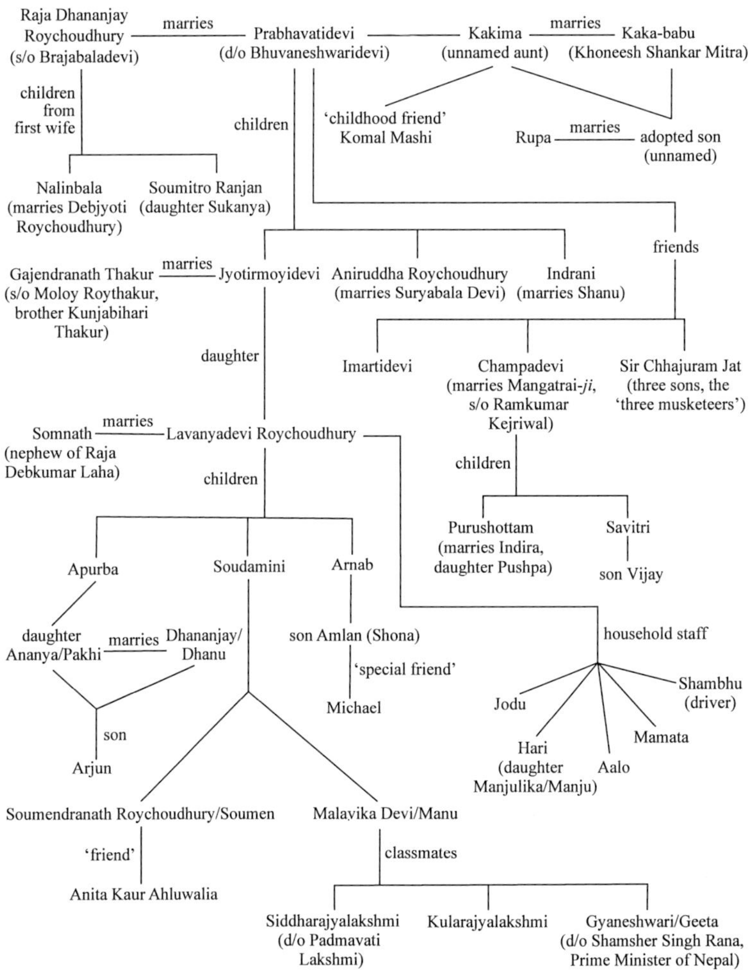

Lavanyadevi

And the next moment that divine, dazzlingly bright figure faded away into the realm of air, water and light...leaving them all standing there, stunned and bereft.

There are people in this world who, it seems, do not belong to this mortal world but to a realm of fairytales, magic and mystery. The souls of such people exude the fragrance of musk and their entire beings seem alight with the halo of knowledge. Their hearts brim with Buddha-like compassion and their inviolable purity turns them into legends in their own lifetime. Isn't Lavanyadevi also one such character?

These were the thoughts I was immersed in when I was rudely interrupted in my reverie by Anusuya Sen's angry voice, "*Ai* Charu! Have you heard what scandal that Lavanyadevi the great has caused? That lady who you consider to be the high priest of virtue, who you say is so austere, so righteous and majestic?"

I was confused and surprised. Chandana, who was sitting beside me, was also taken aback by the vehemence in Anusuya's voice and eyes. I was stunned into silence for a moment. But Chandana immediately rebuked her, "Anusuya! Stop talking nonsense! How can such an intelligent and sensible woman like

Lavanyadevi even think of doing anything that would harm the Roychoudhury family, the family she has nurtured at the cost of her own self? The sun may rise in the west, but Lavanyadevi would never let the family come to the slightest disrepute, leave alone harming them herself! What is it that you have heard about her? All this *aabol-tabol* and utter gibberish you talk is surely because of some grave misunderstanding. What have you heard that makes you spew such venom against her, tell me?"

"Intelligent? Huh! Misunderstanding? *Arey* she is unbelievably pompous, self-centred and totally obsessed with herself! The maharani is possessed by the desire of having her name writ on the clouds. She is hungry for public adulation. She is least concerned with everyday household affairs, with her home and family, or with humanity. She has a heart of stone. If she really had a heart, would she have destroyed the future of a young lad so callously? Just look at her! She behaves like she is Raja Harishchandra incarnate! Oh, my poor nephew, how he cried his heart out! But did she care? You could cut dry wood and still find a drop of sap, but you won't find a drop of compassion in her soul."

Inundated by the torrent of allegations against Lavanyadevi, the fragrance of whose persona had permeated my life right from the time I was a child, I sought refuge in the soothing recesses of my childhood memories, that fairyland of which Lavanyadevi was the uncontested queen.

At school, Lavanyadevi was my senior by three or four years. Her fancy ruffled skirts, her sparkling shoes and the colourful ribbons with which she tied her thick black hair are abiding memories of my school life. I would always be stealing glances at her, greedily taking in the sight of her with adulatory eyes. Yes, you could call it 'hero worship'. This bond of affection endured and though years passed, I kept track of the vicissitudes of her life.

Lavanyadevi not only stood first in every class, she was the only girl in school to secure five double-promotions. Whenever the headmistress would tell Lavanyadevi's mother that it would not be in her daughter's best interests to jump classes so frequently, Jyotirmoyidevi would simply wave Lavanya's report card in her hand and say, "Fine, we are going to another school then. Lavanya stood first in class, and there are other schools willing to admit her to a higher class." She would invariably be brandishing the application form of another school for greater effect. The reputation of the school was due, in large part, to the many students who had done well here and earned a name for themselves in later life. And the heights that Lavanya, a Brahmo Samaj elite, was scaling were well known. Other schools were willing to admit her to any class she desired. The mother did, eventually, carry out her threat. Annoyed by the fact that the headmistress did not agree to promote Lavanya directly from the sixth standard to the eighth despite her insistence, she got her daughter admitted to another school in the eighth standard. Everybody felt that this was carrying things a bit too far. But Lavanya was the wonder girl. She proved all her doubters wrong, and how! Her performance was like that of the heroine of a film. She stood first in the eighth standard. Everybody was left flabbergasted. She was surely no ordinary girl. Was she another Ramteertha or Vivekananda in the making?

The mother had such immense faith in her daughter's abilities that she did not stop there. "From today," she told Lavanya, "don't waste your time. Not a moment will you waste on roaming around uselessly or in training for singing and dancing. Start studying for your tenth exams right away." For the first time in her life, Lavanya answered her mother back, and said—she was just twelve, and no school board in Kolkata would allow her to take the high school examinations. "There has to be some board that will give you permission, if not in Kolkata, then somewhere else. You don't have to worry about that," said Jyotirmoyidevi, and sternly added, "Just concentrate on your studies."

So Lavanya put her head down and started studying. She passed her tenth from Allahabad Board, and before she was thirteen, she was in college. But so many jumps in school took their toll, and during her early days in college, Lavanya did stagger, even fell a couple of times. But then she regained her equilibrium in time for her annual examinations and was able to do reasonably well. By the time she appeared for her M.A. examinations, she was already familiar with the whole terrain. She was placed First Class First and declared a gold medallist.

When the slim, five-feet-five Lavanyadevi, draped in a saree, worn Parsi-style, over a frilled, long-sleeve blouse, sang in her melodious voice, the entire Brahmo society which congregated at the prayer-meetings would be overwhelmed—not just by the music in her voice, but also by her beauty and her poise, and the way she spoke and carried herself. Innumerable hearts throbbed for her. But despite her incredible talent, her transcendent beauty and her refinement, what was most remarkable about Lavanya was the complete unaffectedness of her demeanour. Her whole being radiated an aura of simplicity. Absolutely spontaneous and artless, there was not a trace of cleverness or guile in her. Less educated worldly-wise girls of her age could run their households with a greater degree of wisdom. One of the principal reasons for this was perhaps the fact that Lavanya's whole world revolved around her books, her fixed routine and her extremely sheltered life. She remained wholly ignorant of the real world, and whenever she tried to step out of her sequestered domain into the realities of the world outside, she was quite out of her depth.

Realising wisely that her daughter was not even remotely worldly-wise, Jyotirmoyidevi started searching for an appropriate match for her daughter. When, in accordance with her 'fool-proof plan', she chose Somnath as the prospective groom, sidelining many a celebrated son from renowned families who were interested in marrying her daughter, the decision surprised everyone. Somnath-babu hadn't much to boast of apart from his several degrees. He was neither remarkably handsome, nor did he possess an inordinate amount of wealth that might help one overlook his shortcomings. What was it that made a discerning woman like Jyotirmoyidevi choose so naively, everyone wondered!

In the year 1934, this question, more than many others, was frequently discussed in the elite circles of Kolkata.

Even the normally uninvolved father, Gajendranath, an ICS, usually oblivious to household matters, was left stunned and disappointed by his wife's decision. When he could no longer contain himself, he addressed his wife in a pained "*Ogo, shunchho*? Would you listen, dear?" Divining the cause of his anguish, Jyotirmoyidevi put an understanding hand on his shoulder and said, "Please do not ask me anything. You have unquestioningly trusted me in everything I have done so far, haven't you? Now put aside all your worries and listen to me carefully."

God alone knows what Jyotirmoyidevi told her husband, but the effect of her words was evident from the change in his demeanour. Gajendranath-babu's countenance gradually relaxed and cleared and soon his eyes were shining with joy. Asking for Lavanya's consent was considered a waste of time. The date was fixed. On the appointed day, the *matrivrata* daughter willingly took the seven steps around the holy fire of Saptapadi, and crossing the threshold of her parents' home, bid them farewell and followed her husband to her new abode.

Was Lavanyadevi an embodiment of the philosopher king Janaka, who was so detached from the fortunes of his kingdom Janakpuri that he could remain as unmoved by its prosperity as when it burnt down to ashes? With her familiar evergreen smile, Lavanyadevi touched the feet of her in-laws and embarked on her married life with the firm conviction that her husband was indeed God incarnate, her *pati parmeshwar*. Unable to come to terms with either the choice of groom or the ease with which Lavanya settled into her new life, the perplexed bhadralok society of Kolkata began a relentless and deprecatory scrutiny of the two, and kept at it for some time. However, their lack of success wore out the genteel folk, and eventually they came to accept this unusual marriage.

If fertiliser and water do not nourish a seed, the poor seed soon dries up and becomes one with the soil. Likewise, the complete absence of any incident or rumour led to all the stories about Lavanyadevi dying a natural death.

Lavanyadevi had been brought up in comfort and care. But from the very first day of her married life she readied herself in right earnest for the challenges of her new household. She sent back the car that her mother had gifted. She willingly took upon herself the responsibility of the entire household. Her behaviour endeared her to her husband and her in-laws to such an extent that she soon became the pivot around which the whole house revolved. Ever since she was a child, Lavanyadevi had been made to understand that work is worship. And she had internalised the idea to such an extent and worked with such infectious enthusiasm and alacrity that it seemed like she extracted forty-eight hours' worth of work from a twenty-four-hour day. Indeed, was there any 'speedometer' in the world that could clock how fast she worked? Wonderstruck, everyone around her could only say: "*Hey bhagwan*! How can she possibly work like this?"

As is the norm in the Bengali community, the groom was elder to the bride by eight years. In a short span of time, Somnath-babu's degrees had propelled him to a high position in the Braithwaite Company. A man of few words and gentle manners, his behaviour endeared him to everyone in his office. One day, his English boss asked him in his stilted Bangla-inflected Hindi, "*Mr. Shomnat, Rangoon jaega? Wahan laatshab ka mafik rehne ko, aur poysha bhi khoob milega!* Are you willing to go to Rangoon, Mr. Somnath? You can lead a luxurious life there, and get a handsome salary too!" Somnath-babu was hesitant to break the news to Lavanyadevi, unsure of her response. Would she be intimidated by the thought of going to Rangoon? But he was in for a surprise. Lavanyadevi was overjoyed when she heard the news. The thought of a new place, a life in the jungle, a bungalow by the riverside—her young mind painted the information in the vivid colours of her romantic imagination, and the images filled her with excitement and made her impatient. She happily chirped, "When do we leave? Tomorrow or the day after?"

Somnath-babu was taken aback. "*Hey bhagwan!* What kind of a girl is this? How is it that at such a young age, the thought of encountering strange untrodden paths and the unknown culture of a new land doesn't cause her the slightest consternation or fear? Is she a great fool or a half-wit? Or is she just an 'over-confident' person?" In his heart of hearts, he was repenting why he did not keep the news a secret from her. But he had spoken. And there was no way that Somnath-babu could hurt the feelings of his wife, the wife whom he described only in superlatives—the prettiest, worthiest, most diligent, calmest and sweetest of all—and whom he loved to the limits of his being.

They set off for Rangoon. When the ship docked at the jetty, there was a driver waiting for them with an open-hooded automobile. The driver bowed so low in obeisance that he almost touched the ground. In the blink of an eye, the automobile carried them off to a charming bungalow surrounded by bamboo and cane trees and bedecked with varieties of orchids in bloom. A river ran gurgling right in front, as if joyfully welcoming to its banks the feet of this modern-day woman whose character embraced both the beauty and virtues of mythical women like Ahilya, Shakuntala, Draupadi and many others.

Lavanyadevi, ecstatic at having reached this exquisite destination, threw her arms wide open like a bird stretching its wings to take flight. She pirouetted round and round in joy, singing in her melodious voice. Hearing her, the cuckoo stopped singing, the bees forgot to buzz, and the *papeeha* seemed to have lost its voice. The wind carried her song across the land. A shower of falling leaves drenched her with their love. Somnath-babu stood transfixed in silent communion, wide-eyed, overwhelmed by the beauty of his very own moon, spellbound by the magic of her voice. Some distance away stood the attendant, the coolie and the butler, awaiting orders, their hands locked in front and heads bowed, looking surreptitiously at both—the man mesmerised, the woman in the embrace of her consort, nature. Day had dusked to night when the neighing of the hansom-horses and mules suddenly broke the spell of enchantment cast upon everyone. And Lavanyadevi and Somnath-babu returned from their flights of imagination to the ground beneath their feet.

Lavanyadevi now looked around herself, taking in everything anew, and like a sprightly child started walking towards the beautiful bungalow which seemed to have sprung up like a magical palace amidst the lush greenery and vibrant colours of the tropical jungle.

These British bungalows were aesthetically built and outdid the palaces of smaller kings of the country in opulence. Burma teak, Malacca cane, Italian tiles, expensive bathroom fittings, triple-storied Czechoslovakian chandeliers shining in the reflected colours of rubies, emeralds and diamonds, huge frilled, hand-pulled velvet fans, expensive Noritake cutlery, embossed silver dinner-sets and tea-sets, a huge dining table covered with a frilled cloth of Irish crochet—all these were already part of the décor. Every kind of extravagance, ostentatiousness and exquisiteness that could be imagined and even those beyond imagination were to be found there.

As soon as Lavanyadevi entered the bungalow, uniformed butlers, chefs in toques, maids wearing aprons over flared skirts, porters and attendants, all bowed and rushed forward—someone picking up her shawl, another her purse—to welcome her in. With her characteristic decency and humility, Lavanyadevi spontaneously acknowledged each one of them. Her entry into the house was a sight to behold. Regal in bearing, she moved at a leisurely pace, looking around, taking everything in effortlessly and gently. She was neither overwhelmed by the high splendour she suddenly found herself surrounded with, nor did her young face show any sign of indifference or aloofness. She established an instant unspoken rapport with the maids, which was restrained yet warm. Her loving and affectionate bearing drew everyone towards her while her decorous behaviour simultaneously set a clear line of demarcation for her staff.

Somnath-babu left for office early in the morning and Lavanyadevi went out for her morning walk. She came back, exercised and showered, and noted down her personal and household accounts. As soon as it was evening, she took a phaeton and set off to see the hospital and the school. Burma was a prosperous country and Rangoon, the capital city, its crown jewel. However, Lavanyadevi's keen eye could see beyond the obvious and the visible into the heart and soul of the city.

The hospitals, schools, markets and residences erected there for Englishmen made Rangoon look like London. In a short span of time, Lavanyadevi started wielding considerable influence with the wives of the officers, her housemaids, doctors at the hospital and the nuns who ran the school. She became as familiar with them as if she had known them for years. She directed her gardeners, maids and attendants to pick the best flowers and fruits from her garden and dry fruits from her house, decorate them, and send them to all her acquaintances once in a while. Whether it was the Officers' Club or the tennis court or a meeting of the governing body of the school or the hospitals, everywhere, whenever there was a crisis, the first thing that anyone uttered was "Call Lavanya, ask her!" In the little time that she had been there, Lavanya became the apple of everyone's eye. But she didn't let all this attention and affection go to her head. She had her priorities in life sorted out and worked according to them. Thus, when the Company decided to send Somnath-babu to London for a special training programme and said that his wife could also go with him, she immediately made up her mind to accompany him.

In London, she took all her degrees and started doing rounds of the universities. After giving the matter considerable thought, she decided to apply for the Ph.D. programme at Oxford and a Teachers' Training course from another renowned university. Her husband tried to dissuade her from pursuing two programmes simultaneously, arguing that it would be difficult to manage both courses once she was back in Rangoon, but once again the easy laugh with which she responded reminded him of her capabilities and told him that she had made up her mind. The school in Rangoon ordered all its books from England, and the reference books that Lavanyadevi requisitioned from various libraries were also sent along with the schoolbooks.

The principal of the school was more than willing to oblige Lavanyadevi. It was as if she was always waiting for Lavanyadevi to give her the next list of books—as soon as she received the list, the principal would immediately send the requisition. Both seemed locked in a race of sorts—one ordering books as promptly as she could, the other reading them as rapidly as she could. Lavanya also had to make a couple of trips to London in the interim, but since Somnath-babu's visits to London became frequent, Lavanya could accompany him with ease, and two years of studies passed without strain. Soon it was time for her to take the examination. All her friends were as concerned about her examination as if it was their own. Their involvement inspired Lavanya to work with even greater enthusiasm.

During one of her visits to London, she went to see a lady doctor for a routine check-up. When the doctor told her that she was not just fine but also to become a mother soon, Lavanyadevi and Somnath-babu felt they were in the seventh heaven of delight. It was the happiest day of their lives. Lavanyadevi looked up to the sky with clasped hands to profusely thank that loved one who was beyond the grasp of the senses. "Today I feel truly blessed with your special love and compassion. How else do I explain this wonderful bequest of time?" she said. As if in acknowledgement of her gratitude, a gust of wind showered them with petals as it blew across a beautiful cloud-lined blue sky.

Lavanyadevi got back to Rangoon and resumed her gardening, morning walks and balanced food habits with even greater conscientiousness. She doubled her physical activity and concentrated on having simple but nutritious food, monitoring her activities minute to minute. The anticipation of impending motherhood and the physical changes she was undergoing during pregnancy made her glow and Lavanya appeared more radiant than ever before. Somnath-babu would say on more than one occasion, "Lavanya! I am sure even Lord Indra is jealous of me today. Rambha, Urvashi and all the other celestial damsels in heaven cannot match your beauty."

The family being well-off, no effort was spared in welcoming the firstborn. Even the preparations for Nandotsav, Lord Krishna's birth celebrations at Vrindavan, seemed to pale in comparison. Jyotirmoyidevi would regularly inquire after Lavanya through letters and telegrams and send occasional gifts. Although Lavanyadevi was being looked after well by the English doctors and nurses in Rangoon, Somnath-babu had emphatically declared, "*Bas*! Enough! Either London or Kolkata." It was thus almost settled that Lavanyadevi would be travelling to Kolkata for the birth of their first child, and she had made all arrangements for her travel accordingly. The doctor was not at all agreeable to the suggestion that she travel in such a condition, but faced with Somnath-babu's insistence, had no option but to relent.

On the day she was to depart for Kolkata, Lavanyadevi met every member of her staff and walked out into the garden to caress a favourite plant when she felt a small gush of fluid inside her. Alarmed, she turned towards the elderly female attendant standing next to her. The lady immediately understood what the matter was and brought Lavanya inside. Messengers rushed to fetch the doctor, who, along with the nurse, was beside Lavanyadevi in no time.

The moment Somnath-babu entered the house, puffing and panting, sola-topi in hand, the doctor put the newborn baby in his arms. In his anxiousness, Somnath-babu could only manage to say, in English, "So fast? How come?"

The doctor replied, "All because of Lavanyadevi's excellent planning. She was so meticulous about everything from the very first day of her pregnancy that the child was born healthy, without any difficulty, and at the right time."

As soon as the news reached Kolkata, Jyotirmoyidevi along with her husband, now retired from the Civil Services, rushed to Rangoon. But Lavanyadevi had planned everything down to the last detail. There was really nothing that Jyotirmoyidevi could offer to do. When she expressed her desire to gift a large amount of jewellery and cash to her daughter on the occasion of the birth of her first grandson, Lavanyadevi said, "Ma! Instead of all this jewellery and cash, give me a part of the 100 *kathha* land that you received as dowry. The location of the land is good; it is very peaceful there and full of greenery."

In spite of Jyotirmoyidevi's insistence that she take the entire land, Lavanya took only 30 *kathha*.

When it was time for her mother to depart, Lavanyadevi gave her the layout of a bungalow designed by a renowned English architect. "You get the *bhoomipujan* done and get work started on the bungalow. Employ the best architect and the best engineer. Marble will be shipped to the construction site from Italy, and Burma teak and Malacca cane from here. Ma, your daughter's house will be a replica of the Viceroy's bungalow."

And that is exactly how it was. The only child of wealthy parents, a sharp mind, influence over world-famous architects, an excellent rapport with her husband, a free hand and immense wealth—was there any reason that Lavanyadevi's house would lack for grandeur?

Lavanyadevi gave birth to two more children, and then decided not to have any more children. The first and last born were boys, and the second child a girl. They grew up together amidst laughter and play. All three were sent to Darjeeling for their schooling—Arnab and Apurba went to St. Paul's and Soudamini to Loreto Convent.

Around this time, Gandhi took India by storm and the whole nation was in the ferment of revolution. Judging the gravity of the situation, Somnath-babu decided to give up the lure of the luxurious life and prodigious earnings in Rangoon, and took a transfer back to the Kolkata office of the Braithwaite Company.

Although the income in Kolkata was nothing compared to the earnings in Rangoon, it was still quite substantial.

India achieved independence. Kolkata too had changed a lot in the past two decades. The children were studying in Darjeeling. Life was progressing smoothly. Amidst this order, there was time to laze around, to relax. But could Lavanyadevi just laze around and relax? Did she not need something to do so that her time was well-spent? Without wasting a moment, she applied for a job at Lady Brabourne College and Presidency College. The trustees, after going through her sheaf of degrees, were more than impressed with Lavanyadevi's academic achievements. This lady was a veritable 'masterpiece'! She was immediately called for an interview by both colleges. The interview was just a formality as both the colleges had already typed out her appointment letter. Her accomplishments were simply too many to ignore. Lavanyadevi decided to take up the job at Lady Brabourne for two reasons: first, her teacher-training degree would help her become the principal there within a shorter span of time; second, the college was peaceful, and very close to her residence.

And as always, the moment she became principal, Lavanyadevi impressed everyone with her resourcefulness, her strictness, her sweetness, her discipline, her style of working and her principled conduct. Her fame spread like the fragrance of the *parijat* flower and she impressed the educated and the elite of the city alike. As was her wont, she set her own standards of excellence, and broke them herself to set newer ones. She immersed herself in the task of inculcating in her students all the good qualities of head and heart that she possessed, transforming these tender plants into strong, full-grown banyan trees. The general opinion was that with the kind of work she was doing, she would help the college establish a guru-shishya culture as enduring as the one in Shantiniketan. Of all the things in the world, Lavanyadevi only despised greed, lust, lies, dishonesty and jealousy; her heart was always brimming over with love.

Her three children settled into their own lives. The daughter had been married off well; the sons held prestigious jobs. Apurba, the eldest, had one daughter, Ananya. Soudamini had a son, Soumen, and a daughter, Malavika. Arnab, the youngest of the three, had a son named Amlan, whom everyone called Shona. Shona was the apple of Lavanyadevi's eye, her favourite grandchild.

Lavanyadevi was indefatigable. She administered the work of several institutions, her college and her home efficiently and with ease. She was never seen to panic. She was like Goddess Durga with her many hands—untiring in her zeal, handling all her duties unfailingly, responsibly and meticulously. No one could ever complain of being ignored by her. Shc loved all and treated everyone with the same degree of love and warmth. Scrupulous and hardworking, always upholding truth, Lavanyadevi was the unmatched standard of excellence in all aspects of life, her words worth their weight in gold.

I gradually drifted back to the present. I asked Anusuya, "How can a person like Lavanyadevi do anything wrong? Why would she set fire to her own house? Are you a fool that you talk thus? Look at her past life. Has she ever demanded anything for herself? Ever desired anything or even saved anything for herself? Isn't her entire day spent in caring for others and the world around her? Shouldn't you at least think twice before making such wild allegations?"

Anusuya raised her hand to stop the flow of praise and sternly admonishing me, said, "Enough! You've praised her a lot. Why don't you also recommend her name to the President of India for the Bharat Ratna!" she said bitingly. "*Wah*! What a great actor she is! Arrogant conceited woman!"

Taken aback, or shocked rather, I struggled to make sense of Anu's sarcasm but could make neither head nor tail of it. So I turned towards Chandana, and this is what she told me.

Lavanyadevi's younger son Arnab was allotted a large airy flat adjacent to a lake by his firm. His wife, who was also working, convinced him to move into this company accommodation as it would be compact and easier to manage.

Her grandson Shona's departure from the house left Lavanyadevi without sustenance—no, it left her practically lifeless. Already bereft and lonely after Somnath-babu's recent passing away, succumbing to a heart attack, her grandson's departure now aggravated her loneliness to such an extreme that she was left bedridden. Gradually, Shona's regular visits to see his grandma every Sunday helped her regain her strength bit by bit and she was able to get back on her feet again. But she had no inkling that greater shocks were to follow.

Next, it was the turn of the elder daughter-in-law. Initially, she started staying out for the entire day on the pretext of training poor people to earn their subsistence. Then, one day, she burst out in anger at her husband. "If the firm you work for does not provide you with accommodation, can't you take a loan to purchase a flat? My bones are worn out hollow from running around, taking care of this huge house. Listen to me carefully—I won't stay here any longer! I'm taking my daughter and going back to my parents' house tomorrow."

Actually, it was Lavanyadevi herself who was indirectly responsible for all these happenings. Young daughters-in-law! Modern, beautiful, well-educated. Yet it was Lavanyadevi who was always the cynosure of attention. Even the daughters-in-law's friends would love sitting around Ma as soon as they entered the house. The treasure-trove of Lavanyadevi's diverse life experiences and her inimitable manner of narration could hold her young listeners captive and engrossed for hours. The delicacies she prepared were so tasty that her sons' large circle of friends preferred them to food prepared in five-star hotels and would polish off everything on their plates with relish, exclaiming, "*Wah! Wah!*", "*Ore mori re!* This is food I could die for!" The daughters-in-law's relatives would also join the chorus of praise, and it was not just about Lavanyadevi's culinary skills. Sometimes friends of the daughters-in-law would also say things like, "I see! So you have also started wearing a shawl, just like your mother-in-law!" Or they would ask questions like "Sharmila, did Mashima help you to wear the saree today?" Every such statement and question would upset the daughters-in-law—they felt diminished and inadequate and would experience a strange jealousy. They felt that their education, beauty, culture, sophistication and youth were all in vain—because their mother-in-law was still the cynosure of all eyes, the one whom everyone always admired and looked up to. Outwardly, they never expressed anything but respect towards Ma, of course, but a gnawing sense of inferiority settled softly inside them, like moss, layer by layer.

When the moss of inferiority is acted upon by the fungus of time, it grows like poison ivy and eats up all human emotions.

The two daughters-in-law said, "A house this huge! And spread out like a stable! The rooms are too few! And far too large! It's just too much trouble managing this house. And so much money is needed for its maintenance. Is it really worth it? No! Not worth it at all! This is the age of multi-storeyed buildings. Moreover, the taller buildings all around have stopped the circulation of air and this place now feels claustrophobic. If this ruin is sold off, there would be enough money for all of us to buy spacious flats."

The word 'ruin' pierced Lavanyadevi like a shard of glass. This magnificent, inimitably unique bungalow a 'ruin'? Grandeur and luxury that sent everyone into raptures—"*Wah*! A house befitting a monarch! The polish of the wood! The exquisite and rare artistry of tiles! That perfect milky tone of the marble! The regal splendour of the spiral stairway! The dazzling Belgian cut-glass chandelier hanging from the high ceiling! *Wah*!"—*this* bungalow referred to as a 'ruin'? Lavanyadevi suddenly felt giddy. Steadying herself with one hand she sat down on the big couch. And, as always, she started planning for the future. It suddenly became clear to her that the inheritors of her property were waiting for her to depart. She realised that she needed to resolve the issue before they started chanting the *Mahamrityunjaya mantra* in reverse. Without losing any time, she sent a message to her most trusted lawyer.

The temptation of home-made savouries made the younger daughter-in-law visit Lavanyadevi once or twice a week. Her son Shona, brought up with affection by his grandmother, also had a special liking for her cooking. Lavanyadevi's elder son Apurba too would pay an occasional visit, hesitantly and surreptitiously, though his wife and daughter had boycotted him completely. And yes, Soudamini's son, Soumen, who was very close to Lavanyadevi since his childhood and would call her his 'girlfriend', came to meet her quite often. He was more like a friend to her—hugging her, sharing the occasional laugh, reaching into the darkest recesses of her mind and illuminating them just as a friend would. Somnath-babu's passing away did not affect her as much as her present loneliness, mainly because the house was then full of people. Soumen, through his affection, helped mitigate that loneliness to an extent.

Lavanyadevi asked her lawyer to draw up a will and to make four and a half shares of the total value of the house. Three shares were for her three children; one share was for the Trust and included the expenses for her food; and the half share was for the two servants who had served her ever since they were children and had spent their entire life in her service. Their families were taking care of her even today—especially Hari's flower-like daughter, Manju, who loved Lavanydevi more than life. She would flit about Lavanyadevi the whole day like a butterfly, and feel blessed by just a loving glance or an affectionate touch from her goddess.

Shona, who was exploring opportunities to go abroad for higher studies, had become a rather devoted grandma-lover all of a sudden. These days he had also taken to behaving like a hero.

Lavanyadevi was enjoying these pleasant family diversions, when she was hit by a bolt of lightning. At first she was simply stunned into inaction by the immensity of what was reported to her. As the enormity of what had happened started sinking in, she was horrified. She held Hari's sobbing daughter by the hand, sat in her car, and ordered her driver Shambhu to take her to the police station. They reached there in minutes, and Shambhu jumped out of the car to open the door for her. Lavanyadevi pushed his hand away, got out of the car, and half-walking, half-running, went to meet the O.C. of the police station.

"*Mamoni! Aapni?* Mother! You?" stammered the O.C. in surprise as he bent forward to touch her feet in customary greeting. She ignored his greeting and came straight to the point. "File this report as quickly as possible. I, Lavanyadevi Roychoudhury, testify to the fact that my grandson Amlan has molested this girl, Manju. And I am going home now, but Manju's father is here. If you want to get a medical examination done, go ahead. I will send the car back as soon as I reach home." Turning to Hari, she said, "Hari, keep these thousand rupees, and if you need more, send Shambhu home for it." Saying this, she put her signature on her testimony, and proceeded towards the door.

Hmm…So this is why Anusuya Sen was cursing her! Lavanyadevi's younger daughter-in-law is Anusuya's sister, and Amlan, her only grandson, the heir to her fortune.

Chandana continued with her narrative.

Looking at Lavanyadevi now, one got the impression of a stately figure in utter dishevelment. Her eyes were open but looked blankly into nowhere; her feet just dragged along. Supporting herself somehow, Lavanyadevi managed to drag herself to reach her room, where she collapsed, face-down, on her bed.

A deathly silence enshrouded the whole house. Not a leaf stirred on the trees; the air seemed to stand still. So still was the air and so deep the silence that every breath inhaled or exhaled seemed to disturb it.

Evening deepened into night. Night was followed by morning. Lavanyadevi continued to lie on her bed, unmoving and oblivious to the world. As the sun rose and its rays pierced the darkness, Lavanyadevi got up, went to the window that opened onto the garden, held the bars of the grill tightly and looked out with vacant unseeing eyes. Jodu, her old faithful, came a couple of times with a glass of lime juice or tea, but she dismissed him with a wave of her hand. Thereafter he just sat hunched in a corner of the room.

Jodu dialed Soudamini's number. No reply. He didn't have the nerve to call either the sons or their wives. He tried calling Soumen. Just then he saw Mrinal Didi rushing towards his mistress's room, holding Hari's hand. When Soumen called back, Jodu, without divulging much, asked him to come as soon as he could. Soumen did not ask too many questions. "I'll reach as soon as possible. But I'm quite far from the house and even if I drive fast, it will still take some time. Jodu-*da*, please take care of my Didu till I reach. Please!" he said.

And then Mrinaldevi's imperious voice boomed against the high roof of the bungalow: "Lavanya! *Ei* Lavanya! There's some good news! Will you please listen for a moment to what Hari is saying?"

But Lavanyadevi stood like stone, impassive, unresponsive to everything around her. She seemed incapable of either listening or responding. Mrinaldevi looked towards Hari in dismay. Hari sank to his knees before his mistress, and with his face against her feet, held them with both hands. Tears ran down his face. His breath racked by sobs, he kept crying, "Ma! O Ma! Forgive us, Ma! The fault is entirely mine and my daughter's. It was my dimwittedness that made me take my ignorant daughter at her words. We could not understand what *khoka-babu* was saying, we could not understand his refined gentility. He was merely joking, and my daughter thought he was harassing her. Manju misunderstood what *khoka-babu* was saying. And I! Fool that I was, I believed her without cross-examining her, and levelled such a grave allegation against your family. Ma! I've brought your signed statement back from the police station. Forgive me, forgive this sinner, Ma! Now it is all sorted out, Ma! Everything is okay. Please forgive us, Ma!" Hari's entreaties, his cries, his sobs and hiccups continued unabated. Mrinaldevi went up to Lavanyadevi and holding her by the shoulders tried to shake her back to her senses. It was then that Lavanyadevi heard the words, "Now it is all sorted out, Ma!"

Her body convulsed as she heard the last sentence and a spasm seemed to run through her like an electric shock. She turned and stared unblinkingly at Hari for what seemed like an eternity. The words "Now…Everything is okay" pounded at her eardrums like an insistent drumbeat. She tried to get up, holding on to the window grills for support, but tumbled to the floor, unconscious.

Just then, Soumen's voice was heard calling, "My girlfriend! Where are you, my girlfriend?" Entering her room, he lifted Lavanyadevi up with solicitude, like one picks up a flower, and laid her on her bed, and with folded hands asked everyone to leave her alone for some time. Cradling her head in his lap, he wiped her tear-stained face, carefully splashed some eau de cologne on her forehead and gently ran his fingers through her hair. Lavanyadevi was muttering indistinctly—"Everything is okay…The girl is a fool. I am an idiot. *Khoka-babu* was teasing her. She misunderstood. Forgive this sinner. I've brought your signed statement back. I have committed a crime…Everything is okay." This tangled mesh of words seemed to be giving her more pain than succour. She was unable to decipher truth from falsehood. Never before in her life had she been faced with a situation where her own values and principles collided against each other with such force that sparks flew. Would she have to 'weld' lies of convenience in order to patch the values and principles that she had lived her life by? What crossroads was she standing at today, from where, for the first time, she was unable to see the road ahead? These thoughts racked her brain, disjointed thoughts without logic, without apparent rhyme or reason, thoughts that seemed to make her lose her way in a dark cave. "What is all this? Is my whole life then nothing but a lie? My principles... my integrity...? Is it all just false and hollow? All that I upheld as the governing principles of my life till now and lived my life by, were they just a facade? Was I wrong to believe that truth is the foundation of my life? Was I wrong in refusing to compromise with falsehood, in refuting lies, in rejecting lucrative but dubious offers? Was I wrong to place more trust on my discretion and to love wealth less? My children privilege selfish interests over morals and values. Is a poor man's honesty so cheap that a clever roll of the dice can turn the tables and buy his honesty and integrity? What if my eldest granddaughter Ananya was molested by Hari's son? Would Apurba and Arnab and all the rest of them still react the same way as they do now? Is money indeed more important, more powerful than all moral standards?"

Arguments and counterarguments crowded Lavanyadevi's mind. She tossed around in bed restlessly, turning from one side to the other as if someone had cast a black spell on her. Her delirious mumblings would not have made sense to everyone—and Soumen, though he understood them, did not want to. "Didu! Didu!" he kept saying, all the while gently running his fingers through her hair, caressing her head, trying to comfort her. Despite his efforts, Lavanyadevi's agitation only kept increasing, until suddenly she convulsed once like a fish out of water and then her head fell motionless into his lap.

Alarmed, Soumen checked to see if she was breathing, and was greatly relieved to find that she was. Providentially, the Roychoudhurys' family doctor arrived just around that time. After examining her thoroughly, he administered an injection and advised that she should be allowed to sleep, undisturbed by sound and light. A nurse was instructed to monitor her oxygen level from time to time. The doctor also advised them that when she recovered, everyone should talk to her only about 'normal' things.

The sun brought in a new light that Sunday. The family lawyer of the Roychoudhurys, the famous advocate Shri Shyamal Sen, could be seen seated in the drawing room, dressed in his long coat, briefcase in hand. After him, arrived the families of the three children of the Roychoudhury family and the servants. Each face bore a look of curiosity and surprise, but no one spoke. After a few moments, Lavanyadevi came out of her room dressed in white. Everyone present was startled to see her in this attire. It was as if the grandeur of Lakshmi had transformed itself into the simplicity of Saraswati, a simplicity so pristine so as to make her appear almost transparent. She seemed to be an embodiment of the lines from Saraswati Vandana: "*Shuklam Brahmavichar sar parmamadyam*—Bright coloured and carrying the ultimate essence of thoughts about *Parabrahma*". Each heart instinctively filled with awe and reverence, and the whole family including the lawyer spontaneously and unthinkingly got up as if to pay obeisance to this divine form. After the ritual touching of her feet, which she cursorily went through with a wave of her hand, she asked her lawyer to proceed with the task at hand.

The lawyer started reading the will: "This house is fixed to be sold to a realtor for so many crores of rupees." An inadvertent gasp—"*Hyan!*"—escaped every family member's mouth.

"Of its four and half parts, three belong to the three families and of one half-part, ninety per cent is for Hari and Jodu." Whispers could be heard as soon as this was announced. "What! Oh, Ma! Why do you have to give away so many lakhs to petty servants?" Sensing the mood around her, Lavanyadevi looked long at her sons; her large, clear eyes filled with compassion, and then looked away. As the room fell silent again, the lawyer continued, "Ten per cent for all the new servants who do other work." Those present in the room were no longer surprised and the announcement did not evoke any reaction. "And the one remaining portion is for the Somnath Trust which will be managed by Lavanyadevi and the family lawyer till they are alive, after which Soumen will be its trustee."

This will had been prepared in the presence of Somnath-babu and bore the signatures of the lawyer and Soumen as witnesses.

The daughters-in-law were beginning to get worried. "And will mother-in-law start living with us now?" they thought. Just then, Lavanyadevi's attendant Aalo was seen dragging two suitcases towards the main entrance of the house, where Shambhu had parked the car and was carefully dusting it with a cloth. Everyone was dumbstruck and mystified, unable to figure out just what was going on. They looked at each other in silence. Suddenly Soumen got up, caught his grandmother's hand and cried, *"Ei aamar Didu! Ei aamar pran! Tui aamake chhere kothay chol-li?*—O Didu! My life! Where are you going, leaving me here?" Lavanyadevi laughed her spontaneous laugh, gave him a light pat on his head and said, "My life-partner! I am right here. Wherever will I go leaving you behind? Who do I have except you? Yes, I do have a wish to stop in Rishikesh for a few days, and then go to the upper Himalayas and spend some time with Guru-*ji*. There I must search for answers to so many questions and find solutions to so many of my dilemmas and conundrums. I need to know if the parameters by which I have lived and assayed every moment of my life were indeed wrong or if I have simply tricked myself into believing what I wanted to in order to achieve selfish solutions. What is truth? Is it relative to time? To an individual? To country? To place? Or is truth relative to power? Does it have authority beyond nation, time or place? Is it universal? I also need to think about definitions of honesty, morality, lie, non-violence, sin, holiness, heaven, hell…I need to understand the meanings of all these words and much more in greater depth. If I do not search for these answers today, the python of doubt will grip me in its deathly embrace and swallow me alive. Therefore, my dearest and only boyfriend! Pray do not stop me, let me go."

"And your expenses? You didn't keep even a penny for yourself," Soumen asked desolately, trying hard to control his tears.

"You crazy boy! Do you take this aristocratic girlfriend of yours to be a pauper? See, my mother had donated a huge sum of money to that ashram, and I too have made them some donations, so I don't think they will grudge me my two meals a day. And yes, as to the remaining question of my two sarees a year, I know you will send them to me. Now everything is taken care of. Anyway, I am not taking *sanyas* or renouncing the world. So if I am unable to live there, I promise that I will come back and stay with you."

These reassuring, consolation-filled words which were intended to cheer Soumen up made him try and fake a valiant laugh in response, but he ended up crumpling to the ground, sobbing bitterly, helplessly. But Lavanyadevi was already seated in the car. Like Gautama who was deeply troubled by all the questions that arose in his mind before he attained Nirvana, she too was in search of answers. The depth and conviction of her resolve and its radiance drenched him from head to toe.

Soumen stood up. Then, waving back to Lavanyadevi in farewell, he slowly said, "Lie, just a lie! I know you will never return because, my beloved, my dear life, I know you better than anyone else. A hundred pranams to you! Here, take all my love and take everlasting greetings from the whole world on your journey."

The car had just begun to move when Manju came running, out of breath, and started thumping the glass of Lavanyadevi's window with both fists. The car stopped with a jerk and its abruptness led Lavanyadevi to make the blunder of opening the door. As soon as she opened the door, Manju fell to looking frantically for her mistress's feet. Taken completely by surprise, Lavanyadevi got out of the car, and Manju, in a fraction of a second, encircled Lavanyadevi's feet in her arms and started wailing like a young widow. "Ma! O Ma! Right from birth, I have only thought of you as my mother. I will not live here alone without you. Ma! Please take me with you!" And she started beating her head at Lavanyadevi's feet.

Everyone was stunned. Then Lavanyadevi's calm grave voice was heard, "Get up, you silly girl! If you really believe I am your mother, then show the world that you have been brought up by me. Come, now rise, awaken and stride forward. Everyone is looking at you and wondering—what will Lavanya's daughter do? My doors will always be open for you, twenty-four hours a day." Saying this Lavanyadevi bent down to lift Manju up and held her close, pushed back the locks of hair sticking to her tear-sodden face, caressed her head in blessing and proceeded on her journey.

There must have been some remnant of royal blood still flowing through her veins that made her resist others' browbeating. Lavanyadevi did not, even for a moment, turn back to take a last look at that 'golden world'—the house she had decorated with as much care and painstaking meticulousness as an embroiderer takes in her needlework. Perhaps, even in her grandeur she had retained in her innermost recesses the ascetism of Kabir and Nanak. Or perhaps, like *padma patramivambhasa*—the lotus leaf untouched by water, she had never considered herself a part of that grandeur. Was she, like Lord Krishna, simply upholding the dignity of her duty? Krishna who, after the battle of Kurukshetra, was asked by Bhishma to bear the burden of resurrecting Parikshit who was killed by Ashwatthama's *Brahmastra*? Despite innumerable wives, queens and consorts, Krishna's detachment equalled that of a celibate. Perhaps the level of supreme detachment achieved by Lavanyadevi was similar. That is why she kept moving forward with a gentle smile on her face, radiating an aura of calm. Not once did her feet tremble, her lips quiver, or her eyes grow wet. On the contrary, she had the air of one going to a favourite place to participate in some festivity.

Her demeanour reminded one of the regal bearing of queen Prabhavatidevi of the family of King Santosh who ruled over Bengal decades ago—the resemblance was uncanny. It was so reminiscent of this lady of the ancient royal household that one felt she had been reborn.

In any case, scientists believe that every third generation receives the maximum 'genes' from its ancestors.

Lavanyadevi reached Uttarkashi Ashram. As soon as Guru-*ji* saw her, he said, "Come Lavanya, my daughter! I received news of your arrival from Soumen and was waiting for you. Do you know that you have arrived on a very auspicious day? The gates of your favourite Kedarnath shrine will open today. Have something to eat, and we can straightaway go to Kedarnath Ashram."

Kedarnath Ashram is situated at a beautiful spot in the valley behind the temple. As soon as you open your eyes they are greeted by the sight of pristine snow-capped mountains. Lavanyadevi was very fond of watching the sunrise at Kedarnath and the sunset at Gangotri, and the news therefore gladdened her heart.

The steep ascent to Kedarnath felt almost effortless to her, engrossed as she was in listening to Guru-*ji*'s nectar-like words. And as soon as they reached the Ashram, the loving hospitality of his disciples, his *shishya-sevak*s, made her feel light and unburdened. She had a light lunch, and went into such a deep sleep that it seemed as if she had been awake since an eternity.

The blush on the cheeks of the playful dawn sun as it emerged from behind snow-clad mountains was tinged with Lavanyadevi's joy. Paying her obeisance to the rising sun, she set out for the temple, and met Guru-*ji* on her way. After the early morning *darshan* of Lord Shiva and his infinite grandeur, her heart was filled with rapture. Coming out of the temple, she saw a few *panda*s quarrelling among themselves. One of them came forward and asked Guru-*ji*, "Maharaj, is the patron from Bengal?" When Guru-*ji* nodded in agreement, he delightedly told his companions, "See, didn't I tell you so? Now just ask her: doesn't she belong to the Roychoudhury family?"

Lavanyadevi was aware that *pandas*—men of God who have, over generations, guided pilgrims at temples and pilgrimage sites—could also be veritable archives of one's genealogy and family history, but she was astounded that their keen eyes could recognise her the moment they saw her. Meanwhile one of the elderly priests hurried away and came back with a young lad holding a large bundle wrapped in red cloth.

At Guru-*ji*'s suggestion, everyone moved to the ashram verandah. The elderly priest opened the bundle to tell Lavanyadevi about the various members of her maternal family—her grandfather Dhananjay-babu, her grandmother Prabhavatidevi, her uncle Soumitro Ranjan, her aunt Nalinbala, and her mother Jyotirmoyidevi—and showed her their signatures, simultaneously recounting various incidents from their pilgrimages to Kedarnath. And Lavanyadevi, who had renounced the world to embark on this pilgrimage, got entangled in the eddy of worldly memories.

Possessed of unmatched intelligence and a photographic memory, her mind immediately brought alive a vast swathe of time with the minutest details of incident and dialogue. Valmiki was moved by the suffering of a heron as it wailed in grief at the death of its partner, who was killed by a hunter's arrow as the herons were engaged in making love. The pain that Valmiki experienced flowed out in the form of the verses of the *Ramayana*. The incidents recounted by the priest, the signatures of her family members and their old portraits painted by an artist from the hills carried Lavanyadevi back to the lush foliage of her childhood memories.

The time that she had spent with her mother Jyotirmoyidevi at her *nana-bari*, her maternal grandmother's home in East Bengal, was a priceless inheritance. Jyotirmoyidevi, usually solemn and restrained, would become gay, expressive and playful once she was at her mother's, filling the house with laughter and cheer, and her affection towards her daughter would transport the young girl to the seventh heaven of delight. Lavanya loved these visits. She eagerly looked forward to them and would insist on spending her entire holidays at her *nana-bari*. Even if Jyotirmoyidevi was sometimes unable to accompany her, Lavanya would go alone. There, she would spend all her time with her grandfather, uncle and aunt, listening to stories that transported her into the enchanting world of the past.

Jyotirmoyidevi was efficient, strict and particular in word and deed, and that was probably why she could craft miracles. She was constantly writing something in a large notebook, and would put it back in her drawer and lower the lid the moment anyone entered her room.

One day, finding the room empty, Lavanya quickly lifted the cover of the drawer and peered inside. "Oh! So many notebooks!" she exclaimed as she took out a notebook from the bottom of the pile and hid it in one of her course books, eager to read it.

"*Arey*! Is this a diary or a novel?" she wondered. "The heroine is blessed with the best of virtues and she seems as beautiful as a Raja Ravi Varma painting!"

Surprisingly, Lavanya's maternal grandmother, Prabhavatidevi was the exact antithesis of her mother, being both astute and expressive. She always had a smile while talking to everyone, was ever ready to tease her friends, and was fond of dressing up well, visiting places and loved chatting with people. A platoon of servants was always ready to dance attendance upon her. So she did not have much to do, and spent her time chatting with her mother-in-law and her husband, gladdening their hearts.

One wondered whether Prabhavatidevi was actually from East Bengal. Her appearance, the way she carried herself, her dress, speech, erect carriage and regal neck—all made her look as imperious as the colonial masters of those times. Captivated by her beauty and her qualities, Raja Dhananjay Roychoudhury had sent a missive through his royal priest that he wished to take her as his second wife, despite her not being of royal blood and belonging to a family that, although quite reputed, was financially in dire straits. Though he was fair and handsome and looked young, Dhananjay-babu had already crossed thirty summers, while Prabhavatidevi, who was still into hopscotch and playing with marbles, was just fifteen.

The royal priest asked for the girl's horoscope, and on seeing that it promised *rajayoga*—which meant that she would acquire wealth and fame and live like royalty—he thought it opportune to broach the subject of Dhananjay-babu's proposal with Prabhavatidevi's widowed mother. Bhuvaneshwaridevi, on hearing the proposal, felt what a blind person would if promised vision in both eyes. Her poverty had made her increasingly anxious about how rapidly Prabhavatidevi was approaching womanhood. A large dilapidated old house, in which her three daughters wore the selfsame one or two good clothes and shared other pieces of clothing turn by turn caused the mother so much worry that she was reduced to a quarter of herself. In the absence of the master, the paltry sums of money that the workers who tended to the farms and cattle handed over to the widowed mistress were hardly sufficient to take care of the family's needs. And need one even talk about the customs of respectable Bengali families of the time? Whether the kitchen fires were lit once a day or just once in two days, it was mandatory for daughters of the family to be well-versed in music, dance, studies and embroidery.

As daughters in Bengal are treated with considerable respect and affection, they grow up with an easy openness. Bhuvaneshwaridevi's three daughters would go for a swim not just to the family pond but also to the Padma and Meghna rivers nearby. No one ever seemed to mind or even notice. It was Dhananjay-babu's sight, like Rishi Vaishampayan's, which had placed his Sita-Satyavati Prabhavatidevi in the temple of his heart and had led him to send his family priest to this household with his marriage proposal.

On hearing Raja-babu's message, Bhuvaneshwaridevi was swamped by a tidal wave of happiness and she called out to her daughter with all the strength she could muster, "Prabhavatiiiii! Come here."

The moment Prabhavati, responding to her mother's call, skipped blithely into the room, her two long plaits tied double-fold atop her head with a gay ribbon, the priest was left with no doubts whatsoever about the possibility of receiving a handsome reward from the zamindar family. Without further delay, he promptly placed in Prabhavati's hand a coconut and a silver coin and put a long *tilak* on her forehead to confirm the marriage. On her mother's prompting, she bent down to touch the priest's feet and he blessed her saying, "May you gain in affluence and children." Taken by surprise, she looked questioningly at her mother. Bhuvaneshwaridevi came forward and hugged her daughter, tears streaming down her face. She gratefully thanked the Lord, not just for the present but also for the future.

Dhananjay-babu's immense wealth was much talked about, not just in Dhaka, Khulna, Chittagong and Faridpur, but also in the English localities of Kolkata like Dover Park, Alipore and Belvedere Road. Bhuvaneshwaridevi was constantly thinking of how the person so widely known for his generosity of spirit the world over was about to become her son-in-law, and prayed incessantly to God, "O Lord, please take good care of this harvest moon of *Sharad Poornima* that has emerged from the dark *Amavasya* of my broken fortune."

In keeping with the generosity that Dhananjay-babu was famed for, his diwan sahib arrived the very next day with money and a team of masons who worked night and day to renovate the house in a manner that even Bhuvaneshwaridevi's ancestors showered their blessings from heaven.

On the auspicious day, amidst the sounds of festive bells, ululation and blowing of conch shells, when Prabhavatidevi, her beautiful face hidden behind a betel leaf, weighed down by her jewellery and a brocaded Banarasi saree, stepped into the palace with its tall, round pillars, all the women of the family, near and distant, prayed for her well-being. As she bent down to touch her mother-in-law's feet, the mild lady stopped her from doing so and said, "No, not my daughter-in-law—you are my daughter! Now take this bunch of keys to the household and free me from my worldly responsibilities so that I can devote time to the worship of the Lord." Jealousy arose quick in the minds of the women of the family when they heard the queen mother utter these words and they tried variously to suggest that she should refuse. Though respectful of their counsel, the newly-wed bride gently extended her hand to accept the bunch of keys and, dipping her feet in *alta* as per ritual, entered the marbled courtyard of the house, leaving neat red footprints as she walked.

One, Prabhavati was his wife from the second marriage and, add to that, she was young and beautiful. It was as if the poet Bihari's couplet, "the newly-wed is but a child, yet to bloom into a woman, and if the king is so enamoured of his bride today, what will happen tomorrow?", was being enacted by Dhananjay-babu, who hovered around his wife like a bee around a flower. He started believing that he was luckier than the gods, especially when she developed an easy friendship with the children from his first wife, Soumitro Ranjan and Nalinbala. From morning to evening he would wait anxiously for Prabhavatidevi just to say something. And he would wait eagerly for the opportunity to fulfil her wishes like Aladdin's djinn!

The wooden bridge called Rani Ma's Bridge that one can see even today as one travels from Dhaka to Dhamrai village is Prabhavatidevi's gift. On one occasion when Prabhavatidevi was returning from her middle-sister's village, her chariot had been stopped from crossing a wooden bridge over a small rivulet as the retinue of the zamindar who had built the bridge was passing over it. But she was Prabhavatidevi, the much-adored queen of the palace. She immediately commanded, "Turn the chariot back and camp at the nearest inn!"

The moment this news reached Dhananjay-babu, he raced to the inn on horseback in the blink of an eye. When the queen saw him, as if issuing a decree, she said, "Get a new bridge built immediately, else I am fine where I am."

Almost the entire population of the village set about building the bridge at random wages. What would have taken months to build was completed in just five days, and the chariot drawn by Haryanvi bulls, their horns plated with gold and bells tinkling around their necks, vied with the wind as it crossed the bridge amidst the blowing of conch shells and applause of the villagers.

Instead of scolding her, her mother-in-law embraced Prabhavati and proudly said, "Look how intelligent my daughter-in-law is! Her wish has benefitted so many!"

The soil of East Bengal produced gold in the form of jute. The region was well-known the world over for its delicious *ilish*, handwoven *jamdani* sarees and the softest, sheerest muslin. Combining Sutanuti, Gobindopur and Kolkata, the British made the port city of Kolkata their capital. What more need be said about the prosperity of the city where the Governor General, representative of Queen Victoria herself, resided? All the wealth of India, that golden bird of the British Empire, was accumulated here, loaded onto ships and sent to England. When the English lords plundered not just the material wealth of the country but also its human capital, loading them onto ships as *girmitiyas*, why would they spare what was precious in East Bengal? Some of the exhibits in the London Museum today, like the famed Dhakai mulmul so finely loomed that one can see through seven layers of it and the exquisitely woven Kashmiri *shahtoosh* shawl that can pass through a finger ring, were things that even Lavanyadevi herself had seen being made by craftsmen of the country.

How could a beautiful city scaling such heights in trade not be the centre of attraction for the rich and wealthy of Dhaka? Dhananjay-babu would often travel to Kolkata, and his young sagacious new bride, accompanied by his son and daughter who were almost of the same age as her, would come along with him to visit the English shops selling a variety of rare and precious merchandise, each more attractive than the other. The children were happy because of the mother's generosity; the mother was happy because of what she had gained. There was good cheer in abundance everywhere. It was around this time that Dhananjay-babu fixed his son Soumitro Ranjan's marriage in a well to do family.

Just a few days after Soumitro Ranjan got married, conch shells from the palace announced that Dhananjay-babu's wife Prabhavatidevi would further the family. Almost five years had passed since her son's second marriage, and the queen mother had given up all hope that her new daughter-in-law would give her the gift of a grandchild. She was so euphoric when she heard the news that she immediately bequeathed to Prabhavati the priceless ancestral *naulakha*. The magnificent necklace suited Prabhavati divinely—when she wore it, she looked like the radiant moon garlanded by stars. As soon as she entered her bedroom after touching her mother-in-law's feet, Dhananjay-babu hovered around the string of lights like a moth circling a flame.

Prabhavatidevi continued with her packed daily routine as diligently as before. After tending to the plants in the royal garden, the fruits and vegetables on the farm, swimming in the palace pond, supervising the feeding of the Haryanvi cows and bulls in the cow shelter and tending to Dhananjay-babu's favourite horse, it would be almost evening by the time she would finally enter her bed chamber, and the atmosphere would be pervaded by the sound of conches and the fragrance of burning *dhuno*. She would quickly bathe and start preparations for Dhananjay-babu's dinner before he returned to the inner chambers of the palace.

Apart from the best lady doctor in Dhaka, there was an English lady doctor who would come from Kolkata every fortnight to examine her. Other than being told not to ride horses there were no restrictions on Prabhavati, her slim and sinewy five-feet-six frame attesting to her good health.

On the last day of April, at 5:17 in the morning, Prabhavatidevi gave birth to a daughter, Jyotirmoyi. Although her labour was mostly painless, the way the child was born was the first among many surprises that were to follow in the Roychoudhury family. The baby came into the world intact with her amniotic sac, which seemed coated with a white chalk-like powder. The lady doctor felt that this happened because the mother had taken too much *banslochan*. She quickly removed a bit of the powder with her gloved hand and cut a corner of the sac with her scissors. The sac burst open and fluid spilled out. *Ya* Allah! Is this a human baby or a ball of snow? Or a mass of moonlight? A white lotus blooming in the sea of beauty? This tiny dazzling bundle like sheer white 'organdie'…is it really a baby or some fairy? Oblivious of the astonished and curious eyes of the lady doctor and the host of female relatives surrounding her, the baby let out a brief tentative cry—then she wailed so loud that the whole palace reverberated with her cry. The drumbeats resounded. Dhananjay-babu was naturally very happy, but Soumitro was happier. He could recognise and appreciate beauty. He took the new-born Jyotirmoyi in his arms and held her close to his breast. The unique affection that he displayed towards his infant sister at that moment remained constant lifelong, and he of all the people in the world showered the maximum love on his sister and her family.

Lavanya was greatly impressed by her mother's talent for writing. She was also enthralled as the writing seemed to reveal the most intimate of secrets between mother Prabhavati and daughter Jyotirmoyi, even those that remained hidden in the innermost recesses of the mind. How could a mother reveal to her daughter things that she could not confide even to herself? Such things never ever happen. How then did it happen between these two? Was it Jyotirmoyidevi's extraordinary talent that could hypnotise others into revealing all? Or was it a deep loneliness hidden beneath Prabhavatidevi's dutiful exterior which broke through the dams of self-restraint on finding a genuinely empathetic listener like her own daughter? Whatever be the reason, one thing was certain—if her mother's diaries were ever to be published it would most certainly be banned, just as

Lady Chatterley's Lover was. Lavanya pushed away such fantastic thoughts interrupting the flow of her emotions and picked up another notebook and was soon engrossed in it.

Soumitro Ranjan was affluent and immensely extravagant by nature. His extravagance was well known not only in Kolkata but in Delhi and Mumbai too. When Dhananjay-babu tried to curtail his spending, Soumitro took his entire share of the property in cash, blowing his money day and night in Kolkata. It is said that even today, a huge number of tourists visit his office in Narayanprasad Babu Lane just to see its gilded roof—designed and executed by Persian craftsmen who used liquid gold to do the inlay work. The entire ceiling replicated the design of a Persian carpet, and Soumitro Ranjan, along with many beautiful women of Kolkata, would gaze up at it as they relaxed on his bed.

Soumitro's affection for Jyotirmoyi remained unchanged even after he separated from his father. On one occasion, impressed by a gold and marble table-clock with a lion design, the normally reticent Jyotirmoyi had inadvertently remarked, "*Wah*! What superb craftsmanship! I have never seen such a perfect balance of opulence and restraint!" Hearing this, Soumitro Ranjan immediately instructed the accompanying maid to take the expensive clock, which had reached him from Switzerland that very day, to Jyotirmoyidevi's house. She regretted having voiced her admiration and repeatedly requested him to take it back, but to no avail. The clock adorned her table for a long time.

Soon after Jyotirmoyi was born, Dhananjay-babu got his eldest daughter Nalinbala married to Raja Debjyoti Roychoudhury, who belonged to the royal family of Faridpur. Prabhavatidevi was never one to fail in her duties. In keeping with the proverbial Bengali custom of observing thirteen festivals in twelve months, she unfailingly sent gifts on every festive occasion. The shortcomings that accrue from a lack of institutional education were nowhere in evidence in her person. Prabhavatidevi was always conscious of her personal boundaries and respected others' personal space too. She did not once intrude into Nalinbala's in-laws' house, nor later into Jyotirmoyi's, nor did she ever enter her son Aniruddha Roychoudhury's house without being asked to.

Prabhavatidevi was able to discharge all her responsibilities successfully, and at the same time also win her affluent husband's heart. Of the sixteen qualities that characterise *nayikas* or heroines, a wife must be adept at playing the contradictory roles of being both a mother to her children and an *abhisarika*—the heroine who secretly leaves home to meet her lover—to her husband. That Prabhavatidevi was able to consistently achieve a perfect balance and coordination between these two contrasting roles was an astonishing accomplishment. Even if she had to strike the occasional dissonant note in this ordered melodic symphony of her twin roles, it only seemed to enhance the overall beauty and harmony of her comportment.

In Dhaka, Prabhavatidevi fulfilled her duties as the elder queen of the royal household with consummate ease. And for partaking equally in her husband's pleasure and for his companionship, she chose Kolkata. In Kolkata, if there were opportunities to indulge oneself in leisure and liquor, there were as many opportunities to enhance one's character through the attainment of knowledge, learning and culture. If, on the one hand, there was the racecourse and people were minting money and becoming rich overnight by exporting opium from Afeem Chowrasta and Kaligodam to China, there were, on the other, institutions like University of Calcutta, Medical College and Presidency College which were polishing the real diamonds of Bengal.

Contradictions make life colourful. If all the colours in a palette are equally attractive, they sometimes take away from the beauty of a picture instead of complementing each other. So, the painter sometimes deliberately uses some common or incongruous colour. Gods yearn to become humans because the everlasting spring in their lives, like the fragrance of the *parijat*, like an existence free of all pain and misery, like flowers without thorns, makes their existence dreary and dull. It is true that a life full of unending delight becomes monotonous—the sense of contentment that comes from accomplishing a difficult task and pleasure can only be fully appreciated if it follows pain and suffering. A childhood full of difficulties had inculcated in Prabhavatidevi a strong sense of practicality. Therefore, while in Dhaka, she chose to immerse herself in the Padma of her duties and responsibilities, when in Kolkata, she plunged headlong into the city's 'fashion-Ganga' along with her husband to keep herself duly entertained.

The sight of Prabhavatidevi in spotless white breeches riding Dhananjay-babu's favourite Arabian horse on the racecourse reminded one of a graceful slender-necked swan who had magically transformed a handsome prince into a magnificent white stallion that she rode, her elegant neck erect. Her exceptional beauty and irresistible youth stunned all race-goers and left them dazzled, rendering them incapable of betting rationally. As a result, all the money that was staked went into the hands of Dhananjay-babu.

Soumitro's office on Narayanprasad Babu Lane was just adjacent Afeem Chowrasta, and Dhananjay-babu, befriending the owners of Tarachand Ghanshyamdas, the richest firm in those days, made huge profits in the opium trade. Prabhavatidevi too befriended Champadevi and Imartidevi of the firm Mangatrai Kirorimal and, having learnt from them the nuances of trading in linseed and silver, made two major deals in silver and accumulated such enormous profits that the palace treasury in Dhaka brimmed over with wealth.

If Prabhavatidevi was won over by Champadevi's innate wisdom and understanding of life that stemmed from the simplicity of her rural roots, Champadevi was all admiration for Prabhavatidevi's exquisite persona and refinement. Champadevi was married to a typically wealthy and prosperous Haryanvi, Prabhavatidevi to an aristocratic zamindar from Dhaka, located in the shadow of Kolkata.

One day, when Prabhavatidevi served Imartidevi a *rosogolla*, the latter suddenly stood up and started cursing the former and accusing her of being a low-caste *mlechha* who was trying to corrupt her. Prabhavatidevi was stunned by this sudden outburst and could not fathom what had happened, but Champadevi rolled over with laughter. Even when Champadevi explained to her, "*Arey*, this is not a hen's egg, but a Bengali speciality, a *rasgulla*", Imartidevi disbelievingly said, "I'm sure both of you have teamed up to fool me." And then, when she attempted to stuff the sweet whole into her mouth, syrup from the large *rosogolla* squirted out and fell on her expensive *lehenga*, which only heightened her exasperation. It was a scene worth watching. Imartidevi jumped up and left in a huff, and her two friends were struggling so hard to control their helpless laughter that they forgot even to assuage her anger and stop her from leaving the place! Champadevi later received a small scolding from Mangatrai-*ji* for this.

This friendship intensified during the *adda* and gossip sessions in the *antarmahal*, the women's chambers of the house. In the course of one such conversation, Champa told Prabhavati about Sir Chhajuram Jat, who had in his own lifetime become a legend. On Prabhavati's request, she agreed to narrate an anecdote about him. "In the days that household expenses amounted to not more than five rupees a month, my father-in-law Ramkumar Kejriwal had seen three crores worth of shares kept carelessly in Chhajuram's wooden almirah. Sir Chhajuram was the lord of the princely estate of Shahpura in Hisar and was much admired for his generosity of spirit and his uprightness not just by his own subjects but also by the British lords. Neither his affluence nor the knighthood conferred on him by the British affected his humility. He was a friend of friends, and he extended his friendship to rich and poor alike."

Prabhavati interjected, "But what about the anecdote that you were going to relate?"

"Oh yes, yes," Champa began, "It so happened that a broker from Ganpatrai and Sons once filed a case against him. The news brought the whole share market crashing down! A case against Chhajuram! How? Why? Who is this idiot who has lost his mind? When someone is approaching their doom, they start acting against their own interests! These and similar observations started doing the rounds of the market.

"The case was presented in court. That any judge would not know Chhajuram was unthinkable. As soon as the hearing commenced, the first statement that the judge made in his broken, thickly Bangla-inflected Hindi was, '*Ai Gonpatrai ka dolal! Hum pota kiya ki tum kal tak to kongaal thha, so aaj tumre paas itna paisa kider se aa gaya ki tum Sir Chhajuram-ji ka noksaan ka bharpai kor diya?* Hey you broker for Ganpatrai! I am aware that you were a pauper until yesterday, so how did you come into so much money that you could cover Sir Chhajuram's losses?'

"'Your Excellency, my lord! I…I earned the money through brokerage,' stammered the complainant.

"'In whose deals?' asked the judge.

"The broker replied, 'Sir Chhajuram's, huzoor! I have earned all my money from him. You can see all my accounts, sir!' He proffered his account books for examination.

"Ignoring them, the judge said, 'Okay! So, you have earned all your money from Sir Chhajuram. Right?'

"'That's right, my lord.'

"'Did Sir Chhajuram ever question your integrity?'

"'No, my lord.'

"'Did he settle your accounts according to what you claimed?'

"'Yes, my lord.'

"The judge was so angered by the broker's 'Yes, my lord' that he thundered, 'You shameless man! Go drown yourself in the Ganga! You have filed a case for a few thousands against a man from whom you have profited in lakhs, and that too at a time when he is in difficulty. Does this not embarrass or shame you even a little?' With this, the judge slammed his gavel down and said, 'Case dismissed!'

"Chhajuram was not in Kolkata at the time. He was in Bhiwani. He had not reneged on his payment but had merely asked the broker for some more time. And anyway, Chhajuram was not in any dire straits at the time. Even so, when his condition improved a bit, he walked down to the broker's office and personally gave him a cheque for the amount due, adding the interest accruing to him on account of the delay.

"When he saw the great man walk into his office in person, at first the broker's face went blank. Then his attention was drawn to the partially visible gold watch-chain on his three-piece suit, and also to the blue corner of a cheque in Sir Chhajuram's breast-pocket.

"Making a show of dusting the seat of the chair with his kurta, the broker took recourse to his native Haryanvi as a gesture of familiarity, '*Sa'ab tham! Merey ghaneybhag jo tharey charan mere office me padey*—Greetings, saheb! It is my good fortune that you have stepped into my office. I am honoured! *Arey* Ramkishore! Go order a cup of the best tea. Saheb, please make yourself comfortable and have a cup of tea first.'

"Chhajuram-*ji* said in an even voice, 'Bhai, tea can come later, but first things first. Please accept this cheque and give me a receipt.'

"'What cheque, saheb? My case has been dismissed in court, and therefore I have no claim on this money!'

"'Bhai, the court may have rejected your claim, but I stand right here in front of you, so please take the cheque and give me a receipt for it.'

"After handing over the cheque he also had a cup of tea and then went back without a trace of arrogance or rancour.

"People say there were not just one or two but hundreds who witnessed this incident. Everyone present in the share market at the time that saw or heard the news that Sir Chhajuram was going to the broker's office on foot, and not in his Rolls Royce, had rushed to see what the matter was. In a matter of moments, not just the rectangular office but the road outside was chock full of curious onlookers who thronged the place and were wondering, 'Let's see what is going to happen! Seth got back from Bhiwani this morning and is going straight to that office. Most certainly he will grab the scoundrel by his collar and give him two hefty thwacks with a shoe—he's a Haryanvi Rajput after all!'

"The sum total of the story is that the skies resounded with applause for Sir Chhajuram Jat! And the broker was so humiliated that he had no place left to hide his face."

When Champa told Prabhavati that this was just an ordinary incident in the life of the great man who achieved so many glories that narrating them all was impossible, the latter made a mental note that she would surely meet this remarkable gentleman someday.

Jyotirmoyidevi's diary further read, "I do not know how much of a friendship developed between Ma and Sir saheb, but one day, Gajendra-*ji*, talking about Sir Chhajuram Jat, said, 'Jyoti, do you know about the Viceroy's latest order? As long as Sir Chhajuram is unwell, no one is permitted to use horns in Alipore.'

"'That is hardly news. He is a 'Sir' after all!' I replied mirthlessly.

"*Arey*, don't be silly! Kolkata is so full of 'Sirs' that the title is meaningless. It is Sir Chhajuram Jat's own 'credibility' that has led to this order being issued."

The image of Chhajuram's three sons had stayed with Lavanyadevi from her childhood days, and this made the story of their father more interesting to her. Has Ma written about the 'three musketeers' as well, she wondered. And musing thus, as soon as she rested her head on the table, she was, like Alice, instantly transported to the wonderland of her dreams where a handsome prince suddenly emerged from the star-spangled sky and started waltzing gracefully with a princess. The dance continued for what seemed like aeons, after which the prince asked for the princess's hand in marriage. The king turned down his request saying, "Go and expand your kingdom first, only then can you have my daughter as your bride."

Lavanyadevi woke up with a start and looked around to see if anyone had seen her with her mother's diaries. Assured that no one had caught her reading them, she let out a sigh of relief and, drawn to those notebooks like a magnet, was soon engrossed in them once again.

The pleasures and thrills of reading one's own family history are unimaginable, for the reader has an immediate and personal association with each character; the characters and events are so real that they seem to come alive on the pages, taking the reader with them through the many lanes and bylanes of her own memory, making it an unparalleled and other-worldly experience.

Oh! This prince is none other than the eldest of the 'three musketeers' who bought many a village for the sake of the princess, built her a house that was a replica of the Buckingham Palace and readied a special car for her studded with precious stones which was the exact likeness of Queen Victoria's motorcar. And yet, the king of Kashmir rejected his proposal because his estate was not large enough. Like a god fallen from heaven, the prince took refuge in the arms of an Englishwoman, Camilla, who was only too happy to love him.

Lavanyadevi seemed to be able to hear the echoes of a muted submerged song in this narration: that because of the intimacy between the two families of Dhananjay-babu and Sir Chhajuram Jat, the children were quite close to each other since childhood, and Jyotirmoyidevi was impeccable in her beauty, manners, propriety and decency. But the strong ties between the families and Jyotirmoyidevi's exceptional propriety and reticence held the two younger brothers back and prevented them from saying anything. The tenderness that characterised Jyotirmoyidevi's descriptions of these people gave a clear indication of her feelings for the eldest son. But those were times long past, and all that now fell in the realm of conjecture, of ifs and maybes; all those feelings and emotions remained unvoiced, unsaid.

"Oh! So this is how Ma's love was killed in its infancy. But these boys were brainless. *Arey*! The least they could do was just to ask Ma once, directly or indirectly! And they would have come to know of her feelings."

Though there is no mention at all of any of Jyotirmoyidevi's personal feelings in this autobiographical novel, rather, this record of her life, who knows what emotions she harboured under that serene and solemn demeanour? Is it not possible that she too was attracted towards the handsome, rich and prosperous Jat youth? Even rishis engaged in the severest of penances are susceptible to the tremendous lure and charm of the first flush of youth. Did an ordinary girl, brought up amidst worldly pleasures, manage to stay immune?

Could Lavanya gather enough courage to ask her mother this question? Jyotirmoyidevi would probably kill her! And one thing was certain—asking her this question would ensure that Lavanya's reading of this wonderful eye-witness account of the private and public sphere of Kolkata of those times, written in the form of a diary, would come to an untimely end. And just as the heart of a man driven by passion is fixated on the beauty of his beloved, Lavanya's mind, greedy to know more, was entangled in the pages of her mother's diaries like a moth circling a flame. She therefore decided to brush aside her curiosity for the moment, and went back to reading more about Jyotirmoyidevi's youth.

Jyotirmoyi's younger brother Aniruddha and sister Indrani were both interested in British literature, but Jyotirmoyi found the literature of her own country much more interesting. She was crazy about books from the time she was a little girl, and many a time she was caught surreptitiously reading war stories with a flashlight on, under her blanket.

"Ah! So that explains the river-like flow of her prose!"

Jyotirmoyi was neither as prolific as her mother nor as expressive as her sister Indrani, but she wasn't exactly tongue-tied either. She always sported a carefully cultivated smile; she would clearly say what needed to be said when it needed to be said, and continue smiling. People said she weighed every word she spoke and that you could string her words together like the pearls of

Basra to make a necklace of *gajamukta*, the elephant pearl—the rarest and most expensive of all pearls.

Jyotirmoyi's calm, composed and modest nature reassured Prabhavatidevi; she was never for a moment worried that her daughter could be indiscreet in any way. And it never occurred to her that her daughter had reached marriageable age till, during one of her sojourns to Dhaka, her mother Bhuvaneshwaridevi asked her, "*Mone aachhey Jyoti'r koto boyosh hoye gyachhey? Or biye debe na?* Do you need to be reminded of your daughter's age? When will you get her married?" Struck by this sudden realisation, Prabhavatidevi immediately sprang into action and sent a message to her husband, who was out in the *naubatkhana*, to immediately come to the *antarmahal*.

Prabhavatidevi's wealth of acquaintances contained many gems, each outshining the other. Her personal standing and her family reputation were together like a bejewelled crown that any of these gems would feel privileged to be part of. But was it easy to find a suitable groom for such a beautiful, modest, intelligent and prosperous young woman?

After much discussion, both parents reached the conclusion that they would prioritise intelligence and decorousness. As the blessings of Goddess Lakshmi meant that they had abundant wealth to give to their daughter, they sent back the horoscopes of many suitors whose only qualification was their affluence.

The aristocratic society of those times held ICS qualified, London-returned sons of noble families in high esteem. An ICS certificate was considered weightier that a royal lineage and overshadowed the latter. And Gajendranath Thakur was an ICS as well as the scion of the royal family of Thakurs. Both Prabhavatidevi and Dhananjay-babu agreed that he was the best match for Jyotirmoyi.

The fun of matchmaking lies in the fact that both parties think it is they who have emerged victorious. And Dhananjay Roychoudhury and Moloy Roythakur were both equally exultant. The word in the English dictionary that best described

Gajendranath Thakur was 'perfect gentleman', while the *nayika bheda* of the *Agnipurana* would classify Jyotirmoyi as *uttama*—the best. Prabhavatidevi wanted an immediate engagement and a quick wedding, and she set about her duties with the urgency of a fire-fighter.

Fortunately, around the same time, Dhananjay-babu had made a huge profit in his silver business, much exceeding his own expectations—it amounted to four lakh rupees. Prabhavatidevi, without a second thought, said, "The almighty has sent this money for Jyoti's wedding. We will not spend a single paisa from it on anything else." Did Dhananjay-babu have any option but to nod his head in affirmation?

Lavanyadevi was dumfounded when she read this. "Four lakhs! In those times!" she repeated to herself in disbelief. "That must be more than four crore rupees today! Now I understand why Aniruddha Mama was not on talking terms with grandma and grandpa for six months—he was not at fault. He was naturally upset that such a huge share of the family property was spent on his sister."

Lavanyadevi could vividly recall the day that Gajendra-babu, immediately after returning home from office, called out in an urgent voice, "Jyoti, where are you? Come here, please!" Jyotirmoyidevi, taken by surprise, asked, "What is the matter? Why are you so agitated?"

Gajendra-babu heaved a long sigh and said, "I bumped into Aniruddha today. He told me that he has stopped talking to both you and Babu-*ji*. He claimed that his parents, my in-laws, have cheated him. Is this true?"

Every word uttered by Gajendra-babu seemed charged with disbelief. He was absolutely certain that it was all a big misunderstanding and must be the handiwork of some mischief monger. He could not for a moment imagine that Jyotirmoyi or Babu-*ji* could do anything wrong, even if they wished to! But when the complainant was Aniruddha, could one simply dismiss what he said as a bunch of lies? What had really happened? Who was at fault? As Gajendra-babu kept looking at Jyotirmoyidevi with anxious, enquiring eyes, she spoke in a soft yet serious tone, "It is true that Aniruddha is not speaking to me or Baba. I have tried to reason with him—'Look, Baba is nearing ninety, why are you behaving like this with him?'—but, as you know, Aniruddha and Indrani, being the younger siblings, are too headstrong. They never listen to anyone. Even bhabhi tried to reason things out with him, but he simply refused to budge from his position."

"What exactly is his complaint?" Gajendra-babu the ICS Gazetteer demanded to know.

"The huge amount of money that was spent on my wedding! I tried my best to assuage his feelings. I even gave up my share of the family property, but he was still dissatisfied. It seems only time can bring him around." Jyotirmoyidevi could have also told him a few other things—such as the fact that she couldn't have given her brother the money he was asking for even if she wanted to. The cash she got went into funding the various odd ventures that Gajendra-babu's dear younger brother Kunjabihari tried, unsuccessfully, to set up—it was all used up within a year or two of marriage.

The pages that followed were packed with elaborate descriptions of Jyotirmoyidevi's magnificent wedding and the rituals, spread over almost a month. The brain behind these grand and regal arrangements was none other than her maternal uncle, the affluent Soumitro Ranjan, who had scoured the length and breadth of the country for the rarest, the fanciest and the most exorbitant items to indulge both mind and body, and gathered all these at the venue of the wedding—the Tripura Palace, Kolkata. His exquisite taste was also in evidence in the grand welcome received by the groom's party on reaching Kolkata—the ripples on the Ganga undulated with the heavenly voices of some of the most renowned singers from Lucknow, Allahabad and Varanasi, all of them especially invited to entertain the guests as the flower-decked steamers ferried them into the city.

Prabhavatidevi had asked Soumitro to take care of the arrangements so there would be no inadequacy of any kind in her plans to make this marriage memorable and grand. Not only was nothing amiss in his planning, the scale and magnificence surpassed even Prabhavatidevi's expectations. The arrangements were talked about for years after the wedding. As the past came alive on the pages of the notebook, Lavanyadevi was left astounded by the flawless details of this lavish event and could not help but admire her grandmother's managerial skills, her originality, her zeal for perfection, her taste and her resourcefulness.

Seven years had gone by after this memorable wedding, and Gajendra-babu's mother Brajabaladevi had started getting worried. In these seven years, her daughter-in-law had taken her for pilgrimages to the *char dham* and the sixteen *jyotirlingas*, but in her heart of hearts she longed for grandchildren to play with in her old age. She prayed to God every day to grant her the joy and good fortune of becoming a grandmother. One spring afternoon, Jyotirmoyidevi suddenly got up from her bed and rushed to the washroom. Brajabaladevi was jubilant on hearing the sounds of her daughter-in-law retching, and immediately sprang into action. She blew joyously and vigorously on the auspicious conch-shell to announce the good news. Gajendra tried to tell her to control her excitement and be a bit prudent. "Ma! Have patience till the doctor examines Jyotirmoyi!" But Brajabaladevi brushed his words aside. "*Arey*! Forget the doctor! Take it from me. I am the doctor's grandmother in experience!" The doctor's confirmation, when it came, was a mere formality to her.

On a golden afternoon the following winter, Jyotirmoyidevi gave birth to a bonny baby. What an extraordinarily beautiful baby it was! Two Koh-i-Noor diamonds together could not match her in beauty. When the infant was bathed and cleaned and put in her mother's lap for her first feed, Jyotirmoyidevi, seeing her for the first time, let out a gasp of surprise. Had Prabhavatidevi been reborn in the form of this adorable baby? Her pink complexion, her features, her thick curly black hair, her artistic fingers, long and graceful limbs, her deep-set lotus-like eyes and the regal nose—everything from head to toe seemed a 'carbon-copy' of Prabhavatidevi! A tiny replica! With a quick shake of her head Jyotirmoyidevi dismissed the thought of rebirth as mere fancy and clasped her new-born child tenderly to her bosom.

The urgency with which she hugged her new-born was perhaps partly also because of an obscure shadow of apprehension that lurked in Jyotirmoyidevi's prudent mind. It was, as her diary revealed, occasioned by an incident that took place sometime before the arrival of her daughter.

"Around this time, Prabhavatidevi was struggling bravely to fulfil most of her duties and responsibilities even as she battled tuberculosis, which was incurable in those days. Jyotirmoyi and Aniruddha had been married off; and she had, over time, acquainted Dhananjay-babu with the myriad responsibilities of family and household, before she passed away. When Prabhavatidevi's storeroom was unlocked a few days after her death, it revealed, among other things, dozens of cotton and woollen baby suits of all sizes, a perambulator and a host of other baby items. Indrani, Aniruddha and Dhananjay-babu looked at each other in astonishment, all three searching for answers to the same questions: 'What had come over the wise Prabhavatidevi in her last days? Why would a woman as intelligent and capable as Prabhavatidevi, who had taken the Roychoudhury family from success to success and whose decisions, discernment and meticulousness were not just beyond reproach but unquestionable, fill her storeroom with an odd collection of useless articles when she was about to leave the house and the world?' They all stood around incredulously, but a much greater surprise awaited them. At that precise moment a messenger arrived and presented on a silver tray an auspicious letter from Brajabaladevi, with the feet of Goddess Lakshmi symbolically imprinted upon it, as was the custom. The letter conveyed her felicitations to Dhananjay-babu as he was soon going to become a grandfather. Father, son and daughter were mystified. They could not see this chain of events as anything other than a miracle. But how did this happen?

"Wasn't Prabhavatidevi as earthly as any other human being—flesh and blood, endowed with five senses, corporeal? How then could she possess supernatural abilities? Was it what people term a sixth sense, a differential intelligence that can divine what is imminent? Could she enter a trance when she was meditating and foresee the future? How else could fairytale-like situations like the one they just witnessed happen in real life? Aniruddha was engrossed in these thoughts when he noticed a small red book in a corner of a shelf. Picking it up, he opened it and started reading it aloud: 'The first two lockers are for Aniruddha's wife Suryabala and the next two for Indrani; the small locker and all the baby items are for Jyotirmoyi's child.' Aniruddha did not know how to react; he was stunned. His father gently patted his back as the three slowly walked out of the storeroom."

The next notebook contained the story of Lavanyadevi's birth. The lyrical descriptions of her birth rivalled the beauty and rhythm of the *Agomoni* songs that celebrate the arrival of the goddess during Durga Puja. It is impossible to fully comprehend the flights that the imagination of an impassioned and eagerly expectant mother took as she waited for the birth of the chosen one—one who was pure, one who had imbibed both the energy of the Gods and the unyielding attitude of ascetics—unless one read what Jyotirmoyidevi had written.

While flipping through the pages of the notebook which recounted every incident in Lavanyadevi's life, big and small, down to the smallest detail—her first cry, her first visit to the temple, her first journey, her first school and college—one particular incident caught her eye. As Lavanyadevi read through it, what vestige of playful childishness remained in her character seemed to vanish, to be replaced with gravity and judiciousness.

What she read gave her an insight into the struggles and determination that had gone into Jyotirmoyidevi's efforts in bringing up her daughter. "When Lavanya, without batting an eyelid, turned down that famous director's offer for a role in his film—a role that would have etched her name in gold in the City of Dreams, and the dazzle and brilliance of which would have made her famous not just within the country but even abroad—it filled me with immense faith and peace of mind. This was not just about the fact that she said 'No'. It was a 'no' that assured me about her future. This 'no' assured me that my Lavanya would never ever stray from her path, even for a moment. Her every living moment, every step, every gesture and every word would be bound by the strictest parameters of propriety and dignity. To decline an offer made by a director as reputed and acclaimed as Mr. Sen was something that even celestial nymphs like Menaka and Urvashi would have found difficult. But here was my Lavanya, an ordinary human being…and just a wisp of a girl! She could do what these *apsaras* found difficult! She has actually done it! My Lavanya has shown that she can! I feel truly blessed today. I am trembling all over with joy. Today, for once, I want to dance—in the garden and by the pond, under the tall trees and the open skies. I want to twirl round and round on the green grass! I want to dance! I want to dance until I am exhausted! This fever of joy pulsating inside me has made me so delirious that if I don't keep dancing to tire myself, the pent-up excitement coursing through my veins will cause them to snap!"

What a poignant description of Ma's emotions, thought Lavanyadevi. Ma, who everyone believed was just a 'machine that existed only to work.' And all because no one ever saw her raising her voice, indulging in trivial prattle, laughing out loud, clapping in joy, turning back to see something out of curiosity, leaving someplace in a huff, or getting angry! Which essentially meant that no one ever saw her doing anything that ordinary human beings usually do!! Who could have fathomed the immense ocean of love surging inside her? Lavanyadevi felt the spray from the unruly waves of this unseen ocean drench her to the very core of her being.

Was her mother's toughness, her reserve and her extreme scrupulousness just an assumed exterior aimed to keep her on the 'right path'? Is it not possible that just like other people, Ma too loved the simple pleasures of life and desired to set herself adrift in the stream of these pleasures and let its currents carry her away in any direction they wanted to? Perhaps she did. Perhaps she too ventured out, but the sight of her young daughter Lavanya standing on the banks always held her back and did not allow her to go any further, and she dived underwater and swam back, unseen by anyone.

Being always scrupulous to a fault herself, Jyotirmoyidevi never had to instruct or remind or lecture her daughter about anything—she was Lavanya's role model. Lavanya undertook each and every work with such caution and care that she never ever fell short of the high standards her mother had set. She combined in herself the essence of both her mother Jyotirmoyidevi as well as her grandmother Prabhavatidevi. It was but natural that their qualities combined would prevail over their individual ones.

Lavanya's turning down the offer of a director like Mr. Sen had so astounded and elated Jyotirmoyidevi that she again brought up the incident in her last notebook, written as Lavanya was on the cusp of adulthood, a few pages later: "The issue was not that Lavanya said 'No'. To me, the crux of the issue was Lavanya's discretion, her judgment—the fact that even at her young age, she was able to understand the transience of external appearance. She had intuitively grasped the truth that external form and manifest beauty are but fleeting—ephemeral gifts naturally obtained that decay with time. But if human beings strive to develop their innate qualities to the greatest extent possible—that is earned achievement, and it outlives physical beauty."

"It is my good fortune," she wrote further, "that my daughter is wiser and sharper than I am, and also more dispassionate and balanced. My happiness today is the happiness that Vishwamitra must have felt for the achievements of Rama, Sandipan for Krishna, and Parashurama for Karna. I thank the Lord Almighty for having shaped my child in a way that transcends all my limitations."

Lavanyadevi had accompanied Guru-*ji* and his followers to Mansarovar. As she gazed into the deep calm lake full of stars, she could not fathom why this particular page from the past had suddenly come alive in her memory. But the lake and the stars seemed to know. Stars twinkle in the blue waters of the lake only when the moon is absent; when the moon is in the sky, its soothing radiance obscures all the stars. Lost in the memory that the page had evoked, Lavanyadevi sat gazing into the placid waters of the lake. And it appeared that for once, both the moon and the stars could be seen reflected together in the waters of the Mansarovar—the reflection of Lavanyadevi's radiant moon-like visage, softly lit by the reflections of all the stars surrounding it. In the profound tranquillity of the night, the flickering of the stars that adorned the reflection of her pensive face as she gazed into the still waters seemed to offer a clue to the turmoil deep in her heart. Meanwhile, in Baikunth, even the gods were unanimous that this scene, bringing together the terrestrial, the spiritual and the natural, was the single most beautiful scene that they had witnessed since the world was created.

Lord Shiva and the gods could not shower flowers on her; so they invoked Samir, god of the winds. A strong wind blew towards Lavanyadevi and soon her face was illuminated by a steadily rotating circle of lights. The wind, borrowing lights from the valleys below, had swiftly carried them up to where she sat, and their arc-like motion reminded one of the *aarti* at Haridwar.

An unfathomable silence, the lonely night, the snow-clad mountains, the star-studded sky, the clear blue waters of the lake and the peerless beauty who sat encircled by all these—together, they created an ineffable ambience that brought to mind Tulsidas's admission of his inadequacy in describing the beauty of Lord Rama—*giraanayan, nayanbinubani*—the tongue has not eyes to see, and the eyes cannot speak! The whole scene seemed draped in a delicate, transparent, numinous shawl, and Lavanyadevi sat as if hypnotised by the surroundings. All around her, in every direction, she could sense the powerful presence of the One she had always wanted to meet. It was such a sublime and awe-inspiring encounter with the Absolute, the Divine, that tears streamed down her cheeks and she closed her eyes and raised both her hands heavenward.

Guru-*ji*'s attention was suddenly drawn to the sight of her. Alarmed, he ran towards Lavanyadevi and, lifting her sagging body in his arms as one would lift a child, he gently chided her, "Lavanya, do you want to end your life in these deep blue waters like Sri Chaitanya Swami did? Get up, my girl! Your duties are far from over! There is a lot of good you still have to do."

On opening her eyes after she was brought back to the tent, she felt as if they were someone else's. Her own touch felt unfamiliar to her hands. Even the smallest of sounds felt so loud that it jangled her nerves, and she shuddered. The disciples who crowded outside the room enquired in whispers, "Guru-*ji*! What happened to Lavanyadevi? Why is she in such a state?"

To which Guru-*ji* replied, "A miracle! This is nothing short of a miracle. Lavanyadevi has fortuitously been granted, much in the same way as Arjuna was, what most humans strive to achieve across multiple births and rebirths through great sacrifice and through high penance on the Himalayas. We can argue that this was not accidental. It could be the result of her penances in previous births, or the good karma of her ancestors. But believe me, such miracles occur only when they have to—they are not contingent upon arguments or logic. When He wants something to happen, He makes it happen!"

The curious whispers in the background, like lullabies, soothed her, and she was soon fast asleep.

As she was returning from Mansarovar, Lavanyadevi met Guru-*ji*'s favourite disciple, who was waiting for her. He told her that she should immediately leave for the hospital in Dehradun where her husband's maternal uncle Raja Debkumar Laha was admitted; his life was drawing to an end and he wanted to meet her before his death.

Lavanyadevi was surprised, as she was not really close to this uncle. However, of late, she had increasingly started believing in destiny and was unfazed by the turn of any event. Still, she was unsure what to do. Guru-*ji*'s words resolved her dilemma: "Lavanya, when public welfare is your motto, then why do you hesitate? Go, fulfil your responsibilities."

As soon as she reached the precincts of the hospital in Dehradun, Lavanyadevi could sense that people were waiting for her. This made her quicken her pace and she hastily reached Debkumar-*ji*'s bedside. He was waiting for Lavanyadevi as desperately as the *chataka* bird waits for the *Swati nakshatra* to slake its thirst. He bared his heart to her, telling her his darkest secrets, not sparing any details. The story that he narrated, punctuated by gasps for breath, was startling. Hidden behind the facade of the *bhalomanush* and the Good Samaritan was a chest full of the blackest sins that he had committed. His reputation within the house and in society remained unsullied, but he grew withered and diseased within. He sought treatment in this remote hospital at the foothills of the Himalayas so that his family did not come to know of his condition. But the doctors had given up all hope. The only person who had accompanied him here was his old and trusted *muneem*, who was looking after all the arrangements here.

They were interrupted by two doctors who came in to remove the pus from the sores in his skin. To Lavanyadevi's inquiring glances, they shook their heads in sadly negative response.

The awareness of impending death reflected frankly in Debkumar Laha's eyes was impossible to describe. Suddenly he clasped Lavanyadevi's hand and said, "Bouma! If you say that I will live, I will." Lavanyadevi shuddered to hear these words—for once she did not want to speak the truth. Putting aside for a moment the inflexible principles she had lived her life by, she managed to say, "Don't worry. You will be perfectly all right."

Lavanyadevi had uttered this false assurance more out of compassion than conviction. But the moment he heard her say that he would survive his illness, Mama-*ji* responded as if he had been divinely blessed. His countenance suddenly became radiant and tears flowed from his eyes. In a voice brimming with gratitude he said, "Thank you, bouma! Thank you! May God bless you!"

Lavanyadevi felt a pang of guilt for not having spoken the truth, but soon dispelled any self-doubt arising from this act by convincing herself about its necessity. She wiped the tears off Mama-*ji*'s face. The *muneem* came into the room to give her a scroll.

On seeing the indecision writ large upon her forehead, Raja Debkumar Laha said, "Bouma! Please take them. These are the papers of whatever is left of my property." He told her that he had arranged handsome settlements for his children and his wife, and whatever remained he wanted to donate for some charitable purpose. He further said, "Lavanya! I have never done ill to anybody, but I have squandered my God-gifted wealth and sullied the temple-like body that He gave me. I beseech you, help me rectify my errors. I want this wealth to be used for some significant work for alleviating the sufferings of prostitutes. I want to support institutions which help people to quit alcohol and drugs. Addictive drugs seem to have become common among the poor people living in the hills. Use this money to make them aware of its dangers, get them to quit drugs.

"Lavanya, I know that you are involved in many things. But I cannot trust anyone else with this task and hence I am adding to your responsibilities. I hope you will not disappoint me. I am not entrusting you with this because you are my nephew's wife, but because you are 'Lavanyadevi'—in whom I have immense faith and who, I believe, will not turn down this request of mine."

Having said all of this in one go, Mama-*ji* stopped to take a deep breath, and continued, "Lavanya, go, carry on with your meaningful work. I have already wasted your entire day by asking you to come here, but I hope you will forgive me. I thought perhaps this 'dying person' has some claim over the 'undying immortal', and therefore sent for you. And please take these two black trunks with you when you go. They are full of garbage from the palace—please cleanse them, purify them."

"Garbage?" Lavanyadevi repeated involuntarily.

"Yes, bouma. Garbage. Do you remember the well and its pulley in the courtyard of the house? And the rope with which my mother used to draw water from it to the first floor to worship the gods in her *thakurbari*? That rope, some jewellery, swords and various items that were kept aside to be gifted in marriages and engagements—the trunks are full of such junk. Please sell off everything and put the money you get from it into some auspicious work. This is my dying wish, Lavanya."

Raja Debkumar patted Lavanya's head. What magical blessing did he bestow on her that every pore of her body suddenly came alive? She intuited that he was not a sinful person but a pure *gandharva* soul who had temporarily gone astray and ended up in the land of sinners. But, can remorseful penance destroy the accumulated mountain of sin and atone for wrongs done? These were the thoughts circulating in her mind as she got the trunks loaded onto her jeep. She touched Mama-*ji*'s feet to seek his blessings, and instructing the old *muneem* to inform her if his condition deteriorated further, she started back for the ashram.

After reaching the ashram, when Lavanyadevi opened the trunks, the sight she beheld left her wide-eyed with astonishment—it was as if the wealth of Lord Kubera himself was packed into them. The 'rope' that Mama-*ji* mentioned was pure gold kneaded into thick strands of the kind that jewellers today cannot even dream of crafting. Molten gold was drawn into strands and kneaded so that the rope was strong enough to bear the weight of the golden bucket thirty feet up to the first floor. The rope was then polished with leather to ensure that it did not hurt the hands of the person hauling up the bucket. Gold is heavy in itself, and all these processes made it even heavier. It took four sturdily built *Kahar*s to lift one trunk. Lavanyadevi had scarcely recovered from the shock of what the first trunk contained when she was confronted by the contents of the second trunk. The things kept aside 'to be gifted' reminded her of the Nizam's collection of jewellery. Uncut diamonds, emeralds and rubies from the Golconda mines, aigrettes made of elephant pearl, chokers and necklaces, bangles and bracelets, ornaments meant for the groom and the coachman and the servant, ornaments to adorn every part of the body from head to toe. Lavanyadevi was overwhelmed. "O Lord! What will I do with this property worth billions? How will I ever be able to do justice to what I have been entrusted to do?" The moment questions like these started raising their heads, her sharp mind cut through the dense foliage of dilemma to arrive at a solution. She immediately communicated to her lawyer and to Soumen what she planned to do with this wealth.

A new day dawned. Lavanyadevi prayed to the Supreme Father to grant forgiveness to Mama-*ji*. As she concluded her prayer with "*Om shanti, shanti, shanti*", she saw the *muneem* standing hesitantly in one corner.

The *muneem* greeted Lavanyadevi. He said, "Raja saheb's condition started deteriorating the moment you left, but his face was suffused with a profound sense of peace. Since he had strictly insisted that you were not to be disturbed, I did not inform you. Raja saheb wished that all decisions about his last rites be taken by you; however, he has left instructions that you must not be physically present in any of the rituals. After your departure, Raja saheb also expressed the desire to donate all his organs, as Jyotirmoyidevi had done, and drafted a letter to that effect."

That a less than ordinary person leading an abominable life of debauchery could suddenly turn around and set such high standards was something Lavanyadevi had never imagined or experienced. It added yet another question to her list: "What is more important in a human being—the outer self or the inner? Would I still consider Raja Debkumar Laha a despicable gutter-worm?"

Lavanyadevi was lost in these thoughts when the sound of *muneem-ji* discreetly clearing his throat brought her back to the present. She said, "Ramsharan-*ji*, for donating Mama-*ji*'s organs, it is best to consult the doctors on how to go about it. The funeral rites should be conducted on the banks of the Ganga in Haridwar. Once that is done, please take these trunks to Kolkata and give them to Soumendranath Roychoudhury for safekeeping. Tell him not to sell these rare ornaments just for the value of gold—the owner of Sotheby's will himself come down to Kolkata the moment he has an inkling of their worth. Keep yourself informed about the market value of each of these ornaments, and when he comes to Kolkata, negotiate not just the market value but the antique value of each ornament individually. By that time, my lawyer will have formalised the setting up of a trust in Raja Debkumar Laha's name. Make sure that you understand all the nitty-gritty involved and take due care of it. Put the money that you get from the sale of the ornaments and precious stones to use as Mama-*ji* had desired—for charity. I feel it will be convenient for you if you take on board Soumen, my family lawyer and Ananya as trustees. Ramsharan-*ji*, as you were the one who was dutifully with Mama-*ji* during the lonely last days of his life, it is you who should rightfully take charge of all this."

As he was noting down instruction after instruction that Lavanyadevi gave, Ramsharan marvelled at her level-headedness and her clarity. "Is this lady human or a goddess? She did not hesitate or falter even for a moment in deciding what to do with this immense wealth, and she has already started working towards improving Raja saheb's past! It is true that one cannot undo wrongs committed in the past, but the good deeds of the present can definitely go a long way towards creating a beautiful future. This is the only way that the stigma of the past can be obliterated."

Taking his leave of Lavanyadevi, *muneem-ji* went back to the Dehradun hospital. How could I, so easily, take all these decisions for a person like Raja Debkumar Laha, she wondered! Sometimes, human beings themselves are quite unaware of the workings of their own minds, how subconscious thoughts can lead them to make conscious decisions that surprise even their own selves.

There was enthusiasm all around in the mountains. Lavanyadevi worked through the afternoon. Then, as she sat facing the setting sun, she switched on the computer on her table and began to watch the programmes going on at the various centres. Just then, the postmaster came in running, out of breath, waving an envelope at her, "Madam! There's an envelope for you…from abroad!" Lavanyadevi opened the envelope. A draft for one crore rupees stared back at her. Her utter bewilderment at this sudden benefaction turned into a stunned numbness when she saw the name of the sender—Amlan. *Amlan*? The same Amlan whom she wanted put behind bars? Why on earth would he send such a huge amount…to *her*?

Lavanyadevi looked at the draft again and again, as if trying to convince her own deep disbelief. Arguments and counterarguments circled furiously in her mind. The question that troubled her most was—what entitled her to a gift of such a huge sum of money? That too from the person whose future she had not spared a thought for, so intent she was on getting him punished! Why would he overlook his parents, his friends, his well-wishers and choose to express his reverence to *her* above everyone else? Was it a mistake on his part? But how could a distinguished litterateur like Amlan commit an error like this? Many such questions clamoured for answers inside her, till she reminded herself of what Guru-*ji* had once said: "It is not necessary that you will be able to resolve all your dilemmas and get answers to all your questions immediately. Sometimes, the best course of action is to just wait for time to provide you with the best solution."

Lavanyadevi was not unaware of the course of Amlan's life. She got every bit of news about him from Soumen and from the letters, journals and magazines she read. She was aware that Amlan had permanently settled abroad and established himself as a creative writer of repute. Soumen's letters had kept her abreast of the various awards and recognitions that were conferred on him. When she once asked Soumen if Amlan had also married someone there, his reply gave her a rude jolt—and this despite the fact that Lavanyadevi was considered a modern and progressive woman of her times, and was well-acquainted with the best of world literature. She strongly disliked this new tendency of the open, explicit expression of human sexuality. The mere mention of any such subject would fill her mind with a strange aversion. She had consciously tried to rid herself of this negativity and bias, but had been unable to do so. She couldn't tolerate even her favourite writer Ismat Chughtai's sympathetic attitude towards her characters in 'Lihaaf', and had once gotten into a long-drawn argument with the author over that story when they happened to meet in Delhi. While returning from Delhi, Jyotirmoyidevi, who had accompanied Lavanyadevi, had reminded her of an incident concerning Dhananjay-babu's aunt. This incident was mentioned in Jyotirmoyidevi's diaries as well.

This particular aunt-in-law was very fond of Jyotirmoyidevi and plied her with gifts, but this display of excessive love did not go well with her mother-in-law Brajabaladevi. One day, when the aunt sent a phaeton manned by an impressive looking coachman to bring Jyotirmoyi over to her place, Brajabaladevi, lowering her voice, said, "Jyoti, this aunt of yours is no good. Have you ever wondered why, twenty-four hours a day, she is accompanied by a married woman who has deserted her husband? Do you have any idea what this means?"

"Ma, are you talking about Komal Mashi? But she is such a dear soul!"

Brajabaladevi was incensed. "Dear soul, is it? That no-good rogue of an aunt of yours, and that Komal? God! Do they even know what goodness means? Anyway, I won't stop you from going, but I'm trying to caution you. Stay away from that lady."

But how could she just stay away for no reason? She was Jyotirmoyidevi, daughter of Prabhavatidevi. How could she rest without knowing the truth? The moment she reached her aunt-in-law's house, she asked her point blank, "Kakima! What kind of relationship do Komal Mashi and you share? Komal Mashi is good-looking. She is healthy. Why does she not live with her husband? And why is your daughter-in-law Rupa always after Komal Mashi? Kakima, if you truly love me, please answer me honestly. And I promise you that no matter what the answer is, if it is the truth, I will continue to love and respect you the same way that I always have."

Like a mother holding her child in her arms to explain something, the old aunt made Jyotirmoyi sit next to her and said, "Jyoti, you are pure at heart. Listen to the entire story. I will not twist it or spice it up. I will tell it truthfully, just the way it happened to me.

"My parents, though of a high caste, were very poor. We were four sisters, all growing up quickly. We barely managed to survive on the meagre sums of money that my mother earned by doing housework for some rich relatives. My father was only concerned with keeping his moustaches twirled, preserving his hollow caste-pride and holding court in a house that could crumble any moment. Then, your Kaka-babu's clerk presented himself one fine day, and said, 'Khoneesh Shankar Mitra, a royal and the owner of a jute mill, is desirous of marrying again. Would you like to give away your eldest daughter in marriage?' My father impetuously asked, 'The same Khoneesh Shankar who belongs to the Mitra *rajbari*?' My mother, standing behind the door, was privy to this conversation. She cleared her throat a couple of times to draw my father's attention but my father, it seemed, deliberately ignored her. When my mother could no longer contain her anxiety, she came out into the men's section, and asked, 'What is the reason for this sudden kindness? And what is his age?'

"The *muneem* replied readily, 'He is around thirty or forty, but looks much younger.'

"My mother replied, 'I want to see the groom before I say yes or no to the proposal. If there is any problem in meeting formally, I will be satisfied if I can see him from a distance.'

"They saw him from afar. After my mother gave her consent, the groom's family stipulated that the nuptials would be conducted in the large hall in the jute mill compound. Mother was happy that I was getting married into a reputed family. She wanted to invite all her relatives, but she was told not to, as someone might unnecessarily try to spoil things. She agreed.

"The wedding was fixed for an auspicious Sunday. At the appointed time, a horse-drawn carriage was sent to pick us up. We, all of us in our best clothes, boarded the carriage and reached the mill. Mother was worried when she could not see any noise and bustle, but calmed herself thinking, 'These rich people have their own eccentricities.' But when the groom removed his wedding headdress and the flower decorations that covered his face, an involuntary shriek escaped my mother's lips. 'I did not choose this old man for my daughter!' she screamed, 'I refuse to get my daughter married to him!' But the mill-doors had been shut by then, and half the wedding rituals had been completed. There was no turning back from there."

"But Kakima, hadn't your mother herself seen Kaka-babu?" Jyotirmoyi asked.

With a sad smile Kakima replied, "The person Ma was shown was his nephew! It was not him. I, the eighteen-year-old daughter of poor parents, was tricked into marrying the seventy-year old zamindar-babu."

"Kakima, you must have been very angry with Kaka-babu for having deceived you, for ruining your life?"

"Yes! Initially I was very angry with him! But seeing his immense love for me helped me to gradually come to terms with my anger and bitterness…maybe even to fall in love with him. He would ask me to spit on his palms to counter the bad omens in his life; he would have agreed to bring me the *parijat* flower from heaven had I but asked. You will not believe me, Jyoti, if I tell you that often, on lonely summer afternoons, he would send his young subordinates to keep me company—something I put an end to fearing disrepute.

"Jyoti, if truth be told, I don't have an iota of resentment against the family today. Things were quite different, and difficult, when I was young. But your Kaka-babu plied me with all kinds of comfort, and my resentment gradually faded. There is another thing too. I was not a particularly beautiful woman. Even if a handsome young man had married me, there is every reason to conjecture that his attraction for me would diminish with time, and I could end up in a worse condition than the one I found myself in then. Days after my own marriage, I got my sister married to a young man her age. I spared no expense. But he tortured her day and night for more money. Then one day, he killed her by setting her ablaze, and lied to everyone that the stove had burst.

"As far as Komal is concerned, I'm aware that people say a lot of humiliating and disrespectful things about us behind my back. But then, you are sensitive and thoughtful. Jyoti, just put yourself in my place and think. An eighteen-year-old girl married to a seventy-year-old man—what choices does she really have? Should she fall in love with a handsome young man, get pregnant and commit suicide? Should she kill her old husband? Or should she elope? What can she do? What if, in such a situation, she finds a person in whom she is able to see a soulmate for life? A kindred soul, a woman whose husband trades her for his liquor and indulges in such indescribable and gut-churning acts without precedence as are difficult to even imagine. Komal and I are childhood friends—we have known each other since we were little girls. Our intimacy is the intimacy of shared suffering. Call it by whatever name you wish to, but I can find no sin in this relationship that she and I share.

"Jyoti, I believe that anything that causes harm and suffering to others is sinful. But can any court of law prove that our relationship has caused anyone any harm? On the contrary, the reputation of this household, my husband's standing, the respect of our adopted son, the care and upbringing of Komal's children—haven't all these achievements proved favourable for everyone? But that depends on you. You may still consider me an adulteress. Or, keeping my life, my circumstances in mind, you may choose to take a different view of the whole thing. It depends entirely on you."

"Kakima, I am grateful that you made me aware of the other side of this story," I said, as I got up and touched her feet. "Often, due to our limited outlook, we consider everything from a single perspective. But life is never one-dimensional. From today onwards I will always keep in mind this positive lesson that I have learnt from you. I will never judge any incident or person from a single point of view. I will always consider the diverse dimensions of any situation before I come to any conclusion. I am indeed grateful that you have enlightened me like a guru."

Lavanya, believe me when I tell you that the old lady was not trying to ingratiate herself with me. Nor have I added a word to what she said. This is a truth I have faced earlier too, something that I gleaned from my mother Prabhavatidevi's experiences. Lavanya, you know how close my mother and I were. She used to tell me her deepest secrets, and you know how much faith she had in me—you would have read it in my diaries, or you will. Referring to one such incident, she had suggested a course of action which I later found very useful in my own life practices.

"Ma told me that in course of her conversations, she had come to know that Champadevi's husband Mangatrai-*ji* and his friend used to go on sojourns to Kolkata for three years at a stretch, during which time they celebrated all their festivals on the roof of a *basa*, a lodge, where a *maharaj* used to run a dhaba. In return for monthly payment for their meals, the owner of the lodge had permitted them to sleep on the roof. Every Diwali, the two friends bought a five-*anna* mat each to use as their bedding. With bricks or sometimes their own arms as pillows, they slept on the roof. During the rains they both squeezed themselves under a three-foot wide shed at one end of the roof; in winter, they wrapped themselves up in blankets and looked like two small bundles."

"But Ma! Gulabchand Bhikhraj was such a famous person! There are cities, colleges, *dharmashalas*, temples, wells and so many other things named after him that exist even today!"

Prabhavatidevi did not take too kindly to the question that interrupted her narrative. She responded half-heartedly and said, "Jyoti, all that you mention were achieved when he was mature. I am talking to you about the days when they were younger and used to come to Kolkata to earn their living. *Bas*! No more interruptions! Now listen to what matters.

"One day, in the course of my conversation with Champadevi, I said, 'Champa! Don't talk about your husband to me. For me, a man who loves his friend more than his wife is a truthless man.'

"Champa was stunned into silence, as if paralysed! After being silent for a long time, she gently said, 'So what? Do you or I know about his compulsions? Prabha, let me tell you what my own eyes have been witness to. One night, it seemed that your Jija-*ji* slipped out of the house followed by a shadow. I was momentarily stunned and turned to stone. Then I told myself, Champa, be it summer, winter or rains, year after year this man has been spending his nights on a rooftop so that you can live comfortably. He works tirelessly from morning to night, day in and day out, hard and back-breaking work, a lonely man in a distant city. Spare a thought for how he spends his days! And you are turning against him? What if he had kept a whore? What then? What would have happened to you? Since that day, Prabha,

I have never questioned him. I hold him in greater esteem than I previously did. But Prabha! You are an educated Bengali woman with much greater exposure to the world. How could you utter such stupid words?'

"Lavanya, I still remember verbatim the words that Ma used! 'Jyoti, I used to think of myself as much more intelligent than Champa. But that day, I realised that I was someone who had accumulated her knowledge of life only from books, not from life itself. Champa's practical approach and her wisdom were attributes I could only imagine, not achieve."

The mental commotion aroused by Amlan's draft soothed by these recollections, Lavanyadevi turned her attention to the letter that accompanied the draft.

Respected Maua!

I know that you are more annoyed with some of my later actions than with actions I had committed out of my arrogance. I assume that you will have read that interview in which I have expressed my honest views about sexual relationships. Maua, I will neither present any argument in support of my position, nor will I expect you to pardon me. But there is one truth I want you to know—I have always believed that whatever is good and beautiful in my life is because of you. That is why I am sending half of my prize money to you—so that you can save many more Amlans. I can never even think of freeing myself from the huge debt I owe you. This is just the interest on the first of the numerous instalments that you have paid for me. I hope you will accept this humble offering and bless me.

Yours, Amlan.

There was no way to ascertain the point at which tears started welling up in Lavanyadevi's eyes, but by the time she finished reading the letter, tears ran down her cheeks in a steady stream. That beautiful Guru Purnima evening, every last shred of bad faith was cleansed and washed away by the sacred waters of the Ganga.

Lavanyadevi got up, ate sparingly and went to bed. When she woke up as usual in the wee hours of the morning, her mind was completely free of any agitation. She wrote to Amlan with a calm mind:

Dear Amlan,

Blessings for your long life. Stay happy. I have received your draft beset with apprehensions. To tell you the truth, you were right. I was indeed angry with you and hurt. But whatever is done with good intentions can never be wrong. Which is probably why when I got your letter, the principles of your grandmother and your great-grandmother showed me the right way once again. Both of them made me understand who I am and what my position is in this entire universe. On what basis can I judge people and the world as either right or wrong? Why do I forget that what seems wrong today might also be proved right tomorrow? No, not 'also'—it is almost 'always' so!

Today, I accept this limitation on my part with an open mind and apologise to all those whom I blamed as wrong because of my limited intelligence. While classifying good and sinful deeds, we usually try to follow the dictum that 'any action that does not cause harm or suffering is not sinful'. But if I follow this dictum, I find myself in the dock. What right does a wrongdoer have to pardon others?

I intend to use the money you have sent for the service of literature. I have called a meeting of learned people to find the best way to do this. What I have in mind is a concerted effort to produce writers with the cooperation of schools and libraries. I hope you will find the proposal worthwhile. Everything else is fine.

Yours, Maua.

This has been a year full of surprises thought Lavanyadevi as she came out. She was surprised again by the sound of a car coming up the mountains. Silence is pervasive in these lonely mountains, only occasionally disrupted by sounds like the one that was just heard. Just then, as if concretising her thoughts, Ananya emerged in front of her. "Maua!" she shouted, bent down to touch her feet and pulled her into a tight embrace.

Ananya, the only child of her elder son, was Lavanyadevi's first grandchild, and the centre of the later part of her life. All the affection that she had never even considered giving her own children, she had bestowed on this granddaughter. Ananya studied, read, wrote, bathed, ate, even slept with her grandmother. Ananya was giving back to Lavanyadevi her childhood while Lavanyadevi inundated her with all the affection of an experienced mother. And it was Ananya who first called her 'Maua'.

When her eldest daughter-in-law was intent on moving into a flat, Ananya had flatly refused to accompany her parents. The mother had clearly asked Lavanyadevi, "Ask your granddaughter if she is moving into the flat with us or staying on with you. I won't go in for an extra room if she insists on staying here."

Though she felt broken inside, Lavanyadevi remembered all her elders and their advice, and arrived at the conclusion that the role of Ananya's parents was more important than hers in her granddaughter's future. They were young and more in tune with the world. Therefore, she considered it her duty to free Ananya from the ties which bound them together. Otherwise Ananya herself might regret her decision in the future or worse, hold her grandmother guilty.

After much thought, Lavanyadevi finally told Ananya, "Now that I will not live with your parents and sibling, I want you to stay with them as my representative. Take good care of them, especially of Apoorva, who is too emotional."

Although the physical distances continued to grow due to the hectic schedule of everyday life, the deep attachment between the two remained as it was before.

"*Arey tui*? You? When did you get back to India?"

"Maua! I'm not yet completely back from abroad, just half back. First let me tell you that I did not join Wharton Business

School as Ma-Baba had suggested and joined Princeton instead, and followed it up with a Master's in Social Work from New York. Thank God that for once they did not object, and I was happy. Maua, by now you must have figured out that, since I landed in Delhi today, and from there came straight here to you via Dehradun, I am definitely in a spot of bother!"

As Ananya stopped for a moment, a small boy came up to them with hot tea and snacks. Ananya immediately bought them from him and then, cuddling him, started talking to him affectionately. Lavanyadevi immediately noticed this immense change that had come over her. Is this the same Ananya who was so finicky about everything that she could throw tantrum after tantrum about anything? Today she was as sparklingly clear as flowing water, as gently caressing as mist, and as eager and generous in her affections as mother earth herself! What had come over her?

Without Ananya having said a word, Lavanyadevi could discern that her problem was related to her heart. But unless Ananya revealed the details, she could not understand which direction it was headed towards. Even as she was trying to gauge a few things, Ananya had already started off on her story.

"Maua, you know better than anyone else that Ma is attached to nothing except money. When you filled her coffers with wealth, she started sending me lots of money. But I didn't want it. Both my friend Dhanu and I have already made up our minds that we will spend only what we ourselves earn, and that too sparingly. Well, let me also tell you that I resigned my eight-lakh-per-month job with a New York bank to take up a fulltime job with the Red Cross Society."

Lavanyadevi interrupted her to ask, "But who is this Dhanu?" Ananya blushed as she answered, "Dhanu is a Kashmiri pandit boy born and brought up in Canada and has a degree in architecture from the Cooper Union College. There was lots of money at home, but as the first position holder in every class, he studied mostly on scholarships. And Cooper Union, the best architecture college in the world, admits only scholarship-holder students."

"All that is fine, Ananya. But what exactly is your relationship with him?" asked Lavanyadevi directly, although by now she had understood everything.

"Maua! Why don't you understand?" complained Ananya, lowering her eyes and speaking through her nose, "I love him dearly and I want to make him my 'life-partner'!"

"Oho! Then why don't you say so! And if this is how things stand, I'm sure you must also have brought him along? Where is he? Let me have a glimpse of him! Where is that fortunate boy?" she asked mischievously.

"Dhanu! Dhanu, please come here!"

"Maua, this is Dhanu, and Dhanu, this is Maua."

"I could already make that out, Ananya," said a princely looking young man as he bent forward to touch Lavanyadevi's feet. She stopped him mid-action, ran her fingers affectionately through his hair and embraced him.

What a boy! Nothing less than a diamond—an appearance as luminous as the rays of the sun, shy in spirit, deep-set eyes framed by thick dark lashes, eyes that connected instantly with one's heart. Oh! If only Geeta had found such a good match, perhaps that beautiful, good-natured girl would not have taken her own life. Lavanyadevi tried to banish these depressing memories springing up in her mind at this auspicious moment, but in vain. If only human beings made of earth and mud could control their fickle minds, Lord Krishna would not have had to advise Arjuna in the midst of the battlefield!

Soudamini was in Class I, Loreto Convent, Darjeeling. Lavanyadevi's eyes were often drawn to a trio of girls studying in Class X, whose names were Siddharajyalakshmi, Kularajyalakshmi and Gyaneshwari. All three were connected to the royal family of Nepal. While the first two were the princesses of Jumla state, Gyaneshwari or Geeta was the daughter of the Nepali Prime Minister Shamsher Singh Rana. It is through these girls that Lavanyadevi became acquainted with Maharani Gayatri Devi of Jaipur. An old photograph of a youthful Gayatri Devi in her favourite red *leheriya* saree still revives those memories.

Lavanyadevi found these three girls—tall and lithe, sharp-featured, and with charming faces—very attractive. Gradually and spontaneously she became intimate friends with them. In course of her conversations, she found some unexpected connections too. The same Shamsher Singh Rana whom she had seen more than once in Aniruddha Mama's house, surrounded by his female admirers, was Geeta's father! She even remembered some of Mama's words of introduction. "Jyoti-*di*, all the land adjacent Hogg Market belongs to him. Recently he got two excellent cinema halls constructed there," Mama had said, introducing Rana to Ma. When the trio came to Kolkata after their Senior Cambridge and got enrolled in the same college, Lavanyadevi's house became their second home.

Siddhi and Kularajya once told Lavanya that they were both envious of Geeta. When the rest of the class was struggling with the course and the textbooks, Raja-*ji* (Rana's nickname) would come and take Geeta away—to the racecourse or a ball dance or the derby dance or some other social gathering. The huge amounts of money that he donated to the institution prevented the nuns from saying anything apart from "Yes sir" and "*Yessir*". And they would let him take Geeta out of class whenever he wanted.

In Kolkata, Lavanyadevi too had observed Geeta's rash and careless behaviour, and had asked her two friends, "As far as I know, Rana is a wilful and wayward kind of person and there is a huge difference in age between the two. Why then is he so intent on leading his own child astray and spoiling her?"

"Geeta is Rana's only legitimate child. Incidentally, she is also a late child. Our parents tell us how overjoyed Shamsher Singh Rana was when he heard the good news. He was so happy that everyone in Kathmandu was invited to the celebrations and merrymaking. The wife, whose well-being he had not cared to think of earlier, was suddenly gifted every conceivable thing money could buy."

Lavanyadevi recalled Geeta once telling Arnab, "I feel so jealous when I see you people sitting down to budget your expenses. It is a good feeling to sense that there is someone to whom you are answerable. And I? I am not answerable to anyone. Why? Does that mean that I have no one to call my own? Am I all by myself in this whole wide world?" Lavanyadevi remembered that overhearing this conversation, she had instructed Siddhi and Kularajya to take extra care of Geeta—such thoughts during her growing years could lead her into taking wrong decisions. Those were times in which the city was full of talk of how her wealth dazzled scores of young men who swarmed around her like bees around honey. Every other day one heard that Geeta had left someone and was with someone else. And after a few days the same news would go around again, only the names of the young men would be different each time. Then one day, there was news that Geeta had married an Anglo-Indian boy and, in the following thirteen months, became the mother of two children. This was the completion of the 'Geeta Chapter'—but not the culmination.

Geeta's twenty-fourth birthday was organised with a lot of fanfare in a posh Kolkata hotel. Amidst all the loud music and dancing under showers of French champagne, everyone was missing the birthday girl herself. When guests asked about her, they came to know that she was resting in her suite. It is in this luxurious personal suite that her dead body was found an hour later, with a suicide note.

> *It is now evident to me that no one truly loves me. Everyone around me only pretends to love me. Even the person I call my husband does not love me, he only loves my money. Oh! I wish I was not so rich. If I had been born a poor girl in an ordinary household, I would perhaps have had the good fortune of knowing and experiencing true love. Geeta.*

That evening, instead of swallowing a couple of sleeping pills as she usually did before she went to bed, she had swallowed the contents of an entire bottle. All efforts to revive her were in vain.

Lavanyadevi could not fathom how even the attachment to her two little daughters did not stop Geeta from taking such a step! Upon inquiring, she came to know that verbal and physical conflicts between husband and wife had become daily affairs. Geeta had frequent bouts of severe depression and depressive people are prone to commit suicide. This is what had happened in Geeta's case.

Lavanyadevi was suddenly roused from her stupor, "Maua! Maua! You are lost in your thoughts!" Ananya chided her. "You know this old habit of mine, don't you, Ananya?" she said apologetically. "I frequently leave this real world to stroll through the world of my memories. But poor Dhanu! He must have been slightly worried to see me like this, isn't it?" Saying this, she affectionately drew him close. The tidal waves of affection rising within her drenched Dhanu to the core of his being and his face started glowing with an intense sweetness.

Lavanyadevi rejected their idea of getting married at the Kedarnath Ashram outright. "The proper thing to do is to go down; take your seven *pheras* round the fire in front of all your family members; understand each of the seven promises that you make to each other. If you want to eschew all ostentatiousness, I will instruct Soumen so that the arrangements are in keeping with what you want. But the wedding should be solemnised in Kolkata in the presence of both your parents. I am with you both in mind and spirit and will always be—this is both my promise and my blessing.

"Ananya, there is also a small piece of work that I want you to do. Can you? You have to go to Dhaka and sign the trust deed for my grandmother Prabhavatidevi's colleges. Your great grandma has given this right only to the women in the family and not the men. It will make me very happy if you can go and sign the document."

"Sure, Maua! Of course, Maua!" both shouted in unison and came and clung to her like two leaves desperately trying to hang on to the branch they were parted from and remain there. One of the brothers from the ashram came up to Lavanyadevi and asked, "Should I get the draft deposited at the bank? And post Amlan's letter to London?"

Ananya was happy to hear Amlan's name. "Maua, you have done the right thing by forgiving Amlan. To tell you the truth, of all your followers, it is Amlan who stands most steadfastly with 'truth'. He admits without reservations what he is and what he does regardless of the humiliation, stigma, accusations and ostracisation that he may encounter. For this, he has had to lose a lot, but it has not deterred him from his chosen path. Believe me Maua, I've met him quite a few times, and every time I meet him, I find him grown in stature. I'm glad you too have understood him now. I feel this is not just Amlan's victory but yours too—by accepting him as he is, you too have grown and evolved, Maua."

"Thank you! Thank you, Maua!" Dhanu chimed in, "Seriously, you have done the right thing."

Lavanyadevi was herself amazed that each day in her long life led her to newer pinnacles of success. She also wondered why she had still not been able to identify and weed out age-old biases and irrational prejudices rooted deep within her. Had she created an impenetrable barbed wire fence of rules around herself? "Only that which I experience is the truth and everything else is falsehood"—why did she suddenly find this foundation on which she had built her life-path to be narrow and constricting? Was it due to being reminded of the alternative sexual experiences recorded in the experiential journeys of Prabhavatidevi and Jyotirmoyidevi? Their tacit acceptance of these relationships? Or was it her encounter with the everyday details of Debkumar Laha's life? How was she able to even tolerate the existence of these exceptions in the domain of her Bhishma-like worldview? Where did all of her principles, her strictness, her obstinacy, her inflexibility about what she perceived as the truth suddenly vanish like camphor?

Is this flexibility the 'middle path' that Buddha advocated? Did Mahavira also reconsider his views on truth and non-violence as he was in the process of attaining *nirvana*? Is this a natural process of change that is characteristic to all contemplative people? Perhaps it is merely the ennui occasioned by advancing age in which the mind is ready to accept everything that happens in the spirit of 'whatever happens happens for the best'? Or is it more in tune with Kabir and Nanak's *brahma satya jagat mithya*—the world is illusory and Ultimate Reality is the only truth? Are both ideas true? Due to our limited vision, the infinite dimensions of Truth are always beyond our reach; the one part that falls to our share becomes, in our perception, the sole determinant for the absolute truth.

Was I wrong in how I thought? Or is it the eternal tale of perpetual human progress and evolution? Is it possible that there is a grand layered design to the structure of nature? That nature draws apart the curtain to reveal its mysteries, layer by layer, when the time is right? And that it does this so that our lives are lived in the pleasure of anticipation, and we keep craving to know what the future has in store for us?

Standing on the balcony, Lavanyadevi watched the playful child-sun in the sky. The snow-clad peaks surrounding the ashram were gradually becoming visible on the horizon, just like a child stretching his arms on waking up. And then the peaks were suddenly framed against a magical palette of colours in the sky which reminded one of the Aurora Borealis. One was pink as the *kamedi* bird, another brilliant white, a third like the angry flames of a fire tinged with red, the next also two-coloured, the fifth violet, the sixth green and the seventh adorned with a crown of blue. Each colour appeared like a dancing fairy, the movement of her magnificent skirts transforming the whole sky into a sea where the clouds were the undulating waves moving across it.

Lavanyadevi took in this divine sight as she slowly walked to her favourite haunt, the Shivagauri Falls. She could see, swinging on the numerous rainbows there, the divine pairs of Radha-Madhav and Shiv-Parvati, both contained in each other. She was lost in her own world when she remembered a question she had once asked Swami Akhandanand-*ji*.

"Guru-*ji*, is it true that Radha-*ji* is contained in the idol of Banke Bihari? Devotees claim that Radha-*ji*'s nose-ring can be seen on the idol's cheek. What does this mean?"

As always, Guru-*ji* first laughed his hearty laugh and then answered, "My child, the image of the divine couple in the idol of Banke Bihari? Is that something so unbelievable? *Arey bhai*! You have read history, geography, poetics and God knows how many other subjects. Have you never come across the concept of *ardhnareeshwara*—the form of Shiva which combines the male and female forms? My child, Shiv-Parvati, Radha-Madhav and Sita-Ram are just emblems of our feelings and of our understanding that masculine without feminine and feminine without masculine are both incomplete. The *shakti-tattva* in a woman exemplifies the masculine principle in her while the *prem-tattva* in a man shows the presence of the feminine principle."

Holding on to the railings near the waterfall, Lavanyadevi stretched out her neck to feel the spray of water on her face. Her journey into the world of memories was suddenly interrupted by disruptive voices. Turning around, she saw *Panda-ji*—he was forcibly dragging a young man along and coming towards her. The stream of harsh words coming out of his mouth was lashing the young man like a whip. He was cowering from the blows *Panda-ji* was raining upon him, his hands raised like an umbrella over his head, trying, unsuccessfully, to protect himself from the anger of this Rudradev of the mountains!

The face of the young man appeared vaguely familiar to Lavanyadevi. *Arey*! It was this very boy who had come running to her with a portrait he had painted when she was here last year—she remembered being astounded on seeing it. The youngster had smiled, pearly white teeth showing from behind his pink lips, and said, "I made this portrait based on one that I saw with Baba Sundardas. But I am young, and my imagination doesn't have the expanse of experience. So I imagined the face that I saw in the features and expressions of a young girl who lives here. Isn't it beautiful? Were you like this in your youth? Tell me, does your daughter resemble the face in this picture?" Lavanyadevi was overwhelmed by his artless and direct questions, his talent and his imagination. But could she tell him that her own daughter was angry with her as she was not as beautiful as her mother, and had declared herself an 'unwanted child'?

Distressed by the way the talented young man was being dragged, cursed and beaten, she sternly said, "*Panda-ji*, please let him be and stop all this cursing and shouting. And pray tell me why a gentle person like you who is fond of the lyrical *lasya* dance is performing the *tandava* today?"

"We are doomed!" said he and, slapping his forehead, started crying loudly.

Lavanyadevi had to calm him down as one does a child. But even she was dumbfounded when she heard what *Panda-ji* had to say. There is no saying what turn the human mind can take at any point of time. Perhaps it is never possible for all the pages of the book of life to turn themselves in proper sequence from one to hundred. Some page will invariably get folded, another torn, a third skipped, the fourth turn dog-eared, or several pages might get flipped together instead of one. And because of such breaks and ruptures, humans, disengaged from their contexts, traditions, responsibilities and from any accountability, will sit down to write their stories anew. Is it possible for another human being to step in and alienate him from his own unique creation?

Was this just a passing infatuation for this juvenescent or true love, Lavanyadevi wondered. Is this deep faith that transcends the body? To resolve the matter, it was important for her to know all the details. She came to know that during the winter, *Panda-ji* had sent this handsome youngster to his patrons' houses in Kolkata and Mumbai to learn some trade, as there wasn't much money to be made in the mountains, either as a priest or as an artist, in this age of continual inflation. But the very first place he went to, he got into a relationship with a forty-two-year-old widow who did the housework there. He had gone to learn a trade, and came back having learnt how to clean utensils and sweep and dust the house. God knows what black magic that woman performed on this boy from the mountains; he is now intent on marrying her. Since he was a year short of the legal age for marriage, he had brought the woman along with him so that they could get married when he was officially an adult.

The woman was standing some distance away. Lavanyadevi spoke to her. She was plain-looking and dull, and after meeting her she could only wonder what induced young Gulabchand to fall for her. What did he see in this woman? Certainly not beauty and definitely not any quality! Was it her sluggishness that appealed to him? Her dark complexion? One only had to listen to her loud cackling guffaw to turn away in distaste. Gulabchand Negi had placed before Lavanyadevi's sharp mind a complex puzzle about human behaviour, to which she was unable to find a solution.

To *Panda-ji* who was standing beside her, she said with folded hands, "*Panda-ji*, I'm sorry. I am unable to find a solution to this issue right now. Can you wait till tomorrow morning?" Saying this, she turned once more towards the cascading water, contemplating what could possibly be the right course of action.

She observed how the cascading water bounced off the rocks all around, breaking down the stones that stood in its way and falling downwards to form a river. The river moved rapidly forward, carrying in its current all the small stones it found in its way; when there was a large stone or rock the water did not stop; it merely found a way around the obstacle. If, on the way, any small stream of water got separated from the main body and was stopped by the stones lying in its way, the water would soon stagnate. Would it be right to attempt to stop the flow of water, she wondered? She was reminded of the Prince of Wales who turned down the opportunity to rule over three-fourths of the world so he could marry a commoner. Why then can Gulabchand not have his way? Can the waterfall of intense attraction not be left free to make its way like a river of love? Is it wise to divert it and cause it to stagnate?

Lavanyadevi, caught in the complex dimensions of these thoughts, saw that it was almost dusk and the sun was setting behind the mountains. She saw Gulabchand coming towards her. She had a long, solemn conversation with him after which, with firm steps, she walked to *Panda-ji*'s house. "Bahurani!" he exclaimed, rushing out of the house on seeing her and requested her to come in and have a seat. Lavanyadevi politely refused, sat down on a platform outside and, like one delivering a sermon, said, "*Panda-ji*, I hope you remember what the scriptures have said regarding the role of parents—parents are merely the cannon which shoots the arrow. It is nature that has the first right over the *jiwatma* that parents send into the world. I have thought at length on this matter, and I have just one question to ask of you: will you let this stream of love run unhindered or will you stop the flow and let the water rot?"

"But bahurani, what about other factors? Age, caste, complexion, beauty? Are these not valid considerations too?"

"*Panda-ji*, Savitri had chosen Satyavan for a day, and she is labelled a *sati* by all today. Is it not possible that your son can make something miraculous happen? Who knows what is in store for tomorrow?"

"Bahurani, please! What will happen to our standing in society? What will happen to their children?" *Panda-ji* kept asking these and many such questions, and Lavanyadevi patiently answered them at length with numerous illustrations from the Ramayana, Mahabharata and the Puranas. She finally told him, "Look *Panda-ji*, these places are not isolated any more. Cities are entering the mountains. Television and cinema are also making inroads into lives. In such circumstances, it is not wise to place too many restrictions on your children. Think with all your wisdom and experience. What is the worst that can happen? If it is indeed infatuation, it will wear off in a couple of years and then you will be free to do what you want."

Panda-ji had not expected such an answer from Lavanyadevi. Familiar as he was with her earlier principled and rigid obstinacy, he had gone to her thinking that she would support his line of thought. But her answer left him in a quandary. To top it all, every point that she made was so logical and practical that there was no way in which he could dismiss or refute her suggestions. He simply had no option but to accept what she had suggested.

Lavanyadevi started ruminating over everything that Gulabchand had said and what had prompted her to decide in his favour. He had said, "Bua-ma, I have nothing to do with whether she loves me or not. But I can swear on you this moment that I love her with all my heart. Bua, what do age, looks, caste or creed have to do with true love? The moment I first set my eyes on Sandhya, I sensed that a ray of light emanating from her had entered my being and changed my life forever. Bua-ma, I love her and I will continue to love her till the end. It is possible that she might not, but that doesn't change anything for me."

There was so much truth in what Gulabchand said that it did not take the experienced Lavanyadevi more than a moment to make up her mind about the right course of action. But was not the insight into how to look at these events bequeathed to her by her mother Jyotirmoyidevi?

"Ma, do you know what Mamata has done?" Lavanyadevi's voice was heavy with anger mingled with sorrow and regret. Jyotirmoyidevi, well-acquainted with her daughter's inexperience in matters practical, laughed as she asked her, "What has happened?"

"Ma, you are so casually asking me what has happened! Do you even know? This thirty-five-year-old woman is pregnant! And she is not even willing to reveal the name of the child's father. You know that Mamata is a widow, don't you? The other ayah said that the father is a married man employed in our household. Is she not revealing his name because that man will be disgraced? Just look at her guts! One, she is in the wrong; two, she is refusing to divulge any information!" Lavanyadevi was fretting and at her wit's end.

"That's enough, my girl! Now relax and listen to me. I've sent my car to your place. Send Mamata over for a couple of days."

"Thank God!" thought Lavanyadevi and took a deep breath of relief.

Surprisingly, after a few days, a visibly relaxed and smiling Mamata was back in the Roychoudhury house, accompanied by her mother. Before Lavanyadevi had the chance to utter a word, Jyotirmoyidevi said in her stern voice, "Mamata, you go in and do your work." Then she took her daughter's hand and said, "Lavanya, let us go and sit inside."

Lavanyadevi said, "Ma, how did you sort out the whole matter? Did Mamata tell you everything?" In response, Jyotirmoyidevi gave her some practical tips about how to look at life. "Lavanya, on the hard surface of lived life, the meanings of the physical and material are multidimensional. A poor man is far away from his wife and children, and pines for human touch and warmth. In such a situation, if there is even the faintest possibility of rain in the dry desert of his life, will he not turn towards it? Look at the whole episode from Mamata's perspective too. Does it not stir your compassion to think of a woman married at fifteen and widowed at sixteen? Will she be able to turn down the thought of some warmth and pleasure? She sees you from morning to evening, secure in the love and care of your relationship with your husband, and enjoys a small particle of that happiness without causing harm to anyone—is that a sin? Bring more breadth and compassion into your vision, my child. Don't bring in rites and rituals, honour and tradition as impediments and make your life-path burdensome and inaccessible; use them as steps to take you forward. These are the steps to a successful life, not the goals. And the goal of any person is to become a compassionate and complete human being, not someone who is reduced to being a prudish but broken person brandishing the whip of principles."

"Ma, I completely agree with all that you are saying, but first tell me how you solved Mamata's problem."

"There wasn't much of a problem actually since it has just been a few days. It just needed a small surgery and a vasectomy to set things right. Now there will be no problem in future either."

Lavanyadevi listened in astonishment, deeply impressed by her mother's wise, innovative, pragmatic as well as ultramodern approach to the whole incident. This is what the ancient texts refer to as the right approach to life—being connected to life and standing on the concreteness of reality. It also made amply manifest Ma's broad compassion, as she did for Mamata what she would have done for her own daughter. It was not the time to hold forth on one's high ideals and values, but to take care of a woman and her dignity. A widowed woman wanted to keep her dignity intact in front of her married daughter but was overwhelmed by the demands of her love and her body. To understand a person's limitations and free her from them is no doubt a virtuous deed worth doing, but Lavanyadevi would probably never have understood this if she hadn't seen the way the entire matter was handled.

Jyotirmoyidevi had rightly judged that this incident would fundamentally change how Lavanya looked at things. She also knew that her daughter would now grapple with this idea till she was able to extract its essence. Having said what she had to say, Jyotirmoyidevi got up from her seat, ran her fingers affectionately through her daughter's hair and then moved towards the door. Time proved her right. Without her mother's wisdom, her compassion and her insight, Lavanyadevi could never have imagined being able to resolve the Gulabchand incident the way she had.

Lavanyadevi's entire life had been spent in work and in the din and bustle of the city. The solitude and silence of the mountains were helping her recuperate from life's struggles that had worn her down, revitalising her, making her whole again. Introspection and reflection had always been her favourite companions. The serenity all around heightened her concentration. Lavanyadevi had by now restricted herself within the limits of Haridwar and Rishikesh. She accompanied the mountain gods when they came down to the plains each winter, but never thought about going to Kolkata. Every invitation to the city was politely turned down.

In the midst of her sojourn, she was informed that her mother had willed her the 70 *kathha* of land that she had got as dowry from the family of Raja Santosh. In today's world, the price of that land is beyond one's imagination. Without wasting a moment, Lavanyadevi consulted Mr. Bharti, a sincere administrator from the hills, and on his advice, sold off 50 *kathha*. She used the money to set up numerous elementary education centres in adjoining villages which were grounded in the actual requirements of the population. These centres were very different from the schools of today. Although Lavanyadevi was neither against English nor against higher education, her experiences in the mountains had opened up several novel directions of thought to her. This change was comparable to a well-established allopathic doctor relying on homeopathic and ayurvedic medicine as alternatives.

Could there be a better thinker than the hardworking and studious Lavanyadevi? Harmonious cohabitation with nature became the foundational principle of all these education centres. She decided that they would all be built with locally available materials, on sites chosen so as to make the best use of existing natural resources while also protecting them. Teachers would be trained keeping in mind the kind of elevated role that Maharshi Aurobindo fulfilled. Every child would be encouraged to continue their family profession and the school would not be an obstacle but provide support for this. In sports, kabaddi, football, kho-kho, wrestling, swimming and mountaineering would be given priority. The simple rules of these games were also put down in writing, just like the school constitution.

After she had executed the whole plan and put it in motion, Lavanyadevi felt slightly edgy and restless. There seemed to be no apparent reason for it. Oblivious to where she was going and lost in the mist of her mother Jyotirmoyidevi's memories, she set off in the direction that her legs took her.

Lavanyadevi had taken all possible care of her mother as she grew older. But there was one wish of hers that Lavanyadevi had never been able to fulfil—just sitting together and talking, nothing serious, just banter and trifles. 'We'll talk tomorrow, Ma, not today' was what she said every time, and that tomorrow never came. Jyotirmoyidevi continued to take care of Lavanyadevi's grandchildren till her dying days, nourishing them with the warmth of her affection. The pain of not having been able to spend time with her mother tormented Lavanyadevi no end. She often put herself in the dock for this. Couldn't she have done this one little thing had she really wanted to? She was often consumed by the guilt of having becoming a machine that was only concerned with completing tasks and which automatically 'switched off' when the work was done, leaving no space for human interaction. This is perhaps what led her elder son Arnab, always the emotional one, to remark, "Ma, you have become too business-like!" In retrospect, this was also undoubtedly why she was always an excellent teacher to her children, but seldom an affectionate mother. To offer her some solace from this persistent feeling of guilt, her father tried to console her by saying, "Lavanya, you are Shravan Kumar in the truest sense; you should not give space in your mind to such meaningless thoughts." She also remembered her father saying, "Lavanya! Your mother always said, just wait and watch, our daughter will surpass me in every way. She will go a long way." Lavanya had broken down when her father uttered these words of consolation, which were more like his blessings. She had hugged him and cried for a long time; perhaps her tears provided her some relief from the dull ache in her heart that incessantly troubled her for not having paid heed to her mother's one simple wish.

Today, on this evening of her stay in Gangotri, as she offered her obeisance to the departed soul by praying to the setting sun, Lavanyadevi forgave herself. She then set off towards the cottage of Baba Sundardas, who had gone higher than Gomukh in search of the mythical *neelkamal* flower.

Darkness was fast enveloping the surrounding hills. Lavanyadevi was wearing a full-sleeved cashmere sweater and had draped around a warm shawl, despite which the chill seeped into her bones. She was trying her best to control the chattering of her teeth, but without success. When she finally reached Baba Sundardas's cottage, she found that even in this icy cold weather, the door was open. Peering in, she stared in wonder and awe at the scene in front of her. In this intense cold, Baba Sundardas sat cross-legged in *padmasana*, engaged in some work, wearing just a short dhoti. A large diya burning in a corner illuminated the whole cottage. The walls were plastered with photographs.

This faraway lonely cottage, built on one of the many high peaks that surrounded the Gangotri valley, seemed surreal. This sense was further heightened by the presence of the solitary ascetic and the single large diya burning in a corner—the lone dark cottage and its surroundings were suffused by an ethereal light and ambience. Together with the vast silence of the mountains they seemed to convey an otherworldly sublimity unlike anything that Lavanyadevi had ever experienced. She was mesmerised.

Baba looked up on hearing the rustle of a saree. "You? When did you come?" he asked, in a tone conveying such deep familiarity that it startled Lavanyadevi. Did he know her? Maybe he had just heard people talking about her. She too had heard many things about Baba Sundardas—that he was 150 years old, that he lived in Gomukh for eight to ten months a year, and that he survived on a strict diet of holy basil leaves, among other things.

Whether all this was true or not, Lavanyadevi was convinced that Baba was a seeker of the highest order, and an excellent photographer besides. There was not a shadow of pretence or drama in his manner or bearing. Whatever was there was visible in the photographs, in the surroundings and in his conduct, and stood as firm in its place and as irrefutable as truth itself. Lavanyadevi gathered her meandering thoughts together and focussed her attention on the photographs.

In one of the photographs, ostensibly taken by someone else, of a vast frozen land covered with snow, Baba could be seen climbing down into a pit, like a polar bear, to offer his obeisance to the sun—it was unlike anything Lavanyadevi had seen, a picture worth a collector's prize. The series of photographs on rare species of flowers were outstanding. She could also see carefully dried and preserved specimens of rare plants and flowers in the cottage. Even after gingerly touching a dried *neelkamal*, she couldn't trust her own eyes and fingers to have truly seen and touched the mythical blue lily that she had only read about in stories.

When Lavanyadevi asked him, "Baba, are you really 150 years old?" he did not answer. Instead, he asked her, "Do you know Prabhavatidevi?"

Lord! What kind of question is this? Have I been hypnotised or am I hearing things? Has one of Guru-*ji*'s disciples told him my whole history, she wondered. Disconcerted and in an attempt to compose herself, she asked him, "Baba, how do you know her? Have you met her?" In response, Baba reached for a rusted old tin box kept to his right and opening it, he took out a brittle, yellowed piece of paper on which there was a handmade portrait and showed it to her.

Seeing it, Lavanyadevi involuntarily took a step back in surprise. She had seen the same portrait of her grandmother, life-sized, hanging on the wall of the Dhaka palace. How did Baba acquire a replica of the same portrait?

Like a spider entangled in its own web, Lavanyadevi was progressively getting caught in a web of more and more such questions. Then, quite unexpectedly, her limbs and her entire being felt at once saturated with a comforting tranquillity and her heart was suddenly imbued with peace. In this state of utter peace, she rose above and beyond all questions and answers. Divesting herself of all her fame, her wealth of learning, she prostrated herself before him in a *sashtang pranam*. "Baba! I am Lavanya! Prabhavatidevi's granddaughter. All my questions have been answered, Baba! I have only one last request to make—please bless me so that I always travel on the right path. Bless me so that when I am about to close my eyes to the world, I should not see the face of a single person whom I have caused hurt. Bless me so that I am able to rise above petty considerations of fame and glory and become a particle of dust on earth as I once was. Bless me, Baba!"

Lavanyadevi sat transfixed as tears ran down her cheeks. Gradually her head bent further and further towards the ground. Even in that state of semi-consciousness, her half-closed eyes could discern that the darkness around her kept growing deeper and that the flame from the diya kept growing bigger and bigger. She was almost unconscious and yet her mind seemed to be questioning her why her body was losing consciousness due to this supernatural primordial vibration. How had the light of the diya become so large, so bright? How was it able to illuminate the *shringar* of a huge *lingam*? She was powerless to answer any of these questions, just a mute witness to what was happening around her. Her encounter with the sublime seemed to have obliterated her physical existence and made her one with the ethereal surroundings.

Tansen was singing on his *tanpura*: "The rivers are like different faiths / All merge at last with the ocean / Tansen tells all believers / different religions / worship different gods / but all lead to the same *Brahma*". In the ceaseless tireless praise of the eternal divine there comes one fleeting moment when *Brahma* becomes manifest in all its glory and magnificence in that ephemeral mortal entity, before vanishing once again.

Was she unconscious or was she in a state of pure and absolute consciousness? Whatever it was, these questions beyond the reign of the intellect were taking birth and dying of their own accord in that body. How did this diya, burning night and day, remain eternal? Why did it not extinguish and die down? Is this personified manifest knowledge? Is this what we call the consciousness of the soul? Is this the absolute monolithic power which like the axis of an infinite circle establishes its own circumference and is yet beyond impermanence, beyond time? Is this the greatest of the great, the immutable, the Supreme One? Is this what Kabir raises a hue and cry about when he asks, "Who was it that slept at night? Is he the same as the one who woke up? Isn't sleep death? And waking rebirth? Is our birth just a brief pause then, a temporary stop?"

You may consider *tyag* and *bhog*, renunciation and enjoyment, as truths or as illusions—this is your belief, your destiny. Similarly you can consider the passage of time as true or false. But both have their existence. Your motion, your release, your renunciation and enjoyment are all linked to time like a baby to the umbilical cord. That is perhaps why our ancestors have said: "The story is such that it has no end / the end is the beginning / human beings are but infinitesimal bubbles / imprisoned in this circle".

Echoing like the primordial sound that has no beginning and no end, these words envelop Lavanyadevi completely: "*Buddhimdehi, rupamdehi, bhaktimdehi*—intellect, beauty, devotion—what is it that you desire? Do you wish to be like Draupadi, Ahilya, Shakuntala? Do you desire everlasting life?"

"No, no! Spare me! I do not want to be like Yayati. What will I do with this imperfect mind and body created and woven together with unsteady, crumbling ideas? *Bas*! Enough! Please destroy this intoxicated and scheming existence like you destroyed Daksha's *yagya*, his ritual sacrifice…and if you must grant me Sati-like perfection, please heed my request—when this body, after it rots, melts and burns, becomes one with the earth and sprouts again, may it be free from every small thorn of pettiness and may it spread fragrance in the world."

"Are these words and thoughts mine? Or is it some unfamiliar spirit that has entered me?"

Lavanyadevi remained in the same position, her head tilted to the ground, for time unmeasured. When she opened her eyes, the eastern sky was slowly turning the snow-capped peaks pink and gold and the sun's charioteer was scattering emerald, sapphire and ruby in its wake, and the small cottage too was bathed in this ineffable ethereal light. She rose, feeling light as a flower, and beholding all this beauty around her, she felt it was a boon granted without asking, and set off towards the ashram.

Guru-*ji* was anxiously waiting for her at his ashram. He looked carefully at her face, at those eyes which seemed unearthly—as if they had still not returned to earth and were even now travelling somewhere in the great void beyond. Without waiting for a salutation from Lavanyadevi, Guru-*ji* blessed her, "*Vijayi bhava*! May victory be yours!" Surprised, she looked at him questioningly. "Victory? Whose? Where? Why? What could such a blessing possibly mean?" she wondered.

Reading on her face her unvoiced thoughts, Guru-*ji* said, "Lavanya! May you achieve success in traversing the path of temperance that you have chosen. This is what the blessing means." Hearing this, she touched Guru-*ji*'s feet and took his blessings, stood in silence for a few moments, and then with slow steps walked towards her favourite haunt, the Shivagauri Falls.

Lavanyadevi appeared radiant in the sunlight, her long wavy hair reaching down below her knees as she walked—she seemed as beautiful as Gauri herself. What if Kalidas were to see her thus? How would the poet have described her? Incidentally, there is a connection between Lavanyadevi and the immortal Kalidas. On Shakuntala's beauty, the master of metaphor and analogy remarks, "Analogies may be found for the symmetry in form, beauty and complexion of the picture-perfect Shakuntala, but how is her *lavanya*—her grace, her elegance, her courteousness—the radiance of which illumines her whole being, to be described?"

Lavanyadevi was entranced as she stood gazing at the boundless and infinite spectacle of God. It seemed to her that the eternal beloveds Radha and Krishna were swinging to and fro on the rainbows that hung over the waterfall, while all around them their *sakhis* sang Raag Malhar as they fanned them with the royal *chanwar*. Vidyapati must no doubt be praying to this divine duo and offering his salutations, reciting, "*Nav Vrindavan, nav-nav tarugan, nav-nav vikasit phool*—New Vrindavan, tender young plants, freshly blooming flowers." Lavanya was engrossed in this vision when Guru-*ji* went up to her and gently said, "Lavanya, we are about to depart for Kedar. Aalo has packed your bag; we are just waiting for you."

On the road to Kedarnath in the jeep, memories of her mother Jyotirmoyidevi, her maternal grandfather Dhananjay Roychoudhury and her unseen yet familiar maternal grandmother Prabhavatidevi lifted her spirits. Then, astonished to see Manju coming towards her, she asked, "*Arey* Manju! You have become so beautiful now that it is difficult to recognise you! What are you doing nowadays?", but Manju disappeared even as Lavanyadevi was speaking to her. "What is happening?" she asked aloud, then realised it was a daydream. Lavanyadevi closed her eyes, took a deep breath and was again caught up in the turning wheels of her thoughts.

To come here was the best and the most beautiful decision of my life. This exclusive peace, this heightened attentiveness, the inexhaustible bounty of nature, being able to truly reside in the 'self'—could I have ever known all this had I stayed on in the plains? The resentment that I felt then has turned into gratitude today. If my kith and kin had not made me aware of all the evils hidden behind the curtain of civilised society, which were always present but which I could not see, I would have died having lived the sheltered and convenient life of one who never knew, never experienced life's deepest mysteries, and my presence would have flickered briefly in the mirror of society's memory and then faded. Today I am indebted to my family members—they are the reason I am here. I pray to the Lord to help me repay this debt to them, and to bless me so I can dedicate this body born in human form to the service of others. How had this spirit of forgiveness germinated in Lavanyadevi's mind today without her knowledge?

In this web of thoughts, she was again reminded of Manju. Why had Manju appeared in her thoughts all of a sudden after such a long time and registered her presence? Lavanyadevi had almost forgotten her. Was destiny working to hint at something? Or it could just be that Manju was alive in some corner of her mind, buried under a heap of memories. The mind is the cause of so many troubles, she thought, and firmly told her mind and her intellect: Come out of the corridors of memory and history; forget the past and think about the future.

Lavanyadevi continued this inner conversation with herself until they reached Kedarnath ashram. Guru-*ji* gave her the good news that *Panda-ji* had agreed to accept the Bengali woman as his daughter-in-law. Lavanyadevi was pleased to know that *Panda-ji* had tried to free himself of his prejudices and effect a peaceful compromise. She was also happy that the altercations occasioned by personal differences and their polluting presence in the peaceful environment had been avoided. She moved towards the dining area with light steps and had just pulled a plate towards herself when she saw two beautiful young girls coming towards her. Their haste indicated that they were either desperate to meet someone or in a hurry to get back.

Lavanyadevi went forward to greet them. But before she could say a word, the two girls came and embraced her with the urgency of children meeting their mother after an eternity. She affectionately patted their cheeks and caressed their heads, ruffling their hair. But unable to fathom the mystery of this sudden wealth of affection received, Lavanyadevi asked them, "*Ogo! Tomader naam ki*—What are your names?" From the two heads still clasped to her bosom came the muffled answers in slightly hurt voices, "Didu, I am Malavika, Soudamini's daughter." And "Maua, I am Manju, Hari's daughter."

"*Arey*! How did both of you get here? And I know you must have felt bad that I couldn't recognise you, but one big reason for that is you have both changed so much since I last saw you! And you are now simply unmatched in voice and looks. A person's entire character is reflected in their facial expression and transparency of voice, and your appearance tells me that both of you possess excellent hearts."

They were still caught up in their conversation when Guru-*ji* entered and blessed both the girls and then asked the attendants to get two plates of food for them. Lavanyadevi felt mortified when she realised her neglect. Guru-*ji* tried to put her at ease by putting an affectionate hand on her head and said, "Lavanya! It is natural that such things will happen once in a while. When one becomes seriously focused on good deeds, in *satkarma*, then one is unable to pay attention to anything else and all mundane activities appear to be created from ignorance. One only wants to do more and more work in the shortest possible time without wasting a single moment. It is commonplace for travellers on this path to commit such minor mistakes. Do not take this otherwise and do not let your mind think of this as a mistake or on ways to rectify it. This is quite common when you are focused on your *sadhana*."

Guru-*ji*'s words lifted her sagging spirit. Lavanyadevi blessed both the girls and said, "Come, let's eat first, the rest can follow."

After having dinner, the three of them decided to sleep off the weariness of travel so that they could wake up fresh in the morning and straightaway get down to work.

Just as dawn was breaking across the landscape, the three of them, cups of tea and savouries in hand, came and stood on the ashram veranda from where they could see the sun's rays rouse the entire Kedarnath valley from its sleep. The meadow that stretched out before them was full of small, multicoloured wildflowers. The hearts of these young souls were also filled with optimistic dreams of a conceivable future and with the aspiration to do something meaningful and constructive.

Looking at Manjulika and Malavika, Lavanyadevi wondered whether the role of upbringing and genes in the development of human beings could be so life-changing so as to make it possible for three daughters from three different households to think alike. And if such are the factors that can transform human beings into divine entities, why then do we give such great importance to lineage or to the accumulation of good deeds from previous births? Not one among Lavanyadevi's own children had ever come forward to offer any help for whatever altruistic activities she had taken up for the benefit of society. But the children of her children, how is it that they so strongly support her in everything she was doing, with their minds, words and deeds: *manasa, vacha, karmana*? Even before she can begin to answer this she intuitively knows that all this is *leela*, divine play. She is imbued with an unspeakable peace and instead of clouds of doubt and questions, what stretches ahead of her is the vast clear blue sky. Aware of the fleet-footedness of time, she does not waste a moment more in formalities and asks them directly, "Have you come here with some specific purpose or is it just my love that has brought you here?"

Lavanyadevi's granddaughter Malavika took this opportunity to step forward and promptly commenced bringing her up to date about themselves and their lives in some detail. "Didu,

I know that Ma never gave you the respect that the rest of the world did. In her heart she always resented the fact that you distributed amongst everyone what she considered exclusive to herself. You never loved her less than anybody else, but what can the raincloud do if the vessel is kept upside down? But Soumen-*da* and I had accepted you as the goddess of our dreams since we were children. Soumen-*da* used to say this openly; but I kept the feeling to myself. I kept a mental note of each minute detail of everything that you did and said. My friends often told me, 'Your way of talking, your behaviour, the way you dress, all this makes you look like a younger version of our principal, your Nani—you are her carbon copy.' And Manju here regarded you as her mother since she was a child. You know, don't you, that she was with her parents only when she went to sleep. All her waking hours were invariably spent in worshipping you and following you around." Malavika looked at Manjulika as she said this, and Manjulika diffidently lowered her head in consent.

Malavika went on like an express train. "And Didu, you must definitely have noticed that like your own grandchildren, Manju also addressed you as Maua." Lavanyadevi blinked in consent, and Malavika continued at full speed. "Didu! Manju worked night and day to match up to your strict standards. Imagine the self-taught daughter of an illiterate father appearing for SAT and securing forty-third rank among twelve thousand examinees! How could she dream so big? Where did all this courage, determination and confidence come from? Did it come from Hari? No! You were her inspiration, Didu. A lost wayfarer on a cold, lonely night draws warmth from the mere sight of a glowing fireplace inside a cottage. Manju kept going forward motivated by your ideals. She got some really tempting offers from several foreign universities because of her SAT score, and some were ready to offer her full freeships. But Manju knew that you give more importance to the institutions here. So she took the University of Delhi's CAT examination, and her high scores ensured that she got admitted to Lady Shri Ram College instantly. She had literature and journalism as her subjects. She will appear for her postgraduate exam in social work this year."

A wilted rose, if wrapped in paper and immersed in water, appears to bloom afresh. In the same way, thought Lavanyadevi, despite all the limitations she had been born into, the paper of tireless labour and the water of self-determination had transformed Manjulika into a beautiful, fragrant, blooming flower—a complete person.

"And Didu, I, your granddaughter Malavika, after having studied in some of the most well-known colleges and universities abroad and having secured multiple degrees, have realised that these are all exercises in futility—ultimately meaningless. In the relentless flow of time, what significance do mere pieces of paper and a few silver coins hold? After having been around all these places it seemed that it is all just pretence and show-off. There is nothing more to it. Seen from a distance, you feel that this life is chic, glamorous and desirable. There are no worries, no pain. But such notions are completely mistaken. There is much pain behind this shining facade, there are tears and there is the agony of dying slowly bit by bit. Didu, wealth can help you access all the resources, but it is not an achievement or an end in itself. It can help you buy the softest bed stuffed with eiderdown, but it is beyond its capacity to give us restful sleep.

"Didu, we have both been thinking along these lines and have had many frantic discussions, heated arguments and long-drawn out debates, but couldn't reach a satisfactory conclusion. In the end, we thought that the person we have worshipped since childhood is still active and she can surely tell us the right way out. So, dear Didu, here we are! We have thought it out and have come here as mature and fully aware individuals. We want to give some purpose to our lives, and so we have come to our role-model for help. Didu! Soumen-*da* was initially not ready to divulge your address! But when he realised that we are serious about what we have decided and intent on meeting you, he gave us your address and probably also informed Guru-*ji* about our arrival."

Silently thanking Guru-*ji* and Soumen in her mind, Lavanyadevi cautioned both girls about possible hardships in future, and said, "I do not doubt that both of you are firm in your determination. Nevertheless, considering your age, the ways, customs and milieu of your home-world, always keep in mind that your psyche is still evolving and pay attention to the ebb and flow of your feelings when you make your plans for the future. It is not necessary that you live out the rest of your life as renunciates in the Himalayas just because that is what you had once decided was the right thing to do. However, it is necessary that harmony is achieved between higher values and worldly ones so that life does not appear to be discordant or out of rhythm. Once the right chord is struck, a happy life and sustainability of the tasks that you wish to undertake will automatically ensue. A decision taken in a fit of passion or a plan based on a hasty decision might lead to a barrage of anxieties and upheavals in the future. The right way to live one's life is to live it in its fullness and entireness; any disruption destroys its overall design and permanence.

"So, Manju and Malavika! You can spend the rest of your time today exploring this place. Immerse yourselves in the natural beauty of Kedarnath. We will have a serious discussion on this issue tomorrow morning. I will put you both in the dock for a soul-to-soul discussion and in turn, you too can ask me whatever you wish. If the foundations of belief are firmed up by deliberations, success is guaranteed, else cracks may appear," said Lavanyadevi as she got up. Malavika and Manjulika too got up along with her, and overwhelmed with emotion, embraced her once again.

The two girls found the eddies of love in their hearts difficult to control. Unable to express the intensity of their feelings in words, it was through their bodies that they voiced what their tongues could not.

As soon as it was morning, throngs of people from all across the valley could be seen coming towards the ashram. Lavanyadevi exclaimed in surprise, "*Oho*! It must be the first Sunday of the month. Good! Fortunately, on this day, volunteers from all the centres congregate here. In this congregation, all of us sit down together to share with each other our activities as well as the problems that we encountered in the preceding month. Since both of you are also going to become members of this extended family from today, the issue of your joining will also be discussed at this gathering.

"Look, that is where our discussions will take place," she said, pointing towards a site adjacent the ashram. There was a raised platform-like structure there which resembled a stage. The moment Manjulika and Malavika saw it, they started teasing Lavanyadevi. "Excellent, Didu! Excellent!" they said, in mischievous tones, "You seem to have established a throne for yourself here too!" Lavanyadevi gave them both a loving pat on their heads and said, "That's it! The naughtiness ends right here and serious work begins."

After the initial welcomes and *namaskars* were done with, Lavanyadevi finally began the assembly. She had with herself a long list of items jotted down serially. She gestured to the volunteers from the ashram to distribute copies of that list to all the people assembled there. The efficiency with which the assembly was conducted could give well-organised corporate events a run for their money. Everything was smoothly executed, without commotion or stir; there was not a single person among the attendees who seemed bored or disinterested; they were all excited and enthusiastic. As soon as the pamphlets were distributed, Lavanyadevi's spirited countenance could be seen addressing the gathering in a firm and solemn voice.

"Look! In order to achieve victory over Ravana, you do not necessarily have to endure a long-drawn exile like Lord Rama; you can win this battle of life as vivaciously and as playfully as Lord Krishna. Bound as he was by dignity and decorum, the life of *maryada purushottam* Rama was complex and full of challenges. He, therefore, came to be known as God-incarnate in *satyuga*, the era of truth, when everything was closest to the ideal. On the other hand, Lord Krishna, who was accomplished in all the sixty-four *kalas* or traditional arts, made compromises where necessary and in accordance with his *yugadharma*—the needs of the times he lived in—and yet achieved his goal in complete accordance with his *dharma*. He made all these compromises not for achieving fleeting worldly pleasures but for the greater public good and to ensure the establishment of higher principles. He could get Bhishma to bless Draupadi with good fortune. Furthermore, whether it was directing Bhimsen to strike the crucial blow to Duryodhana's thigh, getting Shikhandi to stand in front of Arjuna while he rained arrows on Bhishma, convincing Arjuna to attack the unarmed Karna or convincing Dharmaraj Yudhishthira to pronounce before Dronacharya, 'Ashwatthama is dead', there are numerous instances that can be drawn upon to argue that Krishna was unscrupulous or that he was a dissembler. But what happened as the Mahabharata war drew to a close is there for everyone to see. Even one as determined and firm as Bhishma ultimately sang Krishna's praises by reciting the hundred names of the Lord—the *sahsranama*—at the end of the war! He praised him as the most venerated hero of the people and requested him to protect the child in Uttara's womb. I cite these examples to convey to all of you that we have to continue our quest for higher values alongside fulfilling our worldly commitments. When one works in governance of one's conscience while giving one's bodily needs their dues, the metaphysical elements remain in harmonious synchrony with the supernatural. Consequentially, one's mind, words and actions become beautiful.

"I acknowledge that the way the youngsters of today function is, and has to be, different from the way I function. I have always been neck-deep in worldliness, and it is only towards the later part of my life that I decided to dedicate myself to doing good deeds and have consequently been able to do whatever little I could. But you people have begun from the central point of your lifespan, the course of which is as long as the Ganga. Therefore, do not be as inflexible or as immovable as the mountains during your time on this earth; let your life chart its course like a gurgling river; that way, it will flow freely towards the sea and will naturally achieve public welfare in the course of its flow. For any goal higher than this one, you must be perpetually alert and keep a sharp lookout for all those creature-comforts which might tempt you and lure you into believing as truth the numerous lies that we encounter in the guise of conveniences and pleasures. However, always remember that it is as dangerous to turn away from the easily available comforts of life as it is to lose oneself in them—it not only makes one dreary, inelegant and uninteresting, it also makes one dull and fills the individual with self-importance and righteous indignation. Therefore, one should love one's physical self and use it as a ladder for scaling and achieving higher goals. One must keep in mind that the unwavering lamp of supreme knowledge—*Brahmagyan*—can only be lit within the temple that is the body. The credo of our mortal existence is best defined, in Kabir's words, by one's ability to be able to return an unsoiled sheet.

"Our existence on this planet is akin to that of insects. How then are we expected to do good for others? Do we even have the capability for such acts? However, it is eminently possible that we do not harm others. We can always take care not to hurt the feelings of others or say bitter words against them. Such things are easy to practise in our daily lives. To think of serving others just by becoming a hermit or by proceeding to the Himalayas is often meaningless; on the contrary wherever the atmosphere has become vitiated by streams of sorrow, misery and torture, it is our manifest duty and responsibility to intervene by contributing towards improving the atmosphere.

"All of you have chosen your own path to do something worthwhile in life. Today, we need to think about our two new members too. For the time being, the areas of work which come to my mind are the elimination of addiction and prevention of prostitution. If these ideas appeal to all of you as well as to the two new members, let us prepare a plan for implementation; if not, we will have to think of something else." Saying this, Lavanyadevi withdrew into a state of complete silence for a while.

The moment she fell silent, a deep hush descended over the assembly as well. It seemed as if all those assembled had suddenly become statues and stopped breathing. The profundity of that brief period of wordlessness created a flutter in the hearts of the two young women. They were now completely convinced that nobody else could guide them with such practicality and generosity as Lavanyadevi. Even more entranced by her after what she had just said, both of them chorused, "Didu! Maua! Please educate us about what needs to be done and initiate us into the work as our guru."

Lavanyadevi once again let some time elapse between their questions and her response. Once again, this silence enveloped in its deep stillness the atmosphere, the surroundings and all that it contained—the earth, the sky, trees, birds and animals, flowers and leaves, dewdrops, the water of the rivers. All seemed sheltered under a vast canopy of peace that stretched in every direction, when the silence was penetrated by the sound of Lavanyadevi's resonant voice. "Everything talked about in today's discussions was your psychic initiation. There is no need for initiation rites like an amulet of charms or whispering mantras into someone's ears. It is all about tuning the strings of one's heart with those of another. Whenever you feel that this *tanpura* is sounding out of tune, you tighten the strings to get the right pitch—which is neither too high nor too low. You do not require a guru for this. As the famous Buddhist dictum goes, *app deepo bhavah*: you will become your own guru and your conscience will always keep you mindful. In order to keep your conscience clear and unclouded by the dust and dirt of illusions, you will constantly have to sweep and swab it. Intelligence creates happiness and conscience leads to joy. If your awareness is pure, you can easily distinguish between the two. You also need to understand that opportunities sent by God should not be refused. Do not act like the protagonist in that old story from the past who pretended to be blind and committed the grave mistake of stepping over a bag full of silver coins. Whenever you think you have met a companion for life who you think is like-minded, co-operative and shares the same beliefs, do not turn away from that person; take the person along. Remember, it is not at all necessary for your life partner to be rich, honoured, good-looking and meritorious. What is necessary is that the person should be the 'right person'. From my experience of the world I have come to realise that this particular 'species' is slowly becoming extinct; however, it is because of the continued presence of some members of this endangered species that the planet is still rotating on its axis even though it is without a base.

"Manju! Malavika! Pay heed! The next link in the chain of the householder's dharma is the offspring. Never sermonise or hold forth in front of your children about those of your deeds that you consider exemplary. However much you are into public service, never deprive your children of their rights. Or else, as the wheels of time turn, you will introduce such citizens into the future who will be averse to good deeds. If your family members are naturally drawn to your activities, it is a good thing; but never cast the burden of your line of thought onto them. Do not recount tales of your golden past, or of someone's deceit, or stories of greed. Try more to listen to what they say; speak less. Be forthcoming with advice, but only if you are asked. And now, if you feel that the understandings of this ignorant guru of yours seem worthwhile, get up and prepare yourselves to navigate the long path that lies ahead of you.

"Manju! Go to Chennai and learn how Priyamvada Rangachary is eradicating addiction there, and train yourself accordingly. For an apprentice, the secret to success is the eagerness to learn. If you are as keen as Arjuna, Lord Krishna might just decide to enter you in this Kurukshetra of life and help you overcome its battles. Never let the fire of seeking knowledge die out."

"Maua, who is this sagacious woman whose name you just mentioned?"

Lavanyadevi thought for a while before responding to Manjulika's question. "Knowing more about this person will be instructive for all of you, so I will speak at length about her. Listen carefully. When I first came to know about her from my friend, the famous author Lalita, I became so obsessed with what I heard that I could not stop myself from going to meet her. When the quiet, beautiful, solemn and aristocratic Priyamvada-*ji* looked at me with her conch-shaped eyes, even I, a woman, kept staring at her as if hypnotised. Such extraordinary beauty! So many degrees! Such noble ancestry! And here was this incredibly beautiful lady in a simple cotton saree and cheap slippers, attaching no value whatsoever to any of these. Head bent over a table like a hardworking clerk, she was completely immersed in writing something, not remotely bothered by the oppressive Chennai weather. She was even oblivious to the fact that the ceiling fan was not working. She was totally focused on tackling the work that had come in for the day, so that whatever would come in tomorrow could be given due attention. My friend had cautioned me in advance, 'Devi! Be sure that she will not even look up from her work, let alone look at you, before it is two o'clock.' Therefore, when it was five minutes to two, I entered her room as quietly and as inconspicuously as possible and tried to take in the feel of the place and the sight of her so that I could corroborate all that I had heard about her with what I now felt and saw. Exactly at two o' clock, the clock sounded a brief alarm. Priyamvada-*ji* set aside the pile of papers she was working on and made as if to get up from her chair; as she straightened her back, she noticed me in the room and looked at me inquiringly.

"Handing over the note of reference from Lalita, I told her very politely, 'I have come here just to have a glimpse of you, but I would be grateful if you could please spare some time for me. Would I have that good fortune?'

"God knows what Lalita had told her about me or whether it was just one of my lucky days. Priyamvada-*ji* replied, 'Come, let's go eat something; we will talk over lunch.' Hopeful that I would get to spend some time with her, I followed her with a gratified look on my face. Her expression was temperate and impassive; it showed no cognisance of the presence of any admirers, nor did it demonstrate any satisfaction at her own achievements.

"After coming down one floor to the dining area, we picked up a plate each and stood in a long queue. She bought a coupon for five rupees and fifty paise and indicated for me to follow her. When my turn came and I reached the table from where we were supposed to serve ourselves, I was, to put it mildly, surprised. Oh God! The daughter of a millionaire! The daughter-in-law of a millionaire! And this is the food she eats! Cold rice, cold thick chapattis, one seasonal vegetable, watery *dal*, curd and some lime pickle. These were the rare dishes beckoning from the table. Priyamvada-*ji* thanked the manager for these excellent dishes in cheerful Tamil, and helping herself to the quantity of food that she needed, softly told me in English, 'Be quick, lots of people are waiting.' While having food, she told me that I could stay with any of the 150 patients admitted to the centre who might be willing to accommodate me, provided I was ready to bear my own expenses. She also told me that since there was comparatively less work to do on Sundays, she usually travelled to any of the nearby villages on Saturday evenings to conduct awareness campaigns. If I wished, I could also accompany her to the nearby hill station of Yercaud the coming Saturday.

"The two days I spent at the centre in Chennai gave me so many perspectives into the possible dimensions of the human mind that I became apprehensive about my own perceptions. I felt that I had done nothing worthwhile till then. Full of drug-addicts, potheads, alcoholics and gamblers, the centre was like a vibrant and colourful canvas on which the artist had been able to distinctively evoke so many hues! But every person in that centre was civil and courteous, and possessed integrity and honesty. All of them described their activities during their conversation sessions as these had happened—they neither tried to conceal anything nor did they narrate their experiences to elicit sympathy. They did not explicitly ask forgiveness during the course of their conversations, but every word they uttered echoed an apology and regret. As I listened to their stories, I was struck by their sheer diversity—from scions of royal families to hawkers selling fruits on carts at street corners, there were people from every stratum of society present there. Each had their individuality and their own place under the sky.

"The image of a guileless, mild elderly woman floats in front of my eyes even today. She was laden with gold all over. She had started drinking to keep her husband company. A spoilt child of a moneyed zamindar family, she had no connection with education. Therefore, she had neither books nor companions to guide her. In the process of giving company to her husband, she gradually became addicted to alcohol and was soon found drinking night and day, inside the house as well as outside. Her husband brought her to this centre so that she could be cured of her addiction. When I asked her, 'Your husband must feel very guilty that you are in this condition today because of him?', she gave me such a withering look that I was silenced. 'It is I who am an idiot and lacked judgment of what is good or bad for me,' she said. 'You can see for yourself how well he takes care of me.' And I thought to myself, what simple guileless minds these people have! They harbour no ill-will for others. She had accepted this man with all her heart as her husband, so how could she ever hold him guilty or in the wrong? I bent down to touch her feet and seek her blessings. Taking leave of her, I started off towards the station to board the train to Yercaud.

"That night, after making all arrangements for my comfort in the first-class compartment, I waited for Priyamvada-*ji*. I scanned the length and breadth of the platform from the window next to which I was seated, but she was nowhere to be seen. The train started moving. Chiding my carelessness, I told myself that my intention was not to holiday in that small hill station and that I should not have made arrangements based on mere assumptions. Anyway, cursing myself and repenting, I went looking for Priyamvada-*ji* from one compartment to another. When I reached the end of the train—the extreme end of the second-class sleeper compartment—I finally saw her! She was sitting quietly on an unreserved seat, a contented expression on her face. Before I could say anything, she made some space for me next to her and proffered two small paper packets. I looked in surprise at their contents. One contained fritters that smelled of stale oil and the other some roasted Bengal gram and groundnuts. With folded hands I requested her, 'A friend has given me more food than I need. If you permit, I will bring it here and both of us can eat together.' She clasped my folded hands and said very softly, 'Thank you very much, but please don't worry. I always eat these snacks. It is my daily routine. Please pardon my refusal. I will meet you tomorrow morning when we reach Yercaud.' I understood that this was a polite dismissal, hinting that I should go back to my seat."

"Maua, how did you come to realise that all your previous experiences were just a drop compared to what you gained at the de-addiction centre in Chennai? The spectrum of your own life experiences has also been quite broad. And even if you have lived the life of the elite, you have also been regularly doing a lot of grassroots social work, isn't it?"

"Manju, looking at pain from a distance and encountering it in person are entirely different. My experiences, including my encounter with Mama-*ji*, can be termed as feeling the pain of others. Seeing and knowing the diverse kinds of pain of others from close quarters were like entering the realm of the real. That is why the agony of that pain spread across my whole being. Today, while talking to a sensitive person like you, that stream of pain which lay dormant inside me for such a long time has suddenly oozed out.

"Alighting at that small hilly place called Yercaud and having arranged to have our luggage sent to the rest house situated atop the hill, we started walking uphill. We had hardly taken a few steps that hordes and hordes of villagers appeared on either side of the road with their hands raised, shouting, 'Devi Ma! Devi Ma!' and fell at her feet. She fondly addressed each of them by their names and asked them about their well-being. I got goose bumps witnessing this sight. Till date, I have not seen such a touching pageant of dedication, love, respect and gratitude. The mere sight of her had most of them in tears. Restless and distraught, hands folded in greeting on their bare chests, each one of them desperately wanted to get closer to this lady whom they revered like a goddess, just to be able to touch her once.

"Manju! Such a poignant scene—of a godly yet mortal figure, deluged by a river of love and reverence streaming in from all sides, assuring benediction to one and all with her hand raised—can be witnessed but rarely in life.

"This incident whetted my curiosity and I wanted to know more about this wonder-woman. My interest was further piqued when Priyamvada-*ji* outright refused to be interviewed by a big corporate house from America which had planned to publish the interview in the country's most popular newspaper. When its senior officials hinted that this could have potential financial benefits for the centre, she laughed off the suggestion, saying, 'Am I short of funds that I should start worrying about how to procure them?' Priyamvada-*ji* was not in need of funds? The same Priyamvada-*ji* who, despite the Chennai heat, did not even get the fan in her room repaired, leave alone getting an air conditioner installed? Was it true then that this was solely because she did not want to allow the serpent of comfort to wrap its coils around herself in any form? Would she be always wearing just two cotton sarees, washing each in turn? Would she never use her hands for any other purpose except to console? Whether it was paeans of praise being sung about her or scaling the peaks of wealth, none of these meant anything to her. Surprisingly, on the one hand, she was so approachable that anyone, whosoever it may be, could easily get in touch with her; but when it came to her personal life, she was as impenetrable as a fortress and not even a bird could breach her defenses. How then could one get past her defenses and approach the frontiers of those fiercely protected regions?

"Concealment creates mystery and the human mind is always eager to unravel mystery. That is why my inquisitive mind was desperately searching for leads to the history of this unique and intriguing individual. I kept pestering my friend Lalita for more information, and I finally got her to tell me more about Priyamvada-*ji*. And to my surprise, she began with the names of two big industrialists and revealed that, 'Priyamvada-*ji* is the daughter of one and daughter-in-law of the other'. 'What…!' I blurted out aloud, to which Lalita chided me and said, 'Listen to me quietly! And promise me that you will never tell anybody about this'. By then my curiosity was so great that I would have agreed to any condition. So I vigorously nodded my assent, and Lalita told me the rest of the story."

Malavika winked and playfully interjected, "Oh Didu! You too are as curious as a child!"

"Malavika, don't interrupt! Maua, what happened next? Please tell us the rest of the story," Manju said impatiently.

"It was a marriage between two wealthy Tamil families. An alliance between a foreign-educated, handsome and eligible prince and an extremely beautiful postgraduate girl! There were celebrations not just in Chennai but across the entire region. But what happened once the auspicious marriage ceremony was over was unfortunate. On the very first night, the bride came to know that her husband was completely wasted due to excessive drinking. The groom, of his own volition, told Priyamvada-*ji* that he had started drinking indiscriminately from a very early age, and this reckless drinking meant that his days were numbered. That night, she also noticed that he was frequently losing consciousness. Priyamvada-*ji*, who was a combination of Lakshmi and Saraswati in human form, immediately changed roles—she transformed herself into Goddess Durga, the embodiment of *shakti* and female energy. Taking charge of the situation the very next day after her marriage, she took her husband to the best rehabilitation centre in America. All she told the family members was that they were going abroad for their honeymoon. For a year and a half, she wandered, often in desperation and sometimes in hope, from one rehabilitation centre to another. But in the end, all she was left with were her husband's ashes.

"Exceptionally beautiful and belonging to the highest echelons of society, Priyamvada-*ji* was again swamped by a long line of eligible suitors, but her resolute 'no' caused grief to her immediate family as well as to other people around her. The wise elders gave her numerous examples from mythological tales and references from ancient times as well as modern, trying their best to convince her to remarry. Her mother-in-law once told her, 'Look at Satyavati in the Mahabharata. I am not asking you to accommodate a man in your life who will bear you a child, but I request you to choose a companion for yourself for this long, mountain-like life that you still have left to live. I give you my word that I will always treat him like my son and you like my daughter-in-law.' But the young lady did not once nod in agreement. Without laying bare the truth of her husband's addiction, she asked for permission from her family members to open a de-addiction centre. Her family tried to dissuade her by enumerating the many difficulties associated with the task. In an effort to convince her to change or postpone her plans, they advised her to begin familiarising herself with the family business first and said they would think about setting up a de-addiction centre at a later date. But despite resistance from both families, the soft-spoken and gentle Priyamvada-*ji* opened a small centre straightaway with whatever personal funds she had. She then applied for land from the government, which she was fortuitously granted. As of today, the first name that comes to mind when one talks of eradicating addiction in the entire country is that of Priyamvada-*ji*."

"Maua, did she renounce everything completely?" asked Manjulika, the trainee, eagerly.

"Manju, she needed neither saffron clothes nor white ones. For her, colours no longer existed. Even if she had worn red, she would still have appeared as sober as if she were wearing white. Seeing her, one got the impression that though she inhabited this world of ours, she did not really belong here; she came across as a transparent, fluid female form made of air and water wafting over the planet like a breath of life. You all think that I am self-sacrificing, don't you? Believe me when I tell you that compared to Priyamvada-*ji*, I am a hedonist. She marks the zenith and I am the bottom of the abyss; it is just that I have received a lot of fame and recognition without really doing much. Today I repent that I made an excuse and deferred going to Pondicherry when The Mother had asked me to come. Why did I allow things to subside? This is momentary detachment—*shmashan vairagya*. The truth is that I have not been able to do anything much in life and now age too is not on my side. With you people around, I will do what little I can do in this dusk of my life."

After completing the story of Priyamvada-*ji* and having given the necessary instructions to Manju, Lavanyadevi gave her a letter addressed to Priyamvada-*ji* enclosing a cheque for a token contribution. She said, "There is a huge amount of money lying with Soumen for this de-addiction work. But the seed capital of this work is total respect, belief and devotion. Think it over. If at any point of time you feel that you do not like this work, change your course without hesitation; don't carry it like a burden.

"Always be in harmony with your family; because if you learn to utilise the twenty-four hours available to you each day properly, no one will have any grievance against you and you will be able to reach the zenith of success with both your own vows and your journey of life."

Manju took the letter and the cheque, bowed down and touched Lavanyadevi's feet with respect. Lavanyadevi blessed her and said, "*Vijayi bhawa*. May you be victorious."

Malavika, who had been a silent spectator to these scenes until now, suddenly blurted out artlessly, "Didu! Leave alone a blood relationship between us it seems that you don't have a relationship with me even as an enemy. I noticed that right from the time we have arrived it is Manjulika who is the centre of your attention. It might be that she has stayed with you and you have brought her up, but if you yourself kept me in a different house far away from yourself, how is it my fault? Even when you knew that my mother, Soudamini, was only concerned with material pleasures, you never spared a thought about whether you should have taken care of me too, did you, Didu? And to top it all, you showered so much love on Soumen-*da*! But what about me? I, the poor thing that kept burdening myself on you for no reason." Having said all this, Malavika pretended to be upset and went and sat in a corner. Lavanyadevi's heart brimmed over with love. Oh, the affectionate tantrums of these loving children! She drew Malavika close, saying, "*O go*, my dear girl! You are the apple of my eye and the love of my heart. Come, come closer to me. From this moment on I will pay attention and I will listen only to what you say and cut off all connections with the rest of the world. Come, let us have tea together and make a new beginning."

"Didu!" said Malavika, clinging happily to her grandmother as a creeper would to a tree, "Yes, let us have tea and snacks together. But first quickly tell me what my task would be, since you are the one who always says that time is flying, and Didu, I do not want to be late anymore." Seeing her enthusiasm, Lavanyadevi's happiness knew no bounds. She visualised the girl's future as bright as the sun. She felt a deep sense of contentment in her heart that, even when she would no longer be physically present, her thoughts would continue to circulate in this world through these children—more accurately, the children of her children. That is probably the reason that the offspring of the soil are called *amritputra*, the undying children—through the eternal values that they impart their subsequent generations, they are present in the world even after they pass away. Since the scheme of consciousness and realisation of soul is beyond the cycle of time, they are therefore adrift in time and eternal.

"Very well! So Malavikadevi, listen carefully then and try to understand. Your task is very easy and extremely difficult at the same time. Don't get confused by this paradoxical statement, for every good deed is beset by the same contradictoriness. If you stand by the seashore and watch the energy of the waves, then the sea looks threatening and intimidates you, but if you swim fearlessly through the waves deeper into the sea, then it becomes calm. That is why you should never be afraid of teething problems. In Sonagachhi, the red-light area of Kolkata, there are many organisations like Jabala, Apne Aap, Swayam and others which are working towards rescuing sex workers. Initially, try to acquire an understanding of the basic issues from them and then get to the root of these problems. Along with poverty, illiteracy and the poor condition of girl children, there are also mafia gangs which operate by kidnapping girls and forcing them into prostitution; they, therefore, have a vested interest in the operation of these red-light areas."

As Lavanyadevi talked, Malavika was absorbing the essence of these instructions with all her senses. "But before immersing yourself in this task you will have to form a coterie of your co-workers—comprising those who have the courage and the understanding to fight against the schemes of the wicked. Debkumar Laha has donated a huge sum of money for this task too. He has also given the names and addresses of some women who live in that hell but who are keen to help others stay away from it. It is true that those who are cleansed by the experience of grief also learn to keep others away from it. You will have to stay away from the publicity of television, newspapers etc. and maintain a low profile in order to effectively make inroads into the innermost workings of the area. Be like the water seeping through walls—enter slowly, unobtrusively and soundlessly in order to be successful, and not like crackling thunder. You will face many obstacles: politicians will try to sabotage your efforts;

police will act openly hostile and barbaric; reputed persons will take recourse to manipulation and underhand means to obscure unpleasant truths. But remember: any attack that is planned well and with caution and agility does not go waste. That is why every plan you make must take into account all the possible resistances and obstacles you are likely to face. Otherwise you may risk endangering your life. You will have to work to turn the police into your well-wisher and aide by using every trick in the book and in this, Soumen will provide you the maximum assistance. He may not be comfortable with the risks involved in the work that his sister is undertaking, but I know that he places my wishes above everything else.

"And yes, Malavika, it is imperative that you discuss this with Soudamini. Convincing your mother will be the biggest challenge. She wanted to master classical music without caring to acquaint herself with either the basics or the nuances of the genre and without ever doing her *riyaaz*—that is why she could never learn to sing. She is averse to any challenging task. And this particular task is not only extremely difficult, it is also not very socially acceptable! She will never permit you to do this work. That is when you will have to gauge your determination in terms of the sacrifices you are willing to make in order to achieve your goal. If you have to get Soudamini to agree to what you are doing, it is important that you never discuss the risks associated with your work; and if you ever achieve success in it, attribute it to her. You should also understand that it is wrong to lie but not to hide facts. Revolutionaries always hid the truth from others in the battle for freedom, and that was not wrong; it was a noble act in the quest of higher goals. Therefore, if you do not give a frame-by-frame description of all your activities to Soudamini, it will not be considered wrong. And Soumen will also be with you. He will manage the rest of the things."

"Anything else, Didu?" To this, Lavanyadevi responded, "Whatever I have told Manju about leading one's daily life applies equally to you; that is why it is useless to repeat. Before we end this conversation, there is one important point I want to stress on: if anybody in the family ever requires your assistance, even if it is for a trivial matter, leave whatever you are doing, however important it may be, and attend to their needs, because in future they will be the ones who will carry the torch of your well-being. Think of such tasks as investments for later life.

"Okay! Now get up, go and have food, rest for a while and then tell me whether you people would like to visit some well-known places nearby tomorrow. Should I make arrangements?"

As soon as they heard this, they said, "Maua! Didu! What visit? We will be done with visiting all the places we wish to by tonight. Tomorrow morning, we will visit the temple and get started on our work. It is you who always keep telling us, 'Time is flying! Run! Catch it! Catch it and run along with it!' So, Maua, there is no time for such indulgences anymore. Now onwards, we will visit only those places which we can accommodate in the course of our work. As for the rest, *khair salla*, this is what is done, and Allah will take care of the rest. As it is, till today we have just been mere spectators; but the time to understand has now arrived. We have accumulated so many words which we have filled our minds with—now is the time to invest them with meaning. Therefore, for our new endeavour, we pay our obeisance to the moon today and the sun tomorrow! We salute you! You have been instrumental in illuminating our beings with the light that will dispel the ignorant darkness within us. Maua, we have become fellow travellers in your journey! But the failure or success of this journey remains in the hand of the unknown unseen." Saying this, both girls touched her feet and went off to their rooms.

Early next morning, when Lavanyadevi returned to the ashram after having bid goodbye to the two girls, Guru-*ji* said, "Lavanya, my daughter, would you like to accompany me to Badrinath for a few days? There is news that the weather there is very pleasant right now. When we reach Badrinath we will inspect the activities of the ashram and from there we will leave for Gangotri." Guru-*ji* was aware that Lavanyadevi did not like the crowds and the hustle bustle of Badrinath. She would always say, "Guru-*ji*! Diesel and transistors have converted this holy pilgrimage spot into a heap of junk. Now this place has lost its spirit and become just another disorganised small town infected with the cancer of urbanisation and modernity; the ill-effects of the disease have spread all over the place."

Lavanyadevi never disregarded Guru-*ji*'s wishes; she immediately called out to Aalo, "Aalo! Pack my things. I am going to Badrinath."

As on previous visits, this time too the first thought that crossed Lavanyadevi's mind when the summit and the flag fluttering atop the Badrinath temple became visible was to wonder what might have prompted Shankaracharya to choose Badrinath over Kedarnath, Gangotri or any other adjacent holy spot as one of the *char dham*—the four most revered Hindu pilgrimage sites. Being deeply influenced by the natural surroundings of these places, she had not been able to comprehend the arithmetic which must have gone on in the Shankaracharya's mind. But today she could arrive at an answer to this question by herself: he must have chosen Badrinath keeping in mind the convenience of pilgrims, as Badrinath was easily accessible and had a relatively large tableland. As Lavanyadevi made her way to the ashram, memories of previous visits flashed through her mind. The first incident she was reminded of was one of pure, innocent humour!

When she was around eleven or twelve, Lavanya, along with her mother Jyotirmoyidevi, her uncle Aniruddha and aunt Suryabaladevi, had come to Badrinath to offer prayers in the memory of her grandmother, the late Prabhavatidevi. Dhananjay-babu was numbed by the loss of his wife. Around this time, one of his knowledgeable pandit friends told him that performing *pind-daan*—the ritual supposed to free the departed soul from the cycle of birth and death thus leading it to salvation—on the banks of the Alaknanda in Badrinath would ensure *moksha* for Prabhavatidevi, and that it was considered better than the *pind-daan* at Gaya. That is why the 'poor English gentleman' Aniruddha Roychoudhury also had to accompany them. Whatever be the reason for their visit, Lavanya thoroughly enjoyed both the trip and the banter between her uncle and aunt.

One day, Suryabala Mami said to her husband, "*Ey ji*, could you please spare a moment to listen to what I have to say?"

Aniruddha Mama could immediately gauge from the tone of the request that there was a catch somewhere. On his guard, he responded playfully, in a nasal tone, "At your service! Tell me, what is it?"

"Listen, stop all this tomfoolery and tell me what is the object that you treasure the most."

When Mama asked her the reason for this sudden inquiry, Mami said, "See, one receives the gains of a pilgrimage only when one renounces the thing that is dearest to oneself, never to look upon it again. I am thinking of giving up eating mangoes. Tell me what will you give up?"

"Oh! You are still just thinking of it! Why haven't you made up your mind yet? But I won't take a moment to give up what is dearest to me. And I am a man who can make great sacrifices and practise great self-restraint. Therefore, following the dictum *twadiya vastu Govindam tubhamewa samarpaye*—all is offered at your feet, Govinda—I hereby sacrifice my favourite and my dearly beloved Suryabala to Him." Saying this, Mama burst out laughing.

Mami made a grumpy face and showed him a slap with one hand, and with her other hand held out a bottle of his favourite brand of single malt whisky. "See! This is your most favourite thing—*this* is what you should sacrifice to God," she implored.

But it was Aniruddha Mama she was up against! Poor Mami was no match for his intelligence or wit. He solemnly replied, "You are absolutely right, Surya! I too am inclined to honour your wish..."

As soon as she heard these words, Mami's face lit up with the joy of the fulfilment of a long-awaited wish. But Mama, like Khwaja Nasiruddin, finished his sentence thus, "but Suryabaladevi! I am always so worried about all of you. See, I can offer this bottle to the Supreme Almighty and, believe me I will not experience an iota of sorrow in doing so. But, what will happen to you after that?" Saying this he furrowed his brow as if in deep worry. Mami excitedly said, "What will happen to me? *Arey*! I will be overjoyed and offer a lot of *prasad* to the Lord!"

"That is all fine. But listen carefully to what I have to say. See, I am like an insignificant clay doll. If I get drunk, I lie quietly in a corner. But if the Master of all the three universes gulps down the whole bottle and starts nodding off in a state of intoxication, what will happen to all of you? Every morning, you keep Him captive in your doe eyes. If He gets drunk, how will you keep your mind occupied? And moreover, what will happen to this planet then? Will not His divine inebriation lead to *tandav* and absolute mayhem and bring about the end of this universe?"

It took some time for Aniruddha Mama's sarcasm and humour to sink in, but it did. Mami slapped her forehead in exasperation and said, "Oh! You are impossible! It is futile to argue with you."

Mama-*ji* took her hand in his, trying to persuade her to calm down, but she jerked her hand away and stomped off, and as soon as she disappeared from the scene, young Lavanya and her uncle were both in splits.

Small, beautiful episodes like these not only repair the cracked, broken walls of human life, they also paint it in new colours and open casements for light to stream in; it is through incidents like these that people garner the strength to move on. Family probably means a protective shell within which a person feels secure—a safe passage indirectly promised.

Lavanyadevi was suddenly reminded of the time when, as a six or seven-year-old, she had accompanied her maternal grandfather Dhananjay-babu, Soumitro Mama and her mother Jyotirmoyidevi to the *shraddh* ceremony of Champa Nani's husband Mangatrai-*ji*.

Champadevi's children, Purushottam and Savitri, had taken great care to nurture their mother's relationship with Prabhavatidevi's family and keep it alive. Champadevi's granddaughter Pushpa and Prabhavatidevi's granddaughter Lavanya played for hours at a stretch at Purushottam's place, swinging on the swings that were hung from the branches of the tall trees in the garden and running around the big lawn in front of the house. Lavanya and Pushpa, both the centres of their respective families, got along well with each other.

Purushottam Mama was dead against petty rituals, but both Indira Mami and Savitri Mashi were acutely conscious of their social standing. Since Purushottam Mama held his father in extremely high regard, he had arranged for the best brahmins with excellent command of the Vedas for the cremation. Mama was, however, particularly ill-disposed to the family priest, Bhagwati Maharaj. Not only was the priest illiterate and uncouth, he also consumed drugs like cannabis and opium with abandon, and was a blot on the image of the brahmin. Purushottam Mama believed that donating money to the undeserving was sin, and felt that the entire sum of money that was ritually mandated to the family priest should instead be donated for some good cause. But Savitridevi and Indira Mami were adamant in this regard.

The rituals finally began. Pandit-*ji* was made to sit on a velvet mattress placed on a silver bed decked with velvet quilts and pillows. There, on one side, were silver dishes, gold jewellery sets, expensive clothing and numerous other items piled up like all those expensive accoutrements placed inside the pyramids of the pharaohs of Egypt. As per custom, Indira Mami made a semicircular motion with the loose end of her sari to symbolically bestow all this on Pandit-*ji* and formally donated everything to him.

Lavanyadevi recollected every detail of how both girls, Lavanya and Pushpa, half-hanging out of the first-floor window of the Merlin Park bungalow in excitement, could clearly see and hear whatever was going on in the courtyard below. Just then they heard Savitridevi's loud voice crackling across the courtyard, "Purushottam! Don't talk rubbish! Why are you after this poor man's life?"

"That's great, Sawaa!" he retorted. "When this good-for-nothing rascal is intent on swallowing all the wealth, then why not the opium too! Who else is it supposed to be for? He has to have the opium too, right here and right now," said Mama. "Gathro!" he called out to Indira Mami, using her nickname, "get a glass of water for Pandit-*ji*."

There was a deathly silence in the courtyard. Indira Mami just stood there, dazed, unable to move, looking in turn at Savitridevi and in the direction of the small gold container in which a ball of opium was symbolically kept. Since Mangatrai-*ji* used to consume a pinch of opium every day, a quantity approximately equivalent to his annual consumption was kept in the container.

Purushottam Mama knew well enough that if this stupid brahmin gulped down the entire quantity of opium, he would surely die then and there; but he wanted to demonstrate his anger about the donation to Bhagwati Maharaj and get even with his family members for wasting money in this manner and hence refused to budge from his position.

However, on the insistence of Dhananjay-babu, Soumitro Ranjan, Jyotirmoyidevi and all the other elders present there, he relented. As he threw the container on a plate and turned to go indoors, Savitridevi caught hold of the *angavastra* on his shoulder and pulled him back, saying, "*Arey* wait, brother! Where are you off to? Get Pandit-*ji* to lie on the *sukh shaiyya*, the bed of comforts, and swing the bed for him. It is only then that Bau-*ji* will be able to get all these things."

"Sawaa, have you gone crazy? This addict! This useless fraud! He will help my saintly father cross the river Vaitarani?" But seeing Savitridevi's entreating eyes and Indiradevi's folded hands, Purushottam Mama relented once again. He called the children who were present. "Devaki! Vijay! Soumitro! Come here and help me lift this bed up," he said. The three young men immediately hauled the bed up, with the priest sitting atop it, as far as they could raise their arms.

The scrawny, haggard priest, already scared at the height to which the bed had been raised, was terrified as it lurched to the left and to the right and swayed dangerously as it was swung energetically by the young men. Lavanyadevi clearly remembered how absolutely delighted she and Pushpa were at the sight of that swaying bed, clapping and egging the young men on. "*Wah* Mama-*ji*! Well done! Raise it higher! Yes! Still higher! Bring it to the level of the window!" they shouted. Ayah Didi, who was standing behind them, smacked them gently on the head and said, "*Ore*! *Chup koro re*! Be quiet, will you! Mama-*ji* has gone crazy. Look at Mami and Ma—they have both turned pale! *Durga, Durga…rokkhha koro*! Goddess Durga save us!"

Meanwhile the poor priest was shivering uncontrollably, as if he was afflicted with malaria. He was perspiring heavily and unable to utter a word. He tried to balance himself on the bed with both his hands and get up, but given the situation, how could he? And even if he did manage to get up, where could he go? He was dumbstruck with terror, but his petrified eyes pleaded with Savitridevi, begging for his life. The God-fearing Savitridevi was unable to bear this sight.

In the end the curtains came down on this scene when, unable to bear what was going on any longer, Savitri Mashi came forward and delivered a stinging slap on her son Vijay's cheek and said, "Lower the bed immediately. Your Mama is out of his senses. If this son of a brahmin were to die tomorrow, what will happen to Bau-*ji*'s soul?" This impact of the slap was felt by the other three as well even though they had not been hit. On being rebuked in this manner by his elder sister, Purushottam Mama abruptly let go of the bed in mid-air and walked off, but the other three, out of their fear of Savitridevi, somehow managed to balance the tottering bed and bring it and the terrified priest down to the ground safely.

Lavanyadevi remembered the incident in vivid detail along with all its 'props'. She also remembered that on their way back from Mangatrai-*ji*'s *shraddh*, Dhananjay-babu had specially instructed Jyotirmoyidevi and Soumitro Ranjan to ensure that his *shraddh* rituals should be conducted as simply as possible. Neither should rituals like *ashouch*, which was the norm in royal households, be followed, nor should there be any *pandal* where relatives were fed every day. All rituals should be done away with as far as practicable and only such rituals as were convenient in the times they were living in be followed to free the physical body from this world. Whatever the family wished to spend was best donated to deserving people. No donation should be made to undeserving candidates, and they should not even be allowed to come anywhere near the pyre, even if they happen to be the family priests for seven generations.

That is why her grandfather sent them to Badrinath for the *pind-daan*. He had great faith in the wisdom of the priests of Badrinath who conducted the rituals without any pomp and show, just as he would have preferred it.

Lavanyadevi had come to Badrinath once more after this trip, with her mother Jyotirmoyidevi and maternal grandfather Dhananjay-babu. She was then a postgraduate student and had begun taking keen interest in anthropology and sculpting. She often accompanied Anand Krishna-*ji* or Bhagwati Sharan-*ji* on their visits to the National Museum in Kolkata. She remembered one incident wherein she had reached the museum at ten o' clock accompanied by both these scholars, a group of four or five other students in tow. There, these two famous scholars got so immersed in analysing a Buddha sculpture in great detail that they forgot the time. When, suddenly hungry, they looked at their watches, they realised that it was two-thirty in the afternoon and they were famished. Their intense discussion had lasted full four and a half hours! Needless to say, that one day was sufficient to teach the accompanying students how to examine sculptures at places like Ajanta, Ellora and the Elephanta Islands on their own.

The inspiring contributions made by these great scholars and her own burgeoning interest were reasons why Lavanyadevi was always eager to learn more about ancient Indian sculptures and iconography whenever she had the opportunity. It was on account of this eagerness that she had asked her grandfather to make reservations for the *mahabhishek* or grand anointment of Lord Chaturbhuj when they were in Badrinath. It was a lengthy ritual conducted over hours, and she would have the time to observe the idol at close quarters.

As Lavanyadevi touched the feet of the priest, who had come from the south, she could once again comprehend the breadth of Shankaracharya's vision. The four *dhams* at the four corners of India! And their priests, all of them twice-born, indubitable scholars of the Vedas, also came from four different directions! What better design for cultural and social unity could there be than this? A learned person, carrying within him his entire cultural inheritance—his language, his customs and rituals integrated within his personality—travels from one end of the country to another, and blending his own inheritance with the local culture of the place where he relocates, establishes a cumulatively higher ideal. One culture thus blends seamlessly with another; and this was essential for the unity of a country as diverse as India.

When Lavanyadevi took the bare idol of Lord Chaturbhuj in her hands, she was startled and whispered to the priest, "Rawal-*ji*, this is not Chaturbhuj Vishnu at all, but an ancient idol of Lord Avalokiteshwara!" Smiling in agreement, the priest replied, "My child! People have worshipped this idol as Vishnu for centuries, and that has led to the spirit of Lord Vishnu being consecrated within this idol. Therefore, you too may rise above this needless bewilderment."

Later when Lavanyadevi broached this topic with her anthropology teacher in Varanasi, she realised that he too was aware of the fact but did not think it warranted interrogating this popularly accepted standard of devotion. He also told her, "Lavanya, wasn't it you who said the other day that the idol of Shrinath-*ji* should not be brought back to Vrindavan from Nathdwara? True, the idol has its origin in Vrindavan, but it has grown new roots in Nathdwara, and the devotion of the pilgrims there has breathed new life into the deity and turned the place into a pilgrimage for Shrinath-*ji*. Uprooting the idol from Nathdwara would never be justified. Lavanya, likewise, we should also accept the idol at Badrinath as that of Chaturbhuj Vishnu and worship it with complete faith."

Walking around, Lavanyadevi admired the influence of Tibetan architecture on the outer walls of the Badrinath temple even as she reflected on the ways in which changes had occurred in the nature and composition of our planet. With the passage of time, entire landmasses broke away from one continent to attach themselves to another, the sea sank and the Himalayas emerged from its depths. When, as a child, Lavanya had learnt that the Himalayas were younger than the Vindhyas of India and the Alps of Europe, she just couldn't believe it. She thought it was impossible. How could any other mountain range be older than Dinkar's *Mere Nagpati, Mere Vishal*—the king of all mountains, the immense Himalayas? It was her geography teacher who had then explained to her, "We are often led to believe that Sri Rama and Sri Krishna are more ancient than they actually are because of the epics, but historical and geographical truths are often different from what our mythologies say. So, don't get caught up in this confusion; just prepare for your exams now, okay?" It was then that Lavanya had decided that trying to scrutinise everything through the lens of rationality was often a futile exercise. That is why one needs to invest one's time only on issues that can make a significant impact on our own lives or on those of others.

Lavanyadevi was not very interested in going sightseeing in Badrinath, which is why the thought of using the spare time to educate Aalo crossed her mind. There was never a moment's delay between her thoughts and their execution. Barely had the breeze carried her voice calling, "Aalo! Aalo! Where are you?" and Aalo arrived like a storm. "Yes Ma! Tell me, what is the matter?" she asked, concerned. Noting the anxiety on her face, Lavanyadevi smiled and said, "Aalo! An excellent thought just occurred to me. Elders say that charity and noble thoughts should be acted upon at the earliest, which is why I called out to you in such haste. Sorry!"

"Oh Ma! Leave aside all this talk and tell me what the matter is."

"Aalo, your family has been connected to mine for the last four generations—your great grandmother, your grandmother, your mother and now you. You have all served my family. Your past seven generations hail from Bangladesh and you too were born there. Although you and your mother were brought up with my mother Jyotirmoyidevi and me, you are still connected to the land of Bangladesh like the umbilical cord to the placenta."

"*Ahha*! I know all of this," said Aalo impatiently.

"All right, then listen carefully. Do you remember when you were very young, you had travelled with us to Dhaka for the inauguration of the schools that my grandmother had set up?"

Aalo promptly replied, "Ma, I am your staunchest disciple, and I remember the event in vivid detail."

But Lavanyadevi's mind had already travelled back in time to those preparations for going to Dhaka some five or six decades ago.

Lavanya must have been about fourteen or fifteen years old at that time. One fine day, there was a message from Dhananjay-babu's house asking the whole family to come to Dhaka for a couple of days. This sudden request had sent the family in a tizzy and the heartbeats of everyone—including Brajabaladevi, Jyotirmoyidevi, Lavanya, Gajendra-*ji* and Moloy Roythakur—racing. Was it some bad news, they wondered, and tried to find out; but they were told nothing, except that it was good news. As soon as travel plans were finalised, Lavanyadevi, who was enamoured of the idyllic countryside, immediately packed her luggage and sent it downstairs. Like a dutiful daughter, she also asked her mother and grandmother if she could help in the preparations in any way. As soon as she got the expected 'no' for an answer, she hurried back upstairs to get back to her only 'addiction', when she saw Jyotirmoyidevi enter. Lavanya looked towards her apprehensively, but the mother hardly paid any attention to the daughter as she took out a new notebook from her cupboard. Having taken her notebook, Jyotirmoyidevi exited the room with the nonchalance of one secure in her knowledge that she had no reason whatsoever to be apprehensive of a person who, she was certain, had no inkling even of the existence of a secret in the first place. Jyotirmoyidevi was completely unaware that her secret was already out. Lavanya heaved a sigh of relief and immersed herself once again in her 'addiction'.

The next day the whole family crossed rivers, rivulets and the Ganga and finally reached Dhaka. Dhananjay-babu's conscientious supervision had ensured that the royal mansion was as well-decorated and maintained as a newly-wed bride. Indrani's husband Shanu, who had recently returned to the country, was always looking at everything and indefatigably exclaiming, "Oh my God! Oh my God!" And Lavanya? The waterfall of her happiness was competing with the length of the Amazon and the breadth of the Niagara. She was intent on packing hours of happiness into every minute that she spent there. One could see her one moment swinging from the branch of a tree; the very next moment she would be in the cowshed, ringing the bells around the necks of cows; and in the blink of an eye she would be seen plucking lotuses and lilies in the pond. Just as during the *raas*, the divine dance of love, Lord Krishna could be seen dancing beside each of the *gopis* at the same time, Lavanya too could be seen everywhere at once—now at the turrets above the main gate, now in the living room, then on the parapet, then again ringing the clock tower bell. Today, neither the stern looks of her mother nor the injunctions of her aunt could restrain her. It seemed that the soul of Prabhavatidevi, whose glorified legends had it that she brooked no restrictions imposed by anyone, had taken possession of her. Thinking that the swirling waters from a broken dam would eventually run their course and calm down after traversing a certain distance, Jyotirmoyidevi kept calm, more so since there was nothing disrespectful in Lavanya's childlike activities that warranted her intervention.

Next morning, the entire family was up early, dressed and waiting expectantly at the main gate for Indrani to join them. Indranidevi, husband in tow, joined them soon after, apologising profusely for keeping everyone waiting. Dhananjay-babu was not a man of many words; in fact, he was mostly quiet and rarely expressed himself. But today, Dhananjay-babu surprised and enchanted everyone with a sudden profusion of feelings. He came and stood in front of the entire family and said, "The court of Lord Indra stands completely overshadowed in comparison to Prabhavati's beautiful and healthy family and its grandeur."

On realising the essence of this statement made by her father, Jyotirmoyidevi came forward and pulling him close, embraced him like a child would, and both of them proceeded to move towards where the phaetons, buggies and cars stood. Everyone else followed. As the convoy of vehicles started moving, the question that was uppermost in everyone's mind was where they were all going. The convoy came to a stop amidst the sudden blowing of conches, ringing of bells, beating of drums and ululation! And as the fragrant smoke billowing from the *dhuno* wafted away, everyone witnessed something magical. In a large enclosure stood two big buildings, on one of which was written Jogmaya Girls' College and on the other, Prabha, Champa, Imarti Girls' College. Everyone was astonished! When did this happen? How did it happen? Where did the funds come from? Whose magnificent idea was it? Who was the architect? The last question came up as all the material used in the construction was found to be local. The stones, bricks and wood used were all locally procured. The labourers were also from nearby areas. When asked, the local people said there was a restriction on the usage of materials and manpower from outside.

Restriction? Whose restriction? Who was behind all of this incredible work? These were the many questions uppermost in the minds and hearts of the family members when an extremely aged priest along with some other people his age, teachers and young inheritors was seen coming. Among them were several old teachers who had taught Jyotirmoyi, Aniruddha and Indrani. The anxiety in all those waiting faces was assuaged for the time being by the Sanskrit teacher who responded, when Jyotirmoyidevi touched his feet, by saying, "All of you, please, watch the ceremony first, then we will talk in detail about everything else."

Everybody sat together after the cultural programme presented by the girls of the school and the refreshments that followed were over. The Sanskrit teacher, who was the eldest of them all, pulled a bundle of eight to ten notebooks towards himself and began addressing them all, saying, "You must all be wondering who has been behind all this? You must also be conjecturing that one amongst you has surreptitiously planned and accomplished all this. But I must at the very outset inform you that it is Prabhavatidevi alone who has wrought this miracle from its conception to its execution.

"When we teachers used to go to the royal mansion to teach the children, Prabhavatidevi too used to learn something or the other from us for hours at a stretch. Once, when all of you had returned from a trip to Kolkata, she had asked all of us to meet her in the library. Handing us a bag of gold coins and two plans, she had said, 'You are all disciples of Mother Saraswati and I am of the firm belief that you will dedicate yourselves honestly to creating this tangibly embodied form of the Mother as outlined in the plans. I request you all to form a trust and be kind enough to bring to fruition this heartfelt desire of mine.' She had already finalised the location—it was to be built near the bank of the Padma, yet some distance away from it, so as to be out of range of the river's erosive destruction. The plans had been drawn up by some French architect, and contained detailed instructions regarding the entire construction process. Residential facilities for students from faraway places were also mentioned in the plans."

When someone asked, "Such a huge setup, and just a pittance for fees! How will the institution sustain itself?", Mastermoshai responded with a chuckle, "The Trust is in possession of shops in Srimani Bazar, the largest market in Dhaka, a complex of 200 shops in Barabazar of Kolkata, the seven-storey *Bahu-ji ki Kothi*—the bungalow of the daughter-in-law—as well as seventy-five shops in Hogg Market. I'm sure you are all aware of the three ladies who, under fictitious names, had rocked Kolkata's bullion market a few decades back. Well, they deposited all the profits they made from the enterprise into the Trust's account. Dhananjay-babu, we do not have permission to disclose the exact amount, but it is a sum that would amaze the richest people around."

An old English teacher who spoke after him remarked, "The inauguration was not the only reason we invited all of you here. Prabhavatidevi had also made a provision according to which, all the daughters of the family would, by birth, be eligible to be members of this Trust. So we also need all their signatures on the Trust documents."

Jyotirmoyidevi, Indranidevi, Lavanyadevi and Soumitro's daughter Sukanya all put their signatures on the documents in amazement. Despite seeing the inconceivable turn into reality right in front of their eyes, they were still not able to believe that something like this had actually happened.

An ordinary girl from a small village in the countryside! How could she develop the kind of administrative vision and acumen so as to match, or even outdo, the chief minister of a state with an entire team of administrators and be able to write pages of clear, detailed instructions and choose with complete confidence a team of people who would unquestioningly and efficiently carry the enormous responsibility forward? This is the kind of intelligence and astuteness that is absent in some of the very best; it is a wonder that Prabhavatidevi, the rustic daughter of a rustic village woman, Bhuvaneshwaridevi, possessed such rare ability. "Maybe this is what a miracle is," everyone there thought silently to themselves.

The Dhaka visit left a deep impression on the daughters of the household. Women's 'simple' minds are conditioned to be easily impressionable, and this was an incident that was directly linked to them. Indrani was enamoured of her mother's social skills and Jyotirmoyidevi found her ability to love everyone equally worth emulating. And Lavanya? She was happier and more confident after seeing her grandmother's efforts towards the emancipation of the girl child. The thought that crossed her mind time and again since then was whether she too would be able to do something as substantial and significant as her grandmother when she grew up.

When Lavanya read how her mother had recounted this incident in her diary, of which, she too was a spectator, she marvelled at her mother's multidimensional understanding of social issues. This is how her mother had analysed the whole incident and its implications.

"My mother Prabhavatidevi was very talented, but she had borne the sorrow of poverty. One can listen to or read about this sorrow and empathise with a person. But when poverty attacks, it creates pain and suffering, the cure for which is not available even with Hakim Luqman, the Wise. That pain can only end or lessen when the situation improves. That is why Ma could empathise with the class of girls who looked to be reasonably all right from the outside but were ragged and torn to bits from inside. Since she appreciated the value of education right from her childhood, she kept learning from the tutors who used to come to teach us. Was it this trait of self-study and self-improvement that inspired her to build these pilgrimages of learning? The biggest benefit that accrues from education is that it gives breadth to one's personality and depth to one's perspective. It enables one to rise above the trivial in life and to develop not only the self but also contribute to the development of others.

"Was not the construction and running of these free residential institutions proof of Ma's spiritual ability and not just, if we go by what the Bhagvad Gita says, the miracle of her *vyawasatmika buddhi*—her resolute consciousness? That an ordinary person could rise above the self and above immediate demarcations of 'yours and mine' on one's own, and engage in doing good for others without craving for name, fame and wealth—was this not an act of spirituality?"

Grappling with such questions, Jyotirmoyidevi subsequently started reflecting on her own actions and that made her realise the fundamental limitedness of her life, which revolved only around her family orbit. Her Guru-*ji*, in whom she had confided her thoughts, tried to explain to her that fulfilling one's duties towards one's family was equivalent to serving God. He had narrated to her the story of a Puranic character to exemplify what he meant. "An ascetic was deep in meditation for ages, engaged in some arduous penance. One day, a bird's droppings fell on him and broke his penance. He looked at the bird with furious eyes and it was scorched to death. The ascetic, impressed with what had happened, was very happy with this achievement and filled with pride, he began to dance. 'My meditation is complete!' he exclaimed, 'But why does God not appear before me yet?' In response, a voice from heaven told him, 'O supreme ascetic! Go to the adjacent village and get ordained by a certain woman, only then you will receive complete *brahmagyan* and get to meet God.'

"'Oh! This is not such a difficult thing to do,' thought the ascetic. He reached the village in no time, flying on the wings of his pride. There, an ordinary woman received him hospitably and washed his feet, but as soon as the ascetic got ready to ask her questions about *brahmagyan*, she apologised and excused herself saying, '*Maharaj*, please forgive me. At this moment, my handicapped husband needs me urgently; only after attending to him can I make myself available at your feet.'

"The virtuous and dutiful wife spent most of her day in the routine activities of looking after her husband. After feeding him properly and making him lie down on a clean bed so that he could rest, the woman appeared before the ascetic, and wiping the sweat off her forehead and hands with the end of her saree, said, '*Maharaj*! Command me, what can I do to serve you?'

"The sun was blazing in the sky and so was the ascetic's anger on earth! In fact, it was more scorching than the sun and almost touching the zenith. Trembling with anger he said, 'You lowly woman! Do you even realise who is standing before you? You have kept a divine ascetic like me waiting just to take care of a wretch? If I curse you just now…'

"Before he could complete his sentence, the woman got up and innocently remarked, 'Forgive me, *maharaj*! But have you assumed that just like the bird sitting on the branch, I too will be reduced to ashes by your anger?'

"On hearing this, not just the ascetic's anger but he himself plummeted back from the sky to the ground. He was stunned, wordless, unblinking! He wondered, how could this woman possess knowledge of something that happened to me in the early hours of the morning? It was then that, with the grace of God, enlightenment dawned on him, and he fell at the feet of that *sati-sadhvi* and begged her for mercy and forgiveness. Consequently, he received *brahmagyan* from that virtuous female ascetic and attained true sainthood.

"Jyoti! That is why your involvement in the betterment of the circumstances of your family members is also a form of serving God. If we do not become a burden on this earth created by the Almighty and try our best not to pollute it, then we are doing what the Almighty wants us to do. If you want to do something more, engage in *daridranarayan seva* and serve the poor, who are the embodiment of God. Out of your body, mind and wealth, you can immediately begin with dedicating your body and mind in this endeavour; so start from there."

Jyotirmoyidevi's character was endowed with the extracted essence of Prabhavatidevi's qualities. She was already determined that she would mould the still clay-like Lavanya into an ideal citizen with exemplary qualities. Now, having taken Brajabaladevi's permission, she started instructing poor girls from the locality in the basics of reading-writing, embroidery, stitching and knitting and other skills on the terrace of her house. The huge terrace of the royal mansion was soon full of daughters and wives from the neighbourhood. After some time, Jyotirmoyidevi, in consultation with her husband Gajendranath, employed a few part-time instructors as well. She managed her social work in such an efficient manner that it never hampered her household chores, nor did she, even for a moment, lessen her attention on the minute-to-minute activities of her daughter. Lavanya was always within the ambit of the *sudarshan chakra*-like vision of her mother. After dropping Lavanya off at school, Jyotirmoyidevi used to go straight to the Rajpur ashram for destitute girls that she later established with the support of a few like-minded women. She, then, turned her attention to several primary schools in Kolkata which had shut down. She got them reopened with the help of the government, got them renovated and transformed them into first-rate schools. It is difficult to be heard, even for a good cause, in government circles, and it helped that Gajendranath-*ji* was an ICS officer.

Young Lavanya could never have imagined her mother doing so many things so discreetly. She was truly a hidden gem! Lavanya had always thought that all her mother's time was taken up in raising her and that she had no time for anything else. "Ma! There was so much you were doing and I never even got a whiff of it!" she wanted to tell her. She wanted to ask her, "Ma! You never mentioned even in passing all these myriad activities that you were involved with, let alone 'glorify' yourself! Why?" But would she dare? Did Lavanya have the nerve to leave the allure of this novel-like history and risk losing the source of her 'addiction' by asking Jyotirmoyidevi these questions? No. Never. Just as the life of the mythological demon lay hidden within a parrot, these precious notebooks now contained Lavanya's life-spirit. So, pushing her questions to the back of her mind, Lavanya picked up the next notebook.

Apart from Lavanya's everyday progress and her all-round development, her manners and behaviour, the company she kept, observations on her friendships, her temperance as well as her independence—everything was recorded in that notebook along with Jyotirmoyidevi's own experiences. It contained descriptions of how she was duped by shrewd people because of her simplicity and sidelined by cunning people in the very institutions that she established. But at the end of each incident, the last note she would record would invariably conclude, "Why should I abandon my character? Let people do what they want to do." And Jyotirmoyidevi would with renewed determination engage herself in creating something new.

Following the deaths of Brajabaladevi and Moloy Roythakur, and after Lavanya's marriage, Jyotirmoyidevi, with the permission of her husband, got a modern hospital built in a third of their royal mansion. The expenses for running the hospital were comfortably managed from the rents she earned from two sources—some shops in a complex in Barabazar that her mother Prabhavatidevi had bequeathed her and the big bungalow that Soumitro-*da* had gifted her. Since she and her husband personally took care of the running of the hospital, the patients were more than satisfied and donated as much as they could, according to their ability. Many a time, the donation box would be so full that it seemed there was a real possibility that the hospital would become self-sustaining. While thus engrossed in thoughts of her Dhaka visit and memories of her mother's life evoked by the notebooks, Lavanyadevi's eye suddenly fell on Aalo.

Poor Aalo! She had been staring expectantly at Lavanyadevi for some time, her mouth slightly open in surprise, and was just beginning to look a little bored when Lavanyadevi returned from her world of memories to the real world, from the past to the present. She addressed Aalo apologetically, "You know too well this irresponsible behaviour of mine, this habit of lapsing into the past, but I guess today I overdid it a bit. You must have been waiting anxiously all this time. What to do, Aalo! I am such a fool!"

Aalo replied with a smile, "On the contrary, Ma, I was delightedly observing the changing palette of colours moving across your face like a mirror, and the emotions they evoked were so real that just by watching you while sitting here, I was transported to the schools of Dhaka." Perhaps this is what is people describe as the effect of good company, one that can endow an ordinary intellect with an extraordinary, multidimensional perception.

"Oh, Aalo!" replied Lavanyadevi joyfully, "I am so pleased by your words. Come, let me tell you what I have planned for your future. I will, at the appropriate time, give you directions to go to Dhaka. By that time, I will also declare you my legally adopted daughter and appoint you as a trustee of my grandmother's Dhaka trust. Apart from managing the schools established by her, your job will be to instill among the girls there a hunger for education that prevails over their hunger for food. The greatest misfortune of our country is its illiteracy, and you have to do everything to uproot it from its roots. Tell me, Aalo, are you willing to perform this task?"

In response, Aalo touched Lavanyadevi's feet to express her consent with the alacrity of the thirsty *chatak* bird which has at last found rainwater to drink in *Swati Nakshatra*. Today, for the first time in her life, Aalo felt proud and complete as a human being. Today she felt that not only was this birth meaningful, but her future births would be worthwhile too. Her heart and body felt light as a breeze and she felt as if she was flying. This incredible stroke of good fortune brought tears to her eyes. Lavanyadevi embraced her. Aalo then turned to Guru-*ji* to seek his blessings. To calm down her excited body and mind, Guru-*ji* placed both his hands on her head in blessing.

Guru-*ji* knew Lavanyadevi would soon start feeling restless in Badrinath, and so he suggested, "Beti Lavanya, should we go to Gangotri tomorrow morning?" Lavanyadevi happily nodded in agreement and got busy preparing for the journey when two emails labelled 'urgent' flashed on her laptop.

They were from Manjulika and Malavika. Having had a cursory look at them, she told Guru-*ji*, "It seems as if the two have gone from here and jumped straight into volcanoes. Otherwise how is it possible to do so much work in such little time?"

This is what Manjulika had written.

Dear Maua,

I have been to a few local centres in and around Kolkata and established connections with them and have found that due to hunger, poverty and illiteracy, the poor and the deprived spend a major part of their income on cheap intoxicants which lead to their untimely deaths. Such people do not have any assistance-centres to turn to, as the few that exist are either too expensive or jam-packed with patients. Maua, the country needs a few hundred Priyamvada Rangacharys; only then will there be some perceptible impact. Meanwhile, I have requested Soumen-da to permit me the use of the bungalow that Soumitro Ranjan Mama had gifted to grandmother. I want to set up an assistance-centre in it. Priyamvada Devi promised that she, along with her team, will oversee the setting up of the centre. Ayesha Khatoon, who is the head of the rehabilitation centre named Antara located in Karimganj, will look after this centre too. Maua, the dedication with which a highly educated girl like Ayesha, who is also from a well-to-do family, works is incredible. That's all for now and I am ending this small report here.

Yours sincerely,

Manju.

If this was a 'small report', how much work would this girl eventually accomplish? Lavanyadevi could sense the urgency in Manjulika, and this delighted her from within.

The second mail was from Malavika and went as follows.

Dear Didu!

Pranam! Namaskar! Adaab! Everything.

Hope you are fine. Okay, I'll come straight to the point. I will not describe the tragedy or pain of the red-light area to stir up its gruesomeness, but the one thing I must say is that if one has not seen the sordidness of the place first-hand, one can never know it. All the novels and stories of the world that describe the place sound inadequate. Here, birth is an expletive and so is death.

Didu, can you imagine that when we took a young man's dead body for cremation, we were not allowed to enter the cremation ground, because the whole world is scared of HIV? He was looked down upon not only when he was alive, but he was discriminated against in death as well.

Recently, with the help of the police, we were able to successfully rescue seven young women who had been trapped by pimps, but their families refused to accept them back and the centres did not accept them either on the grounds that there was no vacancy. But that was just an excuse, the root cause being the stigma that attaches itself to them. Didu! If you permit, Soumen-da and I wish to open a centre for these deprived women in Moloy Roythakur's royal mansion which now belongs to Bari Nani. We can later apply to the government for a land-grant so that we can set up a larger, ashram-like institution away from the city.

We are getting assistance from the centres recommended by you. We are also getting help from all our friends who used to hang out with us. Everyone is taking this task seriously. We have contacted Ananya, Dhanu and Amlan. They have also promised unconditional help.

And Soudamini Ma is also quiet and happy till now, because all your advice and strategies have proved very effective.

Didu, you are unique! That's all for now. Please bless me so that, oblivious to success or failure, I continue to tread the path I have chosen.

So, okay, yours and yours only,

Manu.

Lavanyadevi's eyes turned moist on seeing Malavika's nickname Manu after a long time. These honest and diligent children of mine will surely do something worthwhile, she had thought. But that they would so quickly become the priests performing the *yagna* of social service and get so deeply involved with things was beyond her estimate. Overcome with emotions, she raised her hands upwards to the sky as always and bringing them together, paid obeisance to the Almighty God, and took her seat in the jeep for the journey to Gangotri.

At Gangotri, the mighty Ganga cascades down the Shivagauri Falls with immense force. The water from the Falls accumulates to form a broad but shallow pool slightly further down the river's course. The reflection of the snow-capped mountains in the sparkling waters of that pool reminded Lavanyadevi of her trip to Pokhara in Nepal and the fishtail-shaped peak of Mount Machhapuchre that she had seen reflected in the waters of the lake below. The reflection of the looming peak of the mountain in the waters of the lake below made it seem that there was a gigantic fish in the lake whose tail one could see. The image reminded her of the story of Manu, the progenitor of humanity in Hindu mythology. When the great deluge inundated the earth and destroyed everything, Manu, along with his boat which carried the Vedas, was guided to safety by Lord Vishnu in his gigantic fish incarnation—the *matsya avatar*—to the tail of which the boat was tied. These images evoked for her the entire philosophy of Prasad's epic poem, the *Kamayani*, and conjured in her mind the image of Manu, sitting under the cool shade of a rock on the majestic snow-capped peak, causing the blood to course faster through her veins.

Her mother Jyotirmoyidevi's advice was the reason Lavanyadevi had chosen Hindi as her core language from the very first standard onwards. She was also planning to do her B.A. Honours in Hindi. That was until, on the insistence of her favourite teacher, she abruptly switched to B.A. Honours in English and subsequently did her M.A. in English too. However, three years later, because of her love for Hindi, she had also attained an M.A. in Hindi in the first division. For Lavanyadevi, books were an addiction. However new or serious the topic and whatever the time or situation, she always found the time and excuse to read. Like the glint of lust in the eyes of a rake at the sight of a beautiful woman, Lavanyadevi's eyes would also immediately light up at the sight of books.

Lavanyadevi's journey to Nepal was not mere wanderlust. She had gone there to condole her friend Siddharajyalakshmi on the death of her father. That is why she had travelled to the country in the middle of winter.

Clouds had played amidst the mountain peaks at Mount Machhapuchre then just as they were playing now on the snow-capped peaks being reflected on the waters of the Gangotri, but there could simply be no comparison between the majestic sea of beauty at the Gangotri and the lake at Pokhara. There was no way in which one could one even think of comparing the majestic, divine Himalayas with the fistful of beauty that lay in a small peak! But do we ever find a description that is an exact and absolute representation of the object being compared in any simile? There is always a compromise implicit in a simile.

Lavanyadevi was told stories of characters who figured in numerous illegitimate affairs of kings as she travelled to Siddhi's place. When she finally met Siddhi's mother Padmavati Lakshmi, she was amazed. Plain in looks and complexion, but as haughty as Empress Victoria! And equally anglicised in her attitude and conduct. That notwithstanding, she had had her husband's last rites conducted by priests whom she had invited from Kashi, with meticulous observance of each and every ritual and procedure, and was now going to Badrinath with her entire family and relatives for the *pind-daan*. No matter how much people embrace a modern lifestyle, the culture one is born into is rarely forgotten, Lavanyadevi reasoned. The only princess of the Morvi state, Padmavati Lakshmi had put in great effort to conscientiously follow every religious ritual which she had neither believed in nor followed when her husband was alive. Perhaps it is death that brings you face to face with a mirror in which the good qualities of the dead and the ills of your own self assume enormous proportions—perhaps this is what had happened with Padmavati Lakshmi, thought Lavanyadevi.

The flow of her thoughts was suddenly interrupted when she heard, "And this is my sister Bhanwaribai!" Seeing the incomprehension on Lavanyadevi's face, Padmavati Lakshmi asked her sister to get some snacks for them, and as soon as she had left, addressed Lavanya in a low voice, "You must be thinking that if I am the only daughter, how can I have siblings, right? Well, this is the story of my father, the king! When he used to set out on an elephant across our kingdom, if his eyes set on any adolescent girl living in the *kuccha* huts below, he used to make them the objects of his illicit desire; and then the offspring from them and whosoever among them had poor husbands would be given some royal title, and in addition to giving them *pucca* houses near the boundary of the fort, he would settle them into some occupation or business which had a good source of income. This was a practice common in most kingdoms across the country. In the same way that princesses are married into other kingdoms, these clans too would marry into similar clans which existed in other kingdoms and all their offspring would take the surnames of their legal fathers. This tradition has been continuing for ages. These Rao-Rajas have their own legitimate, independent identity and they are full-fledged personalities in their own right. They are not looked down upon or socially stigmatised in any way. I introduced her to you as my sister with the same sense of equity."

By then, the lady had returned. As soon as Lavanyadevi saw her approaching, she went forward and addressing her as Mausi-*ji* touched her feet and sought her blessings, upon which the lady raised both her hands in blessing and said, "May you live long child." When Lavanyadevi, purely out of curiosity, asked for her address, she unhesitatingly said, "Note it down, baisa! Ms. Bhanwari Devi, c/o Raja Fateh Singh, Jailer, Udaipur Police Station. Baisa, your brother has earned a decent name for himself in Udaipur. If ever you are in Udaipur, promise me that you will stay at our place. This is my earnest request to you."

Lavanyadevi was deeply impressed by Bhanwari Devi's warmth, her love and generosity as well as her self-respect. Irrespective of who was legitimate and who wasn't, the world would be a much better place if it were populated by more people like her, she thought. Her friend and classmate Rani Saubhagyalakshmi of Jodhpur later introduced Lavanyadevi to numerous other people of the same Rao-Raja clan, who, like Bhanwari Devi, were the companions or the offspring of the kings there. This also reminded Lavanyadevi of an interesting incident concerning her friend.

One day, Saubhagya and Lavanya were engrossed in regaling each other with stories of their college days when, all of a sudden, Saubhagya stubbed out her cigarette, slipped on a traditional *ghaghra* over the jeans she was wearing and covered her head and face with a long veil of exquisite *zardozi*. The next instant she was seen bending low in obeisance in the durbar of Rajmata-*ji*, the queen mother, and greeting everyone present there with "*Ghani khamma*." This act lasted for about five minutes, at the end of which she was back in her room. Flinging the *ghaghra* to one side and tossing the veil to another, she lighted another cigarette and was again puffing away vigorously. Before Lavanyadevi could say a word, Saubhagya raised a hand to stop her and said, "Lavanya, now don't start lecturing me about how I should either understand what they expect of me or get them to understand my position. I am perfectly happy the way things are. The fact is, my friend, that except for these five minutes of drill, I live my life precisely as I please—a hundred per cent according to my wishes. Then why on earth should I bother explaining anything to anyone? Let things be as they are."

Listening to Saubhagya's emotional outburst, Lavanyadevi realised that the world is far more interesting and colourful a place because each person inhabiting it has their own unique worldview, their own ideas and eccentricities. Why, then, do we always want everyone to conform to particular ways of thinking and being and living their lives? And supposing that this were to actually happen, wouldn't all human beings become as monochromatic and indistinguishable as factory workers wearing the same dull, drab uniform? Saubhagya is probably right. It is I who need to change myself, for I have become too rigid and bound to the rules that I have made for myself.

The memories of kings and emperors led the pathways of her remembrance to Lalgarh Palace in Bikaner, and Allah Jilai Bai. Lavanyadevi was reminded of how, during a programme in Kolkata, she had to get the microphones in the large hall switched off, so powerful and robust was the singer's voice; but the voice still carried to and stirred the souls of the sea of people waiting outside the hall for a chance to get in. King Ganga Singh-*ji* would be seated on the fourth floor of the Bikaner palace while Allah Jilai Bai sang for him sitting in the courtyard below. Ganga Singh-*ji* was sixty-five at the time; Allah Jilai Bai was sixteen. Some elderly people recounted how enamoured Allah Jilai Bai was of the king on account of his daring exploits and his towering personality. Her songs spun together melodies of intense longing with the throbbing pain of separation in ways that the balconies, fountains, the big square marble courtyard and ornamental windows resonated with the intricate magic of her love songs.

Most people strongly influenced by Western modernity think of spiritual love as a kind of unrestrained delirium. It is important for such people to be aware of the metaphysical dimensions of Allah Jilai Bai's love or the analogous feelings that Siddheshwari Devi had for the poet Jaishankar Prasad. Ratna Shankar Prasad, the poet's son, had an interesting incident to recount in this context. "This happened one winter when the King of Kashi had arranged for a roof-top concert by Siddheshwari Devi at his palace. Prasad-*ji* too was invited; but after waiting for her on the cold terrace for some time, Prasad-*ji*, who suffered from tuberculosis, started feeling cold and returned home to rest. When Siddheshwari Devi arrived, she made it clear in no uncertain terms that she would not sing if Prasad-*ji* was not present. When this was conveyed to the poet, he is said to have replied, 'Go and tell her that I will be listening to her singing from here. Tell her to put her heart and soul into her singing, and once the concert is over, she can come and ask me what she has sung.' When this message was conveyed to Siddheshwari Devi, she instantly bowed in reverence to the absent Prasad-*ji*, strung her tanpura and started singing."

Today's youth which talks so much about telepathy believes neither in such miraculous events, nor in love beyond the body.

Just then Guru-*ji*'s voice pierced through her reveries and brought her back to her present. "Beti Lavanya! It seems that you have once again allowed your imagination to stray into the world of your memories. You have been staring intently at the still waters of this pool for quite some time now. I was keeping a watch over you from the ashram balcony and I realised that while your physical eyes were gazing upon the scene here, your mind's eye was focussed on an entirely different realm of this universe. Actually, this too is a form of meditation, Lavanya. If we can train our senses to do this, then we can traverse the journey of years in moments. I am aware of your spiritual progress but I cannot put the incident at Mansarovar out of my mind, which is why I am at times slightly apprehensive that if you enter a state of intense emotional excitement or trance at an unsafe spot, there could be an accident. But then an inner voice assures me that while the Almighty keeps testing his favourite devotees, he does not ever punish them. And Lavanya, there is no doubt that you are one of His favourites, and the ways of the controller of our destinies are always mysterious."

Guru-*ji* later confided in his favourite disciple, "When I see Lavanya's eyes while she is lost in her thoughts, she does not appear terrestrial to me at all—she appears ethereal. I feel that her love for God is selfless like that of the Sufi saints who are devoted to God not out of their fear of hell or desire of heaven, but because they yearn to be assimilated into His eternal beauty."

After having wandered among the hills and caves in and around Gangotri for five-six days, one day during breakfast, Lavanyadevi began discussing the prospects of visiting Kedarnath and Uttarkashi. It was almost time to discuss, ideate and chalk out the future course of action with the functionaries of the Joshimath, Dehradun, Gaurikund, Hemkund and Sonprayag centres. Leaning on a railing at a turn in the hilly road of the valley, Lavanyadevi was talking to Guru-*ji*, working out the details for the next few days when the breeze carrying the news of an approaching jeep blew past her. There weren't many pilgrims in this season, but one could never be sure about eccentric travellers and foreigners. Both of them looked in the direction from which the sound was coming. The jeep was like a dot which grew bigger and bigger as it climbed up from the valley, and gradually it looked like a toy. As it came closer, they could make out that there were fewer passengers in the jeep than it usually carried. Suddenly, an army man who appeared to be latched on to the rear of the jeep could be seen waving vigorously in their direction. This unexpected movement caused both of them to look at each other, surprised. The air carried some indistinct words towards them which sounded like, "Didu!...O Didu!"

Was it Soumen? But why would Soumen come here? This must surely be her imagination playing tricks on her, Lavanyadevi thought. She had just turned away when the jeep came whizzing up and stopped right next to her, and one muscular monkey jumped out of the vehicle and caught her in a firm hug from behind, cupping her eyes with his palms to prevent her from seeing him.

"O Ma!"

Lavanyadevi protested saying, "*Aha*! Who is this? Leave me!" in mock annoyance even as she relaxed and allowed herself to be enfolded even more completely in that affectionate hug. Her joyful laughter rang out loud across the valleys and echoed in the mountains and forests around her like a jubilant euphony.

It was then that Lavanyadevi saw an excited and coy face peering from behind Soumen. Pushing him aside, she saw a tall, fair, young lady, animated in looks and with sharp features, looking at her. The expression of joy on her face was such that she seemed ready to take wing and fly off any moment. Her looks and her bearing, the symmetry and balance of her body, her supple limbs and smooth skin made it evident she was not a Bengali. Trying to nudge her forward, Soumen said, "Didu! This is my friend, Anita Kaur Ahluwalia."

Lavanyadevi, pushing up the glasses which had slipped down the bridge of her nose with an index finger, spontaneously remarked, "Only friend? Or something more?" Trying to act embarrassed, Soumen said, "Oh Didu! Why must you make me say in words what you already know?"

"Ah, so this is how it is! You want to thrust all the responsibility of assessing and approving on me! But how can I possibly refuse such a lovely and welcome responsibility. Very well! Let's start proceedings right away with the first item on the agenda.

"So then, Anita, you are certainly not a Bengali from any angle. Neither an expatriate, nor a native. Right? Moreover, if you are Anita Kaur, that means you are a true-blue Sardarni, isn't it?

"My dear Soumen, what if your mother opposes your marrying a Sikh girl, and decides to chase her out of the house? After all, she is Soudamini, my headstrong daughter. She will never agree to this so easily. Do not under any circumstance expect her to budge from her orthodoxy which is deeply entrenched in her. Will you be able to convince her?"

"Leave aside Ma for now, Didu. Just tell me what you think, what your opinion is."

"Soumen, perhaps you already know that I love the Sikh community to the extent of devotion. Their self-respect, their heroism, their love for their country, their spiritual and physical beauty—everything about them is dear to me." And Lavanyadevi once again lapsed into her reminiscences. But in her trip down memory lane, this time she took Soumen and Anita along. "I clearly remember that it was three or four years after Independence, and Bengali refugees were roaming around the alleys of Kolkata with sheets in hand, singing poignant songs of the Partition and collecting funds. Champa's daughter, your Savitri Mashi, did not like this seeking aid one bit. One day she told me, 'Lavanya, you wander the whole wide world! This time you should come with me to Bhiwani, Punjab. The fresh air and clean water there will be a pleasant change for you and Pushpa from the Bengali royal households you are accustomed to, and you will also experience the hospitality of Jat landowners.'

"As soon as we reached Bhiwani, Savitri stuffed her phaeton with various household articles of daily use and directed the coachman, 'Take us to the refugee camp.' As soon as the phaeton came to a halt, Pushpa and I were surprised to see a notice board on which was written 'Labour Camp'. We were even more surprised when we saw that all the lanes and houses in the camp looked spick and span. Mothers were seen handing over tiffin-boxes to children going to school. The men of the households were seen going to the market, their wares laden on handcarts and barrows.

"Savitri, standing in front of all those tin-roofed houses, called out to everyone, '*Oye* Harpreet! *Oye* Paramjeet! Issar! Sarabjeet! Come out of your houses all of you. There is a big *masterni* from Kolkata who has come to meet you.' Hearing her voice five or six women with veils on their heads came out of their houses and, greeting us with '*Sat Sri Akal*, behen-*ji*—Greetings, sister and '*Pairi painna,* mata-*ji*—I touch your feet, mother,' brought out stools and chairs for us to sit on and water to drink. One of them went in to make tea for us; another asked us if we would like some sugarcane juice. Pushpa and I both looked at each other wondering what kind of refugees these people were.

"Savitri Mashi affectionately started distributing the items of everyday use that she had brought with her. But what was this? The moment she started distributing the things, all of them got up and withdrew some distance away from where the things were kept. With folded hands and with utmost humility, they said, 'Behen-*ji*! You are like a mother to us, so we request you not to consider this behaviour of ours insulting or offensive in any way and please forgive us for this. Please believe us when we tell you that we are unable to take any of these articles as we have promised ourselves that we will not take anything free, not even water. Sister, we value your love for us, but what can we do—we are helpless. But if you really want to help us, then please hire us to make snacks and grind spices, or for embroidery and knitting. We will happily take whatever wages you give us in lieu of that work.'

"Savitri's eyes shone with pride when she heard this. Turning to us, she said, 'Girls, see this is the kind of self-respect and pride that Punjabis have! You talk of tall concepts like Bengali culture, the nobility and the sophistication of Bengali people and think no end of them, but see, they still spread their sheets and beg like refugees.'

"You know, Anita, both of us thought that the hot-headed Savitri with her regal attitude would be greatly annoyed by the women's refusal to accept her gifts, but the opposite happened. Since what Savitri said was very true, Pushpa and I remained a quiet audience to her pointed statements and continued observing her reactions from the corners of our eyes.

"After having the tea and snacks that they served us, Savitri again pressed the women, 'Listen! I have come to visit you from far off. Please take a couple of things for the children at least.' Polite but firm, their response was, 'Sister! Taking gifts is respectable only when one is in a position to return twice as much as one receives; so please forgive us. We are constrained by our circumstances.' Seeing that they were inflexible, Savitri said, 'All right then! Accept this as advance payment and I will be sending you lots of sewing and embroidery work soon.' But they did not budge from their position. Folding their hands respectfully, all the women said, 'Behen-*ji*, please don't do this. Give us the work first and the payment later.'

"Impressed by their pride and self-respect, yet sad that they did not accept her request, Savitri's face was a curious palette of emotions. Collecting herself, she directed the coachman, 'Brother! Take us to *Kakey di Hatti*.' The phaeton crossed Asaram Gate, then Pataram Gate and stopped right in the middle of the market. Savitri got down and briskly walked into the biggest shop in Bhiwani. Both of us followed her in. After selecting around ten cotton and silk sarees, eight to ten bedcovers and other miscellaneous items, and asking the shop owner to have the bill sent to the mansion of Bhuramal Narsinghdas, she went back to the phaeton and sat down heavily.

"The phaeton dropped us at the haveli and went off to deliver all the shopped articles to the women in the Labour Camp. For many years after that, those embroidered sarees and sheets that she gifted to well-known people in Kolkata's bhadralok society remained much talked about. A few years after that incident, Pushpa once told me, 'Lavanya! You should go and see that Labour Camp we had visited. The untiring efforts of the people living there have transformed it into one of the most modern and prosperous societies in Bhiwani today. Every member of each household there engages in the maximum amount of labour possible and very little leisure.'

"Soumen, there is no doubt that these people are indeed very industrious. There is another incident that comes to mind in this respect. I was strolling in front of Savitri's fortress-like haveli when I noticed a man who had come to fill water. On observing him closely for a while, I simply could not stop myself from asking him, 'Brother! From the manner in which you conduct yourself and go about things it is evident that you are an educated person. How is it, then, that you are engaged in this menial work?' Hesitant at first, after much cajoling, the man replied that he began his day at four every morning. Starting with sweeping the streets, he did various odd jobs throughout the day like vending newspapers, filling water at homes, keeping guard at two schools, giving tuitions etc. He was a well-known doctor with an established practice in Lahore before the Partition, but one night he had to leave everything behind and run from the city to save his life. He was left with no proof of his profession. However, God's grace worked in other ways, and one of his sons was now pursuing a degree in law and the other was studying to be a doctor. On hearing all this, I asked him, 'Do you not feel bad doing menial jobs after having been a doctor earlier?'

"He answered laughingly, 'Sister! First of all, let me tell you that there is no work which is menial according to me. Also, why should I spend my life complaining about what happened in the past when I can use that time to build a better future?'

"There were a couple of other incidents too that happened later in Kolkata, and all these made me a great admirer of this community, just like Savitri Mashi. Soumen, the word 'Sikh' evokes in my mind truthfulness, industriousness and alertness. So, in my books, Anita gets eighty out of hundred chiefly on account of her being a Sikh; and I am sure she will easily secure the remaining twenty as well. After all, I am well aware of the high standards that my grandson Soumen has and how difficult it is to meet them," said Lavanyadevi, and drawing Anita close she embraced her and blessed her from the depths of her heart.

Five years had passed since Lavanyadevi had left the Roychoudhury House. In these five years, neither had she showed any inclination to meet her next generation, nor had any of her three progenies expressed any desire to come and see her; but the subsequent generation had never ceased to express their immeasurable faith and devotion in her.

Does this happen because we spend our entire youth fashioning rules, codes and ideals according to which we must function, and then we ignore the love, the empathy, the time and the patience required to follow them? Naturally, while our children might perforce swallow them like bitter medicine, they do not have faith in these values. But when the same ideals ripen through our experience of life as we achieve greater harmony, sweetness, candour and ease of being, the succeeding generation is drawn to these values and ideals on their own.

Her inner voice seemed to attest to these thoughts. Many factors such as experience, patience, sacrifice, peace, harmony, an expansive foresight, equanimity and pragmatism have all come together to create a new Lavanyadevi who is entirely different from the old one. This new Lavanyadevi is fluid and ethereal. She is capable of concealing all her powers within and suffering the pain of the lowest of the low as her own. Fame, grandeur, nobility and social standards are all hollow notions for her now, and this is the reason that her grandchildren are constantly drawn to her. Then, is she to be held accountable for the attitudes of her own children?

Seeing her trapped in this dilemma, Guru-*ji* intervened. "Lavanya! It is futile to think of affairs of the past. Age and experience play a big role in our lives. If you were never negligent in discharging your duties, never brooked deceit or beguilement, never gave precedence to what is dear over what is right, then in the eyes of a common man, you have not done anything wrong. Lavanya, don't forget that we are all souls within terrestrial bodies made up of five elements, each bringing in its own *samskara*. We are created and shaped by many elements such as atmosphere, ambience, family, society, and in a broader sense, the country, the universe and various other elements. Whatever you have done, you did it with your heart and soul, and that's it—your role ends there. Your favourite philosopher Kahlil Gibran also says the same thing. Then why this dilemma today, my child?"

"Guru-*ji*, it is not about dilemmas, but I don't know why my doubts and fears about my own self are growing day by day. Taking the simplest of decisions has become very difficult. I am constantly anxious, twenty-four hours a day, that unlike bubbles in water which burst when they reach the surface, the upheavals in my mind don't resolve themselves when they come in contact with reality; rather, they keep circling endlessly in the mind like a whirlpool. I am fortunate to have the infinite blessings of the Almighty who has given me a peerless guide like you, whose relentless interventions help me keep my wavering vision of wisdom alert with his *gyananjna shalakaya*—his torch of knowledge—and who is committed to and capable of defending me like a protective shield."

Sensing that she was overwhelmed with emotions, Guru-*ji* adroitly changed the topic and said, "Lavanya beti, the children have been here since yesterday. Come, let us talk to them about their future plans."

The moment Guru-*ji* said this, Lavanyadevi got up and directed a young employee in the ashram, "Please go and enquire if the children are comfortable and if they need anything. Then ask them to join me in the living room."

Soumen and Anita promptly came as they were told, and as soon as they arrived, Lavanyadevi started asking them all that she felt was important. The first question she asked them was, "How long have the two of you been together?"

"For three years now," answered Anita and Soumen in unison.

"Do you both plan to get married to each other? If yes, why?"

Anita replied, "Nani, I personally feel that many a time the plant of love gradually shrivels up and dies out of insensitivity, but if it is given the water of relationships and children and the fertiliser of love, it usually lasts long."

"While sitting together in your courtyard under a star-filled sky, if you express yourself in a lyrical turn of phrase but your companion is unable to appreciate the flights of your imagination or the intricacies of your thought, would it not hurt you deeply? These unstated innocent everyday expressions—will they not gradually inhibit you and embitter your lives? Soumen and Anita, when the flame of the lamp of relationship gets close to you, the heat you feel is more than the light you see. And suddenly the sweet nectar of relationship which could quench your thirst starts tasting sour. Have you weighed your relationship from different angles?"

"Didu, firstly, under that circumstance, we shall transmute the metaphors of our emotionality into simpler sentences, if not words. Secondly, in these three years we have come to know each other so closely that one knows what is in the other's mind without us even having to speak. Didu, do not worry, we have analysed our relationship in every plausible way; it is impossible that we get married today and file for a divorce tomorrow," replied Soumen with complete conviction.

"Do both of you have similar food habits and hobbies?"

"Yes, Nani! Yes! Somu and I have scaled almost all the peaks in the country and both of us are champions in mountaineering. We are both quite good at white-water rafting and skiing as well. Soumen makes films and since I am a senior executive in an advertising firm, I help him market his films. I am resolute in my determination that whenever we start thinking of children, I will give up my job and devote myself completely to motherhood, leaving the rest to the Almighty. *Rab di maya da paar nahin*—One cannot transcend what the Lord wills." Saying this, Anita joined both her hands behind her neck and lifted them up towards the sky. Lavanyadevi looked at Soumen who was looking towards her, smiling gently. Guru-*ji* lowered his eyes in wordless consent, concurring to this relationship.

Lavanyadevi was wary of discussing the issue of marriage in this life of renunciation that she had chosen and apprehensive of the possibilities of her own failure at every step, but she was not in any position to escape from all of this. This was not just about kin or blood relations; it was about two people's lives. She felt that some more discussion was needed before a conclusion was arrived at, and held off deliberating on the issue for the next day.

The next morning Lavanyadevi arranged to have breakfast served in the verandah. The snowcapped mountain ranges, iridescent as the morning sun bathed them in its light, bathed the children of the soil who sat there in their rainbow hues, as if showering blessings on them.

Lavanyadevi started the conversation by saying, "I am in agreement with both of you. Now you people should speak your mind. What is it that you expect from me?"

"Didu! We want a no-frills marriage ceremony in the Kedarnath temple. We want Guru-*ji* and you to be present. If mother insists, we are willing to have a Bengali wedding in Kolkata with rituals like the bride covering her face with a betel leaf as she prepares to meet the groom; and if Anita's parents want a Sikh *anand karaj* at Harmandir Sahib, we have no objection to that either. Didu! When our minds have become one, we want our relatives also to be able to fulfil their long-cherished desires of affection and enjoyment regarding our marriage," Soumen replied.

"When I am not insisting, why do you wish to have the rituals performed here?" Lavanyadevi asked.

"We want to save within us as memory a part of the sacredness which pervades every particle here, but only if you are agreeable to this," was Anita's gracious and sweet reply.

When Lavanyadevi looked to him for an answer, Guru-*ji* again indicated his agreement with his eyes.

"Very well. But if you get all this done by me, you will also have to pay me some tax. Tell me is that okay with you?"

"*Manzoor-manzoor-manzoor!*" they chorused their agreement in a manner similar to the Islamic way of asking for separation.

"Tax number one: you have to periodically review the functioning of the centres here and the work they are doing and help them carry their work forward. Tax number two: by periodically supporting soil research and other scientific research you have to endeavour to ameliorate the difficulties in the living conditions of living creatures and our planet.

"You will have to prepare a dedicated team of service-spirited workers, who will be paid for their work by the Trust, but to whom you will always remain grateful for their public service. Always remember—money can run machines, but to keep people going, you need to love them. Soumen, you being the eldest and most mature among your siblings Ananya, Malavika, Manjulika and Amlan, if you are able to look after them and keep them connected to each other and to yourselves, then understand that you will have achieved the wherewithal to reach for the skies. Soumen! Anita! Always bear in mind that fortunate are those who are able to find somebody like-minded and like-principled as lifelong companion; otherwise, most couples are either mismatched or out of sync with each other. Always keep your eyes open and if you find people who satisfy your criteria, reach out to them and include them your team. If your goals and means are just, people and resources will keep coming to you on their own."

To lighten the atmosphere, Guru-*ji* humorously interjected, "Lavanya, I think it is time to end the graduation ceremony and give them the opportunity to toss their graduation caps in celebration so that they can advance on the path of life shining bright as the sun."

Suddenly shy, Lavanyadevi bowed to Guru-*ji* in obeisance, gratitude in her eyes. Anita and Soumen also paid their respects to both the elders and sought their permission to depart for Kedarnath. It was decided that Guru-*ji* and Lavanyadevi would reach there on the decided date.

After Soumen and Anita left for Kedarnath, Lavanyadevi increased the speed of the vehicle of her life. She slept not more than six hours a day and spent the remaining eighteen accomplishing a range of tasks. Functionaries from the centres at Hemkund, the Valley of Flowers, Pauri Garhwal, Joshimath, Sonprayag, Rudraprayag and other places would come to her to discuss the many problems they faced when engaged with development initiatives, and she worked tirelessly night and day to resolve them.

Lavanyadevi's travels became more and more frequent. Every time she identified a dedicated functionary in any area, she would immediately travel to meet the person, and taking on the complete responsibility of their livelihoods, would make them such a lucrative offer that was well-nigh impossible to turn down, and ask the individual to open a centre there. The person would be left with no scope for refusing. Her magnetic personality tempered with her love, reliability, trust and inner warmth and compassion bound everyone she spoke to in a way that, far from even thinking of saying 'no', people felt fortunate when she addressed them. Her incessant efforts saw a proliferation of centres throughout the jungles, valleys and mountains of the area.

Lavanyadevi also opened centres that focussed on reviving and conserving the centuries-old traditions practised in the mountains. She got traditional organic farming and water conservation practices scientifically validated and worked towards making them an integral part of people's everyday lives. She was very concerned about the unrestrained mining in the Tehri Garhwal region and the abuse of the river Ganga. Deeply influenced by the philosophies and practices of noted environmentalist Sundarlal Bahuguna and other Gandhians, she instructed all her functionaries to emulate these great men and their work. A staunch advocate of the use of indigenous and locally made tools and equipment, Lavanyadevi made one exception to this: every evening she sat in front of her laptop and went through the twenty-four-hour reports that each centre was expected to send at the end of the day. She also mailed them her suggestions and passed on relevant suggestions to other centres. But she did not like using a cell phone and therefore relied on traditional means of receiving and sharing news. This was beneficial as it gave her the opportunity to converse face-to-face with people. She also consciously eschewed the use of cell phones since, according to her, people were increasingly becoming divorced from each other due to the lack of personal connect.

Lavanyadevi's work seemed to increase in proportion to her age! Accompanied by Aalo, she travelled across the entire region to supervise the work being done, returned for a couple of days to discuss a few things with Guru-*ji* and then set off again for other destinations.

Every day, by evening, her fair complexion turned deep pink and her forehead shone with beads of perspiration. When Guru-*ji* once intervened, she recounted to him a Rajasthani folktale. "Guru-*ji*! A very lively, highly accomplished and famous singer-dancer couple once went to perform at the court of a prosperous king, hoping for a rich reward. Their performance began in the evening and the duo put their heart and soul into it, with beautiful dances, heavenly music and spellbinding acts. But the king neither applauded nor gave them any reward. He just sat there sulking through the entire performance. Actually, he was a great miser and fearing that he would have to reward the dancers if he appreciated them, he feigned utter indifference. Evening gave way to night and night was about to give way to the next day, but the king remained impassive and unmoved. Finally, unable to bear his silence any longer, the *natni* sang as she danced,

> The night is nearly gone
> My limbs are exhausted
> This raja refuses to be pleased
> Won't you ease the pace, dear?

"To this, her partner the *nat* replied,

> The night is anyway gone
> Dear woman
> Then why break the rhythm
> When the dance is nearly done?

"Guru-*ji*! Like time in this folktale, most of my time on earth is also almost spent and there is very little left. In such circumstances, I feel the need to put in forty-eight hours of work in a day. And this body? Well, this piece of 'earth' has to ultimately return to 'earth', isn't it; and the more it is kneaded the lighter it will become, and the Almighty will find it easier to give it a new shape. Please don't fret for me. I am a piece of Jyotirmoyidevi and Prabhavatidevi and it is my promise to them that I will never accept defeat. I may trip, I may fall, but I will rise up again and again and continue walking towards my goal. Guru-*ji*, it took only one Lord Krishna to convince Arjuna to fight; I have two goddesses on either side urging me on, and you in front of me, constantly chanting the mantra of *uttishthotishth*, inspiring me to excel over the excellent. Guru-*ji*, you tell me, how can I possibly get tired? How can I permit laziness and laxity to even come near me? Guru-*ji*, please bless me so that I can do even more work. Please keep me in your benevolent favours so that I continue to experience a sense of security."

The idea of streams rising above their sources, or in other words, the disciple moving a step ahead of the teacher was true in this case too. How then could Guru-*ji* or anyone else stop her? Her supervisions, trips and halts kept on increasing day by day and the passion within her grew as well, even as her body grew perceptibly weaker.

Nowadays, one could notice many changes in Lavanyadevi. She would often engage Guru-*ji* in spiritual discussions. She had suddenly become interested in *santhara*—the Jain practice of gradually reducing one's intake of food and liquids and voluntarily starving oneself to death. After Vinoba Bhave undertook *santhara*, the public perception about the practice also changed. The ritual, till then considered a kind of mercy-killing, came to be viewed as a pious act.

Lavanyadevi did not just discuss the ritual with Guru-*ji*, she read whatever literature was available on the subject. Concerned by this, Guru-*ji* asked, "Lavanya beti, nowadays you seem to be absorbed in knowing more and more about *santhara*. I do hope and trust that somewhere in your mind, you have not resolved to do something similar." Lavanyadevi laughed away his concern and said, "Guru-*ji*! Can anyone trust or predict a human mind? It is so dynamic. Moreover, it is extremely difficult to envisage one's own death while one is alive—not because we are afraid of death, but because we love life so much. Guru-*ji*! Life and death are in the hands of destiny. It is not in our power to 'design' or to will destiny one way or the other. The case of certain saints or Bhishma Pitamah was different; they were divine souls. But we are lesser mortals of bone and flesh. Can we even think of *ichhamrityu*—death as we wish—let alone choose it? Please don't worry. I am immortal and I will be here working with you for thousands of years!" Lavanyadevi's innocent childlike smile reassured Guru-*ji* and gave him deep solace.

Lavanyadevi's travels for work grew even more frenetic. Hard work and the intense rays of the sun would turn her face a crimson red even in the chilly climes of the hills. Ignoring all physical discomfort, she immersed herself in more and still more work—as if she were in some tearing hurry to run and board a moving train.

One day, Soumen suddenly received a message from Guru-*ji* which said that he, along with Malavika, Manjulika, Anita, Ananya, Dhanu and Amlan, should reach the Uttarkashi ashram on a particular day. Neither had Guru-*ji* ever sent such a message before nor had they been able to get in touch with Lavanyadevi for a while now. Naturally, they were all suddenly very anxious.

When they started off towards Uttarkashi on the designated date, they found that many people were travelling along those mountainous roads to the same destination either on foot or aboard vehicles. On seeing such large unseasonal movement on these usually quiet roads, all of them got even more worried. They were all apprehensive that Lavanyadevi was seriously ill, and that was probably why all these people were going towards the ashram.

As soon as their jeep stopped before the ashram, Soumen jumped off the vehicle and ran towards Guru-*ji* who seemed to be waiting for them. "Guru-*ji*! Where is Didu? Which room is she in? Please tell me quickly!" Guru-*ji* came forward, held him affectionately by the hand and pulling him into an embrace, ran his fingers through Soumen's hair, saying, "Come and sit down first, son. Let me tell you everything." The other six also joined them by then.

They all sat surrounding Guru-*ji* as he started speaking. "Lavanya's trips were becoming more and more frequent in the last few months and when I asked her to cut down on them, she came up with such irrefutable arguments that it became impossible to say no to her. Around a month and a half back she had left for one of her extended trips. She had said that she would be going to all the ashram centres in the mountains as well as in the foothills. She had also planned to visit a newly opened hospital on her way to Delhi from Dehradun, and would request them to provide some scientific facilities for the centres. Since this would take time, she had asked us not to worry and she had also said that she would keep in touch. For the first fifteen days, we got regular news of her location and progress; thereafter it started decreasing and for the last twenty-five days, we have received no news of her. We tried our best to locate her, but were not able to. It was as if Aalo and Lavanya had been swallowed up by the earth. We tried contacting all the centres, and around fifteen days back we came to know that she had left the ashram's jeep at one of the centres and taken another vehicle. Some people said that she had gone off to a remote cottage in the hills to accept *santhara*; others said that she had admitted herself to some hospital in her last days to donate her organs. Still others reported that she was seen just a day before, sitting with the accounts of a centre in the mountains when she suddenly disappeared. While such unconfirmed news is still floating in from all directions, there is no evidence of

Lavanya's presence at any of these places. We sent people to Baba Sundardas's cottage and even higher, to Gaumukh, but there was no trace of her.

"Suddenly, around four or five days back, I saw a child from the plains whom I had never seen before running towards me with an envelope addressed to me, and another sealed envelope addressed to all of you. Before I could ask him anything, the child had just vanished, gone as fast as he had appeared. It was as if he had come riding a tornado and was carried off by it. This was perhaps what he had been instructed to do.

"The letter meant for me had such detailed outlines of the future course of development and possible projects for the centres around the ashram that my heart was filled with disquiet. I immediately asked a few disciples to go to her special rooms in the ashrams at Uttarkashi, Kedarnath and Gangotri. Leave alone finding a handkerchief, there was not even a piece of thread or scrap of paper to be found in any of the three rooms. Even the floors had been swabbed and the walls and doors dusted clean.

"That was the moment I felt that Lavanya had departed from earth—it was her *mahaprayan*. At that instant my detachment suddenly abandoned me, turning me into a being infatuated with earthly indulgences. I felt that my body had suddenly turned lifeless and I was incapable of any movement. In that condition, I somehow dragged myself to the meditation room and falling at the feet of Gurudev, I started crying. I don't remember how long this lasted, but suddenly the whole chamber was filled with a bluish light and when I looked up, I was surprised to see Lavanya sitting at Gurudev's feet with a gentle smile on her face. Her right palm was facing upwards and her left palm downwards and her eyes were filled with compassion and solace. This vision filled my heart with supernatural peace. It was a strange experience—and one which I had been deprived of until that day." Guru-*ji*'s voice choked as he said this. He handed over the sealed envelope to Commander Soumen and his six soldiers. Soumen accepted the envelope from Guru-*ji* as one would accept *prasad* and looked at everyone questioningly. Seeing that all six pairs of eyes agreed, he tore open the envelope. Clearing his throat, Soumen began to read the letter aloud, but the sight of Lavanyadevi's handwriting caused the dam of his emotions to burst such that it seemed as if water contained for centuries had suddenly decided to break all walls and boundaries and to cross all limits and surge ahead.

Everyone present there had unshed tears in their eyes, but Soumen was sobbing like a little child who, beating his head at the sight of his mother's dead body, unable to comprehend what to do, cries helplessly, inconsolably.

Guru-*ji*, assuming the responsibility of the eldest in the family, consoled Soumen, "My son! These tears will only grieve Lavanya's soul. If you really want her divine soul to rest in peace, then you must carry forward her tasks with a strong resolve. Rise! This is not the time to waste in crying; this is the time to give your Didu the tribute she deserves. In the course of Lavanya's life, the word *vishraam* or leisure had come to carry no meaning in terms of its conventional use. She reinterpreted the negative prefix *vi-* as *vishesh* or special; and by adding it to the word *shram* or labour, she interpreted the word as referring to any task that one finds special happiness in doing. Lavanya always maintained, 'There is no *shram* or hard work involved in doing the things one loves to do. Such work is therefore the ultimate instance of leisure, for good deeds fill us with so much energy that we feel lighter than air as we move around. And therefore, I am always in a state of leisure. Please do not worry about me at all. I am absolutely fine. Please do not be concerned. Nothing is going to happen to me unexpectedly or suddenly. When this river of life eventually meets the sea, it will itself become the sea simply by flowing into it. Its existence will not disappear through this merging; it will merely be transformed into something greater. I do not know what difference the adding of one drop will make to the treasure chest that is the sea. But how the limitless sea that comes to be contained within the singular drop shall transform the drop is something that can only be fathomed by knowledgeable and enlightened beings like you. Where do I have the capacity to comprehend all this?'

"Children! We have studied philosophy only in books, but Lavanya has lived it in person, has invested it with her experiences and has thus enriched it. That is why Lavanya's truth cannot be encompassed in our praise of her." Then, pulling Soumen up so that he was standing in front of the rest, Guru-*ji* instructed him, "Soumen! Read out Lavanya's will."

When the worldly Soumen, lost in the sea of his emotions, stood up to read from the sheaf of papers in his hand, he was overwhelmed at the sight of so many people dressed in bright colours adorning the mountains from top to bottom like beautiful wildflowers. In response to his questioning glance, Guru-*ji* patted him on the back as if saying, "These questions can come later; first complete the task of reading out the letter." Soumen took a deep breath to steady his quavering voice and started reading the letter aloud.

> *My dear, my very own children!*
>
> *This is how I choose to address you because you are all the offspring of my soul. I know that right now you must all be feeling angry and hurt. I agree that your anger is justified. You have all been party to the smallest of my decisions. But today, leave alone asking you, I did not even give you any information about what I intend to do. This is absolutely wrong. I accept this mistake with my head bowed, but I also have a few questions to ask you in return.*
>
> *Would you have allowed me to opt for death-at-will? Would you not have tried to use every scientific means known to you to save this mortal body of mine till my and your own last breath? You know that the only living heir of the Kauravas, King Parikshit, began listening to the Shrimad Bhagvad Gita only out of the fear of death but achieved victory over death simply by listening to it. In other words, he overcame the fear of death. Children! Remember that overcoming the fear of death is akin to becoming immortal.*
>
> *You are all the children of this earth and my immortal children too. You should all happily celebrate the fact that a body made of*

the five elements, with all its shortcomings, has become one with the infinite. The sky, the earth, water, fire and air are all pure expressions of the divine infinite. It is fine if this body made of earth either gets buried in the infinite earth, or burns in fire and gets carried by air into the infinite sky or gets carried away into the fathomless water. One has to ultimately choose a means for this body, confined to a limited time frame, to become one with the absolute, infinite, limitless, endless truth. To stop you people from getting upset, let me tell you that I consider suicide a sin and death as something completely determined by fate.

You are all travellers on the path of knowledge; that is why you will put forward sensible, intellectual arguments which are agreeable to the conscience. But I have become a traveller on the path of spirituality on which, beyond and above all arguments, there is only complete faith and total devotion. There is only one power that rules this path, and that is love. In it, the eyes remain closed, the heart softens, the body is relaxed and all the ten senses become completely inactive. In this state, the inexpressible happiness which one experiences is beyond words. When the entire body melts like ice, disintegrates into particles and starts merging into that Supreme Power, the state is of a mute person tasting jaggery—it can only be experienced, it cannot be put into words. I am fortunate that I was given this boon as prasad. *I am also fortunate that I am able to share this experience with my near ones, and that they are able to understand me. I do not want even a particle of my temporal being to remain on this earth. This effort is only because I want to remain aflame in the lamps of your hearts, not just as a temple lamp.*

So please forgive me, my immortal children. Rise. Fill this earth with the fragrance of your sweetness. I strongly believe that you will take far greater strides than I could because you are endowed with time, intellect, means and a strong resolve for doing good. Only one of these qualities is enough for success, and you have all of them.

Such boisterous enthusiasm! Such boundless courage! And unlimited moral strength! Harmonious in mind, words and deeds— manasa, vacha, karmana*—even if your being strives to capture*

the entire universe and attempts to decorate it, the Almighty Father will use his hands to bless and assure you and help you multiply your deeds. With this supreme belief, once again, lots and lots of blessings to you all.
Lavanya.

P.S.: Having made Aalo one of the trustees of the Bangladesh Trust, I have entrusted her the work of the centres there. She is a daughter of that land and this is the minimum that I can do for her as her three generations have served my grandmother, mother and myself. Please do not try to ask her anything, else you will just end up with mental agony and hopelessness.

By the time they had reached the last sentence of the letter, loud shouts in praise of Lavanyadevi began to be heard. People were cheering energetically across the whole valley—people standing on the roofs and parapets of houses, at the roundabouts, in the serpentine lanes, in the open fields. Like the waves of the sea, just as one wave of euphoric exultation quietened and receded, another one gathered rhythm and force apace and crested, and then another, and then another.

The mountain ranges and their snowcapped peaks echoed with the cheers, as if responding to the applause. The western side was painted crimson in the hues of the setting sun, which seemed to be raining *kumkum* on Lavanyadevi. On the other side, the rising moon and the twinkling stars seemed to be offering their own tribute through the assembled people. This magnificent scene was transformed quite suddenly when a strange stillness enveloped it and night spread its vast canopy and drew everything into its fold.

The very first matter that came up for hearing in the Delhi court, the next day, was related to an affidavit for name change. Seven persons had dropped their existing surnames to adopt Lavanya as their surname.

While leaving the court compound, as if reading everyone's mind, Soumen said, "I think, all of us are surrounded by numerous questions. Come, let's go to some peaceful place nearby, sit down there and chalk out our future course of action.

On hearing this, the creases and signs of worry on everyone's faces were replaced with bright smiles and everyone's voice echoed in unison, "Yes! Yes! Come on, let us go somewhere and sit and reflect."

"Dada! So many strange incidents happening in quick succession have exhausted our senses and induced a kind of numbness within. The pillar that propped us up every time and supported us is suddenly not there anymore. Neither am I able to see anything nor am I able to understand anything now. What am I supposed to do?" Ananya burst out crying as she said this.

Soumen pulled her close to him and signalled everyone to get into the car. They drove to Lodhi Gardens and settled into a secluded corner of the IIC coffee shop. After having ordered tea and coffee he looked around at everyone and started talking in the same manner as his grandmother Lavanyadevi.

"Lavanya Ma has given us our goal, but now it is upon us to decide how best to go about it. At the same time, we must also remember that we are the bearers of her legacy and will have to work in accordance with the expectations that her name evokes. Lavanya Ma always used to say, 'Each of us has everything in infinite quantities.' Believing and accepting this statement wholeheartedly, all of us together should work as much as seven Lavanyadevis, if not seven hundred."

There was absolute silence after Soumen's statement. Everyone was digging their fingers or toes into the table or the ground, looking at the sky or the walls. Then, just as fog clears slowly, the silence gradually filled with conversations in subdued voices. Each face seemed as taut as the strings of a musical instrument that had just been tuned. It was as if their analytical minds were not in harmony with their emotional minds, and while they were all desirous of doing the work, there was somewhere an unnamed hesitation within them.

Sensing their discomfort, Soumen spoke like an elder, "Do not roam in a maze of doubts like one confused. And do not underestimate yourselves by thinking of the huge amount of work which Lavanya Ma has already accomplished by herself. Always remember what she said: 'Build yourself up according to the times and let the flame of your soul-lamp guide you.' Therefore, first choose your areas of work according to your heart's desire, and then we can sit together and plan it out. When you set out on the path of righteousness, you are bound to feel nervous, but as our Guru Ma decreed: 'Charitable work must be done alongside our daily work.' Therefore, freeing our minds of all our doubts from within, we must march forward with the same gusto that the Indian and Pakistani soldiers exhibit at the Wagah Border. When they stride ahead with vigour, feet raised skywards, fists clenched tight, it seems as if they could conquer the world. Come, let us all write a similar script today."

In the fading light, the clearly etched lines of uncertainty on everyone's faces grew softer on hearing Soumen's words. The circle of meaninglessness within which they had been caught seemed to gradually dissolve and their faces became calm, clear and bright once again. They looked at each other meaningfully and all seemed eager and intent on taking a leap into their respective areas of work. Manjulika, however, sat amidst them all like an ice maiden, distracted and detached, immersed in the sea of her emotions. It seemed as if she was picking at the scabs of past wounds, thinking herself to be unworthy and incapable of these great tasks that lay before her. The grey colour of sadness had like *Rahu* eclipsed her bright face, but she seemed oblivious to it. In an instant there was a shared, silent communication between the six faces following which Malavika placed a friendly, assuring hand on her back.

Addressing the Saptarshi Mandal, she said: "Manjulika's shocked state is not unusual. Don't forget that we have all been well fed and taken care of. From the moment we opened our eyes on this planet, we have always got whatever we wanted. Whether we have wasted it or used it for constructive purposes is a different question; but we had everything that a human being on this planet could possibly want, and probably more. On the other hand, think about Manjulika's circumstances. Though she addressed Didu as Maua and wove every dream in life around her, did she get an iota of assistance? Forgive me if my words sting like grit in the eye, but is this not the reality? Have any of us ever considered Manju as a friend or an equal? Was her position in our friends' circle as easy or dignified as that of our other friends? Till date, did any of us ever spare a thought for Hari's daughter Manju? Did she have her food? What is she reading? When does she sleep? Does she need anything? To tell the truth as it stands, we were indifferent to her presence and her needs. But despite that, and undaunted by the odds against her, Manju achieved what all of us here could not even have dreamt of. Our self-confidence is rooted in our families, in our privilege. But Manju? It is entirely to her credit that having stood up to and overcome every single obstacle at every point in her life, she has become worthy of being called Manju Lavanya. She is the most courageous amongst all of us; but her background and her filial dissociation from Lavanya Ma are causing her to drown in the sea of anxiety. This sturdy boat which is rocking midstream just needs a touch of love and respect; and then, you'll see her turn into a huge ship and even pull us all ashore." Then, pulling Manjulika close and embracing her, Malavika enquired, "Am I not right, Manju?" Everyone looked on astonished as Manju, clinging to Malavika, head on her shoulder, tried to smile through her tears like a small child even as Malavika tried to pacify her.

Soumen, seeing Manju struggling to smile, clapped as he cried out, "Bravo! Bravo!" and the other members of the Saptarshi Mandal also clapped, gentle smiles on all their faces. Wiping her face with the edge of her dupatta and composing herself, Manjulika said, "Thank you, Malavika! Soumen-*da*, tell me what I have to do. I am ready now."

Just then, the radiant rose-complexioned Dhanu, with a fit body and sharp nose, spoke up, a slight smile playing on his lips, "Yes Soumen-*da*. Pick up the magic wand and direct us onto our paths of action. I'd also like to tell you my future plans in case it is of help. Ananya and I are in New York but we live like villagers. We stay far from the city and mostly commute using bicycles. Our diet is entirely 'organic' and vegetarian and we don't even drink packaged milk. Our plan is to stay for some time with our parents in Vancouver and then settle down permanently on some tranquil, secluded seashore, either in Thailand or in India."

"And what will you eat? How will you manage your daily expenses, especially since you are averse to even touching the wealth of your parents? And what are your plans for the baby in Ananya's womb?"

In response to Soumen's query, Dhanu showed him a long email that his father had sent him. The relevant part read as follows: *"I would like my grandson to grow up in the lap of nature. For at least two years, he should roll on the sand, tumble on it, eat it and play on it. This is not possible anywhere except in India or Thailand."* Then Dhanu said, "Soumen-*da*, we will choose a place by the sea which is in the vicinity of a city, yet not polluted. I will travel to the city when necessary and market my goods online. That way, there will be no influence of the city on my children. Since Ananya is already an expert on organic farming, rain-water harvesting, etc., she can get our products advertised by leveraging her educational degrees and can easily establish herself as one of the big names in the field of 'organic food'. We can purchase some agricultural land close to any of the cities like Pondicherry, Chennai or Cochin and settle down there. Ananya has exemplary courage and industriousness. Along with managing her daily responsibilities, she will also complete any task you assign her with diligence and devotion; this is what I believe." Ananya thanked Dhanu with her big conch-like eyes and then fixed them on Soumen.

Keeping in mind the significance of what was being discussed, Soumen turned to address Dhanu, "Thanks Dhanu. If your plan is final, this will prove to be a unique proposition for our team. Globalisation and the market have depleted our natural resources, and this has polluted the atmosphere and made it poisonous. In the coastal areas, the intrusion of big trawlers has made life difficult for both fishermen and fish. Businessmen only think about today's profits and have no compunction in killing the small fish that get entangled in their nets along with the big ones for no reason at all. Their activities are aimed at immediate gains but are suicidal for the future. That is why friends, we must unanimously welcome the proposal made by Ananya and Dhanu. And Dhanu, Lavanya Ma has left behind huge amounts of money for good deeds; so, if you ever need funds, you can tell me without hesitation."

"Don't worry, Soumen-*da*," said Dhanu. And when he went on to tell Soumen about the grants he had received for each of his projects, everyone's eyes widened with amazement. Soumen knew that architects who graduated from Cooper Union charged in crores, but Dhanu's perseverance and hard work had made the figure so huge as to be beyond imagination. To top it, Dhanu's pleasant personality and mild manner made him appear more like a sage who was above such things as accumulation of riches. Everybody looked at Ananya and Dhanu with proud smiles and patted their backs. It was decided that they would wind up their work overseas as quickly as possible and come back to India.

All of them were basking in the warmth of the winter sun. They were happy and contented. Seeing the mood of the gathering, Amlan proposed, "Let us take a stroll through Lodhi Gardens and have the rest of the discussions over lunch." Even before he had finished, all of them got up, stretched themselves and proceeded towards Lodhi Gardens.

The monsoons had lent the grass a deep shade of green. The earthy fragrance of the soil, grass and seasonal flowers added to the autumnal feel. The rows of small blooming flowers seemed to be articulating the wonder and delight within the hearts of this Saptarshi Mandal. Careful not to disturb the quiet of the sprawling lawns, they walked in silence with small slow steps, without dilemma and without fear. Their bodies moved in a unified rhythm and, silhouetted against the soft rays of the sun behind them, appeared like a supernatural mass of light. It seemed that the children of Lavanya had seized the entire universe within their fists. This mass of light was moving at a moderate pace when there was a sudden small jolt and one corner of it, disengaging itself from the whole, turned towards the others and stood facing them. She reminded them of the beautiful sculpture of the *salabhanjika yakshini* standing in front of the *sal* tree. Flawless in beauty and tranquil in bearing, Anita did look like a goddess. Everyone turned to look at her. She said, "Listen, Soumen, I do not know whether you will like my thoughts or if you will consider them nonsense and dismiss them as baseless, but I won't be at peace if I keep them within myself, which is why I want to share them with everyone."

Everyone smiled at the spontaneity and simplicity with which Anita expressed herself and responded in unison, "Sure, Anita. Please tell us whatever is in your mind without any hesitation. We will all analyse it on the scales of feasibility and if anything does not sit well with us, we shall lay it before you without mincing words. Don't worry, we won't spare you."

Anita was doubly excited. Addressing Soumen as she spoke, she said, "I am affected by everything to do with the people living in the high mountains—their purity, their genuineness, their backwardness, their harsh living conditions and their poverty. If you all agree, I wish to take up the responsibility of a multidimensional development programme for the hills which will include food, clothing, housing, education, hospitals, organic farming, preservation and restoration of flora and fauna, elimination of addiction and also refinement of local games to make them equivalent to international standards. Cricket, which George Bernard Shaw had once labelled as a game played by fools, is bringing in crores because of media attention. Then why can't we in the Saptarshi Mandal, who have enough resources, promote games like kho-kho, kabaddi, football and wrestling up to international levels? Keeping the conservation of forest resources in mind, if we can present white-water rafting and skiing alongside the sparkling natural beauty of these mountainous regions to foreigners, would they not be naturally attracted towards it? Friends, we only lack in conveniences. I can clearly see writ on the sky of the future domestic and international tourists making a beeline for this place and being ready to spend a lot of money. I understand that so many ideas together might sound too daunting to achieve, but remember what Ma used to say: 'This world is colourful only because people dare to dream. The people who dream are the ones who propel the world forward. If the doyens had not dreamt of anything, we wouldn't have seen any scientific research or the creation of epics either.' The strong practicality on which these dreams are based is a truth that I have myself experienced. I have seen big companies launch ten–fifteen products together, knowing that if even one of them succeeds, they will gather huge profits. Similarly, we too should dress these ideas in the cloth of reality and present them to the public, and leave the rest to the will of God." After this fervent outpouring of thoughts there was, expectedly, silence from the audience.

Breaking that silence, Commander Soumen spoke, "Anita, Ajanubahu himself would not have been able to achieve so many tasks that are so diverse in nature. Remember that if we slip and fall right at the start of a steep mountainous climb, we will lose our confidence and enthusiasm. All your proposals are doable but not defined, and all of us are bound by limits; that is why we need to take decisions after a careful assessment of our strengths and weaknesses, and with patience and deliberation start converting our ideas into action one by one. Any decision taken in a fit of passion or emotion is doomed to failure. There is no harm in dreaming, but presuming dreams to be viable without scrutinising them adequately is a grave mistake. Anita, don't be disheartened. We are all elated that you want, and with such intensity and urgency, to accomplish Ma's tasks. Your enthusiasm is an inspiration to all of us, and we should all consider this a good omen," Soumen concluded as he beckoned everyone back to the table.

As soon as everyone had settled down, the normally quiet Manju said, "Soumen-*da*, can I help Aalo with her work in Bangladesh apart from doing my own work in Kolkata? I have always had a special fondness for Aalo. Both of us have been friends from childhood, right from the time we were at the Chowdhury House. Ma has, in any case, already instructed that I should sign the Trust register there. And the other thing is that, quite honestly, the stories related to Bangladesh have not only become a part of my existence now but they are also central to my life. It is my earnest request that you permit me to work there too."

Seeing the hesitation and diffidence of the gentle, calm, decent and soft-spoken Manju, Soumen the elder, embracing her as a mother hugs her confused child, said, "Good! Bravo Manju! May God always keep you happy and constantly shower you with his blessings. You are blessed that along with your work on de-addiction, you also wish to carry forward the work of our grandmother and great grandmother. Manju, the entire Mandal is with you. Look for us in the middle of the night, and you will find us standing right beside you. The courage you have demonstrated today proves that you are in the truest sense the daughter of Lavanyadevi. May God bless you, my child," said Soumen as he embraced her once again.

The heart of each member of the Saptarshi Mandal was now dancing like the waters of a mountainous waterfall and soaring like the tide on a full moon night. Soumen had just turned around to order for food when Malavika suddenly stood up, "Dada! Dada, may I also say something? Please place your order after you've heard what I have to say." Knowing Malavika's nature, Soumen signalled the waiter who was already bending down to note the order to come back after some time and with full concentration in his eyes and a soft smile on his lips, assured Manjulika, "Yes, my dear child, tell us whatever you wish to say without hesitation. We are all eager to listen to your thoughts."

The talkative but industrious Malavika took a good look around her and, overwhelmed on seeing the eager receptive faces, launched into an extensive preamble to what she had to say, as was her wont. But the young members of the Saptarshi Mandal did not give her this leeway. Covering their mouths with their hands, they made a show of yawning frequently. Seeing this, Malavika was about to burst like a volcano and spew lava when she noticed that, in an effort to contain their laughter by clamping their hands on their mouths, they were no longer able to do so and helplessly burst out laughing. It was a curious sight. Laughter echoed in the background even as they kept touching her feet and saying sorry. The culmination of the whole episode was when Malavika, instead of bursting into tears of rage, also started laughing heartily, saying, "I am like this! Please pardon me. But I will come straight to the point now." Everyone tried to control their laughter on hearing this sweet and welcome statement from her, although sudden peals of mirth still managed to spill in between which, like occasional monsoon showers, were beyond their control.

Malavika said, "You people know that as per Lavanya Ma's directions, my work is with the sex workers in Kolkata. But I feel that, to the extent possible, all of us do this work in our respective areas. Prostitution affects society like leprosy and it rots not only the body but also the soul. My desire is to start a campaign that can lead up to a massive agitation against it. Like the drug cartel, the world of prostitution too is full of ruthlessness. Human trafficking, like the drug trade, is also a heinous crime, and we should strive to get a suitable law enacted that will deal with human traffickers in the same way that drug traffickers are dealt with. We should also involve the media in trying to sensitise people about the issue. Dada, you have not seen the tears and suffering of the innocent children who roam the narrow lanes there. You must surely remember your reaction when you saw the Auschwitz camp. Your reaction will be similar if you see the situation in these places. Though I am younger to you all, my suggestion is that we make a list of all of the programmes for improvement of the society and then, while we all can primarily focus on the specific area of our choice, each of us can also try to devote some time to other works on the list. Lavanya Ma had instructed us to form a core group similar to every corporate business having their 'secretariat', so that we may become a hundred individuals with a thousand arms and are able to take quick, concrete steps to make this planet a beautiful place. Friends, we are also lucky that Ma has educated us on how to go about choosing functionaries and attuning them to our cause. There is just one question that bothers me right now and confronts me like a python with its jaws wide open: where will such huge funds come from? The multifold expenses required for this work would empty even the coffers of Kuber; then what about us?"

Soumen, holding Malavika by her shoulders, shook her affectionately and said, "How did my dear, silly sister grow up so fast that she has started planning for the future? Don't you remember, you stupid girl, how Ma often said—that no good deed ever stops because of lack of funds? Funds suddenly appear from unexpected sources and tasks get accomplished. So, jump into this ocean without doubts and without fears. Believe that the whole world is with you. If you are determined that you *have* to achieve something, God himself will come down from heaven and walk in step with you. And listen—even God is scared of humans, because He knows that a human being is actually a part of Him, and if he is seriously determined, he will build steps to heaven and, unseating God from his throne, bring Him down to earth; therefore it is better that He provides the strong-willed human assistance with all His heart. Therefore, my sister, start threatening and browbeating the Almighty above from now on. And maybe, because of you, we too shall get a chance to meet God." Malavika pretending to be annoyed, tried to hit Soumen, but ended up giggling uncontrollably.

"None of you should worry about funds because I am sitting ashore a sea of wealth. You just have to tell me and I will free it from the sea and divert its flow towards you. The famous painter Michael, who is also a very special friend of mine, has agreed to help us out with the activities envisaged by Ma. Both of us will not only help you with funds but with a lot of other things sourced from foreign soil, in order to nourish our earth-mother. We have been looted for centuries. This way we will at least be able to recover the interest accruing on that loot." Amlan's deep voice pleased everyone. He continued, "My friend and I have done a considerable amount of research into just what is it about India that wealthy Indians abroad and rich foreigners are so enamoured of? Family values? No. They are too rigid. Patriotism? No. To them this country and attire are both foreign. Yoga? Maybe, to an extent. But it has already been flogged quite a bit. Think further."

"Brother, our intelligence has stopped working," said everyone as they put up their hands in mock surrender, admitting defeat. The fun-loving, mischievous Amlan looked at everyone and said, "Okay, does that mean that I should give you the answer?" "Yes, yes dear, do stop this acting and just tell us the answer," chorused the rest of the six voices.

Amlan said, "Listen carefully then and don't mind my commercial slant. If I must use uncivil terminology, I would say that we trade in religion. As an author, I have closely observed that Indians there live their day to day lives like the English, but in their minds, they are unable to let go of their centuries-old religious rituals. Yogis, saints, storytellers and speakers from this country go abroad and earn in crores! Are they even trying to propagate spirituality in the real sense of the term? No, they teach them all kinds of hypocrisy, rituals, decoration of idols, extol the virtues of draping shawls carrying the names of gods on them, sell duplicate *rudraksh* beads at exorbitant prices by harping on their benefits. Commercial concerns take precedence and material things and rituals are thus propagated as the ways to attain salvation. This is cheating. So, are we fools? Can we not teach them the way to salvation in our dignified, educated and modern ways?

"Do you know that the people who burnt alive a dedicated and pure soul like Graham Staines and his two young sons, aged just ten and six, are now instigating Hindus by telling them that in the near future, Hindus will become a minority in this country and people practising foreign religions like Islam, Christianity will become the majority? Their argument is that since these 'other' religions do not allow their practitioners to adopt birth control, their numbers are increasing, and Hindus are progressively becoming a minority. According to them, while educated Hindus were opting for only one or two children, people from other religions had eight to ten. When countered with the question of whether they are aware of the fact that for seventy per cent of Hindus who are poor, sexual intercourse is the only source of entertainment and that for them an additional pair of hands in the family means an additional earning member, they stared angrily at the person who raised the question, with eyes like those of a forest owl that had wandered into the city and was dazzled by the afternoon sun. Once when Michael had intervened, saying, 'If you are willing to listen to me, I can prove to you with figures that these minorities will not be able to become a majority even in the next hundred years,' they had pushed him aside and said, '*Arey hat*! Get lost, you foreigner! You too are a Christian! Why are you so bothered about our religion then?' I intervened and tried explaining to them that Michael was more Indian and more Hindu than they were and that he was not interested in propagating Christianity but was trying to correct their thinking, but Michael cut me short saying, 'Amlan, don't waste your time. You can wake someone who is asleep but not one who is sleeping even when he is awake. Leave these people to themselves and continue towards accomplishing your aims.'

"Ma had once told me: 'Amlan, I am Muslim, Christian, Parsi, Sikh, Buddhist and everything all at once, because without Christ my empathy, without Buddha my compassion and without Nanak my sacrifice is not complete. Then why should I remove any one of them from within and impoverish myself? My teacher's first name was Gangabaksh and this is the miracle of the composite *Ganga-Jamuni* culture to which we belong. Baksh originates from Persian! And then the Ganga! And here they have become complementary to each other. Just think, if I remove Rahim, Raskhan, Kabir, Jayasi, Nanak and so many others like them from my life, what will be left with me? They are the ones who protect me day and night; when I stagger, they provide support; when I fall down, they help me to get up; whenever pride and anger find their way inside me, they help me shake them off. Without these gurus I would be in the same position as Karna without his protective armour and earrings, his *kavach-kundal*. I am sharing all this with you to make you understand that life is about bringing together, not about separating or breaking apart. If you have to leave anything, let it be pride, arrogance and greed; and if you have to add, add love, devotion, respect and humility. Always remember that love adds and brings together, pride leads to removal and separation. Amlan, the philosophical core of Hinduism is its flexibility, spirit of accommodativeness and equal respect for all religions; that is why there is no scope in it for dogma or orthodoxy. And I do not really believe in any religion, but in two special 'isms': humanitarianism and altruism. And I am so blessed with these two that all else follows automatically.'

"Therefore, my Saptarshi Mandal friends, please don't worry. We will neither cheat nor fool anyone. But when it comes to those fools who do not know or believe that a Hindu is born a Hindu and does not need to be initiated to accept Hinduism, we will neither attempt to impart deep knowledge to such knowledgeable fools nor try to make them understand or change their perspective.

We will chant a few mantras and sprinkle Ganga water on them to purify them of their foreignness and get them to donate hundreds of pounds for the Trust." Digressing midway, Amlan suddenly asked, "Ananya! Weren't you a senior functionary at institutions like the UNICEF, WHO and Red Cross at one point of time? Right, then you please arrange for medicines, nutritious food and drinks, quilts, woollen clothes and grants from them for Manjulika and Malavika. You will be able to, won't you?"

"Of course, I will," chirped Ananya. "My close friend Marianne is currently heading the WHO head-office in Geneva. I will approach her directly. I will also request Stuti, who works with the World Bank, to work out some form of assistance which is not riddled by terms and conditions from its Asian Division. Only funds, no rotten grains or useless items. If I train my guns on a lion, I shall at least be able to kill a jackal. Even a jackal would do."

Amlan continued where he had left off. "Lavanya Ma has defined secular not as 'unengaged with any religion' but as 'proportional to every religion'; which is why I shall not overlook Muslim and Christian organisations and shall speak to them in the language they understand. I shall appeal for funds with the plea that if they want to protect and promote their religion, then they should join hands with us. We shall also tell them that we are willing to work towards propagating their religion with all sincerity. Since our team shall help people following all religions without discrimination, we shall easily be able to identify and list those belonging to other religions and give their photos and names to satisfy these groups. Please do not think of this as any kind of illicit jugglery, because even Lord Krishna had to resort to selfish compromises to establish his principles. I promise all of you that since I will not be here and would not be able to put in my share of physical labour, I shall be completely mentally involved with Ma's work. However, communicating from London is quite easy nowadays; therefore, whenever you convene any kind of formal discussion, you will find me present," Amlan said in conclusion, and then fell silent. Amidst the applause of other members, Soumen gently placed his hand on Amlan's shoulder as if thanking him and looked at Malavika.

"Oh Dada!" exclaimed Malavika as she came forward like an overflowing cloud and showered her love on Soumen and Amlan. Her exultant and insouciant voice seemed loud enough to reach the skies. So it was definitely loud enough to rupture ear-drums. Manjulika whispered in her ears, "Malavika, *ektu aaste*—speak softly, please!" As soon as she heard Manjulika's words, the gas balloon of Malavika's childish behaviour deflated, and she solemnly told Soumen, "Dada, order plentiful; I am going to eat a lot today."

The whole atmosphere was festive and fragrant, as if along with Kamadeva's five arrows of desire, spring had set in during autumn. The strings in everyone's heart started vibrating in tune with the *anhad nad*—the primordial sound of the cosmos and human consciousness. The future filled with apprehension was now suffused with the golden possibilities of success. All seven hearts felt blessed with one single thought—that if mere thoughts could lead them to experience such pure bliss, how much more blissful would it be when they actually started walking on the path shown by Lavanya Ma!

Within a few moments of Malavika's wish, varieties of dishes started appearing on the table. When she saw the diced papaya decorated with slices of lemon and the fresh fruit juice, Malavika shouted, "Dada! You can have all this healthy food yourself. We are here for the spicy stuff." Before she could finish her sentence, the waiters came in with dosa, idli, hot fritters made with brinjal and onion, and various other savouries. Squeals of delight and the sound of lips smacking was all that was heard for some time as everyone attacked the food with gusto. Amidst the expressions of delight and enjoyment, Ananya's sombre voice was heard saying, "Soumen-*da*, such extravagance! What was the need for all this? We could simply have had toast and tea. What a waste of money at this costly place."

In the past couple of days Soumen had taken on a new characteristic. Just as an efficient stenographer can understand what the employer means from the slightest of indications, Soumen too could gauge the direction of another's thought from the smallest hint. He had imbibed this quality as he had become observer as well as operator. As soon as he heard Ananya, he responded, "My dear sister, I am happy to see that you have become more sensible. But go through the bill when it comes, and you will see that the entire order has cost us less than what one would have paid for two pots of tea in a five-star restaurant. Firstly, this is a government institution and secondly, this is a place where intellectuals assemble for discussion and debate. Hence, it is natural for things to be more economical here."

Before Soumen could finish his justification, Anita the *yakshini*, looking at everyone through the thick lashes of her bright liquid eyes, started drawing attention to her own plate by humorously imitating street-vendors hawking their goods. When all of them turned to look at her plate, they burst out laughing. Anita's plate was heaped with fritters but instead of eating from her own plate, she proceeded to pretend to stuff her mouth with fritters from the serving plate. Seeing the expression on the six faces looking at her, Anita burst out laughing. And a fritter she was munching on got stuck in her throat and almost choked her, but she was unable to stop her laughter. Seeing her laughing and coughing and choking at the same time, Soumen shouted, "Anita, stop laughing, that's it, just stop!" Soumen's words had the effect of water dousing fire. Anita checked herself, sipped some water, and felt better.

Then she narrated the story behind this episode. "This was when I had gone to deliver the keynote address at a conference titled 'The Importance of Advertising' organised by the plastic industry. I witnessed a strange scene during the tea and snacks break. Whenever some tasty snack was served, people would fill their plates and hold it in one hand, and with the other, take some more from the plate on which the snacks were served. I kept observing these people. Some of them dealt in crores, but they couldn't tame their senses when it came to free food. I just thought of re-enacting that scene today to make you laugh, but almost choked to death in the process!" Anita's voice trembled slightly as she ended her story, but the rest burst out in laughter. Looking at them, she could make out that they had exchanged signals when she was talking and had decided to make her laugh in turn instead of letting her cry.

The scene there reminded one of Lavanyadevi's descriptions of Lord Krishna in the battle of Kurukshetra—grave, yet filled with lightheartedness. The seriousness of their attitude towards their work and the enthusiasm all around was such that people were ready to bring the entire mountain instead of *sanjeevani*, the life-restoring herb. The atmosphere was so full of positivity and creativity that for miles around there was no cloud of despair. The wellspring of love sparkled so bright that the sun would think it to be a reflection of its own self in a river.

The Saptarshi Mandal, as a harmonious body, was geared up like a long-distance runner ready to start the race and run towards the finishing point. The sound of a notification on Soumen's cell phone made him pick it up. It was an email alert. Soumen was flustered. Whose message was it? What was it about? He couldn't identify the sender. Soumen was wondering, drumming his fingers on the table, when Dhanu got up, a smile playing on his face, and putting a hand on Soumen's shoulder, said, "Soumen, please get up. I feel there is some special message awaiting us."

Everyone reached Soumen's studio apartment in Delhi together. They gathered around his laptop, all eyes fixed on the screen. Soumen logged in and opened his mailbox, and then clicked on the last mail he had received. Seeing the sender, his fingers and lips froze. He could only manage to whisper hoarsely, "Message from Ma!"

Seeing the anxiousness on the faces of those present, he immediately started reading it out aloud.

My dear soulmates,

Don't be shocked when you receive this letter of mine or waste your time trying to find out its origins. Like Arjuna, focus on the eye of the bird—locate yourself at the centre of your goal and try to understand what the letter is telling you. Do you know that behind every unsuccessful man is his confused mind, because he gets entangled in so many webs before reaching the core? As a result he forgets that his aim is to rise above the baser things in life and strive for higher ideals. So instead of you researching whether this letter was written in the past or whether I am keeping an eye on all of you from afar, pay attention to what the letter wants to say. For that, the first requirement is that you and I are on the same plane where what I say reaches you and what you have done reaches me. Since the letter is grounded in philosophy, concentration is imperative.

All of you know that you are each a bit different from others, but today also be aware that this is not because of the environment, nor because of your education. The only reason for this is that you have risen above your ego and have connected to the universe. A human being who rises above their own self and starts thinking about others connects effortlessly with all other creatures of the universe. This emotional connect leads the person to a still higher level of functioning wherein the heart is full of compassion. You may be aware of the slight distinction between compassion and pity. Pity is induced when we look at the sorry state of a person, whereas compassion is the zenith of sensitivity and empathy and pervades one naturally and wholly. Compassion connects us to strangers and to people unrelated to us and makes our hearts beat for them. When our personalities develop on these lines, our compassion extends to encompass their existence and becomes unbounded. When we reach that level, the Magician seated above initially taps the earthen pots that are our bodies to examine how well they have been baked. In the well-baked pots is implanted the sweet pain of sarve bhavantu sukhinah*—do good unto others. Since these well-baked pots have* *souls filled with compassion, they make this pain the goals of their lives.*

On this earth, pristine love, devotion and knowledge are scattered all around, but only those who are able to arrive at the conscious vision of understanding others' suffering can understand this. Human beings ordinarily move in three broad directions for their advancement—those of good deeds, knowledge and devotion. None of them is inferior in any way to the others, but devotion has that limitless strength which can liberate a person in a second. The journeys through good deeds and knowledge are lengthy, but a devotee's yearning can instil in him the knowledge of the Bhagvad Gita, in the midst of a Kurukshetra, in a moment. Complete surrender is implicit in devotion—that is why an Arjuna can become one with Krishna. Through devotion we reach the divine sublimity and that empowers us to become one with the Supreme Being who then leads us forward through his antaradesh, *his directions from within.*

I am certain that all of you have understood the three levels. You must have also understood that antaradesh *is the* advaita *stage, wherein the distinctions between* brahma, *the eternal, and* jeeva, *or living beings, is obliterated and there is no distinction left between the two. In Buddhism, the same idea is expounded through* app deepo bhava*—lighting the lamp of the inner self.*

Today I will reveal another secret to all of you. The Lavanya Ma whom you people venerate as a goddess with superhuman powers had only been able to go up to the second level. My emotions and love connected me to others, but it was not at the level of celestial consciousness—it was limited to rationality and to temporal knowledge, which is why even a small incident could hurt me so much. When I look back today, I am not certain whether it was my compassion or my pride which was hidden behind several curtains. This discussion is also necessary to exemplify if the rage, fury, and to a certain extent the detachment that was occasioned by the incident was also an expression of my 'pride'. To tell you the truth I am indebted to life for that stumble, because it led me to an awareness of the celestial consciousness, which in turn, made me realise that what I had, till then, believed to be consciousness was only the knowledge and intellect that I had accumulated over a period of time—it was not prudence and devotion. Today, I perceive this body which I have dedicated to that Sutradhar, *that celestial Puppeteer, as a* sakshi cheta, *a witness, and that brings me happiness which is beyond description.*

The reason I am sharing these thoughts with you is to make you aware. Comprehend in depth the subtle differences between conscience and intellect, pleasure and happiness, knowledge and education, means and goals. Viewed broadly, these dualities might appear to be one and the same, but their final manifestations are vastly different. Only one among each of these pairs is ordinary, the other is extraordinary. That is why you must use your sharp vision to see through the spurious and choose shreya *over* preya*—what is beneficial in the long term over what is short-term, superficial enjoyment—and move towards excellence. I will not discuss in detail the difference between* shreya *and* preya *here again, as I have already discussed this with you at length, in the context of the dialogue between Yama and Nachiketa in the Nachiketa episode in the* Kathopnishad. *If you remember, this was in Uttarkashi, when Malavika had asked me what immortality means.*

With best wishes,
Lavanya.

P.S. I have written this letter in brief aphoristic formulations, which is why you may feel it to be abstract and incomprehensible at times. But I firmly believe that like the annotations of these aphorisms, you too will be able to create your own commentary from these sources.

The letter had been read in one breath, and though it was over, everyone—the reader as well as the listeners—was stunned. All of them were traversing the realms of their inner beings in the quest for meanings of the words they had just encountered, words which seemed lofty and divine, but whose gravity seemed to be challenging their intellect and reason. The words of Lavanya Ma kept coming back to them: "This trouble is inevitable during the first phase of the journey and to keep pressing ahead is the only way one can be free from it. If one can work one's way up fearlessly, resolutely and with absolute commitment, then the flag of success will surely flutter at the summit; else all pursuits will get stuck in the pits of greed, desire and illusion that one encounters along the way." Simultaneously, her words of blessing, "*Vijayi bhava*—Be victorious" also flashed through their minds and seemed to be asking why, at this auspicious moment of commencing on this expedition, were the hearts of the warriors filled with doubts and worries? Wasn't this letter from Ma which had arrived riding on the rising sun giving us all that familiar feeling of blessed protection, that same wall, roof and pillar of strength which we were deprived of after she left us?

Numerous entangled thoughts like these, struggling for expression in their minds, disconcerted them on the one hand, and on the other, also filled them with a strange excitement. They all seemed to intermittently have this feeling that Ma is somewhere very near and that every small component of nature present around them—the leaves swaying in the breeze, the blooming flowers, the burbling water, the love surging in their hearts—all are articulations of her presence.

It was an unusual and intense atmosphere that had been created. The faces were impassive but the eyes eloquent. And the lips held tight to silence, as if they had been forced shut. A 'living-deadness' covered the seven souls from head to toe. The childlike excitement from moments ago was gradually pinioned by the graveness of maturity. Time and again the question—What was Ma trying to say through this letter?—kept rippling across their hearts. Is Ma worried about their limited understanding of the world and trying to advise them through these words of wisdom? Or is she, like the nervous mother of a child taking its first steps, holding their hand so that they do not stumble and fall? Or had she intuitively divined that her *manas-santaan*, the children of her mind, were about to begin the battle of their faith and duty? Had she sent the letter as her words of blessing to encourage them?

Though only a short period of time had passed, the stillness occasioned by chaos and churning of emotions seemed to stretch for ages. Just then, Amlan's deep velvety voice could be heard giving voice to the stillness that had enveloped them: "My dear brothers and sisters, why are you all sitting paralysed on this occasion of joyous celebration? Stand up, dance, sing, play the cymbals and beat the drums! Oh, we are truly the greatest of fools who can't seem to understand the simple fact that someone is effortlessly transforming our 'thoughts' into 'beliefs'. Friends! This letter is a magic box that has come to tell us that we have all chosen the right path and that we will succeed in our goals for sure. Considering these words of blessing from Ma as our capital we should invest ourselves in our respective efforts with twice the enthusiasm. We should also pray to God that Ma keeps interrupting us in this manner so as to guide us. I might not be a man of rituals, but I am a surely a man of faith, and I do believe that there is a special power somewhere in this universe which can, unseen to all, change the course of a person's life in whichever way it chooses to. Let me give you my own example. The maverick that I was, did I ever think that I would become so deeply involved in Ma's spiritual endeavours, and that too, without any conscious effort on my part? The reality of the situation today is that I, who until yesterday saw himself as a sophisticated gentleman, am today transformed into one of the hill-folk. And not just that, I am keen to immerse myself into and become a part of the rivers, streams and soil here. Who, after all, made this magic happen? No doubt it was Lavanya Ma!"

As soon as Amlan completed his little speech, four of those seated there got up, stood erect and holding their right hands to their foreheads in a smart salute started marching in step, singing, "*Kadam kadam badhaye ja, khushi ke geet gaye ja*—Step by step we move ahead, singing songs of joy." This change in scene gladdened the hearts of Amlan, Dhanu and Soumen, who started cheering for the marching women. In the fraction of a second the tentativeness in the air vanished and was replaced with the silky shine of cheerfulness and laughter which was reflected on the faces of all those present.

Sensing the need of the hour, Soumen once again took charge of the situation and, aware of the impatience and restless eagerness of the reinvigorated souls, he started addressing them individually. He first spoke to Ananya and Dhanu: "Ananya, you and Dhanu stop over at Switzerland on your way to America and Vancouver. If you fly from Delhi, the capital city, you will have more options to choose from for your air-journey; you can select whichever flight is most convenient for you."

Then, keeping in mind the distance between America and London, Soumen directed Amlan to take the first flight to London where, in addition to reading and writing, he should also carry forward Lavanya Ma's work. He should not just be thinking about saving money and sending it back here; rather, he should also try to make people there 'self-conscious'. Amlan should address the emptiness within people resulting from the disintegration of families, and try to fill it with his gentle love. If, even while espousing progressive values, his writing remained grounded in the genuineness of his feelings, it would act like a balm for those who have sustained deep wounds from society. It is quite possible that writings of this kind might not win him any awards, but when words written from a true heart help wounded hearts to heal, the satisfaction that would ensue would be greater than all rewards.

When Soumen had finished putting into words many similar stirring thoughts, the other members of the Saptarshi Mandal, who were listening to him with unwavering gaze and rapt attention, were rendered speechless. Was Soumen-*da* always this solemn, clear-sighted and thoughtful? Or has he now learnt to inhabit a body other than his own? Is this the reason why, nowadays, he often speaks in an exceptionally clear and well-thought manner that was the hallmark of Lavanyadevi's style of articulation?

Whatever may be the reason, one thing was certain—there was no option left for Soumen other than to submit. He had now become a traveller on '*prem gali ati saankri*—the narrow lanes of love', and the only way forward was '*sees utare bhuin dhare*—to relinquish all pride'. Was it because he had transcended the dualism between the physical world and the world of soul and spirit and obliterated the distance between them that one could see in him the reflection of Lavanyadevi?

"And, Manju, you can go directly to Bangladesh from here if it is convenient. Apart from the schools and colleges run by the Dhaka *rajbari*, you have to take your work on eradication of addiction and rehabilitation of addicts to the villages and countryside, and work towards the betterment of the condition of poor women. While the inflow of foreign currency has led to the development of the urban regions of Bangladesh, there are still large numbers of impoverished people who populate the countryside, living in as much hardship as in any other developing country. Epidemics caused due to adversities also break out every now and then, wreaking havoc on these rural poor. Request your mentors in Dhaka for help, form an army of people dedicated to the cause you are serving and do your utmost so that your work sounds the clarion call in all directions of the diverse initiatives that you will carry forward. I have complete faith that like a brave commander you will carry Lavanya Ma's work towards its accomplishment, and in the process, you will also carry forward her name, fame and glory, which will resound from the earth to the sky in Bangladesh as well. The flight to Bangladesh will take off in two hours; all the necessary travel documents will be handed over to you at the airport. Get ready and start immediately towards your destination."

Soumen's endorsement of her capabilities lit up Manjulika's countenance, slightly reticent till then, with the sunshine of hope.

His words energised her like an electric current that shot through her body. Every line on her face seemed gently beholden, as if they had suddenly chanced upon a priceless mound of good fortune which was way beyond her wildest dreams and imagination. After hugging Anita, Ananya and Malavika, she touched the feet of Soumen, Amlan and Dhanu, and flew out of the door with such energy that one thought that she would not need a flight to Dhaka at all! She only needed to flap her arms like wings, and her energy would propel her across the skies to Bangladesh!

Everyone looked smilingly at each other on seeing the sudden exuberance of that otherwise modest, quiet and placid girl, and then turned their attention back to Soumen for further discussion.

"Malavika, you have already taken a leap into an ocean brimming with fire; just remember to proceed with caution. It is the grace of God and your good luck that the present police commissioner of Kolkata is an exceptionally honest, diligent and sensitive person. It is because of these good qualities that the wrong kind of influential people talk ill of him. 'This commissioner is an arrogant idiot; he doesn't know how to make the best use of such a high-ranking position. We won't ever let him be promoted, and that's a promise,' they say. And Malavika, such a situation is best suited to your interests, because if this commissioner gets a promotion and goes away to Delhi, he will be of little use to you. So, for the success of some of your big projects, you too should act selfish and pray that he doesn't get promoted to a higher position and posted away from here! There is another good news for you: the Thakur *rajbari* of Bhowanipore that belonged to Jyotirmoyi Didu has now been registered in the name of your Trust. When you had made this request to Ma, she, with her characteristic promptness, immediately forwarded your request to me and advised me to get it done as quickly as possible."

The shower of words from Soumen was to Malavika like drops of elixir, and his animated expression made her ecstatic.

Like a river that had sprung from a new consciousness, a new spirit and a new sense of joy, she submitted herself to the ocean that was Soumen. She felt proud of being the sister of this exceptional brother of hers. Just as monsoon showers create young streams which then find their way forward, Malavika, like an ebullient stream filled with the energy of Soumen's words, started off towards her destination.

Impressed by the enthusiasm of both the girls, all the people present clapped and were wishing them good luck when the voice of 'old' Soumen was heard again. "And you, Anita! Wrap up all your office work as quickly as you can and set off for the mountains, which will be the locus for your mission. Discuss everything with Guru-*ji* and the people there, and whatever work is doable at first, do it with everything you have. If you are able to bring the first work that you undertake to a close with proficiency, then the enthusiasm for the next work will not just be doubled, it will be multiplied many times over. Immerse your 'haste' in the Alakananda, offer the waters of the river with your cupped palms to Swami Ramteertha, and seek from him assiduity, dedication and submission. If your intelligence, capacity for hard work, pace, thoughts and wisdom can all come together to be in a state of peaceful coexistence, then the highest peaks of the Himalayas will be at your feet. This maxim is validated from experience.

"And what about me? I need to think about myself. Indolent as I am, will I actually do something or just keep lecturing and talking to you all? Let me for the moment say that I will think about it, but till the time that I am not doing anything, I shall be at your service. I will be your subordinate and obey every order that you give. You can all ask me to perform any role—that of a watchman, cleaner, attendant, bank manager, executive, anything—whenever you like. You will always find me at your service, twenty-four hours a day, every day. Yes, I do have some expectation from you people too. Just as Lavanya Ma kept track of the activities of all her centres every day, you people too should keep me updated with your day-to-day activities over our daily cup of evening tea." After giving all these instructions, Commander Soumen asked, military style, "*Koi shaq?*—Any doubts?"

All of them shouted back in one voice, "Yes! Yes! A whole lot of doubts!" and clamoured towards Soumen like iron filings towards a magnet.

The swift river of time hadn't flowed too far when detailed news came in from Manjulika in her letter from Bangladesh.

Friends,

Details about the Trust, Aalo and the school will follow; but first listen to this news. As soon as I returned from the village adjacent Rani Ma's Bridge, I was greeted by the sight of a fat envelope waiting for me, and as soon as I touched it, I was filled with a strange thrilling sensation which filtered down to the last pore of my body.

Yes, you are right. That envelope was indeed from Ma. Do you know where it was found? On the very same shelf of the same storeroom where Prabhavati Nani's small red ledger was discovered! Are you now wondering how I got there? Well, that is a slightly longish story, but one well worth sharing and so here it goes.

As soon as my taxi reached the gates of the magnificent Roychoudhury rajbari, *I was taken in by the sight of the huge lake in front filled with lotus blooms—a treat for the eyes. We Bengalis are so fish-tempered, aren't we? Well, I too was strongly tempted to jump into that clean, tranquil lake right away, but remembering the seriousness of the task at hand, I put it off for another time. I first went to the school area and signed the Trust documents. When I learnt that a group of teachers was going to the nearby village, I also went along with them.*

Our carriages were moving along the rough broken roads. The rainy season had just come to an end and the green countryside of Bangladesh seemed even greener. The green fronds of coconut, date and palm trees rustled softly as they swayed in the wind; the smell of the pale green grass and wet earth were intoxicating to my heart and soul. Just then, two divine beauties appeared out of nowhere, caught hold of my hands and started moving so fast in the opposite direction that it seemed as if they were flying. They both jumped into a pond with me and I too started swimming along with them, just like mermaids. An unfamiliar fragrance emanated from the two which reminded me a little of the fragrance of the hari champa *flower. It is impossible for me to even attempt to describe the beauty of those two fairylike belles. Hypnotised, I was ready to renounce everything—body, soul, wealth—they only had to ask. One of them had a body tinged with gold, and the other, silver. Their smiles were so alluring that I could not take my eyes off them. When they caught me staring at them unblinking, they both started giggling, and taking me by the hand, reached the* rajbari *in no time. Within minutes, they had made me so familiar with every nook and corner of the* rajbari *that I started believing I was born there. After walking through the outer bounds of the palace—starting with the* naubatkhana *near the outer gate where music was played, followed by the drawing room, armour room and printing room—they walked me through the galleries, courtyards, doorways and rooms of the palace interiors, and then we entered the ladies' quarters. The golden mermaid pushed gently at a corner wall, and there appeared as if by magic a capacious store-room. She walked into the room and picking up a large blue envelope from the shelf, handed it to me. The moment I held the envelope in my hands and raised my eyes to look at her, there was nothing—no mermaids, no envelope. The sudden jerk with which the carriage stopped told us that we had reached home, and I saw Aalo standing at the door holding the same blue envelope that I had held in my hand just moments before...I learnt that she had found it today while cleaning the house. Believe me, when I beheld that envelope, I couldn't garner the courage to ask Aalo where she had found it. Soumen-da! At certain points in our lives, we avoid seeking answers to questions that could break our illusions. Perhaps for the same reason, I too let this question remain unasked, because I am sure that none of the answers would have satisfied me.*

By the way, I am mailing you the letter in the blue envelope as it is.

Dear Manju,

Since you are my mind-child and have come up through a life full of struggles, my expectations from you are the greatest. You have not just read and heard about the sting of poverty, about honour and dishonour and about various forms of oppression, but lived them as well. So I request this Manjulika, who is standing on the soil of Bangladesh and upholding the motto 'Ekla cholo re—*Walk alone', to journey through those mountains of sorrow which are invisible to ordinary eyes, and which require more empathetic eyes like those of Surdas.*

You are all aware that I am in favour of an approach to issues which is relative not just to the era or period but also to the country, and it has always been the people grappling with issues at the ground level who have impressed me most. When Prof. Muhammad Yunus's micro-banking scheme had startled the entire global community with its originality, I had sent a team of volunteers from the Muslim Mahila Kendra to Bangladesh to gain knowledge and training about its working. The Grameen Bank scheme is successful today not just in Bangladesh and India, but it has hoisted the flag of its success abroad by creating a revolution of sorts even in New York in America, which is generally considered to be a leader among the existing world economies. It is women who are the focus of this scheme and loans are given keeping them in mind. One can participate in the scheme with just a rupee to start off and can even take loans against household utensils. The simple principle behind its operation was that giving loans to women ensured that the money would be spent on the welfare of the entire family, and also ensured security for the bank. Professor Yunus's vision and planning was unprecedentedly successful.

Meet him at the earliest so that you are acquainted with the entire process, establish your centres in every corner of the country and send across a team of volunteers from your centres for training. Since, despite his social commitments, he runs the project as a commercial enterprise, your volunteers will have to pay the requisite fees for their training. Knowledge of this innovative banking scheme will help not just you but all those who have chosen to eschew the highway of comforts in order to travel down the narrow lane of social service which is full of pebbles and stones.

There is no point in holding on to the glamour and glitter of the Roychoudhury rajbari *in Dhaka. Sell off every single item in that palatial property—the Italian marble, the huge Czechoslovakian chandeliers, the Persian carpets, the flooring made of walnut, mahogany wood and Burma teak, the winding wooden staircases and innumerable pieces of furniture, the gold-plated taps and showers, the pure-gold cutlery, the sofas and mattresses from Paris stuffed with bird feather, the frilled velvet curtains, the huge Belgian glass mirrors and the countless other useless articles of ostentation to all those foreigners who are crazy about 'heritage' and run those auctioneering companies abroad—and invest the money earned from their sale into the centres in Bangladesh. My maternal grandfather had willed the palace to Ma and Aniruddha Mama, and Mama had gifted his share in the palace to me; therefore, you can use the entire palace for your social work if you want to. You could also think of handing over the entire building, including the beautiful lotus pond, to the experienced team of do-gooders who are efficiently running my grandmother's educational centres and taking them to new heights. The sixty enormous rooms in the palace would be equal to 150 modern rooms today; and then there are those vast courtyards and hallways where elephants could roam with ease. If you keep alive this careful diligence of yours, you can think in terms of extending the boundary of the palace so as to encompass the entire world.*

Manju, you are the one who has spent the maximum amount of time with me, and you can, therefore, understand what I am thinking about even without my having said anything. Rise then and plant your feet in the battleground of Lanka as immovably as Angad, and blow the conch to declare the war against evil. And henceforth, you will instruct yourself about the next step that you need to take as now onwards you will move from the state of self-instruction to achieve the state of self-order. Remember one thing though—in your passion to make the soil of Bangladesh fertile, do not forget your own soil. Apart from repaying the debt to Priyamvada-ji, there is a lot of work that remains to be done in the southern part of the country; therefore, after initiating the work in Bangladesh, hand over responsibility to the trained teams there and take refuge with Priyamvada-ji. And in any case, the code of ethics demands that every psychiatrist should, for a specified period of time, be under the treatment of another psychiatrist; so, in order to improve and refine your work, keep meeting Priyamvada-ji occasionally and benefit from her training.

Good luck, Lavanya.

Soumen-da,

As our 'definitive centre', please forward this letter and the attached plan for the multipurpose complex to the members of the Saptarshi Mandal. I have also appended the phone numbers and emails of all the soldiers of the Yuva Aazad Fauj. They are ready to help anyone. Please let everyone know that they are willing to help anyone who needs their assistance.

I am planning to leave for Chennai today. I will be unable to keep in touch for a few days as I will be travelling and busy with my work. Please don't mind. I will contact you and enquire about your well-being as soon I reach my next destination.

Till then,

Yours, Manju.

Soumen looked up to the sky with his large 'Bengali eyes' and smiled. Seeing him immediately close his eyes one felt that in the pure and tranquil state in which he pulled down the curtain of his long-lashed eyelids to please his 'beloved', his devotion had reached the stage where, having done away with illusion, he could envision the sight of his 'beloved' reclining in the limitless sky. Was it possible that in spite of being only the 'postmaster' for the instructions of that immeasurable infinite, the Supreme Power would aid him in finding his own salvation? Is it true that even if one simply lives his life with utmost honesty, he will be considered a worshipper of the Supreme Father? Soumen had never consciously done any good deed either through his body or through his senses; then through whose good deeds was he able to flourish and reach the state of ecstasy that he now experienced? How was it that every part and every pore of his body was quivering with excitement? Perhaps it was an extension of the compassion of the compassionate which when it falls on an unnamed, thick leaf in Shantiniketan, makes it soft and velvety, and the poet of the world, Rabindranath Tagore, on seeing this nameless leaf, names it *banpulak*—the happiness of the forest.

Soumen kept thinking: if Ma is giving me so much without my having done anything, if I were to apply myself to some specific work, I would surely achieve this feeling of boundless ecstasy quite easily.

Soumen did not have to puzzle long over these thoughts. The ever-alert sentry within him immediately ordered, "Let go of your greed and immerse yourself wholly in your role. If the president of this country decides to take part in *kar-sewa* to accumulate good deeds for his future, who will look after the country? His service, devotion, good deeds and everything else is to run the country and nothing else. Soumen, throw these foolish thoughts out of your mind and look ahead to the future. Wake up and look around yourself—someone might be waiting for your assistance."

Soumen got up with a start. As soon as he looked at his laptop, he saw two notifications flashing on the screen. At the click of the mouse, a message came up on the screen: *"Hi Soumen-da! What's up? Guess what? I am in Switzerland, and have achieved a lot. Will mail you later in detail. Ananya."*

Having gone through this brief mail from Ananya, Soumen involuntarily clicked the mouse again, and this time it was a mail from Manju.

Soumen-da, Pranam.

I have done what was required in Bangladesh and I am now in Yercaud. As instructed by Priyamvada-ji, I am trying to open a de-addiction centre here. Ninety per cent of the men below the poverty line here are addicts; therefore, the family as an institution is gradually getting destroyed. The government had allotted Priyamvada-ji an old palace down in the valley here for the purpose. It is there that I am going to open Ma's first de-addiction centre. The local women here have promised me their support. Very soon we are also going to start a Grameen Bank. Right now, everything seems to be going fine. If there are any issues later, I will trouble you and the members of the Mandal with my queries. Only this much for now because there is very little time to write. Nowadays, those words that Ma used to repeat are always with me: 'Time is flying! Run! Catch it! Catch it and run along with it!' It is true that time travels at great speed and it is well-nigh impossible to try and catch up with it, but we have to try. So, I take your leave.

Yours, Manju.

Soumen looked around his studio-apartment. He saw that the walls, roof, pillars were all gradually melting, obliterating boundaries and stretching into the infinite. He blinked his eyes repeatedly and palmed them, and then he held his bowed head with both hands as he sat at his table. Soumen had no idea when he left the table and went and lay down on his bed.

The next day, he went about his daily routine semi-consciously like a machine and eventually ended up at Anita's office. Having instructed the people there to send his letter to Kedarnath, he next gave a set of instructions to the lawyer of Lavanya Trust who was stationed at the Delhi office, after which he returned home late at night and slept. He slept a deep and restful sleep, and it was well past afternoon when he woke up the next day. Seeing the clock, he exclaimed, "Oh God! It is 3 pm!" He got up, and helping himself to a cup of black coffee from the percolator, started looking at the mails he had received over the last two days.

The mails from Malavika, Manju and Anita were daily reports, but Ananya's mail was unevenly written and more like a descriptive eye-witness account.

Soumen-da,

I curbed my craving for beauty and my desire to see the beautiful valleys of Jungfrau and Titlis in Switzerland, and called Marianne from Geneva airport itself. As I had expected, she very lovingly said, 'Ananya! Why don't you both come straight to my office? We can have lunch together.' Marianne is presently the chairperson of the World Health Organization. Apart from the fact that we were classmates at Princeton, we were also close friends. So she is acquainted with Dhanu as well.

On the way to her office, we could see the offices of the Red Cross and the United Nations, among many others, which reminded me that apart from the hundreds of banks, some 250 well-known international organisations are also headquartered here. So the streets of Geneva are like a colourful mini map of the world where you can see people of all shapes and sizes in varieties of attire. When I saw the signboard of the WHO office next to a lake in the middle of a street full of flowers, I got so excited that I almost jumped off the taxi there and then. Only, Dhanu held my hand tightly and said, 'Ananya, what are you doing? Control yourself. I will never come between you and your work, but please don't let your enthusiasm make you forget that you are pregnant.' Although I did lower my head and bite my tongue in immediate regret, his advice was forgotten soon after.

Marianne, who was standing at the gate of her office with a bouquet in her hand and a lovely smile on her lips, welcomed us with a warm hug each and then took us straight to the buffet table. When I saw the finery there, inopportune words escaped my lips: Ya Allah! Is this the office of a social work organisation or the seven-star palace of a Hollywood star? Apart from some thirty or forty dishes, there was an assortment of salads, fruits, breads, vegetables, sprouts and desserts laid out, and labels proclaiming that everything was organic. I should have been delighted to see this fabulous spread and should have enjoyed a tasty and healthy meal. But instead, I was furious. 'Look at these shameless people,' I whispered into Dhanu's ear, 'here they are, extolling the virtues of organic food, while back in India they advocate the use of insecticides and foreign seeds. To top it, the World Bank has stopped subsidies to our farmers, driving them to suicide.'

Dhanu whispered back into my ear, 'Ananya! Remember that there is a time for everything. Focus on your aim and do only what is necessary to achieve it.' His levelheadedness brought me back to reality. I gave Marianne an outline of my plans and concluded by saying that if the WHO sanctioned a grant towards organic farming as well as forest and water conservation, it would greatly help in carrying our work forward. And if everything went according to plan, we would be in a position to send out regular supplies of purely organic fertilisers in the future. This would have a two-fold advantage: one, we would gain a foothold in the international market; two, it would help cultivate fertiliser-free products. Marianne, after having heard me out, assured me that she would shortly put the plan into effect. I impulsively embraced her out of happiness and then pressed Dhanu's hands in a silent gesture of thankfulness.

We started back for the airport without wasting any time. As soon as we got into the taxi, I started getting worked up about whether we would be able to board the flight to Washington. Seeing my childish impatience, Dhanu smiled his attractive smile and said, 'Anu, please don't get hyper. Everything is set.' What the hell is set, I wondered. 'What about our tickets to Washington? And our appointment at the World Bank office? How will we manage everything?' But once again I experienced first-hand the managerial capabilities of our reticent Dhanu when I found myself comfortably seated on the flight to Washington before too long.

As always, I was grateful to him for these wordless acts of thoughtful efficiency, but my gratitude peaked when I met Dhanu's first cousin Stuti at the World Bank. Stuti first congratulated me on my impending motherhood and then said, 'Ananya! Do you know how very fond of Dhanu I am since we were kids? All our own brothers and sisters were jealous of the deep bond of friendship that we shared. Ananya, my dear, be assured that the work you have come here for will get done.'

I looked at Stuti and Dhanu in amazement. On seeing my great surprise, Stuti laughed an indulgent laugh and unravelled the mystery—Dhanu had mailed her all the plans and proposals well in advance, and Stuti and her colleagues had already scrutinised our documents closely. Their responses were encouraging, and she felt that they would very soon grant us substantial funding.

As we were coming out, I hit Dhanu fondly on the back and said, 'When you had already ensured that the work was done, then why did you bring me to Washington?' Like a true companion in heart and soul, he drew me closer and said, 'Ananya, firstly, Washington is on the way to New York; secondly, how can I take credit for your work? I am just the clerk who forwarded my owner's documents to the people concerned. The achievement is yours and the pleasure accruing from it should be yours as well.' I bowed my head in gratitude to God for having gifted me with such a clear-hearted soul for a companion in this unpredictable uncertain world. I was indeed fortunate. Whose good deeds was I being rewarded for? 'Thank you, for making my life so wonderful, Dhanu,' I said, but couldn't say a word more as my voice broke and tears blurred my eyes.

Soumen immediately forwarded Ananya's message to the Saptarshis, and early next morning he was with Anita, taking care of the work that had piled up and also making arrangements for upcoming plans. From Delhi airport he proceeded straight to Yercaud to meet Manjulika.

When Soumen saw Manjulika at work, her head buried in piles of documents, he was so impressed by the total absorption and dedication with which she was doing her work that he would probably have stood for hours at the door, just watching her in silence, if a nurse had not come in to disturb her. It was also evident that she badly needed an assistant for her office work, but was probably saving some money by not hiring one.

Soumen held her by her shoulders as she got up, and blessed her by affectionately patting her head and shoulders; then he sat down in a chair in front of her. He requested the nurse to get him a cup of tea, took out his cheque-book and wrote her a hefty cheque. Manjulika, who was startled when she saw the amount on the cheque, tried to say something, but Soumen stopped her. After he had visited the entire centre with Manjulika, he asked for permission to leave. Manjulika said, "Dada, have your food before you leave." Soumen replied, "In the same way that the sage Durvasa and his followers felt miraculously full without having eaten a grain of what was left in Draupadi's cooking pot, the magic of your work has satiated both my mind and body. I do not want to limit that feeling by having food. Goodbye for now."

From Chennai, Soumen flew to Kolkata and upon landing, went straight to the Lavanya Centre in the Sonagachhi red-light area. On reaching the centre he came to know that Malavika had gone to meet the doctor with a HIV-infected child. He went around the centre in her absence and in a matter of minutes drew up an ambitious and comprehensive plan for the centre. When Malavika returned, Soumen responded to her surprised and affectionate, "*Arey*! You here, Dada?" with abundant blessings and motioned her to sit in the big chair. Putting in front of her the paper on which he had chalked out the entire plan, he said, "Execute it. Start working on it immediately. Here is the cheque."

As Malavika quickly went through what Soumen had jotted down on that piece of paper, her eyes widened with surprise. Clinics, schools, hospitals, a police station and so much more, all of which would transform the centre into a small township of sorts! She continued to ponder over the proposal for some time; then she said, "Dada! Where is the space for all this in these narrow lanes? And every house is occupied by a brothel-keeper! Are you planning to implement this fantastic plan here or in some other world?"

What Soumen told her left her speechless. "The whole of Sonagachhi, Rambagan and Darjipara form the outer fringes of

Debkumar Laha's estate. The lines of houses to your left are still owned by the Lahas. Debkumar Laha, in fits of amorousness and inebriation, housed many of the women with whom he had one-night liaisons in these houses, and even today, their house tax, electricity bill, corporate tax etc. are being paid by the Laha Trust. We can first request the inhabitants to vacate them, or if necessary, legally evacuate these houses, get them renovated, and then use them for the larger public good." Malavika got up and ruffled Soumen's hair affectionately, and said, "O Dada! Your brain is amazingly fertile! How are you able to think for ages in just a few moments? I feel dizzy face to face with such an intellect!" and holding her head in both hands, collapsed into her chair.

Soumen laughingly brushed aside all this praise and said, "Sister dear, stop this drama. Enough of your praise. Now get up from your chair, see how much of what I have proposed is feasible, and start implementing them at the earliest." Before Soumen could say anything else, he saw the Commissioner of Police at the door. Getting up he initially proffered his hand for a handshake but ended up embracing him. Soumen handed over all the papers to him without delay and said, "Tushar-*da*! Today onwards take care of this younger sister of yours and help her carry out her tasks. I have to leave immediately for New York. Though no one has actually asked me to be there, I am repeatedly getting the feeling that I should immediately go and meet Ananya. So, I am not meeting Amlan now, and proceeding straight to New York."

When Soumen reached Ananya and Dhanu's place in New York, he realised that his intuition was right—he was really needed there. Soumen's mail, in which he gives a detailed account of the developments that unfolded there, is testimony to the fact.

Friends,

When I reached Ananya and Dhanu's riverside house, I saw Dhanu's parents sitting worried, a hundred wrinkles of apprehension on their foreheads. Complaining about his son, Dhanu's father lamented, 'Dhananjay is very stubborn and headstrong and because of some stupid principles that he has, refuses to listen to anyone's advice. He is intent on handling his child's birth at his house on his own and has refused to call either a doctor or a trained midwife! Both of them are adamant about an unassisted home birth. Since the child is about to be born anytime, they are in that room containing a bathtub, accompanied by a sad looking nurse friend who is here to assist them. We are extremely concerned about Ananya as she also has high blood pressure, and that could be fatal. God alone knows what she is going through! In our entire lives we have never come across such highly educated fools!' The father hit his forehead a couple of times in exasperation. Dhanu's mother was praying continuously. She quickly got up and gently rubbed his forehead saying, 'The One above will take care of everything, dear. Please don't worry.' I was extremely angry with Ananya for the pitiable condition to which these two old people had been reduced, and I don't know what I would have done if she was present there. But for the moment, there was nothing to do but worry! If there was an instrument that measured anxiety, all three of us would have recorded the maximum readings during that wait. Each minute seemed a hundred years long. But we did not have to endure that terrible state for too long, as we soon heard the cry of the newborn.

On hearing the cry, Dhanu's parents both jumped up like wound-up toys and started clapping, 'Congrats Dhanu! Congrats Anu!' they shouted. 'Thanks Dad-Mom!" said two voices from the other room, one heavy, the other thin. I was so overwhelmed by the intensity of my emotions that forgetting all decorum I burst into the room. Dhanu, on seeing me enter, said, 'Hey Arjun! Look at your impatient Mama!' while Ananya, peeping out from behind a curtain, said, 'I was sure that you would come.'

This spontaneous utterance did not have any purpose, and it needed no answer. It was just proof of the profound connection that bound the two of us together. Relationships like these cannot not be explained or defined—they are miracles that transcend all imagination.

I stood on the other side of the curtain running my hand through Ananya's hair and caressing her forehead, and taking my newly born nephew in my arms from Dhanu's parents, I cuddled him for a while. When everything was taken care of, I told Dhanu, 'Brother! My nephew deserves a party from his Mama. Just give me a call when you have talked to Ananya. I'll take care of all the arrangements.'

In all this confusion, I had completely forgotten to greet Dhanu's parents. I touched their feet and sought their blessings and congratulated them on the birth of their grandson. I embraced Dhanu and expressed my love, respect, reverence and gratitude to him. The dark clouds of tension hovering around us a few minutes ago were dispelled by the spring-breeze of the arrival of the new member in the family, and all hearts and minds brimmed over with joy. Dhanu's mother fed us laddus, made some excellent saffron-flavoured tea for everyone and then got busy in preparing food for Ananya. The exhaustion of a day-long air-trip compounded by the killing tension I negotiated when I came in was now starting to make itself felt. I excused myself and went back to the hotel.

The story does not end here; the real fun was about to begin.

What stranger incident still remains to be recounted, the four Mandal members wondered. Is there something crazier than the obstinacy of these two to have an unassisted birth? But Soumen's statement was proved right as he narrated the events that followed.

Dhanu called me the next day and told me that the party would be held not at their residence but in a particular restaurant which, being far from the city was completely free of pollution. I was in a bit of a dilemma as he narrated his plans, but he assured me that he would reach the hotel with his parents in time. The question that was bothering me was: if his parents were coming with him, who would stay back at home with the baby? But thinking I might come across as being too finicky, I decided to remain silent.

When Dhanu entered the restaurant along with his family, I froze in surprise. I could neither take a step forward, nor utter even half a word of greeting. I stood still, wide-eyed, looking at Ananya, who had been so delicately brought up, carrying her three-day old baby in a kangaroo-like pouch strapped to her stomach. I somehow managed to overcome my shock and moved forward to welcome them in. Ananya saw me and came forward to touch my feet. Putting her baby's hand in mine she said, 'Soumen-da! Meet the chief guest for today—Arjun, the Great!' Before I could chide Ananya for bringing him here, I got another shock. 'Soumen-da! Your nephew was looking at the compartments of the train very curiously.' I was convinced that Ananya was joking. 'Compartment? Train? Ananya, what is this nonsense you are talking about? You surely didn't come here from the railway station; then how did Arjun see a train?' Ananya said, 'Dada, we don't own a car and it was not possible for us to cycle down to this place with a three-day old baby. So we took the train. And that is part of our plan to develop his resistance from an early age. We want him to grow up hale and hearty, not as a delicate darling; and I decided that today is as good a day as any to start off.'

When I looked disbelievingly at Dhanu's parents, they spread out their hands to indicate that they were helpless. I really did not know how to respond to what Ananya and Dhanu had said and done. I stood quietly for some time, flabbergasted, and then clearing my throat, could only say, 'I wanted to host this lunch for you at your place; there was no reason for you to take the trouble to come here. Just to think that you people have travelled by train and brought the baby along with you gives me a sinking feeling. I feel guilty for having planned this celebration. God forbid, if something happens to Arjun, I will never be able to forgive myself.'

Instead of looking radiantly happy at the festive occasion, my face was clouded by anxiety and deep creases of apprehension lined my forehead. Seeing me like that, Ananya, Dhanu and Dhanu's parents tried, affectionately, to dispel both my guilt and my fears, saying that I was getting unnecessarily worried. Ananya and Dhanu said they had adopted a plain and pure lifestyle eschewing every kind of luxury. Dhanu's parents consoled me by saying that they had full faith in their son and daughter-in-law, and promised me that my nephew would grow up to be a healthy and hardy individual with a robust personality. Ananya and Dhanu were supposed to accompany them to Vancouver shortly; till the time they were here, they would not pander to any of Ananya and Dhanu's whims and fads, and neither would they allow the baby to be mollycoddled. They would ensure that he grew up to be a balanced and diligent person like his father.

The furrows of concern on my face gradually eased as I heard all these assurances and I could finally manage a smile of gratitude. Ananya had gone inside to feed the child and as soon as she came out, eagerly started ordering some vegetables and herbs for herself. Interrupting her, I said, 'Wait! Let Dhanu's parents order first!' She immediately piped back, 'Soumen-da! Don't stop me. Don't forget that I have to eat for myself as well as for the guest-in-chief. And I'm sure you have no idea how much time it takes to chew raw vegetables, do you?'

Although everyone knew that Ananya was doing this just to dispel the heaviness that had set in, they all played along and said in one voice, 'Yes! Yes! Anu is right. Let's attack the food!'

I knew that Ananya was desperate for information about the status of the grants she had applied for at the WHO and World Bank. So I laughed and said, 'Ananya! Now for your gift!' And raising a glass of water to mimic the celebratory toast so common in the West, I said, 'The first toast is to Ananya. The WHO has approved her proposal. The latest news is that there have been no cuts and the money will shortly be dispatched to India. The second toast too is for Ananya. The World Bank has agreed to everything that Ananya has proposed. And the third toast is for Amlan. He and Michael have devoted themselves completely to their task and the results will show shortly. The two of them together have given lie to the saying one plus one equals eleven—one plus one now equals one hundred and eleven!'

Ananya got up, handed her child to its grandma and wiping tears of fulfilment with the back of her hand came and embraced me like a child clings to her father, holding me tighter than she ever had. Her head rested on my shoulder and her eyes were tightly shut.

I realised it was almost dusk and told everyone, 'Time for all of us, especially this rosogolla, *to go back home. I know that my overenthusiastic sister is intent on making him rough-tough and hardy-sturdy and god knows what else. But she too is a child and should be kept in check by the stick of her elders' experiences.'*

All of us laughed and got up and we were about to leave when I heard the sweet yet serious voice of Dhanu, 'Soumen-da! I too have a piece of good news to share. May I?' I smiled and slapped him on his back and said, 'Yes, of course! Please do. Just to hear you speak is good news to me. And coming from you, it is a fair indication that what you are about to share will be something big. We are all eager to know. Tell us what is it?'

'Soumen-da! I have been able to locate more than 100 acres of agricultural land around 180 kilometres from the coastal town of Mahabalipuram. We will buy the lands which the farmers there are willing to sell off, and as for the rest, we will train their owners about the advantages of organic farming without using any chemical fertilisers, about sustainable farming, water-harvesting, land security etc., so that they are able to double their profits and the soil also remains protected from depletion. And my parents are also considering saying goodbye to their five-decade-old home in Vancouver, and will most probably accompany us back to India.'

I was a bit apprehensive about this last bit and asked, 'Dhanu, they are used to all the comforts and amenities here. At this age, will they be able to adjust to a new life in India?'

It was not Dhanu but Dhanu's father who answered my question. 'Soumen! One big feature of the Canadian government is that it sends a hefty amount as pension to its senior citizens settled in any corner of the world. Dhanu's mother is anyway entitled to a regular pension as she was a government official, but even businesspeople like me are entitled to a pension because we too have watered the soil of this country with our earnings. I have invested in a huge farmland around a 100 kilometres from Vancouver in which I practise organic farming and grow fruits, flowers and vegetables. I have already given my daughter Sarita a lot of land and property in the city of Victoria where she is now settled, and when we go back to India I shall also will her the rest of my property there. As for the question of inconvenience, my son, let me tell you that our roots are in India and we came to Vancouver only after we grew into small trees. Our needs are so limited that there will be a lot left over from the pension that we will get. That is why Vijaya and I have decided to give Dhanu all the money that we have accumulated till date to help him start the venture he has planned. Soumen! What greater joy can there be that we will be back on our own soil with our whole family after so many decades? And to tell you the truth, all of this has come about because of that great soul, Lavanyadevi. Dhanu has been in America for twenty-seven years and almost become a true-blue American citizen. We really don't know whether we should thank our planets and stars or this daughter of ours, whose influence has brought about such radical changes in his personality.'

When I glanced appreciatively at Ananya, she spoke up, clear and truthful as always, 'No, no, excuse me. I cannot accept this false praise. The truth is that we were both walking together on the same path, and we ourselves do not know when this transformation occurred within us. All we wanted was to lead a life that was simple, straight and true—that was the only governing principle for every decision that we have taken. And come to think of it, it is not something extraordinary that we have done. We have merely done what we thought was right, according to our convenience. Believe me, we are neither great renunciates, nor are we particularly sagacious or truthful people. Yes, we do try not to do anything that is wrong, but how successful we are at that only time will tell. Right now we have only just begun.'

Ananya's humility won me over and I ran my fingers through her hair and blessed her. Her mother-in-law embraced her and patted her back. The whole atmosphere was loving and pure, and Arjun's shrieks and gurgles made it more so. I took him in my arms and said, 'Thank you, my nephew, thank you! It has just been a few days since you have come into the world and you have already started blessing us with all kinds of good news.'

When we came out of the restaurant, without paying any heed to their protests and entreaties, I packed all of them off in a taxi. After bidding them all goodbye, I came back to my hotel room and booted my laptop. The first news I read left me stunned: 'A gang involved in the trafficking of women had kidnapped a group of girls, including Malavika, from the Thakur rajbari.*' This terrible news left me cold with fear. I somehow managed to take control of myself, immediately booked myself into a flight back to India and started calling everyone who I thought could help.*

In the skies of Kolkata, the radiance of Soumen was as conspicuous as the moon on a full moon night or the sun at mid-day. But the only way to reduce the distance of a 1,000 miles was to create a commotion in all of Kolkata by knocking the doors of every emergency contact that came to mind, because the slightest delay could lead to the loss of lives of his sister as well as the other girls who had been kidnapped. He was trying to get connected through multiple lines, but today was the first time he felt like crying in helplessness. He had a feeling as though despite being a very good swimmer, he was drowning midstream and his hands and feet were not working. He looked around to see where he was sitting and hiding his face in his palms started crying.

New York airport that remained extremely busy and crowded at all times throughout the day was surprisingly deserted in the middle of the night. There was a strange silence which enveloped the place.

Soumen's face and hair were wet with tears when the unexpectedly soft feel of tissue-paper startled him. He saw that an elderly lady seated next to him was wiping his tears with motherly affection and telling him in a comforting voice in English, "Everything will be all right, my child. It's just a phase. Nothing is static in this world; please relax."

Normally, in these countries, nobody even smiles at another person, let alone comfort them or reach out to them. How, then, did this happen? Thinking along these lines when Soumen emerged from the world of his confounded emotions and turned to look in the direction of the voice that came from his left, there was no one there. Neither was any elderly lady to be seen anywhere in the vicinity. Dismissing the incident as a figment of his imagination, Soumen took out his cell phone which had been ringing for a long time. As soon as he put it to his ear, he heard the Police Commissioner's voice on the other side, "Soumen! Congratulations! We have nabbed the entire gang. Witnessing the courage with which Malavika conducted herself, I must say that your mothers must have 'ingested iron' and given birth to you all. What a brave girl! May God bless her!"

Though the time span between Malavika's kidnapping and the news of her rescue was not very long, Soumen's anxiety had reached extremely high levels. Time and again his hands were moving towards the left side of his chest and he was convinced that he might be experiencing a heart attack. In those moments, the affectionate touch of that unknown woman introduced him to a 'heavenly presence' that had given him solace, but after the Commissioner's call he immediately started feeling better. He regained his composure, and wiping his forehead with the arm of his wet shirt, entered the men's room. After washing his face and hands and coming back to his seat, he looked at his cell phone and found that Malavika had shared a post on Facebook—as if she had just gotten back from an enjoyable outing to some tourist spot. On seeing it, Soumen was suddenly filled with anger and the tension of the past few hours found its release in rebuke. "You feel like laughing and posting on social media while everyone around you is almost dead with apprehension. Malavika, who gave you the right to make us undergo so much pain while engaging with your tasks?" he asked her on video-call. Understanding his anxiety, Malavika burst out crying. The Commissioner, who was still with Malavika, intervened on her behalf. Asking her to give him the phone, he said, "Soumen! You should be ashamed of yourself. *Arey*! You should give your sister the title of Rani of Jhansi. It is only because of her that we were able to nab a whole gang which was involved in the trafficking of girls."

When he heard these words Soumen was filled with remorse for having vented his anger in such a manner. He requested the Commissioner to give the phone to Malavika, and when he did, Soumen held his ears in forgiveness and made a gesture of embracing her. This expression of affection led to a strange scene there. Tears streamed down Malavika's eyes even as there was a constant warm smile on her lips.

Thanking the Commissioner once more, Soumen told Malavika, "Now my flight is about to take off, but remember, as soon as I reach Kolkata, the first thing I am going to do is pull your ears so that you will never make that mistake again. Okay?" When Soumen saw Malavika nodding in agreement like a child, he laughed out loud and said, "Bye! See you soon," and went and took his seat in the aircraft.

Judging this to be a suitable occasion, Soumen immediately drafted an email to Malavika.

Dear Manu!

Today, after a long time, I feel like addressing you by your nickname. As we age and mature, we often feel like delving back into our childhoods, but we hesitate to behave as we once did because we are inhibited by the opinions of people around us. This was probably what happened between the two of us. You suddenly grew up and started taking up the challenges that came your way and handling them with great courage. I, in trying my level best to live up to the responsibility of the position that Didu had entrusted me with, strove and struggled with my promises to her and the responsibilities that followed in consequence. In such a situation, there was no corner left to listen to the footfalls of our childhood except in the seclusion of personal interaction, of which my salutation is a symbol.

Manu, believe me, the pace at which you are progressing in every direction has impressed everyone, including me. But the time has come when you must no longer just remain an influential star in your own right but become a planet which has many satellites and an orbit of its own. But whether you are a star or a planet, there is one eternal, ethical truth—that even though the ultimate aim is to rise above one's body, this journey is possible only through the body. The success of any venture is, therefore, contingent upon the safety of the body. If we are not careful about our bodies, which are like temples, we are also endangering the causative form in the tasks assigned by the Supreme Power. How, then, will we be able to reach our aims and goals?

Manu, the soul is capable of subsuming that vast and infinite power within the container that is the body; through the strength of our consciousness, and directed by that power, the soul leads one towards higher values. Our bodies become blessed when we think not about ourselves but about others, when our breath involuntarily chants the sarva mangal mantra. *When our soul, abundant with intellection and devotion, pulsates with an energy that makes the body execute revolutionary tasks, then we experience eternal bliss. Since at the root of all this lies the human* yoni, *which is our body, we should protect and preserve it keeping in mind the dictum* tvadiya vastu Govindam, tubhyameva samarpayet*—this entire universe is yours and nothing, including myself, is mine, and so Govinda, I submit to you. We are fully accountable for our bodies to the Supreme Soul. We have to use this covering that is our body, this* jheeni chadariya, *in such a manner that it is neither soiled nor destroyed. We have to complete all our worldly tasks and at the same time take precautions to keep this covering safe; otherwise, let alone being able to pay the value of the efforts of the Almighty Father, we will sink it in the debt of fleeting and trivial successes. You might remember that once Ma told us about the best aspect of Savitri. Putting forward numerous arguments to Lord Yama about non-self, self and the ultimate reality, Savitri had been able to wrest back Satyavan's soul on the grounds that she could not make use of* *the boons Lord Yama had blessed her with if the body of Satyavan, the causative form of the soul, was absent.*

If one's aim is to become a moral soul, then one should always keep in mind the fact that the form and attributes of the incorporeal, attribute-less, unknown and infinite are manifested in our human body, and this majestic consciousness seated within it is always engaged in efforts towards one's salvation. And only an unfragmented, unconflicted, firm and determined soul can induce the Supreme Being to reside in its core.

Manu, does this body belong to us? No. It is just an embodiment of that Supreme Being created for a specific time-frame. It is like a borrowed toy, which one will have to return at the stipulated time in the same condition in which it was borrowed. Courage lies in making it more beautiful with your good deeds, not in destroying it by inviting untimely death. Beautifying the body does not mean adorning it with delusional or self-centred elements but caring for it, so that it is successful in virtuous and moral actions. Consider this to be a gift of God and always move ahead watchfully, following the path of truth. This is both my wish and blessing.

These thoughts of mine are not the outpourings of a passionate moment, nor are they a reflection of my recent anxiety. I feel that Ma's soldiers need to be alert and insightful; otherwise our destiny will also turn out to be like that of momentary bubbles in the endlessness of time. As when ascending a cliff, even one small careless act is inexcusable—travellers on this path cannot afford pleasure, laziness and leisure. There is a saying by Chanakya: 'The supreme duty of human beings is to protect their bodies, because not only is it an identification of their being, but also the instrument for attaining knowledge about the Almighty.'

Manu, promise me that in future you will perform your actions with deliberation and without being negligent about yourself, and take forward the tasks of Lavanya Ma.

Good luck.

Your Dada.

As they went through Soumen's email, Malavika and the other members of the Mandal wondered whether Soumen had indeed mastered the art of entering another's body!

Once he was comfortably seated inside the aircraft, Soumen asked for a glass of water. Opening his laptop again, he saw there was a message from Amlan, "Soumen-*da*! Received Ma's letter just now. Forwarding it to you as I received it."

"Ma! So you've now started sending emails too?" exclaimed Soumen as he started reading Lavanyadevi's letter on the screen of his laptop. However, the succession of strange and miraculous incidents that had occurred throughout the day still occupied Soumen's mind. His body was exhausted by these thoughts, and the relaxation occasioned by the immense relief at the good news at the end of these tumultuous events induced a deep slumber. He struggled to keep his eyes open for a few minutes, but the body's condition outweighed his mind and he swiftly drifted off into a deep sleep.

It was only after six hours had elapsed since the flight departed from New York that Soumen woke up. He requested the flight attendant for a cup of coffee and immediately opened his laptop. Amlan had mailed him this letter from Ma along with his own responses; and Soumen, the 'definitive centre', on his part forwarded Amlan's mail to all members of the Saptarshi Mandal. As soon as Soumen opened the mail and saw Ma's salutation—*'Dear Amlan'*—his eyes lit up with sweet memories of Lavanyadevi, his face bloomed like a flower and the accomplishments of the Saptarshis made him feel contented. In a state of such happiness, he began reading Ma's letter.

Dear Amlan!

Blessings! Time is extremely precious; that is why, without wasting a moment of it, I come straight to the point and begin by making a request that you must mandatorily fulfil—please keep the ritualistic aspects of religion limited to the gain of material resources, as the consciousness of the soul has no relation to it. While these external attributes may help to understand that Supreme Consciousness, if our lives remain restricted to and revolve only around those attributes, then it will be like reflexive physical action, and will not lead to the development of our consciousness. If you want to earn money by exploiting the religious superstitions of fools and put it to use in good work, there is no harm in it, but if you also aim to make them understand religion in its proper perspective, then this entire planet will be blessed.

Today, the world is divided into many different sects and is fragmented. This situation is as painful as it is dangerous, and in such a situation, love is the only binding force that can integrate all these fragments. You are a famous author. You should make people understand, in simple ordinary words, that the soul of all religions is love. That which benefits people is religion; that which harms people is not religion. Religion functions by bringing people together and not by dividing them; the very basis of religion is love, and it does not have any room for hate. There is an interesting anecdote that comes to mind in this context, about the Sufi mystic Rabia of Basra. Her house used to be frequented by saints and mystics. One morning, a saint who wanted to discuss something about religion came to her house. Rabia got busy making arrangements for his food; he, in the meantime, took down the copy of the Holy Quran lying on the shelf and started reading. He had read just a few lines when he started screaming loudly, 'Rabia! Rabia!' Rabia rushed agitatedly to see what the matter was. On being asked, he told her in a perturbed voice, 'Rabia! Don't touch that Quran even by mistake; some evil soul has defiled it.' Observing her bewilderment, he added, 'The audacity of that scoundrel! He has struck off an entire phrase which asks believers to hate the devil.' Rabia bowed her head and replied hesitatingly, 'God! Please forgive me. I myself am that scoundrel, but what could have I done? How could I have lied to Allah Ta'ala? The fact is that at present I am incapable of even hating the devil.'

Amlan, temple and mosque, black and white, caste and creed, high and low—are all charades created by humans. The Almighty has instilled the same consciousness in all souls. This body of ours is just like a depository in which all good deeds are saved and from there, they are automatically transferred to the Almighty, who is like the Reserve Bank. Amlan, you know very well that as far as I am concerned, religion is just love and pure conduct. I hold that religion is not just about some rituals but a guide that helps one to maintain a correct conduct in life. For thousands of years, diverse streams of thought and gurus subscribing to them have defined religion in their own ways. Some have created thirty-three crore gods and goddesses; others have opposed idol worship altogether. Those who have created it and those who oppose it have both forgotten what believing in idol-worship or not believing in it actually means. What are these the symbols of? Have we not become ignorant armies of watchmen who police a ubiquitous ethereal consciousness called religion by imprisoning it behind narrow communitarian bars? Maybe, this is what led the famous philosopher Nietzsche to remark despairingly, 'God is dead'.

Amlan, I am apprehensive that being involved in the business of rituals, you too might get lost in its maze like my friend Kulkarni. Let me share his story with you.

I had stayed at Kulkarni's place when I was visiting Rome. Kulkarni was a staunch Hindutva ideologue and could barely endure my religious tolerance. He was frequently enraged by my views and would remark, 'I think you are Christian, Muslim, Sikh, Parsi—everything, except a Hindu.' Even after numerous deliberations and arguments, he would only get angrier with my assertions—that I have learnt this tolerance and flexibility from Hinduism. One day, we were visiting St. Peter's Basilica in Vatican City where, after having had a look at Pieta by Michelangelo, we were moving around from one room to another. We reached the room in which the tomb of St. Peter was placed. At the entrance was a sign which said that only those who wanted to pray should enter the room. Kulkarni blocked my path as I was about to enter the room saying, 'This is not for our people. Let's go and not waste our time.' Firmly but gently I removed his hand and said, 'Kulkarni, just give me a minute.' He kept glaring at me angrily and as soon as I came back, asked me in a harsh and sarcastic tone, 'So what did you pray for from your God, St. Peter?' To which I replied, 'I asked Lord Rama—Lord Rama, bestow some good sense on Kulkarni so that he may love everyone.'

'Really? And how did you find Lord Rama here?' he retorted heatedly.

'Why? Is Lord Rama not present here? But that is not what He told me!'

On hearing this, Kulkarni's face suddenly turned white. The profundity of this reply hit him hard and deep. But the zealot in him did not allow him to accept it gracefully. Unable to handle his discomfiture, he moved hurriedly towards the door; but I tugged gently at his shirt and told him softly, 'Slow, Kulkarni! Slow! Since you are younger to me in age, let me share with you an old saying. Once a stone enters a temple, it becomes a God, but what about us insolent human beings? We go to the temple every day, but remain stones forever. Kulkarni! Joy lies not in becoming a stone-hearted fanatic but in flowing like a burbling spring filled with love. Do test this truth sometime.' Poor Kulkarni! He did not know what to do and was unable to meet my eye.

Amlan, always keep in mind that when talking to people about rituals, you have to also convince them to think of rituals as the means to the attainment of something higher; if people mistake the means for the end, then this planet will become an assemblage of thorny cacti. I must tell you that such people do not for a moment hesitate to term their fanaticism as faith, eulogise it as dedication, and have no qualms about calling it bhakti, *devotion. But* bhakti *is characterised by fluidity and giving, and its spread is not contingent to any form. There is no existence of even a flower—only its fragrance, which is devoid of weight and pressure, can find a place for itself in the idea of* bhakti. *In its subtlest form,* bhakti *can only be experienced in gentleness, flexibility, inclusiveness, politeness and humility. It does not have a fixed form or concrete expression; it is completely formless. Amlan, the two illiterate women who made me understand the correct definition of religion are Lakshmi and Zahida: one a fanatic Hindu, the other a fanatic Muslim. I must acknowledge that their accurate description of what religion truly is weighed heavier than all the knowledge I had accumulated.*

Lakshmi, a mother of three daughters, was a young widow. Her husband died when she was very young, leaving behind a tin-roofed shack and all his debts. To provide for the next meal, she had to start working the very next day after her husband died. With one daughter latching on to her hand, another on her waist and a third in her womb, she worked in people's homes from dawn to dusk. Even after toiling so hard she could barely manage to survive, being able to provide her children food only once in two days. When I met her, her youngest daughter, brought up in such dire circumstances, was six years old. I came to know from Lakshmi how her relatives were intent on physically exploiting her, but were not bothered about her hunger. Her saree, which was in tatters, could not cover her skeletal frame. The three emaciated girls had only some rags covering their small bodies. Even after seeing all this, fool that I am, I could not stop myself from blurting out, 'What about the education of these girls?' I immediately felt very embarrassed for having asked such a question and decided to make some arrangements for their education.

We contacted quite a few charitable residential schools, but without any luck. Observing my concern and my resolve, my driver Frederic, a Christian, told me about a good convent school where destitute children were admitted, provided they belonged to or adopted the Christian faith. Even though he had told me that they would not budge from their position on religion, I tried my best to convince the nuns there in every way possible; but when they handed a copy of the written rules by which they were bound, I gave up. I despondently started walking back when I suddenly heard Lakshmi's determined voice from behind me saying, 'Jiji! Please stop. I have decided that I'm going to stay here with my children.'

I was shocked and stared at her in surprise. The words she uttered thereafter echoed in the air and enveloped the atmosphere: 'Jiji! Does the religion of the body have no meaning for us humans? To preserve and maintain this body—is it not a way to serve God? Please spare a thought for the fact that I can get everything here—work, respect, shelter, food, clothing, education and a good future for my children—just by exchanging the garb of one religion for another Is this not because of the infinite grace of the Almighty Father? Is my faith in the Almighty bound by and limited to just my body? Jiji, please leave behind the fog of this delusion to come out underneath the serene sky of faith and lend me support in my redemption.' Amlan, today Lakshmi and her three daughters are all well-educated and are actively engaged in social work. And the mother of five daughters, Zahida?

Zahida and her husband used to toil night and day to meet ends meet, but were still not able to feed their family of seven. Our centre had advised her about various methods of contraception, but citing religious reasons she refused to accept any of those. Later, when their situation deteriorated further, her husband had a vasectomy done clandestinely. And later, they both shifted to Mumbai thinking that the higher rates of daily wages in the city would enable them to earn more there. I put them in touch with a friend who lived there. However, when in spite of braving struggles and insults, the devout Zahida was unable to turn her fortune around, she registered herself as a surrogate mother with an accredited agency. To be honest, I did not like this development because I had a very grim impression of the act of renting one's womb for surrogacy in my mind. Does a religion which forbids the collection of monetary interest allow a woman to charge for her womb as a surrogate mother, I wondered. Finally, in a roundabout way, I broached this topic with Zahida. 'Zahida, is what you are doing not against the principles of your faith and religion?' Do you know what she said? 'Jiji! How should we define faith? And what does belief mean? Selling one's blood and kidneys, selling one's body—are these sanctioned by any faith? Then how does lighting up the hope of a progeny in a childless person's house become a sin? Jiji! You have always told me that if our actions are such that they do not harm anyone, that is religion. How then can my act of doing good for others make me a sinner?'

The only reason for recounting these incidents is to advise you to protect yourself and others from the fanaticism and dogmatism of religion. Like Lord Krishna, always be flexible enough to evaluate religion in the context of time and situation. No work which is commendable can ever be contrary to what any religion espouses. Your sensitivity and intellect are evident in your writings; hence I believe that when your educated mind dives into the epistemological depths of the sea of information on this issue, your discernment and good judgement—neer-ksheer vivek—*will help you separate the milk from water like a swan.*

Love and blessings,

Maua.

Reading Ma's letter at the same time that Soumen was reading it, Amlan found himself thinking, I might well be a writer, and may have won awards, but this message composed in Ma's simple vocabulary is as fine an example of artistic communicability as any. Conveying complex philosophical ideas and propositions simply and clearly, and being able to exemplify them through stories so that they become easy to follow is a difficult and subtle skill, isn't it? He spontaneously muttered aloud as an afterthought, "Ma, you are just you. There is no one else like you. You are indeed unique." And he bowed his head once more to Lavanyadevi in respect and with pride.

Among other messages Soumen had received was a "Hi" from Ananya. Dhanu then told Soumen that they would be shifting to Chennai the following week. Their parents would book the heavy luggage by cargo to Chennai once they departed. For now, they had decided to leave behind all the expensive and non-urgent items in their apartment. Dhanu's parents had advised him not to sell off the land and houses in America and Canada in haste. This would lead to financial losses; and if at any point of time they wanted to come back here because of any eventuality, it would be very difficult to buy everything again because of the inflation.

Soumen and all the other members of the Mandal were unanimous in their approval. He responded thus.

Dear Dhanu!

This is a very important suggestion from the elders. After five to seven years, if you finally start connecting with this soil and develop roots here, they feel that will be the right time for you to come up with a final decision on this. Dhanu, never forget that it is in those lands that you have grown from seed to tree. Although your cultural moorings and upbringing have been Indian, but your education, business, family, wife, child are all from your life in America. It is true that today your heart beats for India, but every aspect of your life—manners, behaviour, hygiene, a pollution-free environment, surroundings, consciousness towards health issues and many more such small details—have been fostered by the elements and endeavours of that place, and these are so much a part of your daily routine that you can't even consciously realise them or think of them as worth considering. The standards that you are accustomed to in terms of vehicles, roads, houses, electricity, water, food, doctors, hospitals, education—you will find many of these absent in India.

Don't get me wrong; we all have full faith in your decision and perseverance, but many people who have come here to stay in the past have gone back after being disappointed with the conditions here. We have no doubts about the sincerity of your resolution, but we should give due acknowledgement to the experience and advice of parents. Therefore, it is best to plan your trip according to their instructions.

All of us are eagerly waiting for you, especially for Arjun.

With love,

Soumen.

Days were not just passing; they were racing by. Just as little kids get excited when they see ice-cream, chocolate or toys and run to make a grab for them, the soldiers of Lavanya Army swooped down eagerly on their respective consigned areas of work. Each day, the setting sun would see them droop like sunflowers and they would exclaim, "Oh! The day has ended so quickly." At times it almost seemed as if they were competing amongst themselves, each vying with the others to prove themselves the most industrious and efficient, the most favourite and the dearest to Ma. But just then, as if to regulate their motivation and speed, Ananya received a letter from Lavanyadevi with a new set of directives.

Ananya, quivering with nervous excitement, did not know what to do as she asked Soumen, "Dada! Dada! Do I open this letter?" Soumen reassured and calmed her by saying, "*Arey*! Why are you so nervous? Open it quickly. You should be happy that Ma has blessed you too. Open it quickly and share it on mail." Ananya did just that. The letter addressed her by her nickname.

Dear Pakhi,

Lots of love and congratulations. Motherhood is the pinnacle of womanhood, and with the grace of God you have now experienced the fulfilment of being a woman. On this auspicious occasion, I want to brief you about a couple of things. You can consider these as my blessings or as the eccentricities of your Maua. Ananya, whatever knowledge I have acquired and amassed can be summed up in a single phrase—the middle path. I now strictly avoid all forms of fundamentalism and fanaticism, and it is unfortunate that these days, dangerous fundamentalisms exist in various forms and are affecting everyone. I fear that these might soon pervade the whole world like the breath of life itself.

Pakhi! Extremism may be towards any situation, thing or person, and a small domestic experience will suffice to explain how disastrous it can be. Your father Apurva was just a twenty-day-old infant when, in an attempt to make him hardy and strong, I lay him down on the green grass which was wet with dew, and that too when it was freezing cold and there was a strong wind. Many experienced women including my own mother tried to persuade me not to do this, but I was too much of an extremist in my thoughts. And who suffered as a result of it? Apurva. The poor child went down with double-pneumonia and he still carries the effects of the disease on his body—that is why he has to take Cortisone even when he has a mild cold. So Ananya, always remember that neither all old nor all new ways are either completely wrong or completely right. What is needed is the judiciousness to opt for the intelligent middle path, selecting the best of both. Never forget that each person is a product of their time and so may not like things from the past, which to that person might appear to be obsolete. And remember that science and rationalism is not useless chatter and its aim, like that of philosophy, is to search for the truth; therefore, to condemn all scientific and rational beliefs is exceedingly foolish.

Pakhi! Be it family, country or society, or be it ourselves, what is needed to manage all of these is a formula named balance. So, don't let the light of your experience be extinguished by the knowledge of books; strive to maintain a balance between both so as to be able to create something new which, in opposition to rigidity and extremism, is soft, sweet, admirable and spectacular. And always keep challenging the truth that you know and believe, because there is no ultimate truth as such and quite surprisingly, truth keeps changing with time. Even gods like Krishna and Rama defined the truth in accordance with the times they lived in. The quicker you free yourself from the illusion that it is only your truth which is true and that others' truths are lies, the sooner you shall be at peace. Even scientists have now started accepting subjective experiences, traditional prescriptions and natural remedies.

Pakhi! Cherish in the depths of your heart and in the most intimate corners of your mind the fact that flexibility in life is crucial to being able to keep moving forward and this is the greatest mantra to live a pleasant and contented life. Watch everything, listen to everyone, but proceed only after testing things in your own conscience. Don't believe anything that is said or read or heard while keeping your eyes and ears shut. If you keep your conscience awakened, sentient and alert, you will keep getting your answers straight. And it has now been proven that the principles of ancient philosophy and contemporary science are not contradictory; rather, they are complementary to each other.

Congratulations and blessings to both of you on the arrival of the newest member in your family. Special blessings to your sweetheart and life-partner, Dhanu. May you both vindicate the verses from the Rigveda—sangachhadwam sangvadadhwam *and always move in harmony and speak in one voice—thus making your life meaningful and beautiful. This is what I pray to the Lord for.*

Be blessed always,

Maua.

Having read the letter, the question that played uppermost in the minds of all members of the Mandal was: what was the reason for the increasingly personal tone of Ma's letters? Did they signal towards Ma's impending departure? Why did each word in all these letters read more and more like her last instructions to the person concerned? Filled with misgivings, they were discussing these signs among themselves when Manjulika called from Yercaud, "Soumen-*da*! Can we talk about these issues later? There is some very important news that I must share with all of you." Before Manjulika could say anything more, Malavika interrupted her, saying, "I too have some important news to share, but Manjulika is younger, so let us first listen to what she has to say."

What Manjulika then narrated to them over a group call was stupefying to an extent that everything seemed to have suddenly turned to stone and all those listening, wherever they were, frozen into statues. A single question went round and round in their minds: Is this really possible? Is innocent Manju narrating a witnessed truth or did some imposter hypnotise her to plant this incident in her mind which she, then, believed to be true?

"Soumen-*da*! Yesterday night, on returning to Yercaud, I saw that the people here had installed a statue of Ma at the centre as a tribute to her efforts. They had built it surreptitiously behind my back so as to surprise me. They made this mistake because they were completely unaware of Ma's opinion on this matter. Seeing the statue, I found myself in a dilemma about the right course of action. On the one hand there was deep reverence for her and single-minded devotion; on the other was Ma's injunction. Let me concede here that my love for the majestic and divinely beautiful statue made me slightly greedy, and I was searching for a line of argument to contest Ma's proscriptions and justify the installation of the statue. While I was caught thus in the web of these conflicting thoughts, I looked out of the window to take a peek at the statue, but being a new moon night, it was pitch dark and since it was past midnight, the lights at the centre had been switched off. The arduous journey and my agitated mental state had both exhausted me. So I thought I would talk to everyone in the morning and arrive at a decision through consensus. Dada, since childhood, I have a habit of bathing at night before sleeping. This has been a constant even when it is freezing cold; and on that day, I had all the more reason to take a bath since I had just made a long journey. But when I woke up in the morning, I realised that the goddess of sleep had compelled me to forgo my longstanding habit and taken me into her arms just as I was.

"I quickly stepped under the shower, even as my mind flitted between certainty and uncertainty in choosing between what was dear and what was right, when I heard someone pounding on the door. As I turned off the tap, I heard the fearful voices of many women from the centre, 'Didi! Didi! Please open the door! Please come and see what misfortune has taken place!' I was terrified, because in these three–four years here, I had never heard such agitation in their voices. I hurriedly pulled on clothes and came out, and they almost dragged me to the garden. The scene there was so unbelievable that I thought my eyes were playing tricks on me and it was just an illusion. Otherwise how could this have happened? But the truth was scattered all around and I could not turn my eyes away from it. All the faces there seemed to be asking the same question: who harboured such enmity against Ma that they did this to her statue? All the people looked deeply anguished, as if they had lost a young life in their own homes.

"At that point, piercing the inertia of collective bewilderment, was heard the loud voice of Nageshwar Reddy, chief artist and sculptor of Ma's statue. He said, 'Late last night I woke up to a knocking sound, but thinking it was just my fancy, I went back to sleep. I woke up again after a couple of hours, and the sound was now louder and clearly audible because of the silence around. I opened the window to try and make out the direction of the sound—it seemed to be coming from where the statue was. When I ran towards it, I could faintly discern the figure of a woman in the distance, striking the statue with a large hammer. This seemed so very improbable that I almost halted in my tracks, but when I reached the spot, I turned to stone myself. The statue was completely destroyed; its broken head was lying on one side. And there was no sign of any woman nearby. Had she suddenly been gobbled up by the land or swallowed by the sky? I kept staring in turns at the hammer and the ruined sculpture in utter shock and disbelief. After returning to my senses, I got people to look in every direction, but to no avail.'

"Soumen-*da*, after seeing the headless statue and coming to know what happened, I have understood and I believe that this is a definitive expression of Ma's intellect. But the question that this leads to and that is gnawing at my heart is—is Ma still on this earth? Soumen-*da*! I feel completely drained and weak both inside and outside. My mind is clouded; my senses are numbed with fear and misgiving. I have pushed myself with all my remaining strength to share this with you. What will happen to me now only God can tell!"

Everyone listening was stunned into silence. Doesn't Ma's coming in person indicate her final departure? But before deliberating over all this, it was important to support and reassure Manju. So Soumen immediately wrote to her.

Manju,

How blessed you are! Ma came there in person to warn all of us. This act of hers has clearly established her strong objection to any kind of personal glorification. Today, let us all repeat our resolution that in future we will never deify or glorify Ma, neither shall we let anyone else do so. Narrating this example, we should also instruct all our associates that the only way to pay tribute to Ma is through honest work. And my dear, lovable sister Manju! You should be dancing in delight in that compound Ma had stepped into. Silly girl! Do not let fear instil itself in you; fill yourself with joy rather, become fully conscious and bow to the rising sun. Manju, this 'coming' of Ma is an expression of her profound love for you. This is the time to fill your basket with her blessings, to experience wonder and to partake of the divine. Rise, and with renewed enthusiasm get back to your work quickly. Manju, for us, the children of Lavanyadevi, there is no time to rest, sleep or feel tired. Here, hold my hand and rise at once. We all promise you that you are not alone. We are all there with you, every moment. Fearlessly and with a clear outlook, step forward with the full force of your goodness so that the whole earth feels the impact of your steps.

Wait a minute, Manju. Malavika has just sent a message saying that she has received two envelopes. One has her name on it, the other has mine and Anita's. But I cannot provide any further news now as it has been announced that all electronic equipment is to be switched off.

On reaching London, in transit on his way to Kolkata, when Soumen opened his laptop, he saw the note from Malavika.

Dada!

I did not give Soudamini Ma even a hint about my kidnapping. The Commissioner of Police had warned the press and media right at the beginning that my name shouldn't appear anywhere. It was the bureaucracy that got the credit for capturing the gang, which made all the government officers very favourably disposed towards us. When the Commissioner announced that the government had awarded this year's Krititva Samagra prize to our centre, I publicly dedicated it to Soudamini Ma, saying that her unconditional support had been the key to all the work being done there. You know how Ma is—she happily accepted the award without even bothering to ask what it was for! Dada! I am often surprised when I see Ma and wonder: Is she really Lavanyadevi's own daughter?

Anyway, since I have to go for an important meeting regarding a grant for the centre, I shall have to save the contents of the two letters for our next conversation. I will discuss them and everything else in detail when I get back.

Yours only,
Malavika.

Soumen could not sit still. Leaving the laptop open he kept pacing up and down. Despite the fact that he was the captain of the Saptarshi Mandal and everyone was appreciative of his maturity and leadership, he was feeling quite nervous today. The reason for his fear was that this was the first time Lavanya Ma had addressed a letter to both Anita and him. He was also grumbling to himself about how careless it was of Malavika not to send him the letter before she went off for the meeting. If she had even an inkling of how this simple act of carelessness on her part would cause rapid fluctuations in Soumen's blood pressure, she would not have left him to struggle to keep afloat in the ocean of perturbation. He kept muttering aloud over and over again—O Malavika! Come! Please come soon!—and when he saw a notification flashing, he leaped to his laptop. Malavika wanted to tell him about the grant first, but he impatiently interjected, "My dear sister! All the riches of the world are nothing in comparison to that letter, which is worth more than the philosopher's stone. Send me Ma's letter first, please. Everything else can wait."

"Okay, Dada! Okay!" said Malavika and quickly forwarded a letter to Soumen. But in her hurry, instead of sending him his letter, she sent him the letter meant for herself. When she realised what she had done, the mail had already been sent and there was no way she could rectify her mistake. She agonised, O God! What should I do now? Should I call him and apologise? No, if I do that now, Dada will scold me. She finally decided she would simply mail him his own letter, hoping that in his desperation to read it, he would probably forget to scold her. When Soumen got the letter meant for Malavika, he was baffled at first; then muttering "*Uff*, you stupid girl!...as usual, you and your haste!" he started going through the letter.

Dear Manu!

I know what you must be thinking right now—that whenever Didu calls me by this pet name it invariably means that she is going to assign me some complex task. And you are right. There is something I am about to tell you to do. Initially, I thought that I would write to Aalo, Manju and you separately. But then I thought that as these letters would be talking about the same thing, I will include all three of you in the same letter, and I am sending the letter to you Manu as you are the sprightliest of the three.

Manu, the incredible work that all of you have done in the last few days has not only overwhelmed me from within, but I can also see clearly that you have a shining future ahead of you, something which always makes a mother proud of her children.

Aalo, you have worked harder in Bangladesh than you are capable of and have proved that you have not only served me but have felt closely the pulse of each vibration inside me which I myself could not actualise due to my limited capabilities. The untiring diligence with which you have tried to build rapport, love and understanding between Hindu and Muslim communities deserves special plaudits. Also commendable are your efforts towards strengthening the fabric of fellow-feeling by educating the women of both these communities. Aalo, if a woman gets educated and is benefitted, her whole family as a unit benefits along with her; and the collective form of this unit—the society—starts making an effort in this direction as well. The role of a woman is multidimensional. She is mother, lover, wife, daughter, daughter-in-law and mother-in-law; she has multiple roles, and therefore the 'right woman' can make a weak society disease-free and strengthen it to help build a healthy society. Looking at your achievements and knowing your thoughts, I now firmly believe that your abilities and intelligence will not be limited to educational reforms alone, but that you will strive successfully to build an enlightened, conscious and compassionate society.

And you, Manju? You have touched those pinnacles which ordinary individuals cannot even dream of. There is an oft-heard and oft-repeated saying that a philanderer can stop making a pass at other people's wives and a born miser might give up his greed, but it is not possible for an addict to let go of his addiction even if he tries because apart from mental agony he also experiences the acute physical pain of withdrawal, and so he keeps tumbling deeper and deeper down the dark cave of addiction. I know that you are not just committed but devoted to transform this 'impossible evil' into a 'possible good'; so, it is certain that you will eventually achieve success in this task. But unlike other tasks, the success here will be slow and difficult to come by, so don't get discouraged or disheartened. It is my firm belief that like a combat warrior you will not show your back to the enemy even if you have received a hundred wounds and in the face of your determination even Ranchhod—the god who fled the battlefield—will not have the courage to deny you support.

And my queen, Malavika, the work that you have put in to control and reduce prostitution in Sonagachhi and to nurture the futures of the children born there is decidedly admirable. You are battling to secure all three—their bodies, their souls and their minds. Your efforts to stop the trafficking of girls is unprecedented; kudos to you for that. Though the task may not sound that daunting, the truth is that it is a fierce battle to tackle a bitter reality. It is difficult for people like us, who sit on the shore counting waves, to even imagine how difficult it is to swim against the tide. It's true that the tasks that the three of you are handling are challenging and full of struggle; but on top of that, this particular task involves a risk to life as well. But I think that the Almighty probably assigned you this task only after evaluating your potential. After seeing how all of you work, I am fully assured that you will definitely come out of the test of your work as pure as gold.

Aalo! Manju! Malavika! I have a request and a command for all you—get married. Don't be surprised! I personally do not give much importance to the institution of marriage and neither do I look at it as some kind of goal in life, but I do believe that through the bond of marriage a person becomes dignified, controlled and responsible. Unrestrained relations are unconcerned about society and like hill-streams they originate and end wherever and whenever they want and have no accountability; but when waters follow a defined course by restricting themselves between two banks of a river, they bring welfare for the community and retain their distinct identity despite the fact that they flow into the sea. This is precisely why, in Vedic times, Jabala's son Satyakam initiated the institution of marriage so as to curb waywardness and lay the foundation for a healthy society.

If I am to think on your behalf, I would suggest that Aalo should marry Prof. Azhar Alam, Manjulika should get married to Dr. Ravindra Akhilandam and Malavika should choose Shashank Dubey as her life partner. You have all been working with them for quite some time now, and I can see that when one starts saying something, the other one instantly completes it; this means that your hearts and brains not only work alike but also think alike, and that is the pinnacle of love. My understanding of your situations tells me that you must all must arrive at an exact decision without dithering any longer, otherwise it will be too late and you might end up in the depression of loneliness. Remember, if you live life in its natural course, you will be able to focus fully on serious work. Otherwise, untouched by the colours of life, you will end up living a dry and insipid existence and will feel frustrated at every step.

My next suggestion is about your children. Since it is valid for everyone in the Saptarshi Mandal, I will talk about it in my letter to Soumen, the definitive centre, which will reach all of you in moments, as always. I pray to God that you are all happy, peaceful and satisfied—these are my blessings.

Best wishes,

Lavanya.

The letter Soumen was eagerly waiting for followed.

Dear Soumen,

I do not consider Soumen to be the name of a specific individual anymore but of a whole group which thinks alike, walks alike, eats alike, sits and stands alike, sleeps and sings alike, and even breathes in rhythm. This group has synchronised itself with the multitudinous rhythms of the universe and has thus achieved immeasurable expansion beyond its limits so that anyone anywhere can combine their individual rhythm with this rhythm and connect with eternity. One's desire to do something worthwhile results in the violin of one's heart reverberating with the same melody that is playing ceaselessly in this universe in many good hearts that are akin to one's own. One's journey from the limited to the limitless links them with that immense form whose presence can be felt in every grain of this earth—in stationary and mobile beings, trees and plants, sky, land and water, the moon and the sun—in everything visible and invisible.

My children! The elixir of my life! The whole universe is worth worshipping. Every river here is Ganga and every living thing is Lord Shiva. To say that brahm *is the truth while the world is an illusion is false, because how can a part of the truth be an illusion? Neither is* maya *untrue, nor is creation. This world is an extension of the majesty of the Supreme Being—*Parabrahma *himself. To reach that ultimate truth, what you need are not mere eyes but eyes which can look inwards and are filled with compassion. Compassion subsumes everything—kindness, love, reverence, devotion all are* *embedded within it—and comes about without any agent or causal element.*

To be compassionate is the zenith of a person's development; which is why each person who is associated with doing good wants to develop their personality so as to become compassionate. My understanding tells me that the first step towards compassion is to share one's individual self completely with the souls of others. If one is able to completely empty the sense of self from the container of the soul of a living being, it will be refilled with fresh water which will be truly clear, pure and beyond all distinctions of 'yours and mine'. The easier way to overcome this pettiness of 'mine versus yours' is to magnify the feelings of others' affections to the extent that feelings about one's own self appear microscopic or insignificant in comparison and fall far behind. To achieve this, it is necessary that each couple among you should adopt five to six children and nurture and value them all equally. This is indirectly the starting point for acquainting oneself with and internalising the feeling of compassion.

Children, at first, I was unsure about whether I should entrust you with this responsibility, but just as we shut our eyes as we are about to take a leap across a chasm, I too have leapt across my attachment to express my wish.

All your speechless, amazed eyes seem to be asking me the question—how is the divine concept of compassion linked to something as grounded in realism as adopting children? The answer to this apparently complex question is exceedingly simple. We are all aware that all the creatures of the world love their children more than themselves and consider them the carrier of their immortality. All their selfishness and egocentrism is reduced to nothing when faced with their offspring. It is believed that the Supreme Being created all beings on earth in a surfeit of happiness and in the process, blended His self into each particle of this creation. This dissemination of His self is the breadth, the comprehensiveness of compassion.

Children, this process of sharing and participation is the first step towards compassion. The joy that accrues from sharing with one person makes you sensitive to sharing with all as well as compassion for all. The marks of the slap on Majnu's cheek manifesting themselves on Laila's face is compassion, which is the surfeit of love and devotion. It is a mother's devotion which, in spite of the numerous mistakes a child commits, doesn't let her think twice before embracing it, or loving a child more if it is weak or disabled. This 'more' is nothing but the pinnacle of devotion—compassion.

Children, if we want the development and enlargement of the scope of our good deeds, our enlightened children can be of help. Modern research tells us that single or double children from affluent households are usually egoistic and self-centered, whereas children from ordinary backgrounds who grow up among more siblings are more liberal and cooperative in their attitude. They develop tolerant, generous, moderate and balanced personalities and even if they lack in material resources, are capable of enhancing and refining their intelligence, wisdom, diligence and alertness through their dedication and devotion.

I know that you will find the idea of bringing up so many children in the midst of so much work to be well-nigh impossible, but go and peep into a poor farmer's cottage and you will find their children, from a very tender age, participating equally and sharing the work of their parents. The way they live and behave is the reason that they are able to imbibe the positive attributes of their families.

My dear children, you can very well charge me with emotional blackmail. But these are all dreams that I could not live; I have planted their seeds within you. This is true and the reason is that I consider you people to be more truthful and capable than I am. Since the fabric of your being is woven with goodwill, you are all capable of producing harvests of such crops as are the tangible expressions of compassion. The wisdom of the scriptures rightly points out that it is easy to give birth to children but very difficult to bring them up well. It will be still more difficult for you as you have to behave impartially and equitably with both your biological and adopted children in a way that they are unable to even fathom the difference between themselves. If you cannot do this, you will have committed a grave crime. If you adopt girl children, be sure that you have not just done something virtuous, you have also won over the goddess of fortune. The senses of service, loyalty, dedication, devotion, concentration, sensitivity, honesty, affection and compassion are considerably more in women than in men, and if they develop faith in the work that they are doing, they will put their best into it with complete dedication and determination and will strive to justify whatever they are doing. And it is a truth that does not need to be reiterated that girls in a family create melody and in many cultures, it is considered that the presence of girls in a family makes it akin to heaven.

Apart from adopting a larger number of girl children, it is also my sincere wish that each of you adopt at least one child with disability. History is witness to their single-minded dedication to prevail against all odds. Sometimes they are able to carry out such extraordinary feats that an able person can only wonder at it and acknowledge its enormity. One of your children could be one such polestar and create history.

My children, since the time that I have disappeared from the field of your vision you have broken all the established standards of mathematics and redefined them. I feel proud to admit that your achievements have far exceeded my expectations and it is with this pride that I want to tell you how indebted I am to you, and gratefully say dhanyoasmi, anugrihitosmi*—I have been blessed, you have done me a favour.*

Children, I am not sure if I have been able to accomplish all the purposes for which my spirit soul had been given the shape of this body and sent to this earth. In all likelihood, I have not been able to do it, but I firmly believe that your consciousnesses have awakened at the right time and that resplendent in their flames, you are all divine torches now. A long time has passed in these mutual dialogues of ours, and a lot of water in the Ganga, having done infinite amounts of good to creatures on earth, has flowed and fallen into the sea. Now who will decide whether Ganga became part of the sea or the sea became Ganga? We can only pray to our Supreme Father that we are able to create meaning in our lives through our creative efforts and thus make them significant. Remember, the spirit soul connected to the larger good has neither beginning nor end! It always exists in the form of a good idea in every creditable work in this creation within the minds of its enlightened children, and the work done by them leads to continually new eternities in this creation.

My dearest soul-children! One year from now, on the first of January, when the conditions are perfect between the earth and the sun, all of you along with your families come to the valley adjoining the Shivagauri Falls at five in the morning.

Best wishes,

Lavanya.

The sounds of water rushing down the falls and the chirping of birds at dawn seemed to have abated somewhat with the arrival of a group of people. The anxious faces of the adults and the curious playful faces of the children all looked expectantly towards the waterfall. No one spoke a word. They were wary even of blinking lest they miss, even for a moment, what they were all eagerly waiting to witness. The air was thick with anticipation. And suddenly, they saw it—the mystical vision of a woman in luminescent white. They could faintly make out her right hand raised in benediction. It seemed to all those present that she opened her lotus eyes and gazed upon her worthy family with a sense of profound fulfilment and love. And the next moment that divine, dazzlingly bright figure faded away into the realm of air, water and light…leaving them all standing there, stunned and bereft. Aalo screamed, "Ma! Wait…!"

Lavanya's children rushed to that spot. They searched desperately for their guiding deity everywhere—in the rocks, leaves, plants, grass and water—but could find nothing except grains of sand. Distraught and drained, they sat on the rocks adjacent the Shivagauri Falls, and wondered: can one depart in this manner? Is this what is called *mukti*? Their eyes were brimming with tears but they tried their best not to let the tears cross the threshold of the eyes—because Lavanyadevi, while teaching them how to transform tears into pearls, had told them not to cry. "A teardrop born out of pain falling into the clamshell of good deeds becomes a precious pearl!" The mere memory of her words made them restrain their grief and caused their faces to light up. Suddenly they felt a luminousness descend on them from above and embed itself deep in each one of them, and a celestial wave of energy coursed through their bodies from head to toe.

Lavanya's children, almost unconscious for moments, experienced this miracle taking place within themselves. And when they regained consciousness, with radiant eyes, joyous hearts and minds, a sense of feeling lighter than flowers and dancing limbs, they started back for their respective destinations.

Translator's Note

As pilgrims and tourists from all corners of the country jostle through the narrow *galis* that lead them to the Kashi Vishwanath Temple in Varanasi, their attention is invariably drawn to the bustling of shopkeepers hawking their goods in the closely packed shops and makeshift stalls that line these lanes and bylanes. These shopkeepers identify visitors by their language, dress and demeanour, and accordingly switch languages to peddle their wares. The multiple Indian, and sometimes foreign, languages that they use, a skill picked up and honed by listening attentively to fellow shopkeepers and sustained interaction with visitors from different parts of the country and the world, is remarkable. Despite the lack of formal learning, their extraordinary linguistic proficiency is in evidence as they engage with people who pass through these *galis* in multiple tongues, switching effortlessly from one to another, even altering their speech pattern and intonation accordingly. These *galis*, to me, are a microcosm of the linguistic landscape of India, and the interactions between shopkeepers and passers-by a paradigm of the diversity of communication in it.

I have lived my life in translation, if I may put it that way. Childhood onwards, as far as I can recall, my repertoire of languages has been an inseparable part of who I am. Negotiating multiple cultural realities, shaped by personal circumstances, social structures and institutions, I can function, to varying degrees, in six languages. Moving between them plurilingually, the many *khichdis* I made were distinctly my own. While I can claim to 'know' some of these languages, I could never call any of them 'mine'. Yet, each is an indelible part of the life I have lived (across five states), and live. I have, therefore, always been an insider as well as an outsider, neither completely fitting in, nor altogether a misfit in the cultures that these languages embodied. This contradiction has shaped my existence and identity, both as a disadvantage and as an advantage, be it the culture I was born into or those that I embraced.

This paradoxical relationship with language is also the common ground for my kinship with the author, and her linguistic and cultural background. Kusum Khemani belongs to a family from Rajasthan that came to Kolkata some 200 years ago via Haryana and Delhi. As a writer who negotiated this change, she reads and writes in Hindi and English, translates from Bangla to Hindi, and speaks Hindi and Bangla with such consummate ease that one tends to forget she was born and brought up in a Marwari-speaking family. Her rich linguistic inheritance, emblematic of both India and the larger pattern of migrations within the country, is reflected in her novel, as is the cultural diversity it manifests—a diversity that is increasingly under threat today.

Multilingualism is not just about languages. It is also about the consciousness of diverse linguistic and cultural realities, and an awareness of the complexities and conflicts that characterise them individually and with respect to each other. Issues of majority and minority languages, of dominant and subordinate groups, how and why languages are acquired, lost, or subsumed into others, issues of identity and agency vis-à-vis the acquisition of a language, and of voices and positions within it, ranging from gender and sexuality to religion, region and class, are all dimensions of the multilingual condition. It is also about embracing diversity, being attuned to complex social dynamics, and an ability to position oneself beyond narrow regional boundaries and within broader 'Indian' and even global ones. Being a Marwari woman writer in Bengal is about all this as well.

It is with this broad understanding of the author's linguistic and cultural universe, and my own, that I approach the multiple worlds inhabited by the text.

Written in Hindi in Devanagari, *Lavanyadevi* interweaves narratives from different regions, contexts and times through characters who speak in different Indian languages, and the author's own family history. Her Hindi is the everyday Hindi of the Marwari settler community in Bengal today. Her distinctiveness is evident in her choice of words and syntax, in the way her Hindi is peppered with Bangla, Punjabi, Marwari, Haryanvi and Urdu, the occasional Sanskrit and English. While the narrative has references ranging from the esoteric to the commonplace, the dialogues do not attempt a 'high' literary register but aim to replicate the natural cadences and rhythms of speech in these languages, doing so with consummate ease. The spontaneous and organic threading of words, phrases and sentences from these languages into the weave of Hindi replicates the intricate lived reality of multilingual speakers of this language, and at times their pragmatics too (for example, the issue of appropriate marriageable age in the question: *"Money aachhey Jyoti'r koto boyosh hoye gyachhey?"*). This wording and construction can be understood as the author's own unique idiolect, and is something that I have tried to reproduce in translation.

An evident casualty in a multilingual narrative is the notion of 'purity'. While *Lavanyadevi* pulsates delightfully with its inimitable polyphony of languages, voices and registers—much of it warranted by the circumstances of the characters—the use and interplay of multiple languages also leads to syntactic spillages and semantic cross-connections between them. Such spillage is seen, for instance, in the lilt of Bangla in Hindi conversations, in Hindi syntactic structures in Bangla sentences, or in Bangla interjections in Marwari dialogues. These might not always be the author's intent; she may not even be aware of it. Instances of cultural cross-connection and assimilation too are in evidence, as when a Bengali zamindar bride's *jadowa* necklace is referred to as a *naulakha*, or what in Bangla is *mama'r bari* is referred to as *nana bari*, or when customs and habits from the author's lived culture inadvertently replace those of other cultures in the narrative, as when a Bengali wife's '*Ogo shunchho*' becomes '*Ey ji*' (despite the author's liberal use of Bangla), or a nugget of traditional wisdom from the Hindi heartland is articulated by a Bengali woman in a Bangladesh village, or a Hindu Bangla/Hindi speaker exclaims '*Ya* Allah!' or matter-of-factly says '*khair sallah*'.

While there was no way in which I could capture in its entirety the spirit of this multilingual interplay in English translation, I have retained, to the extent possible, colloquialisms, everyday speech rhythms, and how I perceive multilingual characters and societies communicate and interact. That is also the logic for retaining constructions and usages that are syntactically inconsistent or could be interpreted as Indianisms. Adhering to the author's idiom of narrative framing is a creative liberty I have deliberately taken. Morphological possibilities inherent in instances where Hindi and Bangla blend to create words in actual use (as in *aamar hargulo...ghishey jachhey*, where the Bangla *ghoshey jachhey* and the Hindi *ghis ja rahe hain* meld) are, however, lost in translation.

These inter-lingual dynamics also have phonic implications. For example, while the common labial/labio-dental approximant (**व**/*ʋ*) of Hindi phonology is absent in Bangla, and a native Bangla speaker would say La*b*anyade*b*i, Prabha*b*atide*b*i and Mala*b*ika, I retain the sound in names of Bengali characters like La*v*anyade*v*i, Prabha*v*atide*v*i and Mala*v*ika because that is how a native Hindi speaker, the author included, would pronounce and write them, as she has done in her novel. Usages and spellings in the various Indian languages are also retained to preserve textual ambience, or humour, or the immediacy that the author aims for in the original.

Culture-specific interjections, terms of address and kinship have been retained to recreate colloquial speech patterns, and glossed where needed. Kinship terms like Maua, Didu, Mama, Mami, Nani and terms of address, which essentially function as names, are not italicised; while suffixes, such as *ji*, *da*, *di*, where they form part of such address (Guru-*ji*) and where used with proper names (Priyamvada-*ji*, Soumen-*da*) are in italic. Most sayings, set phrases and scriptural references are retained in the source language to convey a sense of their distinct use, with meanings provided alongside or made clear in context. The same approach holds for jokes and repartees, where I have tried to follow a middle path between explaining and flattening humour or nuances of wit. Situational humour was easier to handle. The glossary spans the matrix of languages used in the novel, and is compiled with the logic that some words may be unfamiliar even to Indian readers from different regions.

Snatches of English words, phrases and sentences, a part of how any Indian language is spoken today by Indians urban and non-urban, and used quite liberally by the author in this novel, have been retained from the original; but—barring some exceptions—these are invisible in translation. Single quotes have been used to mark select original English words and phrases, such as 'definitive centre', 'hero-worship', 'heritage', 'girlfriend', 'three musketeers'. In a few instances, English speech in the source text has also been visibilised (quietly, I hope) by mentioning that the character speaks 'in English', such as (p. 103): "Priyamvada-*ji* thanked the manager for these excellent dishes in cheerful Tamil, and…softly told me in English, 'Be quick, lots of people are waiting.'"

Punctuation is mostly retained, except for the rather frequent authorial use of ellipses, interrogatives and exclamation marks, which have been optimised. In a few instances, paragraphs have been adjusted for logic, and chapter/narrative breaks in the novel shifted to align with the run of incidents and the narrative flow.

In at least a couple of chapters, incidents have been rearranged slightly for consistency of storytelling.

I have tried to get as close to the original text as practicable, and except for metaphorical language, which does not quite lend itself to literal translation, I have largely tried to avoid sense translation wherever possible. In other words, between a breezy translation and a linguistically nuanced one, wherever possible, I have eschewed the former and gone for the latter. Friends who read portions of the initial draft felt that aiming for precision of linguistic nuance in English made the novel read more like a prose piece or an essay ('academic writing' was the phrase one of them used), and was not the language of story-telling—an observation that was always at the back of my mind while working on the final draft of the translation.

Finally, there are parts where the native cast of thought and choice of words are rendered from Hindi to English in terms of words/turns of phrase/idioms that, though drawn from a repertoire that is deeply Indian in thought and sensibility, is nevertheless shaped by an Anglophone education. This is something I accept in all humility. It is a hybrid Hindi text translated into hybrid English.

Languages, like the people of the country, too jostle, share space, engage, compete, fight and befriend each other. As every Indian of a certain generation has grown up hearing: *kos-kos par badley pani, char kos par vani*—the taste of water changes every *kos*, and speech (language) changes every four. This fluid coexistence, in the vast Indian linguistic landscape, of an incredibly varied number of languages and dialects fosters spaces where people effortlessly, even unconsciously, become plurilingual. This is despite the fact that we are losing our mother, father and other tongues apace, every day. This leads me to wonder why, even though there are instances of such coexistence in the Indian literary traditions, Indian literature is predominantly conceived of as an aggregation of discrete subsets of monolingual literary traditions in the different Indian languages, falling short of being able to capture this lived hybrid linguistic reality, the many cultural syntheses it enables, and its plurilingual exponents.

I hope that the negotiation of multiple languages within a single text, and thereby the transcending of narrow, defined linguistic and cultural boundaries, fosters the idea of more such assimilative narratives and translations of similar works, not just into a single mediatory language but into all Indian languages. I also see it as a paradigm for bridging divides and for engendering—and reclaiming—a broader, more composite Indian identity through intercultural communication.

Glossary

aarti: (Hindi) Hindu ritual offering of incense and light to deities

aha: (Bangla/Hindi) an expression of either delight or irritation

alta: (Bangla) a bright red dye used by married women in Bengal to ritually adorn palms and feet in simple patterns

anna: (across Indian languages) formerly used as currency in India, equal to one-sixteenth of a rupee

antarmahal: the women's quarter of a palace, mansion or *haveli*

arey: (Bangla/Hindi) an expression equivalent to the English 'hey' or 'oh', typically used to express surprise or disbelief or simply to begin a conversation with someone of the same age, status or younger

ashouch: (Sanskrit) a period of a fixed number of days of isolation and abstinence from customary ritualistic activities usually following a death or birth in a Hindu family

baba: (Bangla) father

babu-ji: (Hindi) father, also father-in-law

bahurani: (Hindi) daughter-in-law; honorific used to address a woman; see *bouma*

bai, baisa: (Marwari) sister; honorific used to address girls and women in Rajasthan

banpulak: (Bangla) a flowering plant; scientific name, *Paretta indica*

banslochan: (Hindi) a secretion from the nodes of the bamboo tree having medicinal properties

bari nani: (Hindi) elder grandmother

bau, bau-ji: (Hindi, informal) father; contraction of *babu-ji*

behen-ji: (Hindi) sister; honorific used to address a woman *beti*: (Hindi) daughter; honorific used to address a woman

bhabhi: (Hindi) sister-in-law; honorific used to address a friend's wife

bhoomipujan: (Hindi) Hindu ritual of worshipping Mother Earth to seek her blessings before beginning construction of a new house/building

bouma: (Bangla) an affectionate address used by the elderly for a daughter-in-law or for any married woman in a household

Brahm: (Sanskrit) the transcendent and immanent ultimate reality of the One Supreme Cosmic Spirit in Hinduism according to the *Vedanta*

Brahmastra: (Sanskrit) a divine indestructible weapon in Hindu mythology

bua: (Hindi) father's sister; honorific used for addressing an older woman

char dham: (across Indian languages) the four most revered Hindu pilgrimage sites—Badrinath, Dwarka, Puri and Rameshwaram

da, dada: (Bangla) elder brother; honorific used for addressing an older man

dharmashala: (Bangla/Hindi) rest-house, usually for religious purposes, built by temple trusts

di, didi: (Bangla/Hindi) elder sister; honorific used for addressing an older woman

didu, dida: (Bangla) maternal grandmother

dhuno: Indian frankincense

Ei: (Bangla) an affectionate address for a close friend or spouse or relative of the same age or younger

Gandharva: (Sanskrit) male celestial beings considered to be the offspring of Brahma according to the *Vishnu Purana*

ghaghra: (Hindi) a women's traditional pleated long-skirt, usually heavily embroidered with sequins, beads or glasswork

hatti: (Punjabi/Haryanvi) shop

haveli: (Urdu/Persian/Arabic) a traditional mansion in the Indian subcontinent, with distinctive architecture and historical significance

ilish: (Bangla) or hilsa, a fish considered a great delicacy in Bengal; scientific name, *Tenualosa ilisha*

ji: (Hindi) an honorific suffix used to address one elder in age or higher in status

jija-ji: (Hindi) elder brother-in-law

jiji: (Hindi/Marwari) elder sister

jyotirlinga: (Sanskrit) a shrine where Lord Shiva is worshipped as a pillar (*linga*) of light (*jyoti*); there are twelve such holy shrines in India

Kahar: traditionally palanquin-bearers, both Hindus and Muslims; a community spread across north India, mainly Bihar, Bengal and Uttar Pradesh

kaka, kakababu: (Bangla) father's younger brother; also used to address an elderly man

kakima: (Bangla) wife of father's younger brother, i.e. *kaku*; also used to address an elderly woman

kar-sewa: (Punjabi) voluntary work at the grass-root levels especially at the behest of some organisation; commonly used in the register of religion

kathha: (Bangla) unit of land measurement in eastern India

khokababu: (Bangla) a term of endearment used for small boys, but can also be used for teenagers

kumkum: (Sanskrit) a red pigment made from turmeric and limestone used by Hindu women to make a round mark on the forehead

leheriya: (Hindi/Marwari) wave-like pattern

ma: (across Indian languages) mother; also a form of address, mostly affectionate, for a young girl, daughter-in-law or older woman

Mahamrityunjaya mantra: (Sanskrit) a verse from the Rigveda which, if recited, is said to be able to forestall death

maharaj: (across Indian languages) great king or emperor; the cook in traditional Hindu households; honorific used to address any male of higher status/stature; here, an ascetic

mama: (Bangla/Hindi) mother's brother

mami: (Bangla/Hindi) wife of *mama* i.e. mother's brother's wife

mashi, mashima: (Bangla) mother's sister; also used to address an elderly woman

mastermoshai: (Bangla) teacher

matrivrata: (Hindi) obedient to the dictates of the mother

mausi, mausi-ji: (Hindi) mother's sister; honorific used to address an elderly woman

maya: (Sanskrit) illusion, a central concept in Hindu philosophy, notably Advaita Vedanta, that denotes the godly (or demonic) power to produce illusions and make mortals believe in what is illusory; the illusion of the reality of all sensory experience

moksha: (Sanskrit) emancipation of the soul from the cycle of death and rebirth in Hinduism, Buddhism, Jainism; also *mukti*.

nani: (Hindi) maternal grandmother

nani bari: maternal grandmother's house

naubatkhana: (Urdu/Hindi) literally, drum-house; a large room or platform built over the outer gate of a palace from where drums or other musical instruments are sounded to mark the time of day or announce important arrivals; orchestra pit during ceremonies; here, it means an outer room of the palace

naulakha: (Hindi) worth nine lakhs

nayika bheda: (Sanskrit) classification of female protagonists in various ancient Indian texts, including the *Agnipurana*

padmasana: (Sanskrit) a yoga posture in which one sits with legs crossed and feet placed on the opposite thighs

panda: (Sanskrit) a Brahmin expert in genealogy who provides religious guidance and, sometimes, also acts as a family priest

pandal: (Bangla, Hindi) a temporary structure, usually made of bamboo and cloth, used for public gatherings and festivals, religious and otherwise

pandit: (Sanskrit) a scholar of the Hindu scriptures who performs scriptural/ceremonial rituals as a priest; also, a caste-indicating address, referring to someone who is a (male) Brahmin

papeeha: (Hindi) the Common Hawk Cuckoo, also known as brainfever bird

Parabrahma: (Sanskrit) in Hindu philosophy denotes that which is beyond all descriptions and conceptualisations; the formless entity that eternally pervades everything, everywhere in the universe and whatever lies beyond

phera: (Hindi) circumambulation round the holy fire during a Hindu marriage; there are seven *pheras*, and each is followed by a vow taken by the couple being married

prasad: (across Indian languages) a devotional offering made to a god, typically consisting of food that is later shared among devotees

rajbari: (Bangla) palace

riyaaz: (Hindi/Urdu) routine practise of an art form, especially music

rudraksh: (Sanskrit) rosaries made out of the dried seeds of a tree considered holy in Hinduism; scientific name: *Elaeocarpus ganitrus*

sashtang, dandavat pranam: (Sanskrit) lying prostrate on the ground in obeisance, face down, with the palms joined above the head and the wrists, chest, knees, thighs, genitals and toes resting against the ground, symbolic of complete submission to God or a spiritual guru

sati-sadhvi: a virtuous female ascetic

Sharad Poornima: (across Indian languages) full moon day of the Hindu lunar month of Ashvin (September to October), marking the harvest festival celebrated on it and the end of the monsoon

shraddh: (Sanskrit) a ceremony performed in honour of a deceased parent or ancestor

Swati nakshatra: fifteenth constellation of the Indian Zodiac in Vedic astrology, ruled by the planet Rahu; in Hindu mythology the *chataka* bird waits the whole year thirsty to quench its thirst only when it rains in this constellation; associated with the advent of monsoon

Tandav: (Sanskrit) divine dance of the gods in Hinduism; here, it specifically refers to Lord Shiva's dance of destruction

tanpura: (across Indian languages) a large four-stringed lute used in Indian classical music chiefly as a drone accompaniment

thakurbari: (Bangla) abode of the gods of the household

tilak: (Sanskrit) mark drawn on the forehead by Hindus, using vermillion, sandalwood paste or ash, among other things, as a matter of practice or on some religious occasion

Vaitarani: (Sanskrit) a mythological river in the Hindu scriptures, separating the earth from Heaven and Hell

Vidyapati: fifteenth-century Maithili and Sanskrit writer, philosopher and poet-saint known for his erudite Sanskrit works and erotic poetry in Maithili; also known as Maithil Kavi Kokil, he was a devotee of Shiva but also wrote Vaishnava devotional songs.